Also by Rachel Butler

The Assassin
Deep Cover

Scorched

RACHEL BUTLER

A Dell Book

SCORCHED

A Dell Book / August 2007

Published by
Bantam Dell
A Division of Random House, Inc.
New York, New York

This is a work of fiction. Names, characters, places, and incidents either are the
product of the author's imagination or are used fictitiously. Any resemblance to
actual persons, living or dead, events, or locales is entirely coincidental.

Dell is a registered trademark of Random House, Inc., and
the colophon is a trademark of Random House, Inc.

ISBN 978-0-440-24337-3

Printed in the United States of America
Published simultaneously in Canada

www.bantamdell.com

OPM 10 9 8 7 6 5 4 3 2 1

Scorched

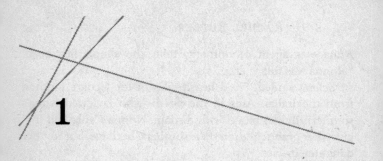

1

"—six, seven, eight..."

"—actually suggested we have another baby..."

"—she's really hot, but she wants to get married..."

Snatches of conversation drifted past Selena, as comforting as the shawl wrapped around her shoulders to protect against the cool October air. She was sitting in a chaise longue on the Ceola patio, with half the family scattered around in an impromptu get-together.

It didn't take much to stir up one of those with the Ceolas. That evening it had been nothing more than Tony and his brother coming over to mow their parents' yard one last time for the season. Selena, along with J.J.'s wife and kids, had come with them, Tony's sister and her family had stopped by, and before long younger brothers Dom and Matt had also appeared at the house. Anna had been happy to switch gears from dinner for two to fifteen, pulling pans of lasagna and garlic bread from the freezer, tossing salads, and whipping up zabaglione for dessert. A spur-of-the-moment party, and everyone was enjoying it, Selena most of all.

Anna sat down in the chair next to Selena's with a grunt, then smiled. "I sound like Nonna Ceola, making that old-lady noise when I sit down or stand up."

"You've done a lot of work this evening. You're entitled."

"Nonna used to say, 'When it's family, it's not work.'"

Anna was silent a moment, then she shook her head. "Nonna was full of crap."

Selena smiled. She'd heard tales of Joe Ceola's mother, from the Italian Alps in the north, who'd viewed Anna's southern Italian blood with disdain. Nonna Ceola had forgiven her grandchildren their southern heritage, but not her daughter-in-law.

Now Anna was *Nonna,* grandmother to a handful of rambunctious kids belonging to her three older children. She was hopeful that the younger four would add to the brood, including Tony. The more Selena thought about the idea, the more she liked it.

After sipping rich espresso from the tiny cup she held, Anna asked, "How is your painting?"

"Fine. I just shipped three canvases to the gallery in Key West." Selena hid a smile. Like her mother, daughter, and daughters-in-law, Anna had always been a stay-at-home mother. Painting was something the kids did with finger paints. Standing at an easel for hours at a time seemed to her an odd way to earn a living, but for Tony's sake, she always showed interest.

Tony's five-year-old twin nieces ran past, giggling and shrieking as Joe lumbered after them, arms outstretched, doing a good imitation of a cartoon monster. He was grinning, having as much fun as the girls, his pleasure lighting eyes that were too often dull.

"How is Joe?" Selena asked quietly.

Anna's smile faded. "He has his good days. With the new medication the doctor's got him on, they're outnumbering the bad. He knew who you were this evening, didn't he?"

Selena nodded. The Alzheimer's that was slowly destroying Joe often left him in a cloud of confusion. Sometimes he remembered that Tony was his son and she was his girlfriend, though just as often he thought they were neighbors from long ago. But this evening he had remembered, had greeted them both by name and asked when they were finally going to get married.

Soon, Dad, Tony had said. The promise had sent a tingle of warmth through Selena that remained three hours later. Sure, they'd talked about getting married, but he hadn't actually asked and they hadn't discussed a date. Selena wasn't in a rush—she knew Tony loved her—but it was a wonderful thought for the future.

"This isn't what I wanted for my old age," Anna said softly. "But I wouldn't have missed a moment of the last forty-some years. Not even the bad ones. I'll make the best of his good days, and I'll love him through the bad ones." She reached over to squeeze Selena's hand. "That's all any of us can do, isn't it?"

With another of those old-lady grunts, she pushed to her feet, making it only a few yards before one of the grandkids attached himself to her. She swung the little boy onto her hip and continued across the patio. Selena watched her ruffle the boy's hair, nuzzle his neck, then say something to make him laugh, and she wondered...

"You look way too comfortable there." Tony slid into the chair Anna had vacated, then claimed Selena's hand, twining his fingers with hers. "What are you smiling about?"

"Am I smiling?" She was, of course. She'd been imagining another little boy in Anna's arms, one with the brown Ceola eyes and her own café-au-lait skin. Anna hadn't been thrilled the first time they'd met—Selena wasn't Catholic or Italian and was half black—but she'd gotten past it, and she would love any children Selena and Tony had every bit as much as her other grandkids.

"Are you ready to go home, babe?"

She could sit there all night, enjoying the evening and the family. But dinner was long over, the cleanup was already done, and a few quiet hours alone with Tony were a marvelous way to finish a good day. She nodded and let him pull her to her feet. Hand in hand, they circled the patio, saying their good-byes, before strolling around the house and out to the Corvette parked on the street.

The top was down, the heater on to take the edge off the chill. They didn't talk much on the way home, but the silence was comfortable. Tony broke it after turning onto Princeton Court. They were passing Selena's house and approaching his at the end of the cul-de-sac when he gestured. "There's a package at your door."

She glanced at the box. She wasn't expecting anything, but that didn't mean Asha, who was running the gallery for her, hadn't sent something.

Tony parked next to the white Impala assigned to him by the Tulsa Police Department. "Why don't you go on in? I'll get the package."

"Okay. Just set it inside the door, will you?" Whatever it was, it could wait until tomorrow.

She brushed against him when they passed at the rear of the car. In the fenced backyard, Mutt was barking excitedly, but everything else was quiet. There were only four houses on Princeton Court—hers, Tony's, and those of two neighbors, neither of whom was home this evening.

She unlocked the door, then opened it carefully. The cats Tony had taken in along with the dog were in their usual places—the calico disappearing up the stairs and the fat black cat waiting just inside the door. She scooped him, purring, into her arms before he could escape, typed in the code for the alarm, then went back to the driveway to watch Tony.

He climbed the steps to her small stoop and unlocked the door before bending to pick up the package. "No return address," he called. "Aren't you curious?"

"Not in the—" As he opened the door, the cat leaped from her arms, streaking toward the house. "Kitty!" she called, but he'd already passed Tony and dashed into the house.

The explosion shattered the evening, the ground shuddering, the very air vibrating with the blast. The concussion pushed against Selena, throwing her to the ground, her eyes closed, her head down against the cloud of debris following in its wake.

The tremors were dying away when she struggled to her feet, coughing, eyes watering. Most of the front central part of her house had been blown away, from the stoop all the way to the roof peak, and glass, bricks, and chunks of wood littered her driveway and yard. Lying unmoving in the midst of it was Tony.

"Tony . . . Tony!" The first came out a stunned whisper, the second a terrified scream. She raced across the yard, dropping to her knees beside him. "Dear God, please . . ."

He shifted beneath her trembling hand, then slowly lifted his head. Dust coated his hair and face and turned his shirt grimy. "Holy shit," he muttered. "That damn cat almost got me killed."

For a moment she stared at him, then she sank down, cupped his face in her palms, and kissed him hard. "That damn cat saved your life." She turned to look at the house. Flames were licking through the entry, dancing along the banister to the second floor and down the hall to the kitchen, sending wisps of smoke into the still-thick air. Upstairs her bedroom was tilted crazily, with much of the floor support blasted away.

Tony sat up, brushing away dust and a fine sprinkling of glass shards. He pulled his cell phone from his belt and called for both police and fire department assistance, while one thought kept repeating in Selena's head.

Not again.

God, she'd thought it was over. William Davis—the man who'd saved her from life on the streets in Jamaica, whom she'd loved almost as much as she hated—was still incapacitated, in what his doctors called a persistent vegetative state. Damon Long, William's right-hand man, was on the run from the law. He hadn't been seen since the night two months ago when he'd escaped FBI custody. The other enemies Selena had made along the way, courtesy of William, were dead, locked up, or had bigger problems on their hands than her—or so she'd thought.

Tony stood, dusted himself off, then helped her up. His fingers tight around hers, he drew her to the farthest corner of his yard, away from the heat and the worst of the smoke, where he wrapped his arms around her, holding her close.

She needed that more than she'd realized.

The fire engines arrived first. Seconds behind them came the first patrol car, followed over the next few minutes by another officer, a crew from one of the local television stations, and, last to arrive, Frank Simmons, one of Tony's fellow detectives and friends.

Simmons ran a hand through his reddish blond hair before shifting his gaze from the house to Tony. "Christ, Chee. Don't I have enough to do without you going out and almost getting yourself killed?"

"If I'd done it intentionally, I would've picked a night when someone who doesn't mind actually working had call."

"Hey, I work," Simmons protested. "I just don't see any

reason to devote myself to the job twenty-four/seven. I have a life." He fumbled in his coat pocket, removed a notepad and pen, then shrugged out of the coat and tossed it on the grass. His tie followed a moment later. "See—this is me working. What happened?"

Tony told him in a few terse sentences.

"Anything unusual about the box? Any labels on it? Any writing?"

Tony shook his head. "Selena's address. No return address. Other than that . . . That damn cat distracted me."

"Sounds like the cat saved your life." Simmons made a show of sniffing. "I don't smell burnt cat hair. Either it's in pieces around here or it used up one of its nine lives and got away."

Selena's fingers tightened around Tony's as she gazed at the destruction. She wasn't overly sentimental. The cat wasn't cute and cuddly like the calico or Mutt, still barking wildly from the far side of the house, sheltered from the chaos. The black cat hissed at Tony every time he came around, and though he let Selena hold him, he remained aloof. Still, she hated to think that he had died because of her.

"Any idea who did this?" Simmons asked.

Tony looked at Selena. He had an idea, of course. So did she. The one person they didn't discuss—couldn't discuss—without risk of arguing. The look in his brown eyes was grim to match the set of his mouth when he replied, "If I had to guess, I'd say that Damon Long is behind it."

Selena shifted uncomfortably. Long had been at the center of the biggest homicide case of Tony's career. His criminal record was extensive—attempted rape, assault, breaking and entering, dealing drugs, and more murders than even he could account for. He'd committed nine of them in Tulsa

County, all on the orders of William Davis—better known locally as Henry Daniels, chief of police . . . and Tony's godfather. Long had faced almost certain conviction and the death penalty, until the FBI had gotten him released from jail in order to help them with a sting operation. *We'll keep him under control,* the feds had promised. *He'll be as much a prisoner with us as he was in jail.*

They'd managed for nine days, and then he'd escaped.

Just as Tony had predicted.

Finally Simmons turned his attention to Selena. "You have any idea when the package was delivered?"

She shook her head. "It wasn't there when we left to go to Tony's parents'. That was about five."

"It'd be damn easy for someone to come in here," Simmons remarked, gesturing with both arms open wide. "Only four people living here, no damn traffic on the street, woods that back right up to the houses. What's on the other side?"

"The Marlowe Mansion," Tony replied.

"Any fences between here and there?"

Tony shrugged and Selena shook her head. When she'd first arrived in Tulsa, she had parked at the mansion and walked through the woods to the edge of Tony's yard, making note of the locations of the other houses, of his fenced-in yard and the dog snoozing there. She liked to know her surroundings . . . especially since, back then, she'd come to town with the intent to kill a man.

"Well, hell, son." Simmons flipped the notebook shut and tossed it on top of his suit coat. "Once the fire department finishes, CSU will gather evidence. Maybe they'll find enough of that cat for a proper burial. Why was it so eager to get in the house, anyway?"

"He used to live there." Tony's expression was somber. "I guess he was going home."

"Well, he's in his final home now. Better him than you." Simmons slapped Tony on the shoulder, then headed off to talk with the fire captain.

Selena sat down on the curb and, after a moment, Tony joined her. For a time they watched the firemen in silence. Finally, though, he glanced at her, his attention a weight she could feel even if she refused to look back. "You don't seem too upset that your house got blown up."

"I only lived there a few weeks."

"What about your paintings? Your brushes?"

"Brushes can be replaced." She hesitated, then risked a sidelong look at him. "You think Long's back in town."

His features took on the hard expression that mention of Damon Long always prompted. "Who else wants you dead as much as he does?"

"Do you really think he would risk coming back to Tulsa?" Long was at the top of the TPD's most wanted list, and the FBI was searching for him, as well.

"Do I think he's arrogant enough to believe he can come back here, kill you, and get away again? Yeah. On the other hand, maybe he hired someone. God knows, he's got the contacts."

Her chest grew tight, and Selena realized she'd forgotten to breathe. She forced in a slow, steady breath, then exhaled it just as steadily. If Tony was right, she could say good-bye to the peace of the last two months. Damon Long was a psychopath. If he was determined to kill her, he wouldn't stop until he'd succeeded . . . or she'd stopped him.

She'd known this day might come. The first few weeks after Long's escape from the FBI, she'd expected it—had curtailed her activities, kept her pistol close at hand, been overly suspicious of everything and everyone. But as the days had passed with no sign of him, her fear had lessened. She'd begun to think that Long had forgotten about her, that all his energies were focused on staying free, creating a new life—a new criminal enterprise—for himself.

She'd begun to think, for the first time ever, that life was going to be normal. She wanted a normal life, dear God, more than she could say.

"If it was Long, he'll try again." Her voice was steadier than she'd hoped for, not even hinting at the fear and distress she felt inside.

Another explosion sounded from within the house, startling her. The firemen, sweaty and grimy inside their turnout gear, fell back and regrouped as flames erupted through the roof at the far side of the house. Like her, Tony watched for a moment before finally speaking. "We'll have to be ready for him."

Be ready. Go back to living in fear. Cowering behind locked doors. Facing every moment of every day knowing that this could be the time he'd strike again. There could be no more lovely evenings like this one; Long liked suffering and wouldn't hesitate to harm Tony's family to punish her. She should stay away from Tony, as well. In fact, she should pack her bags and run. Change her name, change her appearance, give up her life for a mere existence.

Slowly Tony turned to face her, his dark eyes fierce. "Don't even think about it."

"What?" she asked unconvincingly.

"Leaving me for my own good. We'll be ready. We'll face him together."

She smiled weakly, but before she could think of a response, Simmons joined them again.

"Arson investigator's on his way, though they're gonna

have to get this thing knocked down before he can do any-thing. What's the plan?"

"We're going to check into a motel for the night. Tomorrow...we'll see," Tony said.

"We can call the local news stations and get 'em to run Long's picture on the news. If he is back in town, he's gotta be staying somewhere, eating somewhere. Maybe someone will recognize him. You don't need to be driving any of these cars, either. They tend to stick out." Simmons indicated Tony's Impala—obviously a police car with its antennas and grill lights—the red vintage Corvette, and Selena's bright yellow Thunderbird. "I'll take you to the motel, and tomor-row we can see about getting something less flashy for you. Fire captain wants the area evacuated. He says you can go in and grab some clothes from your place if you're quick about it."

Tony stood and extended his hand to Selena. "We'll have to take Mutt and the calico. I'll get one of my brothers to—"

An unholy screech echoed through the air as a streak of sooty black raced across the yard from the back of Selena's house. It cleared Tony's steps in one leap and huddled there against the closed door.

"I'll be damned," Frankie said, shaking his head. "That is one lucky cat."

Tony left Selena to calm the cat while he took the stairs two at a time to the bedroom. He filled the biggest suitcase he had with clothes for both of them, dumped everything they needed from the bathroom into a plastic shopping bag, added Selena's two handguns, and crawled halfway under the guest room bed to retrieve the calico. Downstairs he handed everything over to Simmons, then picked up Mutt's leash. As soon as he let the dog in from the back yard, they could be on their way.

Mutt was always excited to see Tony, and doubly so then. He managed to hook the leash onto the dog's collar, then led Mutt through the double-wide doorway into the living room, where he came to an abrupt stop.

"Fuck," he murmured.

The woman sitting in the easy chair aiming a .45 at him didn't seem to take offense at the profanity. Utterly motionless, she studied him. "Who are you?"

"Tony Ceola. Better question—who are you, and what the hell are you doing in my house?"

She stood slowly and lowered the gun to her side. "I'm here to see Selena. Is she all right?"

"What business is it of yours?"

"We're friends of a sort."

Charlize Pawley. He stared at her—beautiful, elegant, so cool a man might get frostbite. Her skin was a delicate shade of pale, her hair so blond it seemed colorless. Selena had mentioned her a time or two; so had Adam Robinette, the FBI agent in charge of the undercover operation that had almost resulted in Selena's death. Robinette believed Charlize was J.T., Henry Daniels's hitter for the southern region but, with nothing more than an audiotape of a phone call Damon Long made to J.T., couldn't prove it. Robinette also believed that Selena *could* prove it, but wouldn't. Tony suspected he was right, but he couldn't be sure, because while Selena trusted him with a lot, the truth about Charlize wasn't part of it.

"Come on, Chee," Simmons called from the stoop. "The fire captain said be quick."

Tony ignored him. "What do you want with Selena?"

"I came to warn her that Damon Long's put out a contract on her—a half million dollars." Charlize opened the slender handbag that hung from one shoulder and slid the pistol inside. "Apparently, I was too late."

And, apparently, if she knew about the contract, Robinette's suspicions were on target. "Did he offer this contract to you?"

Her only response was a shrug.

"But you came to warn Selena."

Her smile was chilling. "I own one of the most popular restaurants in Savannah. I don't need Long's money."

"How did you get in here?"

"I picked the lock. Disarmed the alarm." Her manner indicated that it had been easy. As if all restaurant owners possessed such skills. "I reset it so you wouldn't get suspicious when you came in."

"Hey, Chee, come—" Simmons halted in the doorway, and his free hand went automatically to his weapon. "Who the hell are you?"

"A friend of Selena's," Charlize replied.

Without taking his gaze from Charlize, Tony said, "She came to warn Selena that Long's put a hit out on her."

"There's a surprise," Simmons muttered.

Another small explosion sounded next door, and Charlize's attention flickered in that direction. "May I suggest we continue this conversation elsewhere?"

"How about the jail?" Tony smiled, but it didn't make his suggestion any less serious.

"And what would be the premise for my arrest, Detective?"

"You kill people."

"You have no evidence of that. And while you harass me at the jail, who's going to protect Selena from the men Long hired?"

Outside the black cat mewed, and a moment later Selena stepped into the foyer. "Tony, what's taking so—Charlize." There was surprise, a hint of pleasure, and more than a hint of uncertainty in her dark eyes. "What are you—" She looked out the door at the burning house, and understanding settled over her features.

The other woman warmed a few degrees. "I came to warn you about Damon Long. Sorry I was a little late."

"We've got to get out of here," Simmons said, "and get Island Girl someplace safe. You want the patrol guy out there to take the blonde into custody?"

"I can help protect her," Charlize said.

As if he would trust her around Selena with a gun, Tony thought scornfully. As if he would trust her without a gun.

"Come with us, Charlize," Selena said. "We'll talk at the motel."

"Selena—" Tony broke off when she looked at him. He knew that stubbornness—had run up against it every time she was in danger. She insisted on doing things her own way. His muscles clenching, he held out his hand. "Give me your purse."

Without hesitation, Charlize handed it over. He removed the .45 and an extra magazine, then gave it back. He considered searching her for additional weapons, but that body-hugging outfit didn't leave anything to the imagination. She couldn't hide a deep breath. Besides, he didn't plan on leaving her alone with Selena even for a second.

"Let's go," he said, gesturing to the door.

After leaving Mutt and the cats in a patrol car, Tony called his brother Dom and made arrangements for him to pick up all three animals and to get the black cat to the vet, though the way he had been purring in Selena's arms, he seemed fine.

Then the four of them climbed into Simmons's car, Charlize up front with Frankie, Selena and Tony in back, where he could keep watch on both women. They drove in silence for a time, aimlessly it seemed, though Tony knew Simmons was making sure no one was following them. It was a good bet that the bastard responsible for the bomb was in the crowd gawking at the end of the block, that he'd seen Selena, alive and well, and knew he'd failed. He would try again.

Finally satisfied that they were safe—relatively— Simmons turned into the parking lot of a motel just off Interstate 44. He went inside and rented two rooms, both at the far end of the second floor, then parked in front of the stairs.

The rooms were standard cheap motel—two beds, television bolted to the wall, disreputable carpet, cramped bathroom. Tony and the two women went into the room on the end; Simmons let himself into the one next to it, then opened the connecting door. "What now?" he asked.

"Get Long's picture on the news," Tony said. "Find out if Garry and Watson can keep an eye outside here, and maybe a couple other guys to relieve them. And we need to see the footage the news crew shot—see if anyone in the crowd seems particularly interested."

"You won't find the man responsible in the crowd." Charlize turned from her position near the window, letting the curtain fall against the wall. "No one Long would hire is amateur enough to hang around to watch. Someone"— annoyance flickered across her face—"must have hired out the job."

"So maybe we'll find the subcontractor," Simmons said, "and find out who hired him."

Charlize was shaking her head. "He won't know his employer's name. Trust me."

Tony barely resisted a snort as he caught Selena's hand, pulling her from her position near the dresser, past Simmons, and into the other room. "Keep an eye on Charlize," he said to Frankie just before closing the door.

Sliding his arms around Selena, he just held her for a moment. He'd gotten complacent these last few weeks. After doing nothing but worrying about her for so long, he'd been stupid to think that the danger was behind them, that everything would be okay.

"Do you believe Charlize came here to warn you?" he asked at last.

The tension in Selena's body was answer enough. She didn't know what to believe, and she knew the woman.

"Robinette thinks she's J.T."

Selena said nothing, but her gaze flickered away for a moment.

"What really happened that night, Selena?"

Restlessly she drew away, paced toward the window, and stood there, her back to him. She didn't lift the curtain, though—didn't expose herself to anyone who might be outside, watching.

"The story you told about killing Yates was so obviously not true. You covered for the real killer, and I let you. I didn't push you even though I knew you were lying." His gut tightened at the last words. It wasn't the first time she'd lied to him, and it might not be the last, but it was the hardest to take. She said she loved him, but she didn't trust him with the truth. "Is Robinette right? Is Charlize J.T.? Did she kill Yates?"

Slowly Selena turned to face him. Her face was expressionless in the dim light, but not her eyes. There was uncertainty in their depths. She was trying to decide whether to trust him or to protect a hired killer.

"I told you what happened."

Disappointment settled in his chest. "You had Yates's blood on you, Selena. There's no way in hell to explain that if you were across the room pulling the trigger." Bitterly he dragged his fingers through his hair, then softened his tone. "I'm not on the job. My only interest in that night is you."

She smiled thinly. "You're always on the job, Tony. It's what you do. Who you are."

"Damn it, Selena—"

For a long time, she remained stiff and still. Finally, though, she inhaled, then quietly said, "She saved my life. I owed her."

Her words eased the tightness in his chest. "She shot Yates."

Selena nodded. "He was going to kill me, and she shot him." Fiercely she repeated, "Charlize saved my life."

Cool was damn sure the right word to describe Charlize. She and Sonny Yates had been lovers, and yet she had killed him to save William's chosen heir.

"You could have told me. Killing someone to stop him from killing someone else is justified." He paused for a moment as guilt flashed into her eyes, then went on. "But she couldn't stand the scrutiny, could she? According to the FBI, Charlize Pawley's not her real name. Her background's phony. The restaurant's a cover for her real business— killing people."

Reluctantly Selena nodded.

Great. So there was a killer outside the motel who wanted Selena dead, and another inside who claimed she only wanted to protect her. Who'd already protected her once.

"What are you going to do now?"

Who the hell knew? He was a cop. It was his job to arrest criminals. But *this* criminal had done the right thing once, and claimed she was trying to do it again. And the only death he knew for certain that Charlize was responsible for hadn't been murder, but the justifiable death of a drug dealer.

"She could have already killed us, Tony. She got into your house without anyone seeing her. She could have left without anyone seeing her. But she didn't try to harm us."

"There were a lot of cops around."

Another smile. "I imagine Charlize would see that as a test of her skills."

"Are you saying you trust her?"

The smile faded. "I don't know. We're a lot alike. William took us both in, offered us both a place within his organization. She was loyal to him, and she seems loyal to me. She killed for me. I feel . . . connected to her."

"Do you trust her with your life?" When Selena didn't respond, Tony changed the question. "Do you trust her with my life? Because the only way anyone's getting to you is through me."

She shook her head.

That left him with three options: have Charlize arrested, throw her out, or keep her close where they could watch her. Arresting her at that point—with no physical evidence, with nothing at all connecting her to Yates's death besides the word of a woman who'd just admitted to giving a false statement to the FBI—would be pointless. Any half-assed lawyer would get her out in no time. She would be pissed, and would know where to find them. Throwing her out would lead to the same problem. They would have to relocate, when they already had security in place at this motel.

Which left the third choice. Guarding Selena and

Charlize would be no more complicated than guarding Selena alone.

"All right. We keep her where we can watch her for the present. When we move, we'll decide then what to do. Okay?"

"Okay."

When he offered his hand, she took it, coming back into his arms. He kissed her—no tongues, just an intensely hungry kiss. Then he let her go, reclaimed her hand, and they returned to the other room.

"I called in every favor I'm owed," Simmons said. "Garry and Baxter are on their way over. Watson's going to relieve them later with a couple of guys from Special Operations. Suz says if we need any real help, she'll get a babysitter for the kids and come on over."

Tony smiled. Suz Simmons was like a yippy little lapdog who thought she was an eight-hundred-pound gorilla—short, slender, girly, but with an attitude that kept her six-foot-plus husband in line. She fiercely protected what was hers, and though she hadn't even met Selena, she obviously felt proprietary toward her because of the connection between Simmons and Tony.

Charlize Pawley claimed to feel proprietary toward Selena, too. The difference was Tony knew Suz could be trusted. He was pretty damn sure Charlize couldn't. But there she was, watching the parking lot through a narrow gap in the drapes.

Keep your friends close and your enemies closer. It was the best choice he could make under the circumstances. He just hoped he didn't live to regret it.

"How have you been?"

Charlize glanced from the scene outside—a mostly empty

parking lot, traffic on the interstate and the access road that ran alongside—to Selena. Looking at her, no one would guess that she'd been the target of a bomb a few hours previously. Selena wasn't the sort of person who readily revealed her emotions. She was cool, calm, and in control. They had that—and much more—in common.

"I'm staying busy with the restaurant." When Charlize had moved to Savannah twelve years ago, she'd spent some of the small fortune she'd amassed on the redbrick restaurant so that she'd have something to do between jobs for William. The place had become wildly successful and, to her surprise, she'd discovered that she liked the business. She could see herself becoming a full-time restaurateur and the upstanding citizen she already pretended to be.

She could see herself becoming a law-abiding citizen. Wouldn't that surprise a lot of people?

Selena stood motionless, a few feet from the window. "That night . . . did I thank you?"

That night. Innocent-sounding words for a most eventful evening. Selena had already survived one attempt on her life by the time Charlize slipped into the third-floor ballroom and saw Sonny Yates about to crush her skull with a dumbbell. For eight years, Charlize had shared her bed and her life with Sonny, but she hadn't hesitated to kill him. He was her lover, and he'd fancied himself in love with her, but Selena was William's heir, and that made her Charlize's boss.

"You did," she replied, "though I'm not surprised you don't remember. Sonny had done quite a number on you." He'd wanted Selena dead—wanted to take over the drug empire he'd thought she was ruining and run it himself, with Charlize at his side.

Charlize never would have allowed him to do that.

"Were you all right?" Selena asked.

Charlize kept her eyes on the window. For all that she and Selena had in common, they were also vastly different in some ways. Selena had never killed anyone, and found the mere idea repugnant. Even if she'd managed to kill Sonny herself that night, if she'd had no choice but to take his life or sacrifice her own, it would have weighed heavily on her conscience.

Charlize, on the other hand, had no such qualms. She'd made her first kill at the age of fifteen and had carried out her first contract two years later. It was a business to her—profitable, challenging, difficult in several ways but not morally. She wasn't amoral by any means. She simply lived by her own code.

"It was just another part of the job," she said with a shrug.

"But he was your—"

"Job," she repeated. "My job was to carry out the hits William assigned to me, to protect his best interests, and to protect him. With him out of the picture, my job became looking out for *your* best interests and protecting *you*."

"Even though I wasn't really taking over the business."

"You were his chosen successor. That was all that mattered."

"And now?" Selena asked quietly.

Was she still looking out for Selena's best interests? Or was she engaged in an elaborate scam to kill Selena and cash in on Long's contract?

The contract that she'd thought was exclusively hers. She didn't accept open offers, didn't take jobs where she was competing against someone else for the paycheck. She didn't need to.

But then Long had offered the deal to one of her competitors.

It didn't bother Charlize that neither Selena nor the two men—especially the two men—trusted her. She'd learned when she was twelve, and again at fifteen, that trust was easily taken and easily betrayed. She didn't trust anyone, nor did she expect anyone to trust her. It was safer that way.

She smiled faintly. "Let's say I'm upholding my own personal code of ethics. I killed once before to save your life. I don't plan to stand by now and let someone else kill you."

"What about the half million dollars? It's a lot of money."

"I have money. Besides, it's never been about the money."

"What is it about?"

She could answer the question truthfully, but it would take time and would require delving into memories and feelings she'd long since buried. Charlize didn't care for such close self-examination. It changed nothing, but made her regret what could have been.

"It's about doing what I do well," she said at last. "You paint beautiful pictures. Your boyfriend is a good detective." Another shrug. "I kill people. Efficiently, reliably, without mistakes."

Charlize knew as she turned back to the window that she sounded cold. She *was* cold. She didn't have a tender feeling in her body...except, possibly, for Selena. They were so much alike. They'd gone through such trauma, and they'd both been rescued by William. He'd taken care of them, taught them, given them what they needed to survive. They could have been friends—sisters, even—if he'd given them the chance.

Of course, he hadn't. He'd had grander plans for Selena. She was to be the heir to his criminal kingdom, while Charlize was merely his hired gun. Selena was to inherit the millions of dollars, along with the dangers, the risks—and

Charlize, who would neutralize them for her. They weren't meant to be friends.

Though they could have been. Charlize found a certain comfort in that knowledge.

But how would it have changed them? Would it have saved Charlize . . . or destroyed Selena?

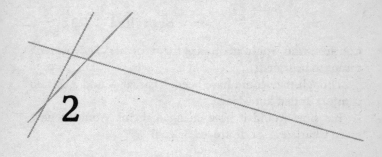

2

Selena sat on the bed farther from the window, eyes closed, concentrating on slowing and evening her breathing. Time was crawling. Tony's fellow detectives were keeping watch from the motel parking lot, while Tony, Charlize, and Simmons took turns peering from the window. Every footstep passing the room brought them all on alert, only for the tension to ease as the intruder proved to be merely another motel guest.

One of the detectives had posed as housekeeping to deliver the footage from the local news stations. The others had watched it, while Selena watched Charlize. If the woman recognized anyone, she hid it well. She'd studied each face in the crowd before shaking her head. *I told you so.* The man who'd delivered the bomb very well might have been in the shots, but the man who'd given the orders wasn't.

After that, they'd had pizza delivered—by another of Tony's cop friends—and now they merely waited and watched. No one seemed in the mood to talk besides Selena, and she didn't know what to say. Except for one thing. "I've got to leave town."

Everyone glanced her way—Tony, standing at the window; Charlize, sitting on the other bed; and Simmons, leaning in the connecting doorway. None of them spoke, until Tony turned back to the window. "You're safe here."

"But how long can we stay here? How long can your

friends give up their free time to provide surveillance? Who will take over when you have to go to work tomorrow? How long can we live in a dingy motel room, waiting for whoever is after me to make another attempt?"

He didn't answer, which meant he didn't have any answers. He hated it, she knew from experience, when he thought she was wrong but had no ammunition to back up his opinion.

"We'll work it out," Tony said flatly. "I'll talk to the chief about setting up surveillance officially. Maybe—"

Simmons snickered. "Come on, Chee. Every division's shorthanded because they don't have the money to hire new officers. There's no way the chief's gonna sign off on this. There's no departmental interest."

"I damn near got killed tonight. How's that for departmental interest?"

Simmons shuffled awkwardly. "But the bomb wasn't meant for you. It's not like your girlfriend's in danger because of your job. *You're* in danger because of *her* activities."

Tony turned and scowled. "Activities she was forced into by the former chief of police. Doesn't that count for anything?"

"Hey, Chee, I'm on your side. If it was up to me, I'd assign a detail in a heartbeat. But it ain't up to me, and it ain't gonna happen. We're on our own."

Tony opened his mouth to argue, then closed it again. He hated that Simmons was right. Selena could see it in his eyes.

She didn't share his feelings. She knew from experience that police officers could be corrupted, that even round-the-clock protection from the FBI didn't mean a person was safe.

Tony gave her a thin, humorless smile. "I could always arrest you."

"You think Long can't get to her just because she's in jail?" Charlize asked.

The mere thought of being confined to a jail cell sent a claustrophobic shiver down Selena's spine. Tony might like to take her into custody, but they both knew he couldn't. One of the reasons she'd gone along with the FBI's plan to put her undercover as a drug dealer was that they'd threatened her with jail. She *couldn't* face confinement and survive.

He stared out the window again, though there had been nothing out of the ordinary to look at for the last four hours. When he finally spoke, his voice was quiet. "Where would we go?"

We. Selena felt a rush of security. He'd promised he would always be there for her, and he'd proven it repeatedly. He was the only person in her life she'd been able to count on, no matter what, and she loved him desperately for it.

Rising from the bed, she went to stand beside him, put her arms around him. "What about your cases?"

"Hell, I can take care of 'em," Simmons said. When Tony looked at him, he scowled. "I can do just as much nothin' on your cases as I do on my own. Don't worry about it. As long as you don't have any court appearances scheduled, I can handle it."

"Thanks, Frankie. You know, you keep this up, we're going to make a detective out of you yet."

"Funny," Simmons replied with another scowl.

"We can't go to Key West," Selena murmured wistfully. Four months ago, her home and art gallery on the island had been the most important things in her life. She missed it, even if it was no longer home. Now "home" was Tulsa or, better put, wherever Tony happened to be.

"Too obvious," Charlize said. "So is Alabama. They'd expect that."

Selena turned to study the blonde. For twenty-eight years, Selena had wondered about the identity of her father. How ironic that once she'd found out, so had everyone who followed the local news in Tulsa and in the small town of Greenhill, Alabama.

Selena had known before that night two months ago that Kathryn Hamilton wanted her dead, but she hadn't known why: because she was the daughter of Kathryn's husband, Grant. The illegitimate daughter of a white, old-money, Southern-aristocracy, descendant-of-slave-holders married man and his black lover.

And following Kathryn's failed attempt on Selena's life, her adopted son Jefferson—known in the shadowy world where he operated as Sonny Yates—had made his own attempt, and died for it.

It had made for sensational news stories in both towns.

"Why don't you come to Savannah?" Charlize suggested.

Selena tamped down the bitterness that had risen inside her. It did no good to hate William, comatose in his hospital bed, or Kathryn, locked up in a psychiatric hospital until the court decided whether she was competent to stand trial. It certainly did no good at the moment to mourn the mother she could never know.

"Savannah," Tony repeated. "People tried to kill her when she was there—twice."

Charlize nodded.

"The story of Yates's death was in the news there. Everyone who worked for him thinks she killed him. Why the hell would she want to go there?"

Selena's arm tightened around Tony's waist. "Because no

one would expect it. I have no ties to the city. On my one visit there, people did try to kill me. Why would I go back?"

"Savannah's my city," Charlize said. "I have contacts there. You'll have a safe place to stay, and if any of my competitors come to town looking for you, I'll know."

Selena's chest was tight. As a teenager, she'd dreamed of visiting Savannah when William's base of operations was there. Nine weeks ago, she'd come too close to dying there. She didn't want to go back. But the argument in favor of it was good.

Charlize rose from the bed. "Why don't you talk about it? Detective Simmons and I will go in the other room and keep watch from there. Is that all right with you, Detective?"

Simmons looked at Tony, who nodded slightly. Her movements elegant and graceful, Charlize walked through the connecting door into the dimly lit room next door. In a low voice, Tony said, "Let her keep watch outside. You watch her."

With a nod, Simmons closed the door behind him.

Silence gathered around them, close and taut. After a time, Selena put a few feet between her and Tony. "What do you think?"

His boyish smile made her heart stutter. "I think loving you is going to make me old before my time." Then he shrugged. "Savannah *is* her turf. That gives her an advantage over us. If we knew we could trust her . . ."

Of course he didn't trust Charlize. Tony had been born a cop. With a father and two uncles who had spent their lives in law enforcement, being a cop was in his blood. He had far more experience with criminals and killers than Selena did . . . though her experience came from the other side of the law. She'd been raised by one crook after another. She'd been taught to pick pockets, steal, and con people the way other kids were taught to brush their teeth and comb their hair. She knew some crooks could be good people in spite of their lawbreaking ways. Some crooks had their own ethical code.

Was Charlize one of them?

"What do you suggest?"

He took one last look out the window, then grabbed her hand and drew her over to the bed with him. "I think I'd rather stay here. Tulsa is *my* turf. That gives *me* an advantage."

She waited for the *but...*, as he turned her so he could work on the tension that knotted her shoulders.

"But...contract killers work a lot like cops do when they're looking for someone. They'll go to the last known location. They'll talk to friends and neighbors and coworkers. They'll use whatever leverage they can find, including family."

And while she had no family in Oklahoma, Tony did—parents, six brothers and sisters, aunts and uncles. Every Ceola listed in the phone book was related to him.

And Damon Long was intimately acquainted with Tony's younger sister, Lucia. He'd seduced her, intending to use her against William, godfather to all seven of the Ceola kids, but it had been a miscalculation on his part. Lucia had inadvertently led Tony to the discovery of William's true identity—police chief Henry Daniels.

"If I had enough help...but Simmons was right. There's no way the department's going to take on the job of protecting you. Much as they'd like to see Long back in jail, to them you're just one more of his victims, and we don't have the budget or the manpower to provide protection to victims. You're not even a good witness against him. You know a lot about what he's done, but you have very little firsthand information."

She considered herself lucky for that as her head fell forward, exposing more of her neck for his touch. His fingers kneaded deeply into the stiff muscles, a moment of pain followed by an easing of tension. She loved his touch. He could calm her, soothe her, arouse her, satisfy her, comfort her, love her.

"So you agree I need to leave."

His hands stilled for a moment before resuming their movement. "I think the smart thing for both of us is to get the hell out of Dodge."

"I—" She hesitated, then went on. "I can go alone. Your job is here, your family, your life. I've been on my own before."

This time his fingers didn't even slow. "You're not going anywhere without me but the bathroom until this is over. And when it's over, I'm going to look for that island Frankie keeps talking about and hide us both away there forever."

She wasn't sure which sounded better—the island or simply the *forever*. One of these days, she *would* be free to live a normal life. She would...or die trying.

"So..." Finished with the massage, Tony lay back on the bed, stuffing pillows under his head. She stretched out next to him, resting her head on his shoulder. Through the fabric of his shirt, she imagined she could feel the scar where she'd shot him over three months ago. She'd done it to save his life—if she hadn't, William would have shot him in the heart or the head—but she still regretted it.

His voice rumbled in his chest when he spoke. "To fly to Savannah from here, we have to go through Dallas and/or Atlanta. Dallas was Damon Long's last known location, so we don't want to spend any time there, but Atlanta..."

Atlanta was a good place to get lost in, as well as a good jumping-off point to any other destination in the world. "So we let everyone, including Charlize, think we're going to Savannah, but we get off the plane in Atlanta and go into hiding." Disappear. Go on the run.

Everything in her wanted to protest. She was tired of running and hiding. She wanted to stand and fight...but not as much as she wanted to live.

Tony kissed her forehead. "Sounds like a plan."

"Not much of one." Disappearing in Atlanta wouldn't discourage Long's assassins. It would merely delay the inevitable.

"No, but it'll give us time to come up with something else."

Time to plan. Time to be together. Time to live.

Before it turned into time to die.

Tony pressed the button on his watch to light up the dial, then suppressed a yawn. *Two A.M. and all's well.* Traffic had slowed on the interstate, and only an occasional car passed on Fifty-first. Most people were home in bed asleep, where he wished he and Selena were.

He wished he'd killed Damon Long the first time he'd laid eyes on him. God knows, he'd had good reasons: everything the bastard had ever done to Selena—trying to rape her, beating her, taking part in Henry's plan to kill her—along with what he'd done to Lucia. Tony's baby sister drove him nuts more often than not, but he didn't like anyone screwing with her, and Long had done just that, in more ways than one.

Maybe Tony would get another chance to kill the bastard.

Not arrest him. Kill him.

There was a brush of sound behind him, along with the aroma of strong coffee, and Simmons appeared in the shadows, two cups in hand. "You wanna get some sleep?" he asked as he offered one cup. His voice was pitched low so he wouldn't disturb the two women resting in the beds behind them.

"I'll sleep on the plane tomorrow." At least for the brief duration of the flight, he could be sure Selena would be safe from gun- or knife-wielding attackers. Maybe they could spend the next however many days hiding out on airplanes and in airport terminals, he thought, and knew he really did need sleep, because the idea didn't sound as ridiculous as it should.

"You cleared being gone with the chief?"

"Yeah." The boss hadn't been happy about him taking off on such short notice, but since the only alternative had been to accept Tony's resignation, he'd agreed. "Don't fuck up any of my cases."

"You can't fuck up what you don't mess with."

A minute passed before Tony glanced at Simmons again. "Keep in touch with my sister Julie, will you? And tell her to warn Lucia about Long."

"You think he might send someone around to find out if she knows where you are?"

"I wouldn't put it past him." Lucia would never deliberately do anything to put him or Selena in danger, but she hadn't deliberately fallen in love with a psychopath, either. Long had hurt her enough. Damned if anyone else was going to.

"You gonna come up with a plan while you're in Savannah?"

Tony looked over his shoulder. Selena was asleep in the far bed—he could tell as surely as he knew he was awake—while

Charlize lay in the closer bed. Though her breathing was even and her eyes were closed, it was impossible to say whether she was sleeping or putting on a good act. Either way, he wouldn't risk sharing their plans in front of her.

"Right now we're just playing for time." And right now that was enough. But they couldn't put their lives on hold forever.

"We're gonna have to stop Long to put an end to this. If the feds can't catch him—and they haven't even had a sighting in nearly a month—he's gonna have to be lured out into the open. And if we get him in the open . . ." Simmons's expression was grim as he stared outside.

"He's got to die," Tony finished for him.

Simmons looked at him. "It's the only way Island Girl will be safe. And any way you look at it, it's justice."

Any way you look at it, it's wrong. It was nothing more than vigilantism—judging, condemning, meting out punishment. No matter what Long had done, he had a right to a trial, a jury, due process.

But his right to due process didn't outweigh Selena's right to live. Long was responsible for untold deaths and violence. Not just Selena but the world would be better off without him in it.

And Tony was willing to remove him. Without an arrest. Without a trial or a lawyer or civil rights. He was ready to be judge. Jury.

Executioner.

If it kept Selena alive, if it made her safe, he could live with it.

"I'm leaving my cell phone," he said, relieved to change the subject. "When I get a new one, I'll let you know."

"Sure. I'll notify the feds tomorrow about Long's

contract. You'd think with their vast resources, they'd have already heard about it."

"Who says they haven't?" Tony's smile was thin. He didn't think highly of anyone who'd put a cooperating witness like Selena in position as a target...though wasn't setting up Selena as a target now the best way to lure Damon Long out of hiding?

"Yeah, and they probably didn't think it wise to notify the intended victim." Simmons shook his head. "Damn feebs."

In the silence that followed, Tony drank half his coffee. By the time they got on the plane in a couple hours, he was going to be exhausted. He hoped a few hours' sleep would be enough to keep him alert while he and Selena found a place to hide.

Down below, a car turned into the parking lot. Tony watched idly, and knew Simmons was doing the same, when the vehicle stopped near the stairs. A second car pulled in behind, headlights off, and an occupant from the first car climbed out and trotted back to the second.

"You guys awake up there?" a quiet voice asked on Simmons's radio.

"Yeah, we see 'em."

"That punk outside...I remember him from my days in Street Crimes. Name's Lorenzo."

"What do you think are the odds he's got legitimate business here?"

A snort was the only reply from the detective outside.

With the hairs on the back of his neck standing on end, Tony watched as three more men got out of the cars. Despite the mild chill, they all wore bulky jackets—the better to conceal their weapons. They talked a moment longer, then started up the stairs.

He slid his pistol from the holster, barely breathing. Simmons did the same, then headed for the adjoining room.

The men had just reached the landing when the squeal of tires broke the silence. Two marked units, emergency lights flashing, turned into the parking lot from opposite ends and screeched to a stop, blocking in the two cars. As the officers jumped from their sedans, weapons drawn, the Special Operations Team guys came from their own cars, shouting, "Get down, get down!"

Three of the men on the stairs jumped over the railing and raced off in different directions. The fourth one, in the lead, took the last steps two at a time. He ran past the window where Tony stood watch, then, an instant later, sprawled back on the floor.

Simmons approached him, gun in his left hand, shaking off the pain of the punch in his right hand. "Give me a reason to shoot," he said before flashing a grin through the window at Tony.

"What's going on?"

Tony stiffened as Charlize joined him. "They found us."

"How?"

"Damned if I know." They hadn't been followed from his house—he and Simmons were sure of that.

Maybe Charlize had some kind of GPS transmitter on her. She didn't have a cell phone and hadn't gone near the room phone. More likely, someone in the crowd watching the fire had taken note of Selena leaving in Simmons's shit-box Ford, and they'd tracked it down in this motel parking lot.

He crossed the room to wake Selena. She was already stirring when he sat down next to her. "Hey, babe. Time to get up."

Her gaze shifted around the room—still dark except for

the red and blue lights shining through the parted drapes—
and immediately she came alert. "What happened?"

"We can't stay here," she said when Tony had filled her in.
If she was really as calm as her voice, he was impressed. If she
was only acting that calm, he was still impressed.

"No. As soon as they get those guys out of here, we're
moving."

"To where?"

He glanced at Charlize, whose attention was turned outside. "I'll tell you when we get there." It would be another
few hours before the airport opened for business, but UDE—
Uniform Division East—was always open. It wasn't quite as
good as placing Selena under arrest and locking her away in
a cell downtown.

But it came close.

After the stress of the last few hours in Tulsa—looking at
every car, watching every person in the airport terminal
with suspicion—the flight to Atlanta provided Selena with
the luxury of feeling safe. The knotted muscles in her neck
eased and the hyperalertness that had held her body stiff for
so long relaxed.

She sat in the window seat on the very last row in coach,
with Tony beside her. Though Charlize could have had the
aisle seat, she opted for one some thirty rows closer to the
front. She wanted to be able to see everyone who came onto
the plane.

"What are we going to tell her?" Selena asked as the plane
taxied to the gate at Hartsfield International.

Tony looked ragged, his eyes bleary from too little sleep,
his jaw stubbled with beard. He'd ducked into the lavatory
shortly before landing to splash cold water over his face, but

he was still pretty worn. "That we've changed our minds. We'd rather go it alone."

How would Charlize feel about the change of plans? Anything at all? Their rejection of her assistance might not matter either way to her. After all, she'd made the offer. The blame didn't fall on her if they didn't take her up on it.

The plane came to a stop, and virtually every passenger immediately stood, except her and Tony. They remained where they were, his fingers wrapped tightly around hers. "I hate being out here without a weapon," he remarked.

"I know the feeling." Though he could have checked his gun in the suitcase, the bag was going on to Savannah. They weren't. In light of that fact, he'd left both his and her weapons in Simmons's care. Replacing them was high on her list of priorities.

As the crowd slowly thinned, Tony stood. "We'll say good-bye to Charlize and get a cab to a motel. Later today we'll get some clothes and see about picking up new pistols. Then we'll decide what to do. Where to go."

Selena immediately had an image of a shady backroom deal, netting them at least two very illegal firearms. It wouldn't take more than a phone call to someone who knew someone to get directions to that back room, but Tony's mind worked in other ways. No doubt his plan was more along the lines of using his police resources to acquire the guns legally.

"And then?"

His expression was grim. "Then we come up with a plan."

Selena watched as the passengers moved slowly down the aisle. She already knew the best plan: she needed to come out of hiding, to lure Long into the open. To put her life on the line. It was the only way she could be free. And Tony would never agree to it.

As their turn came, they left their seats. Charlize fell in in front of Selena; Tony brought up the rear. They walked up the jetway and into the terminal, where Charlize stopped to locate the gate for their connecting flight. "We're this way," she said, turning to the left and taking a half dozen steps before realizing they weren't following. She turned back, looking from Tony to Selena. "What's up?"

"We appreciate everything you've done—"

Charlize's gaze shifted to someone behind and to the left of Selena and she muttered, "Shit. Walk with me. *Now.*"

Selena followed her gaze to the man who had caught Charlize's attention. He leaned against the wall ten feet away—good-looking, blond hair, jeans, white button-down shirt, sleeves rolled up to reveal muscular forearms. With one sneakered foot propped against the wall, a backpack slung over one shoulder, and a newspaper open before him, he looked like any other traveler waiting for a flight, except for the intensity with which he watched them.

As Tony took Selena's arm and pulled her along, the man pushed away from the wall, tossed the newspaper to the floor, and followed them.

"Who is that?" Selena asked, matching her steps to Charlize's long strides.

"His name's Luke Morgan." Charlize replied.

"He's one of you," Tony said grimly.

Charlize glanced at Selena. Selena didn't regret telling Tony about that night. It had been a tremendous relief, in fact. Still, she wished she'd warned Charlize that the truth was out.

Charlize shrugged dismissively. "We're in the same business. I wasn't aware he had also been offered this job." Where the broad corridor they were traveling was bisected by another, she steered them to the left and into a crowd of just-deplaned passengers. Weaving around the slower ones, she led them onto the escalator seconds ahead of a couple with three small children and a stroller. Morgan was left waiting.

The escalator led down to the train stop, which looked too much like a trap to Selena. Charlize had a plan, though. "Go to the far end," she ordered. Selena and Tony watched as she rushed up to a waiting group of young men, her gestures frantic, her expression distressed. Looking as if she might break into tears at any moment, she pointed to the escalator, then, in a nice touch to whatever tale she was telling, she clutched the arm of the biggest, brawniest man and made one last plea. He patted her arm with reassuring words, then the five men surged around her on their way to the escalator. When Morgan stepped off, they manhandled him to the side as the train pulled into the station, its doors opening with a whoosh.

Her cool and efficient self again, Charlize herded Selena and Tony onto the first car. As the train pulled out again, Morgan, still surrounded by the young men, waved good-bye with a one-fingered salute.

"What did you tell them?" Selena asked.

Charlize's mouth quirked in a half-smile. "That I ran into my ex-husband and he'd threatened me. Young men do like to play the hero."

"How did he know we would be here?" Suspicion darkened Tony's voice and his eyes as he scowled at her.

Charlize braced herself against the steel pole as the train took a curve. "I certainly didn't tell him. I didn't have the opportunity—or the reason. Think about it, Detective. If I want to keep Selena alive, I wouldn't tell Luke Morgan how to find her. If I'm merely trying to keep her to myself so I can kill her, I'm certainly not going to tell anyone else who's interested in killing her."

After an icy smile, she went on. "My guess is he's had someone watching you for a while. They followed us to the airport."

"We weren't followed," Tony disagreed.

"Not by an individual, but there very well could have been two, three or more cars working together. The most observant person in the world wouldn't have noticed."

Two stops passed in silence before Tony spoke again. "We're not going to Savannah."

"No," Charlize agreed. "Now that Luke's seen you with me, that'll be the next place he looks. We'll take a cab to a motel, then I'll pick up weapons and a car for you. I'll go on to Savannah, and you...hide."

Hide like a coward, Selena thought, then immediately amended that. Like a strategist. They needed time to formulate their plan—when she would step out into the open, where, how they would maximize her chances of survival. Staying safe in the meantime—hiding—was the smart thing to do.

No one paid any attention to them when they stepped off the train or when they left the terminal to get a cab. If the driver thought it strange they had no luggage, he didn't mention it. If anyone followed them as they left the airport and headed into the city, Selena couldn't tell.

The motel Charlize chose was on a street lined with other motels, fast-food restaurants, bars, and convenience stores. It had a budget price, and a budget look to go along with it, but that was fine with Selena, because right now no one else in the world knew they were there. Right now they were safe. But that didn't stop her from looking over her shoulder far too often.

She could do it a thousand times a day for now. As long as she didn't have to do it for the rest of her life.

While Tony slept, Selena stood in the corner, watching out the window, scrutinizing every passing car, every person who came into sight. She'd been doing it long enough for her muscles to stiffen when Charlize returned, carrying a folded paper bag under one arm and a half dozen plastic shopping bags in her hands. Selena didn't give her a chance to knock, but opened the door as she approached, staying out of sight, then closed and locked it again.

"I have food and some clothes," Charlize said. "Take the paper bag."

Inside were three weapons—a Glock .45, a Smith & Wesson 9-millimeter, and a .22-caliber Beretta. The last two were Selena's weapons of choice. Coincidence? Or had Charlize learned that about her before they'd met? There were also holsters, boxes of ammunition, and a thick wad of twenty-dollar bills. Selena sat down on the bed near Tony's feet and began loading the magazines for each of the three guns while Charlize laid out the food on the dresser.

When Selena was done, the Glock and the Beretta went on the nightstand, while she holstered the Smith and clipped it onto her waistband. Now she felt safer.

"I know you're not a jeans sort of person," Charlize said as she dumped the contents of the other bags on the bed, "but changing your appearance even a little can't hurt." She sorted everything into two piles. For each of them she'd bought a pair of jeans, three T-shirts, a package of underwear, and socks. She'd also purchased a pair of inexpensive running shoes for Selena, and toiletries.

Selena glanced at her flowing silk skirt and tank top, then

at the new clothes. Jeans and T-shirts. Could there be another outfit that blended in as well?

Leaving the clothing on the bed, Charlize unpacked food from a Chinese buffet. They each claimed a pair of chopsticks and a foam carton, then used the dresser as a bench, sitting at opposite ends. After taking the edge off her hunger, Selena glanced at Charlize. "Why are you helping us?"

For a long time, the other woman seemed too preoccupied with her lo mein to respond, but finally she looked up. A distant smile curved her lips. "I went to work for William eighteen years ago. I knew about you from the start. I knew when he went to Jamaica to 'rescue' you."

Selena slowly chewed a bite of egg roll. It had been a literal rescue. She'd chosen the wrong man to rob that night as a child on the streets in Ocho Rios. He'd hit her, threatened her, ripped her clothing . . . and then fallen lifeless on top of her. William had stepped out of the shadows, retrieved his knife from the man's back, and helped her to her feet. He'd taken her to his hotel, procured fraudulent papers for her, then brought her to the United States, and she had been oh, so grateful.

Until she'd discovered two months ago that William had paid the man to attack her in the first place.

"I thought no one knew about me but Damon Long," she said, surprised her voice was even.

"William told me more than even Damon realized. Our relationship was more than just professional."

"You weren't . . ." Selena couldn't finish the sentence. She knew Charlize had been lovers with Sonny Yates, but cold-hearted snake that he was, he was still a vast improvement over William. She couldn't imagine anyone being intimate with William.

Charlize's blue eyes glittered like ice. "No. Nothing like

that. He was old enough to be my father." The disdain faded from her voice. "I told you that night in the ballroom, after I shot Sonny, that my father had been William's hitter before me. They were friends, as much as William could be friends with anyone. My father was killed when I was fifteen, leaving me on my own. My mother had left us years before, and my father had had no contact with his family since before I was born. I was having a tough time until William took me in. He gave me a few odd jobs, then hired me on permanently."

"To kill people for him."

Charlize shrugged. "The idea of becoming an assassin wasn't as repugnant to me as it was to you. My father had done it. It wasn't hard to learn the ins and outs of the game. As you know, William could be a good teacher."

My father was killed . . . Selena prodded at the vegetables left in her carton. That night in the ballroom, Charlize had said that her father had gotten sick, that when he'd realized he was dying, he'd trained her himself. Which was true?

Selena understood better than most the reasons a person might lie about her upbringing. She'd done it herself—to the girls at the exclusive boarding schools William had sent her to; to the occasional friend; to Asha, who ran the art gallery for her; and to Tony. Shame, wanting to fit in, wanting to forget . . . she had her share of memories too painful to face without good cause.

She wouldn't intrude on Charlize's. "So William told you about me."

"He did some of the same things for me that he did for you. Not the formal education, but teaching me how to dress, how to walk, how to talk, how to stand out, how to blend in. He occasionally asked my advice regarding you."

"He 'rescued' us both."

"For his own purposes." Charlize took one last bite, then

tossed her carton and chopsticks into the trash. "Wake up Sleeping Beauty. We need to talk before I leave."

Selena hated to do it. If the tantalizing aromas of the food hadn't awakened Tony, then he seriously needed the rest. But she went to the bed and gently shook him awake.

When he opened his eyes, they were dazed and fatigued, but he still managed a smile for her. "Hey, babe."

"Charlize is back with food. She wants to talk to us before she goes."

He sat up, combed his fingers through his hair, leaving it standing on end, then scowled—at the room, at Charlize, at life in general. "The sooner we talk..."

Charlize heard the words he didn't say as clearly as Selena did. *The sooner you can go.* If the sentiment, his tone, or his frown bothered Charlize, she didn't let it show. Instead, she opened her purse, withdrew a photograph, and laid it on the bed. "I thought this might come in handy. It's a picture of the man Long hired to kill you." She gazed at the photo a moment, her features expressionless, then added, "Or, at least, one of them."

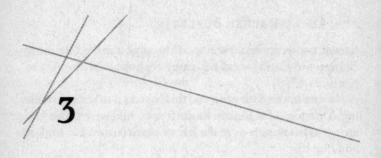

3

Tony had already committed Luke Morgan's face to memory in those few minutes at the airport, but the photograph *would* come in handy, since that likely wasn't his real name. He was six foot or so, blond with blue eyes, tanned, a scar across his jaw, and a tribal band tattooed around his left bicep. He was probably in his late thirties, and looked more like a surfer than a hired killer in the Hawaiian shirt and khaki shorts he wore in the photo.

"Where does he live?"

"He's not exactly settled, though he has a fondness for southern belles and beaches. Charleston, Miami, Tampa, Pensacola." Charlize lifted one shoulder in a shrug.

"He looks harmless," Selena remarked, though clearly she wasn't fooled. No one would guess to look at her—tall, slender, with curly black hair and coffee-colored skin, with big eyes and amazing delicacy—that she had a black belt in tae kwon do, could deliver a punch as well as she could take one, and was an expert pistol shot.

"Morgan's not his real name, of course," Charlize said, "but it's the one he uses most often. In our business, one name tends to be rather limiting."

Tony glanced at Selena, who'd had numerous names her-self, though not for the same reasons, thank God. All her names had been given to her by the adults controlling her life, except for the current one. She'd chosen that one for herself two years ago. He hoped she would make one more change—to Ceola—and be happy with that for the rest of her life.

Selena nudged his arm, and he looked up to see her holding a carton of Chinese food. It was lukewarm, but the aroma was enough to make his stomach growl. He took it and dug in.

"Is a bomb his style?" Selena asked.

"He's an equal opportunity killer. Whatever works." Charlize began gathering trash into one of the empty bags. "I'm catching an afternoon flight to Savannah. I'm going to see if I can track down Damon Long."

"How?" Tony demanded. "Cops and the feds have been trying to do that for two months."

She gave him a dry smile. "I have resources the Tulsa Police Department and the FBI are lacking."

"You have a phone number for him?"

"No."

"How did he contact you to make the offer?"

"By E-mail."

No surprise there. E-mail addresses were easy to set up, identities easy to conceal. The FBI's computer geeks could eventually follow the electronic trail back to its owner, but by then it was usually too late. He was long gone.

"And if you find him?"

She looked around the room as if determining whether she'd forgotten something. When her gaze connected with his again, her expression was blank, cool, and distant. "If Damon's dead, the contract is null and void."

She was willing to kill Long to protect Selena. Tony had that much in common with her.

If she could be trusted.

She walked to the door, then turned back. "I almost forgot...the car's a silver Toyota, parked at the bottom of the stairs." She tossed the keys and Selena caught them with one hand. "You guys stay put. I'll be in touch."

"Thank you," Selena murmured as the other woman walked out the door. She secured the two locks, then replaced the chair before sitting on the dresser. She sat there a long time, hands curled around the edge of the wood top, watching Tony eat, before finally speaking. "I want Damon Long to die in prison."

He polished off the last bit of an egg roll, wiped his hands on a napkin, then flatly said, "That's not going to happen."

"It's what he deserves."

"He'll get what he deserves. Whether Charlize finds him or I do...he's not walking away from this, Selena."

"You can't kill him."

"It'll be justifiable."

"Tony—"

"He's trying to kill you, Selena. He's been trying to kill you for months. This is the end of it."

She looked so troubled by the idea that he couldn't resist going to her and wrapping his arms around her. "It *will* be justifiable. He's not going to meekly surrender. The only way for this scenario to play out is for one of you to die, and I damn well won't let it be you."

"But—" Breaking off, she pressed her face to his chest as a small shudder vibrated through her. In a heartbeat, it was gone. She was afraid, but she wouldn't let it make her weak.

After a moment, Tony set her back and went to the phone. After asking the desk clerk to call a cab, he began stuffing the clothes Charlize had brought back into their plastic bags. Selena watched, then, without a word, started tidying the room so that it looked as if they'd never been there.

"Where are we going?" she asked after straightening the rumpled covers where he'd slept.

"To another motel." Finished packing, he went to watch out the window. When a cab turned into the parking lot, he picked up the bags and gestured for her to follow him.

"You don't trust Charlize," Selena said quietly.

He glanced at her. "Do you?"

"Part of me wants to. Part of me does, I think." She said the last with a faint smile. She was used to conflicting feelings. She had both loved and hated William for years.

"The gut instincts that have kept you alive all these years... what do they tell you?"

"Not to trust anyone." She opened the cab door and slid into the backseat before smiling at him. "Except you."

He told the cabbie to drive and kept his attention on the traffic behind them. After a few miles, they left that cab and flagged down another to return in the direction they'd just come. Tony directed the driver to the motel across the street from the first. He wanted to keep an eye on the place Charlize had chosen for them, to see if anyone came looking.

The second motel was nicer, with indoor hallways and security cameras inside and out. Leaving Selena just inside the door, out of sight of the clerk, Tony rented a room, requesting the second floor, facing the street and overlooking the entrance.

The room was cleaner, brighter, and smelled better. It wouldn't be a bad place to hole up for a while—after he'd taken care of business. Setting the bags on one of the beds, he said, "I've got to go out. We passed an office supply place a couple miles down the street. I want to fax Morgan's picture to Frankie and pick up a cell phone."

"I'll go with you."

"No. You draw too much attention. I'll take the Beretta

and leave the Glock with you. Keep the door locked and don't open it to anyone."

Selena rolled her eyes. "I've been taking care of myself for a long time."

"But you've never been in a situation like this, babe. None of us have." He kissed her forehead, then took the Beretta. He checked the magazine to make sure it was loaded before sliding the compact piece into his jeans pocket. After gathering the room key, the photograph, and a handful of twenties, he looked out the window, then left. He waited to hear the lock click before he headed downstairs, out the door, and started walking. Three blocks away, he waved down another cab.

At the office supply store, he bought and activated a prepaid cell phone, along with a couple of backpacks, then made arrangements to fax the photo to Simmons. While the clerk was sending the fax, he called the Detective Division and got Frankie at his desk.

"Where are you?" Simmons asked, his voice hushed.

"Atlanta."

"I thought you'd be in Savannah by now."

"We're not going. One of Long's goons was waiting for us at the Atlanta airport. Apparently, we'd picked up a tail neither of us recognized in Tulsa."

"Damn. He must've had more than one person working it. So what now?"

"We stay here for the time being. I'm sending you a photo of the man from the airport. Goes by Luke Morgan, maybe lives in the South. See if you can find out anything about him. And while you're at it, see what you can get on Charlize. Last name's P-a-w-l-e-y. Owns a restaurant of the same name in Savannah."

"You think she's legit?"

"I think she's a stone-cold killer. She's gone on home. Says she's going to try to track down Long." Tony glanced at the clerk, still standing at the fax machine, then turned away. "Says if she finds him, she'll void his contract."

Simmons was silent while that sank in. "Well...then she's not all bad. Listen, the ATF guys have been going over the house. It was definitely a bomb, but not in the package. That was just a lure to get Island Girl to open the door. There was a trip wire inside that your damn cat set off. By the way, I talked to Dom, and the vet said the cat's fine. Just a little singed."

"Selena will be glad to hear that." She was too kind-hearted. She hadn't wanted the cat hurt, didn't want Damon Long killed.

He wasn't surprised about the bomb. If a blast that size had been packed inside the box, as close to it as he'd been, he wouldn't be standing there now. At best, he'd be in the hospital. At worst, the medical examiner's office.

"I also talked to Julie. She said to tell you to be careful and to not worry about your folks or Lucia. She'll take care of 'em."

Tony smiled wryly. That was his older sister's primary job in life—taking care of everyone. She helped their mother watch out for their dad as Joe's Alzheimer's worsened, and bossed everyone else in the family as well.

"She was gonna go down to the university this morning and warn Lucia about Long."

Six months ago, Lucia had been too hell-bent on having fun to listen to warnings about anything. After her experience with Damon Long, she was more subdued. He hoped that meant more cautious, as well. Snatching her would be one quick way to bring Tony out of hiding, and Selena with him. She would never sit back in safety while someone else was threatened on her behalf.

"Anything else...oh, yeah, those guys we arrested last night. They don't know nothin' 'bout nothin'. They was just going to visit a friend there at the motel, though they didn't know his name or what room he was in, and they was only armed because, hell, Officer, it's a dangerous world out there." Simmons snorted in disgust. "They're still sitting down at the David Moss Center, though I imagine they'll be out on the street again before long."

Tony paid the clerk for the fax, took the photo, and walked out to the waiting cab. "Listen, I've got to head back to the motel. Call me if you find out anything, and I'll do the same. Thanks, Frankie."

Once again he instructed the cabbie to drive. Two blocks past the motel, he got out and walked back. No one seemed to be paying any particular attention to him, but that was the trick of good surveillance, wasn't it?

He took the stairs two at a time and, after a knock, let himself into the room. He closed the door, secured the locks, turned, and stopped abruptly.

Selena had changed clothes while he was gone, from the sexy, silky skirt and tank top that clung to her every curve into a pair of low-rise jeans and a T-shirt that also clung before ending an inch or two above the jeans. He'd seen her on rare occasions in shorts or capris, but never in butt-hugging denim that stretched around her like a second skin. His tongue was thick in his mouth, and that wasn't the only thing swelling.

He had definitely been right earlier. This room wasn't at all a bad place to hole up in for a while.

———

It was nearly seven o'clock when Charlize pulled into the driveway of her house. She parked near the entrance, then sat for a moment gazing at it in the waning light. Two stories, square, painted white with dark green shutters and doors, it was nearly two hundred years old. It had been built in the middle of an expanse of lush green lawn a hundred yards from the river by a merchant who'd done quite well for himself.

Just as Charlize had done quite well for herself. She'd bought the house twelve years ago, when William had transferred her from Charlotte to Savannah. Simon Bernstein had been in charge of the Savannah operation at that time, but William had had doubts about both Bernstein and some of the people he'd hired—Sonny Yates, in particular.

He'd had good cause for concern. Not long after Sonny had learned the business, Bernstein disappeared. Sonny had admitted privately to killing him, but his body had never been discovered. It was Bernstein's own fault, William had said when she passed the information on to him. He'd trained Sonny to take over, and naturally, Sonny had done just that.

She went inside, reset the alarm, then turned in a slow circle. She never entered the house without taking a moment to bask in its old-money elegance, to appreciate the workmanship and care that had gone into it. But she could walk away that day if she had to without a single regret.

She saved her regrets for more important things. Selena was one of them. Though it bewildered the younger woman, Sonny was not.

As she'd explained, Sonny had been a job to her. Nothing more, nothing less. She'd enjoyed his company, had shared his bed and enjoyed that, too. She knew he'd imagined himself in love with her, knew he'd envisioned a future where the two of them ran William's enterprise side by side.

But she hadn't shared that vision. Hadn't loved him. Hadn't let whatever affection she felt for him distract her from the job she'd been given. She'd spied on him; she'd reported his every casual comment to William; and, when the situation required it, she'd killed him. She'd done it for Selena, and for William, though he would never know. It was what he would have wanted.

In the library that served as her office, she sat down behind the desk and picked up the phone. She hadn't lied when she'd told Ceola she didn't have a phone number for Damon Long, and she was confident that the E-mail address from which he'd contacted her had been deactivated soon after. But there were still ways to get in touch with him.

The phone rang three times before a familiar voice answered. It was female, southern, and belonged to a woman named Ruby Dee. Charlize had never met her and didn't want to. Long-distance anonymity suited her just fine. "Ruby Dee, it's J.T."

"How are you, sugar?" Blues music played in the background, an appropriate soundtrack to Ruby Dee's husky, too-much-whisky voice.

"Fine. And you?"

A smoky laugh. "Better 'n fine. What can I do for you?"

"Pass a message on to Damon Long. Tell him to give me a call about his offer."

"I don't know when I'll hear from him, but I'll tell him. Anything else?"

"No. Thanks." After hanging up, Charlize turned on the CD player on the credenza and made her own blues selection. It was an appropriate soundtrack to her life, as well.

Ruby Dee was one of a handful of people who knew that

J.T. was a woman. The initials were Charlize's father's—John Turner—and those who knew thought she'd chosen the name to honor him. They were wrong. She didn't use his name to honor him.

Merely to remind herself why she killed.

Luke Morgan knew the reasons why.

When she'd seen him in the airport, for one helpless moment, she'd been at a loss. She'd wanted to just stand there and study him. Wanted to snap his spinal column. Wanted to hurt him. *Badly.*

Thank God, it had been only a moment. Otherwise, it might have been Selena's neck that was broken. Like her, like Damon Long, Luke didn't need a weapon to kill someone. His hands were dangerous enough.

Charlize hadn't been so shaken in six years.

Hadn't seen him in six years.

And very well might have no choice but to kill him, if he found Selena before Charlize found Long.

He might be one she would regret.

But she wouldn't bet on it.

Selena rolled over, curling into Tony's body to share his warmth, but found nothing besides cool empty sheets. Raising herself onto one arm, she checked the bedside clock—11:43 P.M.—then shifted her gaze to the shadow at the window. Fumbling into the T-shirt Tony had shed a few hours earlier, she pulled it over her hips, then padded across the room to slide her arms around him from behind. "Seen anything interesting?"

He didn't turn, but laid one hand over hers where they were clasped. "I'd guess a great deal that goes on in Atlanta after dark is interesting."

"Anything that concerns us? Charlize? Luke Morgan? Any strangers skulking about?"

"No."

"Then come to bed."

"I will. You go back to sleep."

She kissed his bare shoulder, then moved around to stand beside him. "Tony, no one knows we're here. We're safe."

Though he nodded, he didn't look convinced. Truthfully, neither was she. She felt better knowing that he was watching, because someone very well might have had the other motel under surveillance—might have followed them even with the cab changes. Might even know what room they were in at that moment.

Never underestimate your enemies, someone had once told her—maybe her self-defense instructor at home in Key West, maybe William. William had underestimated her, and was in a coma as a result. Underestimating Damon Long and his hired help could get her killed.

"Why don't you rest and let me watch for a while?" she offered, leaning against the window so she could see his face. His brown hair stood on end, as it usually did, and there were shadows under his eyes. He'd napped for a few hours more after they'd settled into this room, but it hadn't been enough.

He spared her a brief glance before returning his gaze to the street. "I'm fine. Go back to bed."

She took part of his advice—she did return to the bed, but only long enough to pull the spread free and wrap it around her. Shoving her feet into her running shoes for warmth, she returned and took up the same position, back to the wall, facing him. "When am I going to come out of hiding?"

Suddenly very still, he looked at her.

"You know that's the only way to draw Long out into the open. I have to make myself visible. I have to provide him with a target that a blind man couldn't miss." Though she tried to keep her voice steady, she didn't succeed. Thanks to the FBI, she'd had some experience at being a target, and she didn't like it. She hated the constant awareness, the uneasiness, the fear. She hated even more knowing it was pure luck that had kept her alive. Despite her own skills, despite the FBI's protection, she could have just as easily died.

Tony remained silent and still.

"We have to give them the chance to take me out," she went on, shivering beneath the bedspread that enshrouded her. "And we have to be ready to stop them. Charlize can help us."

"She'll help us most if she kills Long."

Another shiver. Selena didn't want anyone to die because of her, not even Damon Long. If a jury found him guilty and sentenced him to death, that was fine. That was justice. But for Charlize—or Tony—to simply kill him . . . It was the way William had done business: If someone caused a problem, he died. Problem solved. It was the life she'd struggled to avoid. Yet it was the only way she would be safe.

But it was wrong.

"If we go to Savannah—"

"No. They'll be watching for you there."

"That's the point, isn't it?" she asked softly. "To set a trap. To lure him in."

"You're not playing bait for a killer. Not yet."

"Then when? How long can you stay away from your job, Tony? How long can you stay away from your parents? Your mother depends on you to help out with your father. I know Julie's filling in, but Anna still needs *you*."

His jaw tightened until she thought she would be able to hear his teeth grind if the air-conditioning wasn't humming in the background. "Don't worry about my job or Mom and Dad. And don't be so anxious to put your life on the line. Just trust me, Selena. I'm not stupid. I have some experience at dealing with killers. I know—Fuck."

Immediately she turned to look out the window. Everything was quiet in the parking lot below, and traffic seemed normal on the street. But outside the motel they'd left earlier, a dark vehicle had parked behind the silver Toyota, and two figures were checking it out, looking in the windows, trying the doors. They met back at the darker car, talked with the driver for a moment, then headed for the stairs.

Selena was barely breathing as she watched the men climb the stairs. They moved purposefully, with no glancing around, no overt caution. When they reached the landing, they went directly to the room Charlize had rented. Dim light glowed around the curtain edges; Selena had straightened up, but she hadn't turned off the lights.

Neither man knocked. One stood guard, facing the parking lot, while the other bent over the lock. An instant later, he straightened, pulled a sawed-off shotgun from beneath his jacket, and signaled to his partner. They went inside, one behind the other, and closed the door behind them.

Less than sixty seconds later, they came out again, obviously angry. They stomped down the stairs, spoke to their driver for a moment with wild gestures, then got inside the car and drove away.

Finally Selena exhaled.

"You get a look at that shotgun?" Tony asked quietly.

She nodded.

"You still so anxious to set yourself up?"

Of course not. But what she wanted to do and what she had to do were two very different things. She wanted to live a normal life. But if she was ever going to have that, she had to come out of hiding so Long could be stopped. It was a risk, but a calculated one. If they were prepared, if their trap was set...

"You think that was Luke Morgan's people?" she asked, rubbing her arms inside the blanket to chase away the bumps that had gathered.

"Or Charlize's."

"Someone could have followed us from the airport. Morgan might have had an accomplice outside. One cell phone call..."

Tony nodded.

"Or Charlize could have been followed when she picked up the car and supplies."

Another nod.

"Or..." Selena's jaw tightened. "She could have told those men where to find us." Selena didn't want to believe it, but she'd been on the receiving end of betrayal often enough to know how easily it came to some people.

"She could have," Tony agreed. "Though it seems doubtful they would have waited this long. She had to suspect that we would move." With a grim smile, he let go of the curtain and turned on the lamp before extending his hand. "Whoever hired them, in the end, they're working for the same guy."

She peeled off the T-shirt, handing it to him, picking up her own shirt from the dresser. They dressed quickly and left quietly by the rear entrance, picking up a cab a short distance away. This time Tony left the choice of motels to the driver, asking only for a place on the outskirts of the city.

Within an hour they were in the new room—their fourth in twenty-four hours—and once again in bed.

Just trust me, Tony had said. She didn't always take his advice—Damon Long was proof of that—but she did trust him, more than she'd ever trusted anyone. He would never betray her, never turn on her.

"You don't trust Charlize—"

He snorted.

"—but you're willing to give her a chance to track down Long and kill him. What makes you think you can trust her to do that?"

"If we see his body, or if the authorities verify his fingerprints, we'll know."

And if he was dead, that would take care of Selena's enemies—at least, those with a professional interest. With the promise of a big payday gone, Morgan and the others would forget about her, and William was never going to wake up from his coma. No one else could possibly care enough about her to want her dead. She would be safe. She could marry Tony. Make a home. Have a family. Live a normal life.

It was a sweet dream to fall asleep on.

Bayou Blue was the kind of place people would rather be leaving than coming to—poor, shabby, southern Alabama at its worst. The kind of place where Damon Long felt right at home.

It was located at the end of a county road in bad need of repair—the only way in or out, unless you had a boat and were familiar with the waterways that surrounded it. There was little to bring anyone to town—a general store, a gas station that serviced both vehicles and boats, and a bar. Damon parked in the shadow of a massive live oak near the bar.

Spanish moss drifted from its branches in ghostly tendrils that gleamed silver in the moonlight.

A glance at his watch showed it was a quarter of two. The bar, identified as Ruby Dee's by a hand-painted wood plank over the door, would close in fifteen minutes. Rolling the windows down, he settled in to wait.

The bar's windows were open, as well, throwing wedges of yellow light to the ground below and allowing music to drift on the night air. Ruby Dee didn't care that not everyone loved the blues like she did. It was her bar, and the customers would damn well listen to her music.

Since the next nearest bar was forty miles away, the customers listened.

Damon let his head sink back against the headrest, his eyes closing while he remained alert to the sounds around him. Water lapped against the shore, insects buzzed, and far off in the distance, a motor skimmed across the water. The bayou was tricky to navigate even during daylight. Anyone out at night was almost surely up to no good.

Damon knew that for a fact, since Bayou Blue had once been an important part of William's network. Mitch Gautier had headed the crew based here, and he'd been a good worker...until William had learned that one of the crew was skimming. It had taken Damon all of two days to identify which one, but he'd been too late. William had ordered the whole crew taken out, shotgun-style, leaving Ruby Dee Gautier a widow.

Damon never had been able to make the old bastard see that murder was bad for morale.

From the bar's porch came the slamming of a screen door, followed by voices. The customers were leaving in twos and threes, some fairly steady on their feet, some barely remaining upright. A few had vehicles parked in the clearing; the rest disappeared into the night shadows.

At 2:01, Damon climbed the steps to the porch, opened the screen, and stepped inside. The room was square, with tables scattered around two pool tables, a bar that ran the length of the back wall, and a speaker system hooked into a compact stereo. Forty-watt bulbs dangling here and there didn't do much for illumination, but that was fine with the people who frequented the joint. Neither they nor their business held up well to the light of day.

Ruby Dee was standing at the bar, totaling receipts. She wore a faded denim skirt that rode low on her hips and hit so high on her thighs that her legs looked endless. Her shirt was white, V-necked, and clung snugly to every curve. With wild hair the color of a new penny, soft eyes, pale skin, and a damn sexy body, she looked strong enough to break a man and delicate enough to make him bleed. She was the best fantasy Damon had had in a while.

He stayed where he was, just inside the door. Unless someone was in the storeroom or the john at the back of the building, they were alone. And unless someone was waiting for her at home, they would be alone there, too. They always found damn pleasant ways to pass their time alone.

After a time, she looked up, her gaze coming straight to him. Even though he hadn't dropped by in months, she didn't look surprised to see him. She never seemed surprised by anything. "Damon Long," she said in that husky, sexy voice that always made his cock quiver.

He walked across the room, weaving around tables. "Ruby Dee Gautier."

"What are you doing in Bayou Blue?"

"Just passing through."

Her laughter was low and rich and sent a rush of heat

through his veins. "Bullshit. This wide spot in the road isn't on the way to anywhere, except maybe Hell." Moving behind the bar, she took a beer from the cooler, popped the top, and set it on the scarred wood, then got a bottle of water for herself. "I thought I might be seeing you soon."

"Why's that?"

"Anytime people start calling, you're bound to turn up." She pulled a sheet of paper from beneath the bar and laid it next to the beer.

He glanced at it as he picked up the bottle. Two names, two numbers. Good news or bad?

Ruby Dee straddled the line between law and disorder. Her business was legit, even if most of her customers weren't. She knew they were on the wrong side of the law, though she avoided particulars. She made introductions, served their booze, and took their messages, but she asked no questions and tolerated no answers. The less she knew, the safer she was. Deniability could save her hide, she believed.

Damon figured any half-assed prosecutor could make a case against her for conspiracy, but that wasn't his concern. He had only two interests right now: avoiding arrest and seeing Selena McCaffrey dead. He'd had a damn good life before the bitch had screwed up everything—money, power, control. He still had plenty of money, but she'd destroyed the business he'd spent half his life building. No one fucked with Damon Long and lived to tell it.

"I heard about Mr. Davis," Ruby Dee said, arms folded under her breasts—and damn nice breasts they were. She'd been way too fine for that dumb fuck she'd married, and must have realized it. She sure as hell hadn't hesitated to take Damon to her bed before Mitch died, and he didn't kid himself that he was the only one. "It's a shame."

He had to think for a moment what she was referring to,

then he shrugged. He didn't have any sympathy for the old bastard. If anyone had ever needed killing, it was William. Of course, the SOB had refused to die, but wasting away in some hospital bed was almost as good as dead. He was out of Damon's life either way.

"Is there any chance he'll ever get better?"

"Nah. He's a vegetable. The only thing keeping him alive is the machines."

Emotion flitted across her face. Disappointment? "He gave me a lot of money after Mitch died. Enough to buy this place and not care whether it makes a profit. He said it was life insurance. Because Mitch died working for him."

It was money to salve the old goat's conscience—what he had of one. But Damon didn't tell her so. It was too late to avenge Mitch's death on William, and who knew how she would react to living off money soaked in her husband's blood?

"You staying over?" she asked.

"Depends on whether anyone's got a comfortable bed to offer."

She was neither coy nor flirtatious. "You're always welcome in my bed, Damon."

"Then I'm staying." His cock had already started swelling at the promise of pleasure to come.

"You need to return those phone calls first?"

He checked the time again, then the numbers. Middle-of-the-night calls were such pissers, especially when there was likely no urgency. He'd already found a news story on-line about an explosion destroying a house on Princeton Court in Tulsa, miraculously with no injuries. No doubt, the bitch was in hiding, which meant this job was going to take longer than he'd expected.

"Yeah, I guess I should."

"You know your way to the office. The prepaid cell's on the file cabinet."

Taking his beer with him, he walked down the narrow hall to the storeroom, where one corner had been partitioned off. He dialed Luke Morgan's number, answered by a sleepy female.

"I saw your girl in Atlanta yesterday," Morgan said when he came on the line. "Came in on a flight from Tulsa with a connection to Savannah. She and the boyfriend left the airport here. They took a cab to a motel, but left without checking out. I haven't caught up with them yet."

Imagining Selena's cool, smug smile, Damon rubbed the spot between his eyes. "You didn't have surveillance on the motel?"

"Not quick enough." Morgan covered the phone to say something to his companion, who giggled. "You didn't tell me they were traveling with J.T."

Damon stiffened. "J.T.? You sure?"

"Of course I'm sure. You think I don't remember the bitch who threatened to cut off my dick and serve it up to the old man on a platter?"

According to ancient history, Luke Morgan had trained under John Turner Thomas—had been the son John Turner Thomas had never had. Once, with a few too many beers in him, he had hinted that life in the Thomas household was whacked. But he hadn't offered details, and Damon hadn't pushed. Whatever had made such an impression on Morgan, it was obvious there was bad blood between him and Charlize. One time William had brought them both in on a job, and she *had* made just that threat, knife in hand. She'd left no doubt in anyone's mind that she wasn't blowing smoke.

"They were traveling together?" Damon asked. "She didn't just happen to run into them there like you did?"

"I didn't 'just happen' to run into them. I had people watching them. It was the result of first-class surveillance. But, yeah, they were together. They came off the plane together, and J.T. created a distraction so they could get on the train together—without me. Is she in on this or not? Am I gonna have to kill her to get to the McCaffrey woman?"

Damon didn't know the answer. Charlize had accepted the contract, just as Morgan had. For all he knew, she could be in the process of carrying it out. It seemed overcomplicated—getting the target to trust her, to go off to a strange place with her—but sometimes killing *was* complicated.

Sometimes so was betrayal.

"You have a problem with killing her?"

There was a moment's silence. Was Morgan remembering the good ol' days with John Turner, the father he'd never had? Debating loyalty to John Turner against a half million bucks?

"No," he said at last. "I don't have a problem with killing J.T."

"Then do the job I hired you for before someone else beats you to it." Damon ended the call, then gazed at the other number. Maybe Charlize was executing some complex plan . . . or maybe she was helping Selena escape her hunters. William had been convinced of her unwavering loyalty, but Damon didn't believe in unwavering anything. Loyalty could be bought or sold, won or lost, destroyed by disregard, or simply betrayed.

Charlize was a coldhearted snake, but even snakes could have soft spots. His was Ruby Dee . . . and she was waiting for him to take her to bed.

He would make a decision about Charlize later.

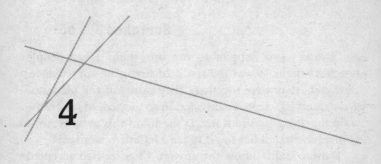

4

Selena and Tony's first stop the next morning was Atlanta's biggest and busiest mall. She was wearing jeans again, along with a red T-shirt that was too short to cover even the compact Beretta. "You'd think Charlize would have thought about that," Tony had muttered as she tucked the .22 into her purse along with the Smith.

"She's not a jeans sort of person, either," she'd replied.

They'd gone to a department store first, where she'd bought shirts long enough to conceal either weapon, along with a jacket for extra coverage. They'd stopped at the food court for a late breakfast and were now standing in an alcove that held two pay phones. On one side was a video arcade, on the other, a music store, ensuring a heavy flow of teenage traffic past the alcove. Still, Selena kept her back to the wall as she dialed Charlize's number.

"How are you?" Charlize demanded the instant Selena identified herself. "I called the motel this morning, but there was no answer in your room."

"We went out for breakfast. Have you found out anything?"

"I've left a message for Long in the usual place. I sent an E-mail to the address I had for him, but it bounced. I knew it would. So things have been quiet?"

Selena glanced at Tony, but his attention was on the

crowd. "Not particularly. Someone broke into the room last night."

"But you're okay...because you weren't in the room. You changed rooms—or, knowing Ceola, motels."

"It was a precaution that paid off."

"I should hear from Long soon," Charlize said. "Once I find out where he is, I'll...well, I won't be able to let you know unless you keep in touch."

"We will." Selena hung up.

"Any luck?" Tony asked without glancing her way.

"She expects to hear from Long soon. She wants us to keep in touch." She went to stand beside him, watching the shoppers pass by. Everyone seemed so relaxed, having a nice Saturday morning, and all she wanted was to hide away someplace where she didn't have to worry about blending in or being recognized.

All her life she'd stood out in some way. Her café-au-lait skin and long black curls had marked her as an outcast among her Latino families. Later, at the boarding schools William had sent her to, she'd been surrounded mostly by white girls who found her somewhat exotic with her island accent. In her advanced martial arts classes, she'd been the only woman among the students. Even being with Tony earned her a few glances. Because she was beautiful, he told her. Because he was white and she wasn't, she knew.

She couldn't do anything about her skin or her features, but she could make one change that would alter her appearance far more than the switch from feminine tropical silks to denim and cotton.

"Come on," she said, then cut between shoppers to the hair salon across the way.

Tony caught her hand when she would have walked

inside. "What are you—" He glanced at the nearest stylist, scissors in hand, and his eyes widened. "You aren't—"

"What is the first thing about me that catches people's attention?"

"But—" He liked her hair. She knew that. He liked to tangle his hands in it when they kissed, liked the way it tickled along his body when she made love to him, liked to stroke it when he soothed her.

"It'll grow back." She freed herself, went to the desk, and asked for the next available stylist.

Twenty minutes later, the floor underneath the chair where she sat was littered with curls, and her head felt light—or was it that she felt light-headed? She stared at herself in the mirror so long that the stylist shifted nervously. "I told you it was drastic, cutting all that off at once," the woman said defensively.

Her hand trembling, Selena raised it to touch the short curls that were all that remained. "No," she said softly. "I needed drastic. It's . . . nice. I just need time . . ."

Forcing a smile, she rose from the chair, paid the receptionist, and gave the stylist a good tip. Next she made a stop in the bathroom at the rear of the salon, put on a new shirt and the jacket, then tucked her Smith into her waistband. For the first time in more than forty hours, she felt comfortable. Even without her silk clothing and beaded sandals. Even without her hair.

When she approached Tony, waiting restlessly at the salon entrance, he stiffened at the touch of her hand on his shoulder, then slowly faced her. The set of his mouth turned grim.

She kept the smile in place through sheer will. "Come on, Tony. Anyone who's looking for a woman with long black curls won't give me a second look."

"Of course they'll give you a second look because you're so damn pretty, and when they take that second look, they'll recognize you." Grudgingly, he took her hand and pulled her toward the end of the mall opposite from where they'd entered. "We're meeting a cab at the far end."

He was wrong, she thought as she matched her stride to his. Even people who knew her would walk right past without slowing. Strangers tended to fixate on one dominant feature, and for most people, it was her hair.

She doubted the predators stalking her were any different.

She was counting on it.

The Gautier house was the fanciest one in Bayou Blue—not that that was saying much. It stood across a narrow inlet from the rest of the town, spanned by a rickety footbridge. Built on stilts, it was similar enough in style to the bar to prompt a guess that the same person had designed both— square, a lot of windows, deep porches front and back.

Damon sat in a rocker on the front porch, watching the town through the pines. One vehicle every couple hours constituted heavy traffic in this burg. Except for the dogs running loose, the place pretty much looked deserted. Because it was just a quiet place, Ruby Dee said.

Yeah, right.

He couldn't figure out why Ruby Dee chose to stay in Lower Alabama hell. She didn't have any family around the bayou since Mitch's old man had died in the last hurricane. Hot as she was, she could have her pick of men in any city across the country, and smart as she was, she could make good money for herself, too. Why choose a place where half the inbreds didn't have the teeth they were born with and were dumber than dirt as well?

It was a shitty place to live . . . but not to pass a little time. Damon wasn't the first fugitive to take up temporary residence there, and he wouldn't be the last. But he intended to get the hell out just as soon as he figured out what to do about Selena. The longer it took Morgan to find her, the longer Damon had to stay in hiding himself.

He was already tired of it.

He had to come up with a way to lure her out into the open.

The screen door closed with a bang, and Ruby Dee came out with two mugs of strong chicory. She handed one to him, then perched on the railing to the side, leaving him a clear view of the town . . . and her. She wore a man's T-shirt, white, threadbare, with nothing at all underneath. She wasn't trying to look sexy or sultry with those long bare legs dangling in front of him, or the cotton pulled tight across her breasts, or the shirt inching up toward indecency as she scooted farther back on the rail. She just *was*.

"When you're ready for lunch, I'll put some steaks on the grill," she said after taking an appreciative drink of her coffee. "How long can you stay?"

She wasn't much for asking questions, so when she did ask, he figured she deserved an answer. "I don't know. Maybe a day or two." Or maybe he'd leave in a few hours. After those steaks and another go-round in her bed.

The sound of an engine rumbled across the water a moment before the vehicle came into sight. Damon saw the light bar first, then the shield for the local sheriff's office on the door. Any other time, any other place, his muscles would be taut and his pistol would have already cleared the leather of his holster, but this was Bayou Blue. "That Sheriff Beaufort?"

"Uh-huh." Twisting on the rail, Ruby Dee gave the man a wave that he returned lazily. The sheriff was potbellied, wore mirrored sunglasses, and made a hell of a lot more money looking the other way than he did enforcing the law. He turned around in the clearing in front of the bar, drove back a short distance, then shut off the engine. "He's come to have dinner with his mama."

Damon propped one foot a few inches from Ruby Dee's hip. "The corrupt old sheriff has a mama?"

"Who taught him every corrupt thing he knows."

"What about you? You have a mama?"

"Do you think I just dropped from the sky?" she asked drily. "My folks live in Shreveport. What about yours?"

"They're dead." He knew for a fact his mother was dead. Seeing that he'd never known who his father was, he was just guessing about him. Didn't matter to him either way. The man had been a sperm donor, nothing more. Not knowing him hadn't affected Damon any more than knowing him would have.

"Even though I don't see them too often, I can't imagine my parents not being there. They're kinda my anchor." Her cheeks turned pink, and she shrugged as if to dispel the sentimentality. "Maybe it's because I'm a girl. Maybe girls feel more connected to their mamas and daddies than men do."

Damon didn't know too many "girls," but he'd probably agree. Lucia Ceola—the good detective's little sister and the last woman he'd fucked before Ruby Dee—had been her parents' baby even at the age of twenty-five. Selena was older than that, and she'd been eager enough to find out something about her old man that she'd come to Damon for information. Like he'd have told her anything if he'd known it.

Now she knew. That had been in the news stories, too—about William's sister, Kathryn, getting caught in a murder-for-hire scheme. That Selena was her husband's illegitimate bastard. That Kathryn had killed the mother twenty-eight years ago and had trusted William to do the same to the baby. That Kathryn had even tried to shoot Selena herself.

The family that kills together . . .

The murder twenty-eight years ago had apparently been the beginning of the transformation from respectable law officer Henry Daniels to global drug lord William Davis. Covering up his sister's sloppy killing and spiriting the infant Selena out of the country must have given him a taste for the darker side of life.

In the end, all Kathryn had accomplished was reuniting her husband Grant with the daughter he'd thought was long dead. Now Selena had the father she'd always believed would want her if only he knew about her. Now she had family. Family was so very important to her. She would risk everything for them.

Including her own life.

"Son of a bitch," Damon muttered, his foot hitting the floor with a thud. "Do you have a state map?"

Wearing a speculative look, Ruby Dee went inside, returning a moment later with a road atlas.

He flipped it open to Alabama, located Montgomery, then studied the area until he found the tiny dot marking Greenhill. Grant Hamilton lived there, only fifty miles northwest of the city. Nothing would bring Selena out of hiding faster than to find out that Damon was so close to dear old Dad.

Aware of Ruby Dee watching, he turned to the Georgia map and pretended to study it a moment before shutting the atlas and surging to his feet. "Come on, darlin', let's put those steaks on. I'm ready to eat."

To eat. To fuck. To set a trap for Selena.

And damned if she would escape this time.

Sunday morning dawned bright and warm, the sun doing its best to penetrate the rubber-backed drapes at the window in yet another motel. Tony sat on the bed, the wall at his back, and watched Selena fiddle with her short curls.

She was right. It made a huge change. He'd catch a glimpse of her from the corner of his eyes and think, *Who the hell*— before remembering.

He didn't like it. Even if it did make her look younger, more innocent, and sexier, too. Even if it suited the delicate lines of her face.

She gave up trying to do something with the unruly curls, left the mirror, and sat down on the other bed—just sat and watched him. Uneasiness crept along his spine. Whenever she got so damn serious, he got edgy. Things between them always went downhill when she got that look.

She was waiting for him to get impatient, to ask *What?* He refused to do it, but merely held her gaze.

Finally she broke the silence. "We need a plan."

"We have a plan. Charlize will try to find and kill Long."

"We need a plan in case that one fails. Damon Long is very good at not being found. How do you think he's avoided prison for so long?" She folded her hands primly in her lap. In her snug-fitting jeans, Braves T-shirt, and running shoes, she looked like a typical young woman... though he'd bet she was the only typical young woman in the city of Atlanta whose shirt concealed not one but two weapons.

"We need to be ready with Plan B. I still think Savannah would be a good place. Charlize can set us up with the help we need. I could . . . I don't know . . . offer to meet with Morgan—offer him a better deal than he's getting with Long. I could even offer to meet with Long. And when he shows up, we're ready."

Tony pushed away from the wall and stood up. When he did, the scar where she'd shot him early in the summer twinged. Phantom pain. She was an expert shot; she'd done as little damage as possible and he'd made a complete recovery. It was only because he was angry—worried—that it hurt.

The bed where she sat butted against the outside wall. He rested one knee on the mattress and lifted the curtain an inch or two for a quick look outside. Nothing had changed since the last time he'd looked: The day was still sunny, the same cars were parked in the lot, nobody was paying attention to the motel.

He paced the length of the room to the mirror and sink, then came back. "You think it's that easy to set the kind of trap you're talking about? With a woman we don't trust calling the shots? With people we don't trust providing backup? With targets who have so damn much to lose that killing us all wouldn't trouble them in the least?" He raked his fingers through his hair. "Damon Long and Luke Morgan are professional killers. They're too smart to walk into a trap. How do you think they've avoided prison?"

Her jaw clenched when he turned her own words back on her, but she didn't respond to the question. "Okay. What's your plan? Besides waiting?"

Again he dragged his fingers through his hair. Truth was, he didn't have one, beyond hopefully staying a few steps ahead of the killers. She was right: As long as the offer was good, she would never be safe. If Charlize or Tony didn't kill Damon Long, the only other option was to use Selena as a target.

The odds of successfully capturing Luke Morgan might be reasonable . . . but Morgan *and* Long?

So what was Tony's plan? If he could find a truly safe place to stash Selena—a cell for one, buried six feet under the jail sounded good—he could borrow Charlize's plan for his own. He was good enough at tracking down people who didn't want to be found that he'd had the best record ever on the fugitive apprehension squad. He would make it his one goal in life to find Damon Long and stop him.

Kill him.

In cold blood if necessary.

Two months ago, the idea never would have occurred to him. When Long's murder spree had started in Tulsa, people had called Long a vigilante. They had praised him for cleaning up the scum that the police department couldn't keep off the streets, and wondered why the cops didn't just let him continue his work. Even Simmons had wondered why they were busting their balls when the guy was actually doing society a favor.

Their job was to find the killer, Tony had told him. Not judge or condemn him. That was the court's job.

But even in jail, Long had arranged an attempt on Selena's life. He had rights—to visitors, to phone calls—that he would continue to use to put her in danger right up to the time the state put a needle in his arm.

One way or another his rights, and his threats, were going to end soon. For good. If there were consequences, Tony would live with them.

Impatiently Selena said, "You don't have a plan besides waiting, do you?"

"My plan is to keep you alive, and using you as bait to draw out a hired gun doesn't figure into it." His smile felt pretty damn phony. "Do me one favor. Trust me. You generally don't, and it generally gets you in trouble."

"I trust you with my life!" she argued, rising from the bed.

He loudly blew out his breath. "I told you not to listen to the feds, and you did. I told you not to work with them, and you did. I told you they'd make you a target. I told you getting Damon Long out of jail was a mistake. I told you the feds couldn't control him. I told you he would try to kill you, and here we are."

"I *had* to work with them! If I hadn't, they would have arrested or deported me!"

"You're *American*!"

"But we didn't know that then. I couldn't prove *what* I was. And if I *hadn't* worked with them, I never would have found out. I never would have met my father. I never would have known the truth about my mother. I don't regret what I did at all, not even now with Long's killer out there searching for me."

He smiled cynically. "No regrets when those bastards ran you off the road in Savannah? When they chased you through the streets with guns? When Kathryn Hamilton took a shot at you? When Sonny Yates beat the hell out of you?" He lowered his voice. "No regrets at all for not trusting me?"

"Tony..." She reached toward him, but stopped short of touching him. After a moment, she lowered her hand to her side. "I trusted you. I just had to make decisions that you didn't approve of."

"Yeah. Like getting Long out of jail so he could try to kill you again. He's the single most dangerous criminal I've ever met. He makes your run-of-the-mill murderer look like a Boy Scout. To capture him I had to get shot, I had to watch you get beaten, and I had to shoot Henry . . . and now Long's loose again, free to kill whoever he wants, including you, and he has you to thank for it.

"And what did you accomplish, Selena? Is Savannah drug-free now? Was there a shortage of drugs for even a day? Have the dealing and the money-laundering and the killing and the intimidation and the corruption stopped, or even been affected at all? Exactly what did the great undercover FBI operation achieve?"

She stared at him a long time, her gaze as chilly as her body was tense. Finally, folding her arms across her chest, she said, "Two corrupt FBI agents have lost their badges and their freedom. One killer is dead. Several others are awaiting trial. The woman who murdered my mother is locked up in a psychiatric hospital, and I met my father. I wish Long hadn't escaped. I wish it hadn't been necessary to use him. But I'd do it again in a heartbeat to learn what I learned."

Tony knew it was past time to shut up—his brain even gave the command—but the snide words came out anyway. "Right. Finding out that you're the product of an adulterous affair between a woman who's now dead and a man whose wife tried to kill you was well worth unleashing Damon Long on an unsuspecting public. Hell, the man's only killed more people than he can remember. But knowing who your parents are is so damn much more important than that."

Selena simply stared, then quietly said, "I'm sorry you find my curiosity about who I am and where I came from so trivial."

"I'm sorry you find it a fair exchange for the escape of a psychopathic killer."

Her dark gaze frigid, she spun around, walked to the

door, and reached for the security lock. Her fingers rested there a moment before lowering to her side. She was angry, but she wasn't stupid enough to leave the room and put herself in needless danger because of it. Instead, she returned to the second bed, dropped onto it in a huff, and turned on the television.

Tony dragged his fingers through his hair. He was sorry he'd said anything. He could hardly imagine what her childhood had been like—not knowing her father's name, constant abuse from the bastard who was her stepfather, and no love, affection, or protection from the woman she believed to be her mother. How much damage had it done to a child to face the proof every day that her own parents neither wanted nor loved her?

Enough that she'd been an easy target when Henry had tracked her down in Ocho Rios. She'd been grateful for the slightest kindness, and he had lavished her with it in the beginning.

Enough that she'd been driven to learn what she could about her past. She'd put her life on the line—had put their relationship on the line. It was that important to her.

But it wasn't worth letting Long run free again.

Tony sat down on the bed where they'd slept the night before, catching a whiff of her perfume from the sheets as the mattress shifted beneath him. Just a whiff, and he could damn near feel her in his arms...not that he was likely to find her there anytime soon. "Selena."

She'd settled on a movie, something with a lot of explosions and loud sound effects. When he spoke, she turned the volume up a few notches.

"*Selena.*"

The volume went loud enough to vibrate the air. Muttering a curse, he crossed to the television, yanked the plug from the socket, then looked in her direction. "I'm going out to pick up lunch. Lock the door behind me." After plugging in the TV again, he left before he could say more things that he shouldn't.

Even if he believed them.

For June Ravenel, going to church on Sunday was one more in a long list of chores she had to accomplish each week. She didn't find peace there, or hope, or sustenance for her spirit. It was just something she did, because it was expected of her. Because practically everyone in the black community of Greenhill, Alabama, attended Sunday morning church, no matter what they'd done the rest of the week.

Her mother, Oda Mae Ravenel, gone thirty years this summer, bless her heart, had seen to it that both her daughters were present for services three times a week for as long as she'd had a say in it. Through winters when cold air had seeped through the cracks and summers when all the open windows and all the fans turning hadn't lessened the heat one bit, June had sat on the same hard pew, sung the same hymns, and prayed the same prayers. So had her sister, Amelia.

For all the good it had done them.

Sweat trickled down her spine as the pastor finished the final prayer. Clutching her Bible in one hand, she took her father's arm with the other. "Come on, Daddy. Let's go home."

Luther let her help him to his feet before shaking her off. "You're always in such a hurry, girl. What do you think's gonna happen if we don't rush right home? Is the house gonna fall down? Is the world gonna stop turning?" His broad, affectionate smile gleamed against his ebony skin. "You gotta learn to take it easy, girl."

Grudgingly, she smiled, too. "Taking it easy comes natural to you," she retorted. "Living a life of leisure, playing dominoes with your buddies and dropping a line in Possum Creek . . . life doesn't come much easier than that."

"Don't forget drinkin' beer and chasin' the ladies." He winked as he hooked his arm through hers. "That's the best part of my week."

She snorted as they shuffled down the aisle to the door. On the steps outside, the pastor and his wife were shaking hands and working the crowd, Luther liked to say.

Her daddy didn't really chase the ladies. Besides the fact that Oda Mae had been the love of his life, he was seventy-nine years old and stooped from years of backbreaking farmwork. He'd given the best part of his life to Hamilton Farms for very little return, but he didn't mind. He'd done an honest day's work for an honest day's pay, he claimed, and he had his house and his own little piece of land to show for it. He still talked about "Grant this" and "Grant that," as if they were more than distant boss and unimportant employee.

If fate hadn't intervened, they would have been father-and son-in-law.

And now they had blood between them. Amelia and Grant's daughter, long believed dead, was alive and well in Oklahoma.

June's stomach clenched and heat rushed through her. She snatched off the hat that covered her short graying hair and fanned herself with it, not that it did much good. It was round and compact and ugly, but she just didn't have the features to carry off the big-brimmed beauties that some of the other ladies wore—that pretty, delicate Amelia had always worn. "Lord, I don't know why we don't air-condition this church," she fussed as they finally reached the door and a hint of a cooling breeze.

"Because there are better things to do with the Lord's money than put air-conditioning in a hundred-and-fifty-year-old building," the pastor said. "Miss June, how are you?"

"I'm fine, Brother Hawkins. How are you?"

"Couldn't be better. Brother Luther, it's good to see..."

June tuned out the chatter as she smiled at Sister Hawkins and shook her hand, then descended the steps and found a cooler spot in the shade. In thirty years, the pastors had changed, but the question hadn't: *How are you?* Or her response: *Fine.* When she was angry, when she was hurt, when she was bitter, when she was beyond forgiveness, the answer was always the same. Always a lie.

Thanks to Amelia, she couldn't remember a time in her entire life when she'd truly been *fine.* Beautiful, funny, smart, sassy, flirtatious Amelia. Even dead, she'd made June's life hell. And now her daughter was back to do the same.

Oh, she hadn't shown up in Greenhill yet, but according to Grant, it was just a matter of time. When he'd broken the news to them upon his return from Oklahoma six weeks ago, Luther had wanted to jump in the car and head straight to Tulsa, but June had refused. She couldn't take time off work, she'd told him—a lie that Grant had exposed right in front of her. She was the best executive assistant in the world, but she could be spared for a few weeks.

She had managed to persuade Luther to wait. The girl might be the baby they'd loved so dearly all grown up, but to her, June and Luther were complete strangers. Plus, the girl had just gotten out of the hospital, and she'd gotten some tremendous shocks about her people. She needed time. She knew where they were, and when she was ready, she would find her way there.

Dear God, June hoped she was never ready.

Still fanning herself with the useless purple hat, she smiled and nodded to folks who passed by on the way to their cars. Luther was standing under a live oak with his old buddies, his shirt buttoned up to the collar and his tie still tight in spite of the sweat that gleamed on his forehead. He'd gotten new life with the news about the girl. Amalia, she'd been named. Selena, she called herself now. There was a spring in his step, and laughter came more readily. A piece of his precious Amelia had been found, and it had rejuvenated him.

Pain radiated through June's jaw, and she forced the muscles to relax. It was a wonder she hadn't ground down her teeth in the past six weeks. Bad news had a way of making her do that.

The sun slowly claimed the spot where she stood, and she moved to keep up with the shade. Her lightweight lavender suit and sandals with chunky heels were well suited to the muggy weather, but she was growing more uncomfortable with each passing moment. She liked to blame the heat and the humidity, but they weren't the cause. Lately she'd been uncomfortable in her own skin. She didn't think it was the news about Amal—Selena, though certainly that didn't help. Maybe it was just age. Growing old and growing tired. The sins of the past catching up.

Finally, when fewer than a dozen people remained in the yard, Luther and his great-nephew, Tyrone, came toward her. "Girl, why don't you go on home?" Luther suggested. "Ty and I are gonna get us some sandwiches and head down to the creek."

She wanted to protest—not that he'd decided to skip out

on dinner at home but that he'd made her stand there sweating all this time before deciding. But she smiled instead. "Have fun. And be sure you clean what you catch. Tyrone, you watch out for your uncle."

Luther rolled his eyes as Tyrone saluted her. "You're a natural-born mother, Junie," the boy said with a grin.

"Natural-born boss is more like it," Luther muttered.

June watched them cross to Tyrone's pickup, where he helped Luther into the high seat, then she went to her own car. The heat inside was searing, so she rolled down the windows and turned the air conditioner to high.

It took less than five minutes to drive home to the house where she'd been born. When she was a girl, they'd walked back and forth to church. She'd always been sedate, wanting to look her best for Sunday school, while Amelia had all but danced there and back, shoes in her hand instead of on her feet, looking wild and mischievous and reckless. *Ain't she something?* people had always said with an affectionate shake of their heads.

She'd been *something* right up to the moment she died.

The house was set in a grove of tall pines fifty feet off the road. It had been a sharecropper's cabin when Luther and Oda Mae moved in after their wedding some sixty years ago. Soon after Amelia's disappearance, Grant had deeded it and ten acres to Luther. Luther had built a coop out back where he kept a few chickens, and laid out a huge garden every spring. June had thought that after spending his whole life growing food for other people's tables, he would have given it up in retirement, but he was a stubborn man.

Thanks to the dense trees, there wasn't a yard. June parked next to Luther's ancient pickup, then sat there for a moment. Knowing Luther and Tyrone, they would stay away all afternoon, whether the fish were biting or not. There was no reason to fry chicken and mash potatoes just for herself, and no chores that demanded her attention right away, but there was work at the office she could get caught up on.

Shifting into reverse, she backed out again, but instead of turning onto the highway, she followed the dirt lane that disappeared into the woods behind the house. Less than a half mile away on the other side, past fields and barns, was her destination: The Gardens. Though Grant had an office in town, he did much of his work at home, which meant she spent time there, as well—more now that Grant's wife Kathryn was no longer in residence.

Crape myrtles marched in rows along all four sides of the yard, screening the residents of the mansion from all signs of the manual labor that supported them. June followed the gravel drive through a break in the hedge, parked beside the house, and climbed the steps to the veranda. The first time she'd ever come to the house, she'd been told to use the back door, like a servant. Today she strolled past rockers and benches and walked right up to the front door. She was about to put her key in the lock when a vehicle approached from the west side of the hedge.

The car didn't look familiar, and neither did the man behind the wheel. It couldn't be a friend or a client of Grant's—everyone in town knew he went to his mama's after church on Sundays. A farm employee or one of the house staff, all of whom had Sundays off, would have used the service entrance a half mile farther down the road. So either this man was lost or he was snooping where he didn't belong.

He parked along the driveway, careful to stay off the grass, and climbed out. His smile was bright and a little too polished. "Good afternoon, ma'am. How are you this lovely Sunday?" He wore dark trousers and a white shirt, the sleeves rolled back, the tie loosened at his neck. His hair was a little too shaggy, the color a flat auburn. In contrast, his beard was dark brown and neatly trimmed. Tortoiseshell glasses perched on his nose, and a long, skinny notebook was sticking out of his hip pocket.

She folded her arms over her chest and set her jaw. She was right: He was snooping. She'd been harassed by enough reporters when the news about Kathryn Hamilton having killed Amelia first broke to recognize one a mile away.

"This is the Hamilton place, right?" He didn't seem to notice that she hadn't yet spoken as he climbed the steps and extended his hand. "And I'm guessing you're June Ravenel, Mr. Hamilton's executive assistant. Am I right?"

She looked pointedly at his hand, then back up to his face. "I am, and I don't recall inviting you to come on up."

Letting his hand drop to his side, he backed down a couple steps. For an instant, his smile faltered, then it came back with more wattage than before. "No, ma'am, you didn't. I apologize." Drawing a business card from his pocket, he offered it to her. "I don't suppose Mr. Hamilton is in."

David Jones, *Modern South Magazine*. She'd seen the glossy publication. It was a slick, snooty rag for slick, snooty people, and, according to Kathryn Hamilton, who had long subscribed, it attracted its readers as much with the down-and-dirty gossip it covered as with the society stuff.

And they wanted to write an article about the Hamilton-Ravenel scandal. Wouldn't that serve Kathryn right, to be skewered on the pages of her favorite magazine for all her friends to see?

Of course, David Jones's plan might be to skewer Amelia as well. That would be fine with June—Amelia certainly deserved to suffer the consequences of her affair, even this long after the fact—but it would break Luther's heart.

"Mr. Hamilton is out," she said curtly as she tapped the card against her palm.

Mr. Jones nodded. "Of course. It's Sunday afternoon. He's probably visitin' with his mama. At least, that's what I'd be doing if I was home in Birmingham. What about you, Miss June? Can I have a moment of your time?" He had a hungry look in his eyes, greedy and sly, that he tried to hide, but she recognized it. It reminded her of Amelia. Beautiful, sassy, manipulative Amelia.

After one more glance at the card, she slipped it into her pocket, then gestured toward the nearest pair of chairs. It couldn't hurt to find out what he wanted, now could it?

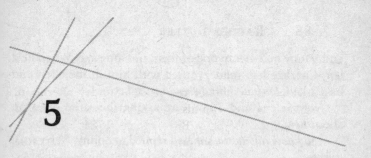

5

Charlize wended her way through Pawley's busy dining room and out into the courtyard, greeting regulars with a warm smile and a gentle touch. When she'd bought the building twelve years ago and turned it into a small café, her only experience with the restaurant business had been dining out. She hadn't cared whether she made a success of the place. She had merely been looking for something to do between keeping an eye on William's business and taking care of William's hits.

If she'd cared, would she have been so successful? she wondered as she chatted pleasantly with the mayor and his wife, who were sharing a table near the fountain with a local senator and her husband. If the business had truly mattered to her, would it have come so easily?

Probably not. In her experience, things that mattered were rarely easy.

In the years since, the restaurant had doubled its square footage and picked up a regular clientele that included the rich and powerful of Savannah. Charlize was on a first-name basis with them all and knew a lot about them, while they knew nothing of her.

Once she retired from her other line of work, she intended to keep it that way.

Back inside the restaurant, she turned down a narrow hall that led to one of several private dining rooms. Selena and Sonny had met in one of them not long ago. When he'd left, Charlize had rendezvoused with him in the alley, and he'd asked, *Do you think I should trust her?*

Now Selena and Tony were asking the same question about *her.*

You know my motto, she had replied to Sonny. *Never trust anyone.*

Her first lesson in trust—in betrayal—had come from her mother. Two weeks after Charlize's twelfth birthday, Mary Elaine Thomas had sent her off to school one day with a hug and a kiss, the same as always, then loaded her car and disappeared. Charlize had come home to find everything of value gone, and to the knowledge that her mother—the woman who said *I love you* every day—hadn't loved her enough to take Charlize with her.

The second lesson and betrayal had come from her father. When John Turner had returned from his business trip and found out that Elaine was gone, the first thing he'd done was go on a three-day drunk. Then he'd resumed life as usual. But instead of Elaine cleaning and cooking for him, it was Charlize. Instead of Elaine running his errands and taking care of things during his frequent trips out of town, Charlize did. And instead of turning to Elaine for comfort and love, he'd turned to—

Grimly, she forced the memories to the back of her mind. *Never trust anyone,* she'd told Sonny, but he hadn't listened. He'd trusted her.

And she'd killed him. And it really had been just a job. Loyalty to William and Selena.

She didn't miss Sonny. Wasn't sorry he was gone. Didn't regret anything about him . . . except occasionally late in the night, when she remembered the feel of his arms around her, the quiet whispers. *I love you.* Though there were exceptions, for the most part she knew love was a fairy tale. It was a pretty word people used to cover up ugly, dark emotions—an excuse to justify their actions. *I love you, little girl,* her father used to croon to her right before the pain started.

He'd paid for his crimes. So had Sonny. So would Damon Long.

Realizing she stood motionless outside the private room, she gave herself a shake and quickly strode to her office at the end of the corridor. It was hardly big enough for a desk, a chair, and file cabinets. She had larger closets at home, but she liked the coziness of the space. It was painted a soothing peach, with cream-and-coral-striped drapes over the one window. The top of the desk held her computer and phone, and inside the drawers were the tools of her trades: notepads, pens, paper clips, and stapler; dagger, pistol, pepper spray, and Flex-Cuffs.

Sitting down, she slipped off her heels, took a few deep breaths, then fixed her gaze on the painting on the opposite wall. It was a Selena McCaffrey original, a gift six years ago from William. She suspected it had been a gift to *him* from the artist herself, but he'd hated Selena's passion for art too much to keep it. It was a waste of her natural talents, he'd complained.

It hadn't been the first time Charlize had disagreed with him. Anyone could learn to run a business, to carry a gun and give orders. But creating scenes such as the one that hung before her . . . such beauty, such serenity and peace . . . *that* was Selena's real talent.

Sometimes Charlize fantasized about finding the cove featured in the scene, with its sandy beach and lush, tropical growth. If the house didn't exist, she would build it—a sprawling white structure with windows and porches and paddle fans and gauzy white curtains that floated on the ocean breeze. She would pack away her weapons and her conservative clothes, along with the last twenty-three years of her life, and she would discover her own passion. She would live. Grow. Heal.

After she fulfilled her last obligation to William and gave Selena the chance to live and heal.

The ring of her cell phone was soft, melodic, in the quiet room. She flipped it open without checking caller ID. Few people who called this private number wanted their own number displayed. "Hello."

"J.T.? This is Ruby Dee. You hear from Damon Long?"

Straightening in her seat, Charlize slid her feet back into her heels. "Not yet. Have you seen him?"

"He was here. Left again yesterday. I gave him your message, among others. He said he'd called."

Charlize wasn't surprised that Long had lied. That was what he did—he lived, he breathed, he lied. But she did wonder why he hadn't returned her call. Had he heard that Selena had left Tulsa with a woman matching her description? Or had Luke Morgan tattled to the boss that they'd been together in Atlanta?

If that was the case, Long had probably written her off. There were other hitters. He didn't need her, didn't have to trust her.

"Did he mention where he was going?" she asked, still gazing at the white house in the painting.

"No. He asked to see an atlas, but I couldn't see what area he was looking at."

"I appreciate the call, but...why?" Ruby Dee owed Charlize no loyalty, and from all accounts, she never took sides. She stayed on the fringes, minding her own business both literally and figuratively.

The telephone line fairly hummed with silence before

Ruby Dee exhaled audibly. "You ever hear of Mitch Gautier?"

"Your husband? Yes, of course. He worked for William." Everyone on the job had heard about Gautier's crew and the missing merchandise after the executions had been carried out. William hadn't given her the contract. He'd said it was too simple; he would have it handled locally.

"Yeah, him and his cousins, Benny and T-Bone. Turned out, Benny was stealing from Mr. Davis, but instead of punishing him, Davis had all three of them killed. My husband didn't do anything wrong, and he was damn near cut in half by that shotgun." The emotion in Ruby Dee's voice was thick, vicious. "Davis gave me some money and told me how sorry he was. He thought I was too stupid to figure it out. Hell, people talk. Within a few days, everyone around here knew what really happened."

Charlize felt compelled to point out, "Long wasn't involved in that." He'd argued the case with William, but William was so damn arrogant. Life meant nothing to him, especially someone else's. He'd taken the easy way out, then tried to make up for it by giving money to the families of the two men who had needlessly died. He'd thought that would make everything all right.

There was a moment's silence, then Sippie Wallace began singing in the background. "Maybe Damon didn't pull the trigger. Maybe he didn't agree with doing it. But he didn't do anything to stop it, either."

And for that, he had to pay. Long had committed so many crimes for which he had to pay.

But hadn't they all?

"Thank you for calling," Charlize said.

After a moment, Ruby Dee replied. "Yeah. Sure."

Then the line went dead.

"I'm sorry."

Selena stared at the television, her gaze narrowly focused on the screen. Her head throbbed, her eyes were gritty, and her jaw ached from clenching so long, but all the deep breathing exercises in the world couldn't help her relax.

After returning with lunch and the Sunday *Journal-Constitution,* Tony had made several efforts to talk to her, but she had refused to acknowledge him. Finally she faced him.

"How dare you imply that I'm selfish for wanting to know who I am?" she demanded, and the rest of the words followed like water bursting through a crumbled dam. "You *know* your entire family history, everything about your parents, everything about *their* parents! You know that your grandparents immigrated here, you know the villages they came from in Italy, you know every major event that ever happened in their lives. You've never been tossed away like—" Her breath caught on a sob. *So much garbage.* That was all she'd been to Luisa and Rodrigo Acosta—one more worthless mouth that they'd had to feed. Even the money William had paid them to take care of her hadn't made her matter.

"Selena—"

She raised her hand to keep him from approaching her. She was a strong woman who didn't cry, but if he touched her, if he held her, she would surely break down.

"It's not as if I set out to—how did you put it? 'Unleash a psychopathic killer on an unsuspecting public.' Getting Damon Long out of jail wasn't my decision. His escape isn't my failure. If you want to blame someone for that, blame the FBI."

"I do blame the FBI." His voice was quiet—because he sensed she was on the edge? "They knew how dangerous Long was, and they got him released anyway. I just wish . . ."

As his gaze fell away, her stomach knotted, and her fingers followed suit in her lap. He sounded so regretful, and, God help her, she didn't want to give him regrets. She didn't want him to think about how much trouble she'd been, how much danger she'd brought into his life. She didn't want him to consider for even a moment that he might be better off without her.

He looked at her again. "I love you, Selena. I want to spend the rest of my life with you. I want to have kids with you. I just wish you trusted me. Just once give me credit for knowing more about something than you do."

She swallowed back the lump in her throat. "I do trust you, but . . . this is my life."

"No. It's *our* lives. I've got as much at stake here as you do."

She shook her head, dimly aware of the absence of curls brushing her skin. "Long doesn't want you dead."

"But his guy is gonna have to kill me to get to you," he pointed out. "I've been a cop a long time, Selena. I'm not operating completely in the dark. I'm good at what I do. I understand how the feds think, how criminals think." His voice lowered and grew husky. "You're not alone in this."

She hugged her middle, rubbing her arms to chase away the sudden goose bumps there. Except for the first few months of her life, she'd always been alone. She'd had William making decisions for her but offering nothing in the way of a normal relationship, had had acquaintances but no real friends, had dated but had never seriously cared for anyone. She'd handled everything herself because she'd had no one to turn to, no one to rely on, no one who was always there.

Tony had always been there. Even when he was angry, even when he disapproved of her decisions, he'd never let her down.

She didn't know what to say, how to explain, so she said the only words that came to mind. "I love you."

His grin came and went. "I know you do."

"That's still so very new to me. There's never been any-one . . ." No one to love, to laugh with, to make a life with. "In twenty-eight years, there's never been anyone," she repeated in a whisper, then smiled bleakly. "I sound like some sort of emotional cripple."

This time when he moved, she didn't try to stop him. He sat beside her, close enough for his leg to bump hers, and reached over to clasp her hand snugly in his. "You're not a cripple. It's the way you had to live. Blame Kathryn. Henry. Luisa and Rodrigo and all the others in your past. But re-member that it *is* in the past. It's all over now, Selena. You've got me and all the rest of the Ceolas, and we're not that easy to get rid of. Maybe you don't know enough about where you come from, but you'll know all you need to know about where our kids come from."

Her fingers tightened around his before letting go, mov-ing to stroke his jaw. Beard stubbled his chin, raspy against her skin. "I love you," she said again, then brushed her mouth over his. She cupped his face in her palms and kissed him, sliding her tongue inside to thrust, taste, stroke. Heat flared inside her and her nipples grew taut as her lungs con-stricted. When the need for air forced her to end the kiss, she stood, removed the pistols from her waistband and laid them on the night table, then kicked off her shoes.

Tony's gaze never left her as she drew the T-shirt over her

head, folded it neatly, and laid it on the bed. The jeans were next, sliding down her legs into a puddle on the floor. She picked them up and folded them, too, before adding them to the shirt.

Her lingerie at home was all satin and silk and lace in vibrant colors, soft, sensuous, luxurious. There was a certain sensuality to cotton, too, or so Tony seemed to think. She undid the plain white bra and laid it aside, then hooked her thumbs in the elastic band of the plain white panties. She slid them over her hips, down her thighs, past her calves, then folded them neatly.

Grabbing a handful of Tony's shirt, she pulled him to his feet and backward onto the other bed with her. As they tumbled, then settled into the soft mattress, he tried to push back, protesting, "No fair. I want to look."

She traded her hold on the shirt for a hold on him, wrapping her arms around him, moving sinuously beneath him. "I want to fuck."

His cock, already swollen, jerked against her, and his gaze went dark and smoky. He kissed her hard while they fumbled with his jeans. One of his shoes hit the floor with a thud, followed by the other, then his button was undone, his zipper unzipped. She left pushing the denim and briefs away to him and instead wrapped her fingers around his penis, caressing the hot silky skin, drawing a groan from him.

"Ah, damn, don't—" He tried to capture her wrist, but she brushed his hand away.

"Now," she demanded.

"Just—" The strong muscles in his legs flexed against hers as he freed himself from his jeans, then braced his hands alongside her shoulders. Wearing a sweetly pained look, he thrust inside her, filling her with one hard stroke, then stared down at her. His breathing was ragged, his muscles tight. "Haven't you heard of foreplay?"

Smiling wickedly, she slid her hands from his hips to his chest, then scraped one nail across his nipple. "You're a man. I thought 'I want to fuck' was all the foreplay you needed."

"I didn't even need that, babe. You had me when you touched me." He moved inside her, drew out, then sank back in, finding a slow, easy rhythm that she matched . . . until he lowered his mouth to her breast. The kiss made her quiver. The bite arched her back and flooded her with hot need.

He teased and tormented her, and she returned the favor. Every nerve ending in her body was tingling when she finally came, and that was enough to make him come, too. Their skin slick with sweat, their breathing harsh, their bodies quivering, he lowered his forehead to hers, gazed into her eyes, and said, "We forgot the condom."

His erection was softening inside her, but with a thrust of her hips, it grew hard again. She rolled with him until he was on his back and she sat astride his him. Hands braced on his chest, she slid lazily along his length and back again, then bent to rub her mouth gently over his.

"Well, then," she said softly. "If I get pregnant, I guess you'll just have to marry me."

Monday morning found Damon in a diner in downtown Greenhill. It was just like every other little Southern town he had been in, Bayou Blue excepted—just a little cleaner, a little more prosperous. There was a major logging operation to the west of town and Hamilton Farms to the east. Each employed about a third of the town, and the final third provided services to those two thirds.

He sat, back to the wall, his laptop, his cell phone, and the remains of his breakfast in front of him. The color he'd used to turn his hair from brown to "warm auburn" made his scalp itch, and he idly scratched it. Between the hair, the beard, and the glasses, though, he could probably walk right past the people looking for him and they'd never give him a glance.

Well, Selena might. But she felt more passionately about him than the others did.

He'd been in town since Saturday afternoon, and had located Grant Hamilton's office three blocks down the street, his mother's house on the ritzy south side of town, and his church two blocks off Main Street. He'd looked up the police station, the sheriff's office, the courthouse, and the jail. He'd gotten the general layout of the Hamilton plantation before June Ravenel had spotted him, and seen for himself how easy a target Hamilton was—multiple unguarded access routes onto his property, no obvious security at work or home, and the guy had been oblivious to Damon following him the afternoon before and again that morning.

Grant Hamilton didn't have a clue. He was harmless—defenseless—and Selena knew it.

Damon had also spent two hours talking to June and learned more than she'd realized she'd said. She wasn't happy about her long-missing niece coming back from the grave, and wasn't sad about the confirmation that her long-missing sister was actually in the grave. She'd said the right words. They just didn't ring true. There'd been bad blood between the Ravenel sisters, and it wasn't likely to be any better between aunt and niece.

That might come in handy, once the trap was baited.

Damon had given it some thought over the weekend and decided Charlize was likely fucking with him. She'd accepted his offer, then turned around and offered her assistance to

Selena. For more money? Or for some twisted reason that made sense only to her?

Didn't matter. She was still part of his plan. He intended to call her and tell her where he was. If he was right about her, she would pass on the information to Selena. If she didn't, he would have to come up with another plan.

Draining the last of his coffee, he dialed the number Ruby Dee had given him, then braced the cell phone loosely against his ear. Charlize sounded cool and elegant when she answered. She was probably wearing one of those pale dresses that made men hot, with her hair pulled back like some kind of schoolmarm, looking so damn untouchable. She had always been untouchable—damaged goods, William used to say.

He'd said the same thing about Selena. Were they teamed up now, two of a kind? Women standing together against the men who threatened them? Had Charlize transferred her unwavering loyalty from William to Selena?

Truth was, he didn't give a shit. "This is Long," he said curtly. "I heard you wanted to talk to me."

"You're a hard man to find."

"Life is safer that way."

"Isn't it," she agreed drily. "Last I heard, Selena was in Atlanta. You have anything new?"

Last I heard, she was in Atlanta with you. *You have any explanation?* "No. But I'm thinking she might come to Alabama soon."

"Why would you think that?"

"Because her father's here." He paused. "And so am I."

"Hmm. But if she doesn't know . . ."

Damon smiled at the waitress as she brought his check. The redhead, maybe eighteen, and pregnant, smiled back before leaving. "Oh, I'm thinking she'll figure it out. You know her and that damn Ceola—they've got sources every-where."

"Don't you think it's a little dangerous, hanging out in the town where her father lives?"

"I like to live dangerously. So do you."

"You're wrong. I prefer to minimize the danger."

Yeah, right. She was double-crossing *him.* That was only slightly safer than playing Russian roulette with an auto-matic instead of a revolver. "Yeah, yeah," he said impatiently. "You call for any reason other than to tell me Selena's in Hotlanta?"

"No. That was it." She sounded level, believable, but he figured she was lying through her teeth.

He grinned. "Just for the record, I'll be hell and gone be-fore you can get here, so if you're entertaining any ideas about taking me out, you might as well forget them now. You can work for me and maybe take home the half-million-dollar prize, you can sit this one out, or you can be-come one of the targets, Charlize. It's up to you."

If his distrust surprised her, she gave no sign of it. After a moment's silence, she said, "Just don't forget, Damon, that the hunted often become the hunters."

He chuckled again as she disconnected. He didn't give a goddamn if Selena had somehow turned Charlize against him. He'd accomplished what he'd come here for. Either Selena would soon show up to protect her precious father, or she wouldn't. Either way, Damon was going right back into hiding someplace where no one would ever find him.

Selena hated waiting. Hated confinement. Hated someone else controlling her life. She'd had her fill of it from William, from the FBI, and now from Long and his cohorts. She just wanted to be free. Was that so damned much to ask?

It was their third day in Atlanta, and they were in their fifth motel—or was it the sixth? She was tired of the sameness of the rooms—the layout, the cheap furniture, the smells. She was tired of keeping the curtains closed and staying away from the windows and not going out.

The only thing she wasn't tired of was making love with Tony, she thought with a smile. They'd made up for all the sex they'd missed after she'd shot him in June, when he wasn't speaking to her, when she'd been working with the FBI and living in William's house, and when she'd been too sore after her fight with Yates.

But they couldn't spend the rest of their lives making love in cheap motel rooms in Georgia.

The ring of the cell phone made her stiffen, then look over her shoulder as Tony answered. His end of the conversation was uninformative, his expression difficult to read. That meant bad news. He wouldn't be so guarded otherwise. Stomach knotted, she waited for him to hang up, waited until he reluctantly met her gaze.

"Well?" Her voice sounded rusty. She didn't know whether to hope for the best or fear the worst, and settled for trying to feel nothing.

"That was Frankie. He got a call from Charlize." The grimness in his expression intensified. "*She* got a call this morning from Damon Long."

Selena's muscles tightened. "And?"

Tony dragged his fingers through his hair before finishing. "He's in Alabama. In Greenhill. Charlize is on her way there."

She shot off the bed, crossing to the dresser in two strides. Snatching up the nearest backpack, she went to the sink and began sweeping toiletries into it. She ducked into the bathroom to get the items there, then turned to find Tony blocking the doorway.

"What are you doing?"

"Packing."

"Are we going somewhere?"

"I don't know about you, but I'm going to Alabama." She pushed, and he let her pass. After shoving the shampoo, shaving cream, and razor into the bag, she started toward the dresser, but again he blocked her way. This time he didn't let her go.

"Selena, we can't go there. It's a trap. Long knows you've gone into hiding. He obviously knows about you and Grant. He's just trying to use your father as bait to get to you."

"And guess what? It's working." She tried to sidestep him, but he caught her arm. She clenched her fingers around his biceps. "Damn it, Tony, he's dragged my family into this. I've waited my whole life to know my father. I went through hell to find out who he is, and damned if I'm going to stand back and cower while Long—" She couldn't put it into words: *hurts him, threatens him, kills him.*

Muscles knotting, she forced a deep breath, forced the panic down. "You can come with me, you can stay here, or you can go back to Oklahoma—I don't care. But *I'm* going to Greenhill." She saw the hurt in his dark eyes and knew the cause: *I don't care.* But stubbornly she refused to take back the words.

He pushed the hurt aside for the moment, too. "Your being there could put Grant in more danger. It'll bring Luke Morgan to town, as well as Long, and they won't hesitate to take out anyone who stands between them and you."

"Maybe." Probably. Logically, the best thing she could do was stay far, far away from Grant. But he was her *father,* damn it! She'd just met him. She could protect him. She would kill anyone who threatened him.

"He's setting a trap for you, Selena. Why else would he go to Greenhill? Why would he tell Charlize? Because he's trying to bring you out of hiding."

"So we'll turn the trap on him. He wants me out of hiding? Fine. He'll be sorry he did." She took a breath and forced her fingers to relax. "Tony, I have to do something. I can't hide forever. This is my chance. For the first time in two months, we know where Long is. We can find him. We can stop him."

Not kill him. Just stop him. Unless he hurt Grant and left her no choice.

Pulling away from Tony, she scooped her clothing into the second backpack, then picked up a handful of his clothes. "Are you going with me?"

He stared at her a moment, then snatched both the clothes and the bag. "That's a stupid question," he muttered. "Of course I'm going."

While he finished packing, she scanned the room. They didn't have much to take. Other than the three pistols on the night table, they had it all.

As she secured both backpacks, Tony called the front desk and asked for a cab, then watched at the window. When a low-riding taxi pulled into the lot a few moments later, he left the room first, looking around quickly before motioning for her to follow.

She hadn't given any thought to how they would get to Alabama until he directed the cabbie to drop them at the nearest car rental agency. Other than paying for the flight, they'd avoided using their credit cards for fear that Long, through one of the corrupt cops they knew had been on William's payroll, would manage to track them. But what did a paper trail matter now? Charlize knew she would go to Greenhill. Long expected her there, and he would tell Luke Morgan. The trick was to get to Grant's house before Long and Morgan found out what kind of vehicle to look for.

At least Grant would be all right.

Tony wasted no time throwing the packs in the rental's backseat, then leaving the lot. "There's a map in the glove compartment," he said tersely. "Tell me where to go."

It took a few minutes to get her bearings, but at last they were headed in the right direction. She watched the city pass by—a lot of green, tall buildings, rundown areas—and periodically checked the outside mirror for traffic behind them. Tony was driving the speed limit, and no one was interested enough in them to do the same.

As they left the city proper behind, he braced his knee against the steering wheel, plugged the cell phone in to charge, then handed it to her. "Call Grant. Don't tell him we're coming. Just . . . warn him."

"If he sees or hears from Long, he should . . . ?"

"Call the local police, then the FBI. There'll be a number for the Montgomery office at the front of the phone book."

She knew Grant's numbers—office, home, cell phone—by heart. Her *father's* numbers. Weeks after meeting him, it still seemed unreal. So many years she'd wondered about him. So many years she'd been told he was black, and she'd built an entire fantasy around that. She'd given him a large, loving family who hadn't cared that her blood was mixed; she'd imagined him greeting her with open arms and making up for all the years they'd missed with more love and acceptance than she'd ever dreamed.

In reality, he was as white as could be. Old-money, plantation-holding, southern-aristocracy white. He was only a few inches taller than she, made soft from a lifetime at a desk. His brown hair was heavily brushed with gray, and he wore thick glasses that emphasized the weariness around his eyes. He was totally different from the image she'd clung to so long.

But he was her father. He had loved her mother. He had loved *her*. Wanted her. Missed her as desperately as she'd missed him.

After his adopted son had tried to kill her, he'd visited Selena at the hospital and at Tony's house, and they'd talked on the phone, as well. He'd talked about his family, his law practice, and the farm that had been home to generations of Hamiltons. She'd learned so much, but there was so much more she wanted to know. So much she'd missed—

"This is Grant." He sounded distracted—had sheepishly admitted that he often was. It had seemed the best way to live with Kathryn. Without Amelia.

Selena swallowed the lump that had arisen in her throat. "Hello, Grant. It's Selena."

Pleasure warmed his voice. "Hey. I've been thinking about you. How are you feeling?"

He'd asked that question every time they'd spoken since their first meeting. He'd wanted her to recuperate at his home, where he could see that her every need was met, and had reminded her regularly to take it easy. For someone who'd never known a parent's concern, it was a lovely feeling.

"I'm fine." *My house was blown up, I'm on the run, a psychopath is offering people a fortune to kill me, and now he's in your hometown.* "Listen, Grant, I can't talk long. I just wanted to tell you . . ."

"Tell me what?"

She could imagine him sitting in the office he'd described to her: crimson walls, built-in bookcases, a marble fireplace, and a mahogany partner's desk that had been in the family for generations. His brow was furrowed—she'd seen it often enough to match the voice with the expression—and he would be rubbing the finger where, for thirty-six years, his wedding ring had rested. He'd discarded the ring the night Kathryn had tried to kill Selena, but it was going to take a while for the reminder to disappear.

"I just found out that Damon Long is in Greenhill."

After a moment's silence, Grant sounded sharper, more alert. "Damon Long. The man who worked for Henry, who escaped FBI custody the same night Jefferson . . ."

"Yes."

"And he's here . . . to somehow get to you?"

"Yes. If a stranger shows up, don't talk to him. Don't let him in. Just call the police."

"What does he look like?"

"I can't honestly say. I've known him with brown hair and blond. He might be clean-shaven, have a full beard, or anything in between. His eyes could be blue, brown, or any other color. He changes his appearance as needed." She reached up to tuck her hair back. Startled anew by its shortness, she smiled grimly. Long wasn't the only one who understood the value of blending in.

"Are you safe?" Grant asked.

She glanced at Tony, one hand on the wheel, dark glasses covering his eyes. "Yes, I am."

"Good. If anything happened to you . . ." Grant coughed to clear his throat, then said more heartily, "I'll keep the alarm set and stay on my guard."

"Don't rely too much on the alarm. Long is very good at bypassing them. I don't mean to worry you . . ."

He chuckled. "You're my daughter. Of course I worry. Will you stay in touch?"

She cleared her own throat. "I will. I'll call you again soon."

"I love you."

Misty-eyed, she whispered, "Good-bye," then disconnected. When her father had been without substance or form, she'd loved the idea of him almost fanatically. Now that he was real, she still loved the idea, and there was much about the man she liked, but there was so much she didn't know. They were still, for practical purposes, strangers.

And she was damned if she would let Damon Long keep them that way.

The miles to Montgomery passed in silence. At times she fancied she could hear them clicking down in her brain: 130, 110, 90. *Too far, too far, too far.* Once they reached the city, it was another hour to Greenhill. How much damage could Damon Long do in an hour?

He could kill in less than sixty seconds.

Anxiously she shifted as much as the seat belt would allow. "Do you have any suggestions for once we reach Greenhill?"

Tony glanced her way, brows arched above the sunglasses. "Are you just asking for my advice or is there a chance that you'll actually take it this time?"

She stared down at her hands, clasped tightly in her lap. She couldn't blame him for being annoyed. His arguments made sense: he *was* a cop; he *had* experience. His advice was generally good, if a bit on the overprotective side.

But she had experience, too. She'd lived half her life on the wrong side of the law. And she had to live with the decisions she made. If she stayed away from Greenhill and Grant was hurt or killed because of it . . . she *couldn't* live with that.

She looked at him again—the hard line of his jaw, the

taut muscles, the grip he had on the steering wheel. "Please, Tony..."

A mile or two passed before he spoke again. "I'm not like you, Selena. Whether you stay in Atlanta or go to Greenhill, whether you hide or walk down the street at high noon—whatever you do, whatever happens to you, I care. It would kill me to lose you."

Guilt flushed through her for the careless hurt she'd caused in the motel room. "I didn't mean—"

His attention locked on the highway ahead, he interrupted. "The first thing you—we—need to do is buff up Grant's security, for his sake as well as yours. I'll get Frankie to send Long's and Morgan's photographs to law enforcement in the region, as well as to the media. If Grant's house can be made secure enough, you're going to stay there. You'll still be a prisoner, just in a fancier room this time."

The quality of the room didn't matter. During the FBI's operation in Tulsa, her prison had been William's Riverside Drive mansion, a beautiful place filled with great treasures, and she'd hated every minute of it.

Because Tony wasn't there.

"If Grant's house can't be secured, the two of you will have to leave. You'll have to go into hiding someplace else. We can call in the FBI if you feel more comfortable—"

"*No.*" In her only experience with them, rather than keep her safe, they'd exposed her to more danger than she'd been prepared for. "We don't need their help."

He nodded curtly. "Greenhill's small. It won't be easy for Long to move around unnoticed. Unfortunately, Grant's house is a mile or two out of town. Woods, fields, a lot of places to go unnoticed. All Long and Morgan need is one clear shot."

"So all we have to do is make sure they don't get it," she said with a smile that was steadier than she felt.

And a small town might be just the place to set their own trap. It might be the perfect place to put an end to the hiding, the threat, and Damon Long.

Seconds dragged past. Tony opened his mouth, but in the end, he didn't speak. He simply laid his hand over hers and squeezed once.

He wasn't convinced. Logical as that was, it made her chest tighten and stirred the fear in her gut. She wasn't just saying words. She had been ready to sacrifice her own life to save his. He *was* her life.

And damned if she would let Long or anyone else come between them.

Not even herself.

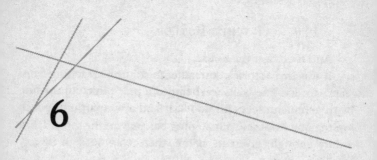

6

Tony slowed the car as a turnoff came into sight ahead. The entrance to The Gardens was 1.8 miles east of Greenhill, off a winding county road. A white board fence gave way to a short section of black wrought iron, with an iron gate in the middle. The gate looked as if it had been there for generations, and in the same open position. Bushes grew behind the fence, and a small guard shack stood empty to the left.

The only mention of their destination was on a worn historical marker a few yards off the road.

> The Gardens, built in 1823 by Cyrus Hamilton,
> governor of the State of Alabama.

That governor's blood flowed through Selena's veins... along with the blood of the slaves who'd made him prosperous. From which one did she get her incredible stubbornness? Tony wondered drily.

The gravel drive ran in a straight shot for a few hundred yards under a canopy formed by the dense trees on either side. It dipped through a low marshy area, then curved around the edge of a pond. Through occasional gaps in the trees, he caught glimpses of cultivated fields, then a roof here, a balcony there. Finally the road passed through rows of tall shrubs and into the open again.

And there was the house.

It was three stories, square, with columns reaching from earth to sky. The walls were tinged a pale pink, contrasting with green shutters and doors. It had a wraparound porch on the first floor and a matching balcony on the second, but oddly enough, given its name, there was no sign of any gardens.

"Nice place," he said, hoping the understatement would ease the tension that had held Selena rigid for the past thirty miles. She looked as if a smile might crack her face, as if she would give anything to turn around and run the other way.

If Kathryn Hamilton hadn't been such a greedy bitch, this could have been Selena's home. Instead of going hungry, sleeping on the dirt floor of a shack, and stealing to survive, she could have been the pampered daughter of one of the state's more influential families. It wouldn't have been perfect—that family was white, she was half black, and that still mattered—but it would have been close.

She would have been a different person. He might never have met her. She might never have loved him.

Gravel designated space at the side of the house for parking. Tony pulled in next to a burgundy Chevrolet, cut the engine, then looked at Selena. She was pale.

He hoped Kathryn Hamilton rotted in hell.

He got out, circled the car, opened the door, and offered his hand. After a slight hesitation, Selena took it and stepped out. She slung the purse with its two pistols over her shoulder, wrapped her fingers tightly around his, and started for the steps.

Chairs and small tables lined the porch, and stands held pots of bright red flowers. Every ten feet a pair of French doors broke up the wall, giving glimpses into formal rooms that looked too much like Henry's house for Tony's tastes, decorated for historical context rather than comfort.

At the front door, he rang the bell, then looked around. The yard was large, a smooth expanse of green that offered no place to hide—no trees, bushes, fountains, or statuary. With good lighting and strategically placed motion detectors, it would be impossible for anyone to approach the house unnoticed.

The door was opened by a stout woman with graying hair and a pinched face. "Can I help you?"

Since Selena remained silent, he spoke up. "I'm Tony Ceola, and this is Selena McCaffrey. We're here to see Mr. Hamilton."

"Do you have an appointment?"

Unsure how forthcoming Grant had been in his hometown, Tony said, "No, but I'm sure he'll want to see us."

"I'll ask. You can wait right here." She stepped back so they could enter, then disappeared down the hall, her shoes squeaking on the gleaming marble.

She left them in an entry hall broad enough to rival the rooms on either side. Family portraits hung on the walls, and a staircase on the right rose to the second floor. Everything was oversized, overly luxurious, and impressive, but Tony was more interested in Selena. He'd never seen her so nervous and showing it. She always looked so serene, no matter how much turmoil she was really in.

"Come on," he said softly, bumping his shoulder against hers. "It's Grant. Your father."

"And his house. His home. His history. His family. Amelia's family. . . . *My* family," she whispered.

She hadn't yet met any of her other relatives, though now that she was here, they would want to see her. Despite his need to keep her safe, Tony knew he couldn't stop that from happening.

He'd never had particularly strong feelings for anyone outside his family. He had a lot of friends and few enemies, and got along with most people, including most of those he'd arrested. But he hated Damon Long with an intensity he hadn't known he was capable of.

Just as he loved Selena more than he'd thought possible.

From somewhere down the hall, a door closed, then footsteps approached. Not the housekeeper's—these shoes made a sharp rap against the marble. Not Grant's, either. The sound suggested heels. Tony felt Selena's tension ratchet up as they both turned toward the door. A soft hum became audible—an old gospel tune—then the woman walked through the arch.

She was black, average height, a few pounds over average weight. Her hair was short, black mixed with gray, and reminded him of a sprayed and lacquered helmet. She wore a business suit in red and shoes with the thick, sturdy heels Tony's mother preferred. Her features were too strong to call her pretty. In fact, his first impression of her was *solid.* Reliable.

A bulging purse hung over one shoulder, and she was carrying an armful of file folders along with a tall glass of iced tea. She was halfway across the foyer before she noticed them, and when she did, she stopped abruptly and stared. The glass slipped from her grasp and tumbled to the floor, shattering on the marble, tea splashing her stockings and puddling around her feet. An instant later, the folders slid free, papers flying loose, some landing in the puddle with a splash, others drifting lazily down.

"Oh, dear Lord," she breathed, one hand raised to her

chest. Eyes wide, she stared at Selena with shock, surprise, and confusion. "Dear God up in heaven, *Amelia*..."

Abruptly, the woman realized there was a mess at her feet. She started to kneel, but Tony caught her arm. Instinctively, she snatched it back, and he let her. "Watch out for the glass."

"Glass...oh, yes, of course." Flustered, she glanced around, then retraced her steps to the arch. "Nell, could you bring some rags and a broom?"

While she composed herself, Tony crouched and picked up a handful of papers, letting the tea drain from them. The ones in his hand appeared to be part of a contract; another batch, still soaking, was a will. Grant was a lawyer, and June Ravenel was his assistant.

She was also Selena's aunt.

Finally June came back to the center of the foyer, skirting Tony and the spill, and stopped a few feet in front of Selena. Clasping her hands tightly, she drew a loud breath. "You must be Selena. You gave me a start. You look"—another shaky breath—"*so much* like your mother. Her skin was darker, of course, but she had that same curly hair and those eyes...dear Lord, you could be her twin."

Tension hummed around the two women, as if neither knew what to do next. June took a step toward Selena, raised both arms a few inches, then stepped back again and extended her hand instead. Selena shook hands with her, let go quickly, then clasped her hands together in front of her.

Such a warm greeting, Tony thought as he fished the last of the papers from the puddle. He couldn't remember a time he'd ever seen one of his aunts without getting hugged, kissed, pinched, or all three. But he'd grown up with his aunts. Selena and June were strangers.

"I wasn't prepared," June said, her voice unsteady. "Grant didn't tell us..."

Finally Selena found her own voice. "He didn't know. We just decided today."

"So you drove all the way from Oklahoma."

"Atlanta, actually. We'd been there a few days."

The housekeeper bustled in, tutting to herself as she mopped up the tea, then swept the ice cubes and glass fragments into a dustpan. Tony used the extra towels she'd brought to blot the worst of the liquid from the papers. He'd just laid the final one aside when Grant came in.

"Selena!" There was no hesitation on his part. He enfolded her in his arms, brushed a kiss to her forehead, and murmured, "I'm so glad to see you!" before hugging her tightly again.

Selena didn't squeal, or even say anything at all, but her arms went around him, her muscles flexing as she held him. For her, Tony knew, that constituted an emotional display.

Tony's attention shifted to June, standing motionless, still staring, still stunned. There was something not quite pleasant in her expression. Grief? Sorrow? Was she remembering her sister? Recalling Amelia's affair with their married neighbor? Thinking about all those years they hadn't known what had happened to Amelia or her daughter?

Finally Grant released Selena, stepped back, and extended his hand. "It's good to see you, Tony."

Tony shook hands. "Sir."

Smiling broadly, Grant gestured toward his assistant. "I see you've met your aunt June. Isn't Selena as beautiful as I said, June? Doesn't she look just like her mother?"

June's smile didn't reach her eyes. "Just exactly," she agreed. She took a deep breath, got a better hold on her emotions. "Are you staying just for the night?"

"No, no," Grant said, then beamed at Selena. "Now that you're here, I can't let you go without having you meet all your family and showing you around and catching up on the last twenty-eight years. You've got to stay longer than one night."

"Actually, we were hoping to kind of hide out here for a while," Tony said.

Immediately Grant's expression turned grim. "Because of Damon Long?"

Selena exchanged glances with Tony. Some of the serenity was back in her gaze, her manner, as she gave him a small smile before turning to her father. "He's put out a contract on me—a half million dollars to the man—"

Or woman, Tony thought.

"—who kills me. We've spent the last four days in motels, but now that he's been spotted in this area, we would like to stay here . . . unless you'd rather avoid the risk."

Grant looked offended. "Of course you'll stay here."

"It could be dangerous," Tony pointed out.

"You're family. You'll stay. We'll do whatever is necessary to make this place impenetrable. Tony, I assume you'll want to handle the security?"

"Yes." He gave Selena a pointed look. At least someone valued his opinion. "Do you mind if I have a look around now?"

The room Grant showed Selena to was on the south side of the house, large and airy, with French doors leading to the balcony. The colors were peaceful—pale yellow, soft blue, muted green—and reminded her of the watercolors she hadn't touched since last week. A long time for a woman used to painting every day.

He didn't bother hinting that she and Tony shouldn't share a bed while in his house. She thought she might have been amused if he had. She definitely would have felt guilty, because she had no intention of sleeping apart from Tony. She'd become too accustomed to the warmth—the security—of his body next to hers.

"My grandparents used to vacation in the Bahamas," Grant said as she drew her finger along the gleaming dresser top. "They brought this furniture back with them. It makes me think of you."

She smiled faintly. Island Girl, Frank Simmons called her. All her adult life people had thought her exotic—half Puerto Rican, half Jamaican, with a faint tropical lilt to her voice. And in reality, she was as American as... well, apple pie. She didn't have a drop of Latino blood, was no more Jamaican than Grant. She could trace her family tree back for generations and find nothing but native-born Alabamians.

She *had* a family tree now. Ancestors with names and faces and stories to learn. A father, a grandmother, an aunt, a grandfather. She would meet her grandfather soon. Grant had invited June and Luther to join them for dinner.

Opening one glass door, she stepped outside onto the balcony. Grant followed.

A pair of wicker chairs flanked a matching table, occupying the space between doors. More sets of furniture in each direction marked the rooms on either side. Crape myrtles lined the far edge of the lawn, and behind them, pines stretched to the sky. Through their branches, the fields of Hamilton Farms were barely visible.

"June wasn't particularly happy to meet me, was she?" she asked as she idly fingered a vine trailing from the nearest hanging basket.

"Of course she was. She just wasn't prepared for how much you look like Amelia."

Selena wanted to believe him, but there had been something about the woman.... Maybe it was just shock. Or maybe Selena was being overly self-protective. For so many years, she'd dreamed about being welcomed into a family. Now that it was happening, maybe she was afraid to wholeheartedly embrace it for fear of losing it again.

Off in the distance, she saw Tony, walking with the farm foreman, and smiled. They were deep in conversation, both gesturing. By the time he came in for dinner, he would have mapped out a comprehensive security update for Grant... and she would be grateful.

As the two men disappeared through the hedge, she faced Grant and leaned against the balcony railing. "Tell me about my mother's parents."

She had asked before—in the hospital, while recuperating at Tony's house—and he'd complied, but there was a certain comfort in hearing it again. This was how family histories were passed down: from parent to child or grandchild. One day her own child would say, "Tell me about Grandpa and Grandma Ravenel," and she would.

Luther had been born on Hamilton Farms and was a third-generation employee. His wife, Oda Mae, had come down from Chicago to visit relatives, met Luther, and never gone back. She'd been only sixteen, but she'd known what she wanted: Luther and a houseful of children. They'd been blessed with just two: Amelia and, three years later, June.

And while Luther and Oda Mae had loved both their daughters, they had absolutely adored Amelia. "Everyone adored her," Grant said, a tender smile curving his mouth, a distant look in his eyes. "How could they not? She was beautiful. Outrageous. Funny. Daring. Exciting. She loved people, loved life, loved herself and everyone else, and she especially loved *you*. She was the light of Luther's life, and you were the light of her life."

Selena's artist's eye made it easy to imagine a young woman who looked like her, cradling her baby girl, crooning to her, dancing barefoot with her. Amelia hadn't sat when she could stand, hadn't walked when she could run, and hadn't run when she could dance. She'd embraced life, and Grant, and Selena herself.

And Kathryn had snatched it all away from them.

Rubbing away the chill that raised bumps on her arms, she quietly asked, "Have you spoken to Kathryn?"

Lines bracketed Grant's mouth. "No. After she found out about Jefferson, she pretty much lost interest in living. I doubt she'll ever be competent to stand trial."

She wouldn't be judged for killing Amelia, for trying to kill Selena. But she'd lost the son she doted on and, with him, the ability to cope. Wasn't that punishment enough?

Not really, Selena thought with a thin smile. But it would do.

"Are you still married to her?"

A flush crept along Grant's cheeks. "I've drawn up the papers."

"But you haven't filed them, because it seems cruel to divorce a woman in her state." She smiled again. "You're a kindhearted man."

"You don't mind?"

"Divorcing Kathryn won't bring back my mother. It won't undo everything she's done."

"She'll never come back here," Grant said, watching her. "Kathryn, I mean. She's not welcome here. You, on the other hand..." Smiling broadly, he swept his arm across the horizon. "One day all this will be yours, and you are always welcome."

"Even when the odds are good that at least one hit man will follow me here?"

"All the hit men in the world can follow." He frowned, then repeated, "Hit men. I don't believe I've ever said those words seriously. It's a concept so far outside my experience."

"It's become an everyday part of my life."

Moving closer, he put his arm around her shoulders, then nodded toward the driveway below, where Tony and the foreman had reappeared. "Don't worry. Between Tony's expertise and my money and determination, we'll keep you safe."

It wasn't her own safety she was worried about.

You're my daughter, he'd told her on the phone. *Of course I worry.* It was what fathers did—and, she was beginning to learn, what daughters did, too. At least they had that part of the relationship down to a science.

If she and Tony were successful at stopping Damon Long, she would have a long life to explore the rest of the daughter/father relationship with Grant. If they weren't successful...Her jaw clenched grimly. She'd waited too long, wanted too much.

Failure wasn't an option.

Ordinarily, by eight o'clock on a Monday night, June would be settling in to relax for what was left of the evening. Dinner would be over, the dishes washed and the kitchen put back in order. Luther would be stretched out in his recliner, ready to doze off during whichever television show she chose. Everything would be quiet and peaceful. Satisfying.

But this Monday night found her sitting stiffly at the table in Grant's dining room. The chandelier overhead and the wall sconces cast overlapping shadows, and the veranda doors were open an inch or two to let in the cooler night air. The occasional breeze caused the candles in their glass globes to flicker, and sweetened the air with the fragrance of roses.

Grant sat at the head of the table with Selena and Tony on his left, Luther and June on the right. Even on such short notice, Nell had prepared an excellent meal, or so everyone had said. It had tasted like sawdust to June.

Luther was in heaven. He had cried when June had told him he was finally going to meet his granddaughter. He'd taken his time getting dressed, changing into a dove gray suit, carefully knotting a tie around his neck in spite of his arthritic old fingers, slicking back the strands of his thinning hair, giving his shoes a quick shine. "It's just dinner," she'd chided him, and he had responded with an ear-to-ear smile.

"It's the most important dinner of my life."

The chill those words sent up her spine had extinguished the guilt for chastising him.

Silence fell over the table, broken after a moment by Luther. "Isn't she just beautiful?" he asked of no one in particular. He was gazing at Selena as if she was his precious Amelia.

In all her life, he'd never told June she was beautiful. Oh, she knew she wasn't. She straddled a line between plain and just plain homely, but if a woman's own daddy couldn't see beauty in her, who else would? Even if he didn't believe it, even if it was a bold-faced lie, it would have been nice to hear just once.

But, no, in Luther's eyes, Amelia had been beautiful. Selena was beautiful. And June was dependable. A good daughter—that was the best compliment he'd ever given her.

Looks aside, Selena didn't seem to have much in common with Amelia. She didn't appear flighty, greedy, or selfish...though coming to her father's house with killers on her trail wasn't the most considerate thing she could have done.

If there really were killers.

June's head was throbbing by the time Grant suggested they move to the parlor. She pushed her chair back, then turned to help Luther to his feet, as she always did. He shrugged her off, though, and offered his arm to Selena instead. "Walk with me, baby girl," he requested. "Make an old man happy."

The knot in June's stomach tightened. He'd always called Amelia *pretty girl*, and the fragile daughter she'd brought into the world was *baby girl*. His nickname for June was just plain *girl*. For much of her life, she'd been happy to hear even that from him, because it was proof she hadn't disappeared entirely into Amelia's shadow.

Judging by the pure love shining in his old dark eyes, she just might disappear into Selena's shadow. After all she'd done, all she'd struggled for, she could end up right back where she'd started. Forgotten. An afterthought.

And it was all Amelia's fault.

Grant led the way from the dining room, with Selena and Luther following him. Tony Ceola waited to walk at June's side. "How long have you worked for Grant?" he asked as he matched his pace to hers.

"Twenty years. How long have you known Selena?"

"We met in June."

Less than five months, and already he was in love with her. He didn't have to say so. A blind man could see it in the way he looked at her. That was one more thing Selena had in common with her mother—the ability to captivate a man.

Along with the foolishness to exercise that ability on a white man.

"Grant says you're a police officer."

"Yes, ma'am."

"Do you believe it's safe for her to be here? For my father and Grant to be around her?"

"We're taking precautions."

She'd seen a few of them. For the first time in memory, the gate between Ravenel property and Hamilton property had been closed when she and Luther had come for dinner, and an armed guard had stood watch. He had actually asked to see her driver's license before letting her pass. They'd seen other guards along the way, and the drapes inside were closed, the glass doors covered to block the view in.

"I don't want anything happening to my father because of that girl," she said in a hushed voice as they entered the parlor.

Tony gave her a level look. "I don't want anything happening to anyone. That's why I'm here."

She swallowed hard. "I'm sorry. I didn't mean that the way it sounded. Of course I don't want anything to happen to her, either. It's just . . . he's my *father*." He was old and frail, and she'd devoted her entire life to taking care of him, both before Amelia disappeared, when he'd hardly noticed June was around, and after, when he'd finally come to realize what a good daughter she was. He'd thought Amelia was his light, but he'd finally realized that June was the true blessing.

And Selena was going to change that.

They settled in the parlor, Luther and Tony looking out of place on a petit-point settee, June feeling out of place in one of Kathryn Hamilton's treasured antique chairs. Selena sat in a matching chair, and Grant chose an ancient rocker that had been in the family for generations. June's however-many-greats-grandmother had rocked his however-many-greats-grandfather there, back when his people had owned hers. And now here he sat with his half-black descendant-of-slaves daughter. How many of Selena's ancestors, both black and white, were spinning in their graves?

"You are a lovely girl," Luther said for at least the fifth time with an awed shake of his head. "I just can't get over . . . Tell me what you've been up to since the last time I saw you."

He laughed at the idea that she could cover twenty-eight years in the time they had, and Selena smiled with him. "School. Work. The usual."

He laughed again, and June recalled how frequently that had happened before Amelia had passed. It had been months, maybe even a year, after she'd disappeared before he'd managed even the faintest of smiles, much longer before he'd laughed again. "A woman of few words. I like that. It leaves more talking for me to do."

Again Selena smiled, a quiet, confident smile. Even without people telling her all the time how beautiful she was, how wonderful she was, how perfect she was, she knew. It showed in the way she moved, sat, held herself.

June had never had that kind of confidence.

Amelia had been brimming to overflowing with it.

"Seriously, baby girl, after that—that man"—Luther couldn't bring himself to say Henry Daniels's name—"took you away, how did you live? What did you do?"

Selena looked for a moment at Tony, then Grant, before lifting her slender shoulders in a shrug. "He left me in the care of a family in Puerto Rico. I stayed with them until I was nine, when I went to live with a family in Jamaica. I came back to the States when I was fourteen to attend boarding school, then college. Now I have an art gallery in Key West, and I paint."

And upset people's lives. Because of her, Kathryn Hamilton had suffered a breakdown. Her son was dead, and her brother might as well have been. Because of her, there was upheaval in Tony's life, Grant's, Luther's, and most especially June's.

But no one would ever guess to look at Selena that there was any upheaval in *her* life. She had what she wanted and didn't care what it cost others around her. Something else she had in common with her mother.

"Boarding school," Luther repeated. "You hear that, June? Bet you never thought baby girl would live in some fancy boarding school."

June forced a smile that sharpened her headache. "No, Daddy, I didn't." How could she, when she'd thought baby girl was dead?

As ashamed as she was to admit it, it had been an easy loss to accept. She'd never spent much time around Amelia after the baby was born. It had been too hard to watch everyone fuss over them as if Amelia was the first woman in the history of the world to give birth. As if her child wasn't the biracial product of an adulterous affair.

It isn't fair! The words had echoed through June every moment of every day twenty-eight years ago. If any other woman in the community had done what Amelia had done, Luther would have shaken his head in condemnation. If June had gone out with a white man or a married man, he would have told her how sorely she disappointed him. If she'd borne that married white man's child, he would have scorned her.

But not Amelia. Never his precious Amelia.

Or his precious Selena, apparently.

The girl's return threatened disaster. June was certain of that.

And it had nothing to do with the killers after her.

"Hey, Frankie. You have any news?"

"Not anything that helps."

It was Tuesday morning and Nell had just cleared breakfast from the dining table, but Tony had already been at work for several hours. He'd gotten a referral to the best security company in Montgomery and dangled enough of Grant's money in front of them to move to the top of their day's jobs. He'd done a walk around the grounds with the head of the crew that had arrived an hour earlier, explaining the precautions he wanted—motion-activated lights, ground motion sensors, infrared thermal imaging cameras, perimeter alarms, armed guards. The men who'd filled in the night before were trusted employees of Grant's, comfortable with the weapons they'd carried, but untrained in security matters. Tony wanted the best bodyguards money could buy.

Now he was ready to start on the background checks.

"ATF hasn't learned anything we didn't already know," Simmons went on. "The bomb that destroyed Island Girl's house contained Semtex—not your typical pipe bomb. The goobers we arrested at the motel still aren't talking, but they haven't bonded out yet, either. Makes me wonder if they think they're safer in jail, seein' as how they screwed up their job."

The displeasure in Simmons's voice was familiar—damn near comfortingly so, Tony thought with a wry grin.

"I ran those names and got nothing. Charlize Pawley's history goes back twelve years—all clean—and there are too damn many Luke Morgans to count. We need something else—a birthdate, middle name, Social Security number."

"We're just striking out all around, aren't we?" Tony said sourly. "I'm going to fax you more names—people employed by Grant Hamilton. Can you get criminal histories on them?" The only people with routine access to Grant's house, aside from his family, were June Ravenel, the housekeeper, Nell, and a young woman who came in twice a week to help with the heavy cleaning, but if anyone who set foot on the property had so much as a parking ticket, Tony wanted to know.

"Sure. I live to serve. So ... how's it feel to be staying at an honest-to-God plantation?"

"Weird." Tony preferred the claustrophobic closeness of the motel rooms. Smaller space, easier to secure. "Don't tell anyone, will you?"

"Christ, Chee, come on. I'm not as big a putz as that." Simmons sounded wounded, and Tony felt guilty. For all his faults, Frankie was a decent detective and a damn good friend.

Then he went on, slyness coming into his voice. "I wouldn't give out information like that ... at least, not for free. D'ya think Long would offer enough that I could pay off my house?"

"You'd have to find him first." No matter how many people searched for Long, if he was hidden well enough, he could escape capture. He could be holed up in any of a thousand hiding places right there in the area and no one would ever know. "Listen, I'll send those names now. Get back to me as soon as you can."

Tony hung up, then swiveled the chair to face the fax machine. Hamilton Farms had a lot of employees. It was good he wouldn't have to be there in the Detective Division to hear Frankie piss and moan when the machine started spitting out page after page on that end.

While the machine worked, Tony gazed around Grant's office. He did as much work there as in his town office, and it was every bit as well equipped, with printer, fax, copier, and law library sharing space with leather, antiques, and art. The room reeked of money and privilege. Kathryn and Henry had stolen the privilege from Selena, but one day the money would be hers. One day Tony's kids would be wealthier than any Ceola had ever dreamed.

He wasn't comfortable with the thought. He'd seen firsthand how money and the desire for it could corrupt. It would be his and Selena's job to ensure it didn't happen to their children.

Their children...

Once the fax was completed, he left the room in search of Selena and found her and Grant in the only comfortable living space he'd seen so far. The sole antique in the family room was the armoire that held the television set. Furniture made for sprawling sat on Berber carpet, and soft jazz played from the stereo speakers mounted in the corners.

Selena and Grant were sitting at a table in one corner of the room, and lying on the glass top between them was a photograph of Amelia. It wasn't the first picture of her Tony had seen—Grant had shown them several back in Oklahoma—but he was still taken aback by the resemblance. It was no surprise Kathryn Hamilton had needed only one look at Selena to know who she was.

He bumped against her as he sat down, then reached for the photo. It was a glossy picture of a beautiful, sexy, sultry woman with a smile that lit her entire face. She was darker than Selena, her hair was coarser, and her eyes carried a mischievous gleam. She looked like a woman who loved life, but Kathryn had stolen it from her, and Henry had helped.

What had gone through Henry's mind when his little sister told him that she'd killed her husband's lover? Had he suggested she call the authorities? Had he been stunned, appalled? Or had he told her it was all right, that he would take care of it?

The Henry whom Tony had known his entire life—his father's best friend, his own godfather—would have been shocked. He would have called the sheriff and a good lawyer, though maybe not in that order. He wouldn't have cleaned up the crime scene or gotten rid of the body or secreted away the victim's baby.

But the Henry he'd known had never really existed.

"That picture was taken a year before…" Grant's gaze was on the photo, a distant smile on his mouth. "We didn't know it yet, but she was pregnant then. Probably not more than a few weeks, but…"

"What did you think when you found out?" Selena asked. She looked calm as usual, but her voice was guarded. She'd asked the question, but wasn't sure she wanted to know the answer.

"We were ecstatic." He gave her a chiding look. "It never occurred to either of us that it might be a problem."

"But you were married."

"I was. Unhappily so. Amelia's pregnancy was the push I needed to end it."

"But you're still married twenty-eight years later."

Grant rose from the chair and walked to the nearest set of French doors, lifting the filmy curtain to gaze out. "I was ready to leave Kathryn the day your mother told me. I made plans—for the practice, for the farm, for my mother and the others who relied on me. We were going to move away, far from here, where no one knew us or anything about us. Where no one would care that she was black and I was white.

"But this was home, and Amelia loved it. She couldn't bear to leave her father and take his only grandbaby away from him. She was afraid, I think, of going someplace new and different." He smiled faintly. "It was the only thing she was ever afraid of. She didn't just wait for things to happen. She rushed out and made them happen. She was bold and brave and fearless, except when it came to leaving Greenhill."

It was easier to be bold and brave when everyone knew and adored you, Tony thought. In a new place, she would have been surrounded by strangers who might not have been as delighted with her as the people who'd watched her grow up. They wouldn't have spent a lifetime saying, *That Amelia. Isn't she something?*

"But in the end she was willing to go," Tony commented.

"It would have been better for her if she kept refusing." Grant turned back to them, his expression sorrowful. "I spent as much time with you"—he nodded to Selena—"and her as I could, but it wasn't enough. Amelia decided that living together as a family was better, even if it meant moving away. I told Kathryn I was leaving her, and..."

Desperate to keep her marriage at any cost, she'd killed Amelia and demanded that Henry kill Amelia's baby. She had thought it was no more than Amelia deserved, no less than *she* deserved.

A knock at the open door was followed by Nell stepping into the room. "There's a man out here who wants to talk to the security chief."

Selena smiled as she squeezed Tony's hand. "That would be you."

"So you say now," he grumbled. Rising, he pressed a kiss to her forehead, then started toward the door.

"Mr. Grant, they called from the main gate," Nell went on. "Miss Rosalind is here, too, and her feathers are ruffled at being detained."

"Who is Miss Rosalind?" Tony asked, stopping halfway to the door.

Grant stood, too, and extended his hand to Selena. As she took it, then rose gracefully from her seat, he said, "She's my mother. Selena, sweetheart, you're about to meet your grandmother."

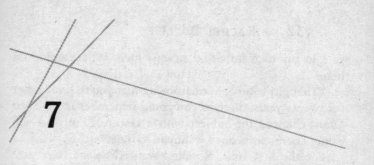

7

Rosalind Harper Hamilton swept into the house all aflutter, the feathers on her hat swaying in her self-generated breeze, the fringe of her shawl gently swinging. She ignored Nell, who'd held the door for her, except to hand her the hat, and Selena, and strode across the entry to Grant. "Who are those men, and why are they trying to keep me from my own home?"

She was several inches shorter than Selena, slender and dressed in a hot pink suit that fitted as if custom-tailored. She was seventy-nine, Grant had told Selena on the short walk from the family room to the foyer, but she looked ten years younger. Her hair was pure white, striking against the healthy glow of her skin, and she wore close to fifteen carats of diamonds as easily as Selena wore wooden beads.

Her grandmother. They shared the same blood, the same history. They were *family.* Selena couldn't quite wrap her mind around that. Suddenly she wanted to be anywhere else but there. She wanted to know her family, but these first meetings were proving difficult.

"Hello, Mama. It's good to see you, too." Grant bent to kiss the woman's cheek, then slid his arm around her shoulders. "What brings you to The Gardens today?"

"I went by your office and that girl said you were working at home today, so I came here, only to be stopped at the gate to my own home by strange men. What's going on here?"

"That girl is June, Mama. Seeing that you've known her for twenty years, it seems you could remember that." Then Grant changed the subject with a gesture. "I'm glad you came. There's someone I want you to meet."

For the first time, Rosalind noticed Selena. Her gaze started at Selena's curls, moved over her face, her T-shirt, jeans, and sneakers, then slid back up, touched by distaste. "Is she replacing Colleen? Really, Grant, you shouldn't let the servants dress just any old which way."

Grant's expression grew strained and his smile faltered, but didn't disappear. Rosalind was a product of her environment, he'd also told Selena on that short walk. The translation for that had been simple enough: a wealthy white woman, descended from Old South aristocracy, a firm believer that everyone had their place—and most black folks' place was serving wealthy white folks.

"Mama, this is Selena McCaffrey. My daughter. Your granddaughter."

"Well." Rosalind studied her again, this time focusing on her face. "Grant has told me about you, and, of course, all the dirty details about Kathryn's exploits in Oklahoma were in the local newspaper. I just didn't expect you to be quite so . . . black."

Her blunteness was momentarily jarring. In Selena's experience, people tended to tiptoe around issues of race as if color didn't matter. In her experience, it did—tremendously.

She treated Rosalind to the same study, then softly replied, "I expected you to be very white."

Rosalind's blue gaze sharpened as the implied criticism struck home. "Hmph. You can call me Rosalind or Grandmother, but not Gran or Grandma. No one gets away with calling me that, not even my grandson from my other son's marriage." She put a slight emphasis on the last word, then breezed on. "So what brings you to Greenhill? Getting a look at all the money Kathryn cheated you out of?"

"Mama," Grant admonished, but Selena didn't mind. She preferred blunt words over polite deception.

"I wanted to see my father's home, my mother's home, where I came from."

"You come from a little Alabama town that's like every other little Alabama town. Nothing special here."

"My father's here. My grandfather. My aunt. My grandmother." Family counted with Rosalind Hamilton, Selena knew. At least, legitimate family. Whether *Selena* mattered waited to be seen.

She wanted to matter.

"Hmph. I've been here five minutes. Why do I not have a glass of tea, Nell? Why am I still standing in the foyer? And *what* are those strangers doing outside?" In another flutter of movement, Rosalind stepped away from Grant and strode into the formal parlor.

His expression still strained, Grant gestured for Selena to follow. He was a few steps behind her when the phone in his office rang. He looked that way, then at Selena. She smiled. "Go ahead. We'll be fine."

Relief crossed his face as he turned. She watched until he was out of sight, then entered the parlor.

Rosalind was sitting on the settee, legs crossed. She patted the cushion next to her, but Selena went instead to the same Louis XIV chair where she'd sat the night before. Her action amused the old woman.

"My son doesn't seem to have any answers for me, so why don't you tell me about the men? I doubt it's coincidence that they arrived at the same time you did. It seems from the news stories that you have a knack for attracting trouble, like your mother."

"Did you know my mother?"

"No, but I heard talk."

"Of course, gossip is the best way to get information about someone."

Rosalind stiffened, then slowly smiled. "Are you in trouble?"

"Yes. There's a contract out on my life."

If Rosalind was surprised, she hid it well. "How much?"

"Five hundred thousand dollars."

"Not a bad amount. It shows you have value."

"I always wanted to have value to a psychopathic killer," Selena said drily.

"So these men are security guards. Good idea. One can never have too much security."

Oh, yes, one could. Selena had been smothered by security during the FBI's undercover operation, and again in the past few days. She longed for the time when safety hadn't been an issue. Going out whenever she wanted, wherever she wanted, without looking over her shoulder, seemed a distant memory. A woman couldn't live her entire life this way. Couldn't raise children this way.

Rosalind twisted a ring on her right hand. It was habit, not a nervous action, but it drew Selena's attention to the large diamond nestled in the band. It looked very much like one of the rings Kathryn had worn—and twisted in the same way—the day they'd sat in a similar, formal parlor and talked for the first time. Soon after, Kathryn had decided the only way to deal with Selena was to have her killed.

Hopefully, Rosalind wouldn't reach the same conclusion.

Rosalind stopped the twisting to shake one finger in her direction. "Don't go coveting this ring just yet. It's a family heirloom—been in my husband's family for generations. He gave it to me when we were married, and I wore it until Grant married, when I gave it to his wife." Her mouth quirked. "When she was admitted to that place, I reclaimed it for safekeeping."

"It's lovely," Selena said. "But diamonds aren't my style."

"Oh, you'll be surprised by what becomes your style once you get accustomed to being your father's daughter."

Selena shifted in the chair, crossing her legs. "You seem to think, Rosalind, that I'm some poor waif your son has rescued from the depths of indigence. I'm not. I have a home. I have a career. I make enough money to fulfill my needs as well as my desires. If I wanted diamonds, I could buy them. I don't need family heirlooms." She just needed a family who wanted her. That was all.

"Desires change when money becomes available. So do needs."

Rosalind fell silent as Nell entered the room carrying a silver tray holding three glasses of tea and an insulated carafe. Selena was surprised. She would have guessed the woman was the type to talk in front of employees as if they were invisible.

Selena thanked Nell for the tea and took a sip of the heavily sweetened, mint-flavored brew, then waited for Rosalind's next assault. It came once the housekeeper had left them alone again.

"I wasn't happy to learn about you."

"Imagine that," Selena murmured.

Rosalind gave her a warning look. "Don't get smart, young lady. I'd heard rumors about Grant and your mother all those years ago. He thought they were being discreet, but I couldn't walk into the club or even church without hearing whispers. Everyone knew except Kathryn, and she didn't want to know. She ignored it as long as she could, until Grant told her himself. And then poof!" She snapped her fingers. "You and your mother disappeared. Kathryn said she had paid your mother to take you and go, and we believed it. Kathryn was the sort to buy off any problem, and your mother was the sort to be bought off."

"No, she wasn't," Selena quietly disagreed. "If she'd been that 'sort,' she would have taken the money and left."

"She was flighty."

"She was young."

"You're young, and you're not flighty." Rosalind paused a moment. "Are you the sort to be bought off?"

The thoughtful question made Selena's stomach knot with disappointment. She hadn't expected open arms and unconditional acceptance from any of her new family—though she'd gotten just that from Luther—but she hadn't quite expected this, either. "No, I'm not."

"I could make it worth your while."

"No," Selena said flatly. "You couldn't."

Rosalind studied her a long time, then nodded. "I hope that's true. I'm not thrilled to welcome a full-grown half-black girl into my family." She made a rueful gesture. "I wasn't thrilled to welcome that boy Kathryn adopted, either, but I tried, for Grant's sake. Jefferson never did warm up to anyone besides Kathryn, but then, nobody but her warmed up to him. And look how that turned out.

"But Grant *is* thrilled to have you. I love my son, and because he loves you, I will endeavor to treat you no differently from the grandchild I've known all his life. But do not disappoint your father, because that will disappoint me, and when I'm disappointed, I am a force to reckon with. Have I made myself clear?"

"Yes." Though Selena wasn't clear at all. Was the offer of

money truly an attempt to get rid of her or merely a test of her loyalty? Would the woman really accept her, for Grant's sake, or simply put on a good act? Did it even matter?

"Very well. We'll have dinner this evening so you can meet the rest of the immediate family. I'll invite them here— best that they get accustomed to seeing you in this house. Don't expect much warmth, but they'll be civil. I'll make certain of that." Rising from the settee, Rosalind stood in front of Selena's chair. When Selena stood, too, she enveloped her in a less-than-enthusiastic embrace.

"Welcome to the family, Selena."

Charlize parked in the motel lot, climbed out of the car, and took a look around. This was her first trip to Greenhill, though she'd seen so many small towns like it that she felt as if she knew it. The courthouse likely sat in a grassy square downtown, with a war monument or two for decoration. The older churches would be on side streets, close to the center of town, and the cemetery marked the city limits on one side or another. There would be distinct neighborhoods—for old money, new money, middle class, and no money.

The Thomas family had always lived in the middle-class part of town, even though John Turner Thomas had earned a substantial living killing people. Nobody paid attention to the middle class, he'd said. No one would wonder how he paid his bills.

Besides, his vices hadn't included material things. Drinking, gambling, and molesting his daughter—those had been his idea of fun.

Her jaw taut, she went inside the office of the motel, one of only three in town. The clerk—middle-aged, balding, glasses sliding down his nose—greeted her with an effusive smile, then typed her name into the computer. She paid a week's rent in cash, took the key, and returned to her car.

Her room was on the first floor, about halfway down the building, sandwiched between adjoining rooms. It was a standard motel room—a step up from the one where she'd left Selena and Tony in Atlanta, a whole damn flight of stairs down from what she was accustomed to.

She hung her clothes on the small rod that served as a closet and laid out her toiletries on the chipped tile that surrounded the sink. Except for the pistol in her purse, the most important items for this trip remained locked in the trunk of the car: a SIG SG-550 sniper rifle for distance shots; a .22-caliber handgun for up close and personal with maximum concealability; ammunition; a double-edged dagger, its blade honed razor-sharp; burglar's tools, duct tape, a flashlight. Whatever she might need to get the job done, she had . . . though, truthfully, the only thing she needed was her mind. As long as she had her wits about her, she could always find something to use as a weapon.

Lucky for her, she never got so involved that she lost her edge.

Once everything was in its temporary place, she made a phone call, leaving a brief message on Detective Simmons's voice mail. Selena and Tony might not want her to know their location, but she wanted them to know hers. Then she went back to the car. Her first destination was The Gardens, though she didn't intend to stop. She merely wanted to know where the farm was. Where Luke Morgan's target was. Where, sooner or later, Luke himself would be.

One way or another, she was going to stop him from carrying out Damon's contract. She was going to stop them both.

With whatever force was necessary.

Unlike her, neither Luke nor Damon would check into an area motel. They would both stay under the radar until it suited them to surface. Damon would hole up someplace—a house whose occupants were away, a seldom-used barn on someone's back forty, camped out in his car in the cover of thick woods. Luke would probably find a woman, pretty and not too bright, who wouldn't hesitate to invite a charming, handsome, sexy stranger into her home for a few days. He was a hound dog, Charlize's father had said with some sort of stupid pride, as if Luke's luck with the ladies was important. Though maybe if John Turner had been half as interested in women as Luke was, he would have left *her* alone. And if he'd left her alone, maybe he would still be alive today.

Charlize shook off the thought. Her father had paid for his sins—not enough, but he'd paid. He was in the past. Her focus at that moment was one narrow sliver of the present: finding Damon and Luke.

Clearly, Damon no longer trusted her, and Luke had doubted her for twenty years, back when she was a desperate girl. He'd been her last hope, her last chance at stopping the pain and the fear, and he'd let her down. He'd broken her heart, but not her spirit. She'd put a stop to the situation herself. She'd coped. But she hadn't forgiven.

She would find Damon and Luke, and she would take care of Selena's problems—her own problem?—once and for all.

June was grumbling as she got into her car. She didn't mind being summoned to The Gardens. Heavens, since Grant spent so much of his work hours there, so did she. But

Tuesday was her day for catching up in the office, and being called out not for business but for private matters annoyed her no end.

Private matters. A fancy way of saying Selena. No doubt this little meeting was about her and her precious safety. Frankly, the only concern June had for Selena's security was how it would impact Luther's and her own. If there wasn't a risk that the danger trailing Selena would spill over onto them, June would say let the bad guys have at her.

When she reached the main gate to The Gardens, it was closed, and a dozen or more men were working in the area. The bushes that had lined the fence for years were gone, and cameras had been mounted to catch both incoming and outgoing cars. Workmen were busy around the guard shack, installing what appeared to be new electric and phone lines, and others were working along the fence where it stretched off in either direction.

Grant was sparing no expense to secure his daughter's safety, she thought grimly as she was waved through the gate. Just as he'd spared no expense for Amelia. He'd bought her a house, a car, jewelry, and clothes, paid all her bills, and set her up with the best obstetrician and pediatrician in Montgomery. June and Luther had argued about the impropriety of it on more than one occasion, but he'd refused to see. Amelia could do no wrong in his eyes.

Mr. Grant's gonna marry my pretty girl. Gonna make her his wife.

Why should he? June had responded time and again. *He's already made her his whore. He's paying her for her services, and she's happy taking his money. He'll never marry her. You wait and see.*

She'd been right. There had been no marriage. Just a

death, a disappearance, and twenty-eight years of grief. Sorrow. Guilt.

Did being right count when she'd taken matters into her own hands?

She parked at the side of the house, and a moment later one of the security firm's pickups pulled in beside her. Tony Ceola and one of the firm's men got out. Tony fell into step with her. "Ms. Ravenel."

She gave him a sidelong glance. "You can call me June."

Acknowledging her with a nod, he went on. "Grant said this would be a good time for you. I hope it is. Your father's already here, and—"

She stopped so abruptly at the foot of the steps that the other man almost ran into her. "What do you mean, my father is already here? Why is he here? Why are you involving him in this?"

Tony stepped aside to let the security guard pass, then said, "Because he is involved. Everyone who comes to the farm, who has contact with Selena, is involved."

"He shouldn't be burdened with this. He worries enough as it is. He's a frail old man. He shouldn't—"

Tony raised one hand. "My father is sixty-one, and he has Alzheimer's. About half the time he doesn't know who I am or even who he is. I understand worrying, believe me, but the more Luther knows, the safer he'll be."

She stared at him a moment, then climbed the steps. "I'm sorry about your father," she said grudgingly. Luther might be old and frail, but his mind was as sharp as ever. That was a blessing.

"Frail" wasn't the word that came to mind when she walked into the foyer and heard Luther's hearty laughter coming from down the hall. She followed the sound toward the family room, realizing as she drew closer that he was telling a story about Amelia.

Dear God, she hated those stories. She'd heard every one so many times that she knew them by heart. And he told only the charming tales, the cute ones, the funny ones. He never told anyone about the time Amelia had been brought home by the sheriff, only fifteen and too drunk to stand. Or the time a year later when she'd run off for three days in Nashville with a college boy. Or how she'd sassed her elders, flirted with everything in pants, couldn't hold a job, wouldn't hold a job. Life was just one big amusement for Amelia.

Realizing that Tony was waiting for her to enter the room, June unclenched her fingers, forced her jaw to relax, then walked inside. Luther and Grant were sitting on the sofa with Selena in between. Nell sat uncomfortably on a straight-backed chair she'd pulled over from the table, and the security guard was sitting on the arm of an overstuffed chair.

"Hey, girl," Luther said, catching her hand when she approached. "I was just telling baby girl about the time Amelia entered that talent show. You remember that?"

"How could I forget?" Fourteen, beautiful, and even then aware and taking advantage of her sexuality. She'd gone up on that stage barefoot, wearing a white cotton dress that clung to her breasts and the curve of her hips. She'd sung some long-forgotten tune, swaying her body to the music, making every one of the male judges think she had eyes for only him, and she'd walked away with the grand prize. "Amelia couldn't carry a tune in a bucket."

"She sure couldn't," Luther agreed with a laugh. "But she won. She always won."

No, Kathryn had won. And for a time, June had won. Until Selena had reappeared.

June took a seat, crossed her ankles, and said, "I have a lot of work to do at the office. If we could get this over with..."

Tony straightened from where he'd leaned against the fireplace, photographs in his hand. "We're putting in a top-of-the-line security system. The alarm in the house is being upgraded, and they're installing electronic gates and surveillance systems. There will be motion-activated security lights around the house and the yard, motion sensors along the perimeter, and guards at all the gates. Everyone coming in will be IDed and, for the present, access to the property will be restricted. These photographs"—he held them up—"will be passed out to every guard and posted at the gates. We're also going to show them to all of the employees. If you see either of these people, you need to let us know immediately."

He handed the pictures to June, who was closest, and she studied them, though not for Selena's sake. She didn't care what happened to Amelia's daughter, but she damn well cared if anything happened to Luther.

Both men were white, young, handsome. The one identified as Luke Morgan looked harmless, as if having a good time was all that mattered to him.

There was nothing at all harmless-looking about the second man. It was an arrest photo, and showed short-cropped blond hair that spiked on top, a stubble of beard, and soulless blue eyes. Even in the flat dimensions of the photo, his gaze was intense. Greedy. And familiar.

June's fingers trembled, fluttering the picture. She clenched it tighter and stared harder, mentally changing the hair to shaggy auburn, growing the stubble into a neat beard, adding tortoiseshell glasses. He could change the color and style of his hair, add a beard and glasses, but he couldn't change the ice in his eyes.

Dear God, David Jones, nosy reporter, was really Damon Long, drug dealer, criminal mastermind, and multiple murderer. She'd sat outside with him on Sunday, no one around for miles, and talked nearly two hours. He could have killed her right there and no one ever would have known it was him.

Except that he wasn't interested in killing her, not unless she got in his way.

"Have you seen him around town?" Tony asked.

She stared a moment longer before jerking her gaze upward. "Wh—No." *No, I saw him right here.* She took a breath, opened her mouth, then closed it again.

Was she absolutely certain it was the same man? Wasn't it possible that David Jones simply shared a remarkable resemblance with Damon Long? Selena looked so much like Amelia that it stunned everyone who saw her.

She couldn't be positive. She had good instincts. If David Jones was Damon Long in disguise, wouldn't she have felt something? Wouldn't she have known something was off about him?

Deep inside a small voice whispered, clamoring for her attention, but she steadfastly ignored it. She didn't want to face the weak logic of her arguments.

No more than she wanted to tell everyone that Damon Long had already come to the house. Not yet. After all, he was probably long gone. It was the other man they had to worry about.

And if he wasn't gone, it wasn't as if he could drive, or even walk, right up to the house as he'd done before, not with all the new security measures. Selena would have to leave the grounds for him to threaten her, and Tony and Grant didn't intend to let that happen.

She handed the photographs to Grant, who leaned closer so Selena could see them, as well. Luther leaned closer, too, resting his arm around Selena's shoulders. June hadn't seen that look on his face—peace, contentment—in twenty-eight years. He looked happier than she had ever made him. Happier, even, than Amelia had made him.

Her fingers curled into fists again. If Damon Long and David Jones were one and the same, and he was still in the area, maybe she could turn that to her advantage. All she wanted was Selena gone and the past left in the past. She didn't care how it was achieved.

Just as long as it was.

After the meeting ended, June gave Luther a hug and a kiss, exchanged a few words with Grant, then headed for the door. Rising from the sofa, Selena followed. She caught up with her aunt under the arch that led to the foyer. "Do you have to rush back? We'll be having lunch soon. We'd like to have you join us."

Slowly June turned to face her. For an instant, the emotion in her eyes was intense and ugly enough to make Selena step back. Then the older woman closed her eyes, took a deep breath, and the look was gone so thoroughly that Selena thought she must have imagined it. "Thank you for the invitation, but I have work to do."

"You have to eat."

Her gaze skimmed over Selena, then she smiled grimly. "No, I don't. There's never been a time in my life that I couldn't afford to miss a meal or two. Amelia was always telling me so. Of course, that wasn't a problem for her."

The bitterness in her voice was faint, but very real. She didn't give the impression of heaviness exactly, but rather solidness. Neither, though, would have pleased a young woman when her sister was willowy and slender—and apparently willing to criticize.

"I'd like to talk with you sometime."

June studied her a moment, then shook her head. "The things I have to say about your mama aren't the things you want to hear. Stick with your father and Luther. They paint a prettier picture."

"I want to know everything about her, good and bad."

"You have any stepbrothers or sisters?"

Selena shook her head. She'd believed the eight children with whom she'd shared Luisa and Rodrigo's home were half siblings, but there had never been any real emotional connection. They'd known she didn't belong, and they had, for the most part, shunned her as their parents had.

"Sisters don't always get along the way you see in books and on TV," June said. "They came up with the term 'sibling rivalry' for a reason."

"You and Amelia were rivals?"

June's laughter might have made her pretty if not for the resentment in it. "Good heavens, no. I couldn't compete with her in anything. She was smarter, prettier, skinnier, more daring, more adventurous, more popular, more feminine, more everything. I was just an afterthought. There was 'pretty girl' and 'girl.' Amelia and 'that other one.'"

June walked a few paces toward the door, then pivoted back. "Do you know what her full name was? Amelia Jamila Ravenel. Jamila's an African name that means beautiful and elegant. And do you know what my full name is? June Ravenel. Three guesses what month I was born. They couldn't even be bothered to pick a real name for me because of her." The anger drained from her and her shoulders rounded. "She was the only one that mattered."

Selena didn't know what to say. She'd had little enough experience at receiving or giving comfort. "Luther told Grant he and your mother wanted a lot of children, but were blessed with only two."

"With only one. And stuck with another." June straightened her spine. "I suspect they thought another daughter would be as beautiful and wonderful as Amelia. When they saw how wrong they were, they decided against having any more."

Movement down the hall drew Selena's attention that way. Tony and the security team chief came out of the family room and took a few steps their way. When he saw them, Tony said something to the other man and they reversed direction, disappearing into the kitchen.

Turning back to June, Selena gestured toward the broad doorway leading into the parlor. June hesitated, then went inside and sat stiffly in a chair.

"I know what it's like to feel unwanted," Selena said as she took the nearest chair. "The people who raised me the first nine years were Puerto Rican—husband, wife, all eight children. I was a nuisance, a burden, and a curiosity to everyone who saw us together. When the husband grew tired of beating me, he sold me to another couple." Her only value to that couple and to her next set of "parents," had been her nimble fingers and fleet feet.

Not that there was any real comparison between her upbringing and June's. June may have felt unwanted, but there was no doubt her father loved her. She'd had a safe home, and her physical needs had been met. If her parents had favored her sister, that was sad, but it hadn't been life-threatening.

"When Daddy asked you about your life, you said——"

Selena headed off the accusation. "I didn't lie. I simply glossed over the more unpleasant parts. What good would it do him to know the details? It wouldn't make a difference. It would just fill him with regrets."

Staring off into the distance, June nodded slowly. "It wouldn't make a difference," she murmured in agreement. "You can't get those years back. You can't undo what's already been done. When the truth can't change things, when it can only hurt, why stir it up?"

"But knowing the truth about Amelia—all of it—won't hurt me. I have no illusions to lose. I know she wasn't perfect. She wasn't the best sister she could have been. She had an affair and a child with a married man, and no matter how much she loved him, that was wrong."

"It was wrong," June said. "But Amelia never cared much about right or wrong. She wanted what she wanted—Grant, that pretty little house, you, her secret life playing family with the two of you. Then, finally, marriage. She'd had an affair. Taken another woman's husband. Had his baby. And he was going to marry her. She'd sinned and sinned, and she was going to get it all in the end. She always won."

There had been amusement, pride, and love in the words when Luther had said them earlier. Not so with June.

"But she didn't win."

June's mouth thinned, and her voice was harsh. "No, ma'am, she did not."

Instead, Amelia had died, and Selena had been stolen away. Grant's heart had been broken, William had discovered the satisfaction in committing an unsolved crime, and Kathryn had gotten away with murder.

And Luther had finally remembered he had another daughter.

The first question to ask in a homicide, Tony often said, was who would profit from the victim's death. There was no question that Kathryn had killed Amelia, just as there was no doubt that June, however unwittingly, had profited. She'd gone from being the daughter who didn't matter to the only daughter. The only hope for Luther's future.

Exhaling suddenly, June pushed to her feet. "I've got to get back to the office." Without waiting for Selena to rise, she started toward the door, but turned back when she reached the foyer. "We'll talk again sometime, baby girl."

A shiver rippled through Selena as June closed the door behind her. The words sounded more like a threat than agreement, the pet name more like a slur.

Selena walked to the French doors and lifted a filmy curtain to watch as, a moment later, her aunt's car passed down the drive. "Consider yourself warned, baby girl," she murmured.

As the fabric fluttered back into place, footsteps sounded behind her. She didn't startle, didn't turn, but waited for Tony to slide his arms around her from behind and nuzzle her neck.

"No surprise? No self-defense moves?"

She tilted her head to one side to give him better access. "I knew it was you. I don't want to hurt you."

"You think you could?"

She twisted to face him, then slid her arms around his neck. "You know I could." She'd trained intensively for more than two years to become an expert at all types of self-defense—her response to an assault and attempted rape by Damon Long. She hadn't worked out regularly for more than two months, though—no sparring, no target practice, no jogging. Nothing but a little yoga since the night Sonny

Yates had beaten her to a pulp. If she hadn't been in such good shape, he would have killed her.

Even being in such good shape, she still would have died if not for Charlize.

"How's the work going?" she asked.

"Fine. I miss you."

"You've been in and out all morning." But she understood. They'd had little enough private time since arriving at The Gardens—less than eight hours in the guest room they shared, and they'd slept most of that.

"How did your conversation with your aunt go?"

She leaned back in the circle of his arms to gaze at him. "My *aunt*. It doesn't feel like we're family."

"You're strangers," he pointed out, drawing her close again. "It takes more than blood to make family."

"Luther doesn't seem like a stranger."

"That's because he adores you. So do I."

"How much?"

He paused in the act of kissing her earlobe, straightened, and fixed a stern gaze on her. "Not enough for that."

"For what?"

"Letting you do whatever it is you want to do that makes you think you need to manipulate me with how I feel."

"I want to visit Amelia's house."

He studied her a long time before flatly saying, "Of course you do."

"Neither Long nor Morgan has been sighted in the area, have they?"

"They're professional killers. Part of their job is not being sighted."

"It's safe to go now. You've made it so."

"It's safest to wait. That house has been there a long time, Selena. It'll still be there when this is over."

She folded her arms across her middle. "When will that be? Next week? Next month? Next year?"

Tony mimicked her position. "Don't get greedy. I agreed to having the Hamiltons over for dinner tonight."

"Forget the dinner. I'd rather see the house."

His grin was unexpected and stirred a pang of intense emotion in her chest. "If I didn't know better, I'd think you were teasing."

She wasn't. Sitting down to a meal with Rosalind would be difficult enough, and the behavior of the others, apparently, would make Selena's grandmother look warm and fuzzy. She didn't have to meet *all* her family just yet. Some of them could wait for another time.

She didn't respond to his comment, but simply waited and watched him, and he watched her back. After a time, he shook his head with dismay. "You're something. You know that?"

She gave him her fullest, sultriest smile. "I get that from my mother, they say."

"We'll take some of the security guards with us."

She nodded.

"If we run into anything at all suspicious, we come right back. And you don't say anything to anyone until just before we leave. Grant will have to give us directions, but don't mention it to Luther or Nell. Okay?"

"Okay."

Grudgingly, he snaked his arm around her waist and pulled her snugly against him. "Enjoy the trip, babe, because it's the last time you leave this house until Long and Morgan are in jail or dead. Understand?"

Without waiting for her answer, he kissed her hard, stealing her breath, making her hot and edgy and hungry. He didn't stop when Grant called their names from down the hall, not until footsteps grew dangerously near. Finally breaking the kiss, he gave her a long, hard look, then took her hand and pulled her out into the hall just as Grant cleared the arch.

"There you are," Grant said, either not noticing, or pretending not to notice, that they'd been otherwise occupied. "Lunch is ready, and Nell is too good a cook to let it grow cold."

"We were just on our way," Tony said, sounding remarkably normal, considering that Selena's heart was still pounding, her chest still tight.

It wasn't just the kiss that made her feel shaky all over, though his kisses were quite capable of that. It was the grin, and her own responding punch of emotion. She loved him. She'd known that for weeks now, but sometimes it struck her anew with such force. It was so different from anything she'd ever known, and the intensity could take her breath away. She'd waited all her life for something like this, and damned if she would let anyone steal it from her. Not Long, not his hired killers.

Not even herself.

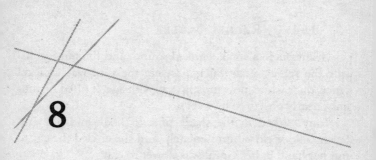

8

Location was everything in real estate, and had definitely been the deciding factor in the house Grant had purchased nearly three decades earlier for Amelia. It was nearly ten miles east of Greenhill, located outside a quiet little wide spot in the road, at the end of a narrow dirt lane.

Tony sat in the driver's seat of Grant's Cadillac, his fingers loosely gripping the steering wheel. The drive over from The Gardens had been uneventful. Other than the three security guards who'd followed them in an SUV, no one had paid them any attention. Now the guards were checking out the house, out of sight a half mile down the road. When they came back with the all clear, they would wait here where dirt met pavement while Selena and Grant revisited their past.

Grant sat in the passenger seat, staring off into the distance. Behind him, Selena looked apprehensive. When Tony reached back, she took his hand, squeezed, and gave him a smile she clearly didn't feel.

The SUV approached slowly, the driver pulling onto the shoulder, then stopping. He nodded once before driving past to block access from the highway.

Weeds grew waist-high on either side of the ruts and brushed the undercarriage of the car. Tony drove slowly to minimize the jarring, skirting the deepest holes. The road dipped down after cresting a hill. When they reached the top, the house came into sight a few hundred yards ahead.

Grant made a small, choked sound, and the tension inside the vehicle grew thick. Circling the yard was a picket fence, once white, now mostly gray with age. It tilted drunkenly, nearly obscured by weeds.

Tony parked in the shade of a live oak and got out. Selena's door closed immediately, and she circled the car to put her hand in his. Grant was slower to exit.

Silently they walked to the front yard. The house was small, board and brick, with a deep front porch and tall windows flanking the door. Like the fence, it had once been painted white. The shutters were dark and hung crookedly, and the withered remains of irises—his mother Anna's favorite flower—filled the beds that abutted the porch.

Grant had bought the house for Amelia a year into their affair, he'd told them on the drive. It had given them a place to meet and had made her happy. More than anything, he'd wanted her to be happy.

Then he should have left his wife for her, Tony had thought. Shouldn't have worried about the scandal. Shouldn't have waited until Amelia was pregnant to make up his mind. Tony would face any scandal necessary to be with Selena. Hell, he'd faced death several times since meeting her and would likely do so again, and that was okay. As long as they ended up together when it was over.

Turning his gaze to Selena, Tony studied her. The sunlight gave her coffee-and-cream skin a warm glow that was cooled only slightly by her innate self-control. There was no obvious tension on her face, but he could see it in the shadows that darkened her eyes, could feel it in the way her fingers clenched, then eased in his.

She swallowed hard, released his hand, and made a path through the weeds to the porch. There she touched a brick column, adjusted a shutter, drew a finger over one of the sidelights beside the door. The house couldn't compare to The Gardens, but to a woman who'd grown up in a share-cropper's cabin, it must have been special. Her own home, cozy and snug and filled with love.

Grant fished a key from his pocket and followed her trail to the steps. Tony stopped beside him when he hesitated. "You don't have to do this. You can wait out here."

Grant's smile was weak. In that moment, he looked years older than fifty-eight. "I want to."

Maybe he'd lacked courage back then. But he'd paid for it in the years since.

He climbed the steps, put the key in the lock, and opened the door. Selena was the first to cross the threshold.

The door opened into a large room—living area on the left, kitchen and dining space on the right. Straight ahead a short hallway led to three doors—bathroom, Tony assumed, and two bedrooms. The room didn't look like a crime scene. There was no sign of a struggle, no bloodstains, nothing out of place.

She lived in a shack. Kathryn Hamilton had told Tony in an interrogation room two months ago. *The kitchen was so small she kept the pots and pans stacked on the stove.*

Obviously, the house was no shack. Filled with comfort-able furniture, done in shades of red and white with a little navy blue, it was more welcoming than The Gardens could ever be. As for the kitchen, there was plenty of space for a family of two, sometimes three. Had Kathryn realized that the pots and pans were stacked on the stove because Amelia was in the process of moving out, of leaving Alabama with Kathryn's husband? Had she not noticed the half-packed boxes on the kitchen floor?

Probably not. When Tony had asked her to confirm that she'd killed Amelia to keep Grant from leaving her,

Kathryn's response had been a dismissive shrug. *That never would have happened. I was a Daniels.*

As if being a Daniels made her special. She and Henry had lived privileged lives, but in the end, they'd proven to be no better than any common criminal. Just more heartless than most.

Selena walked around the room, touching things. The red-and-white-striped chair. The television. The brick of the fireplace mantel. The frame of a painting. The long-dead flowers still in their vase.

After she'd completed a circuit, she glanced at Grant. "No pictures? Nothing personal?"

"Luther and I took the pictures, the souvenirs. The baby things are in storage—your crib, toys. The other things— clothing, her purse, your stroller—were all gone, along with her car. Presumably, they were dumped with . . . with her . . ."

Her body. Along with cleaning the crime scene and dumping Amelia's body, Henry had made it look as if she'd just taken a notion to leave. Almost everyone who'd known Amelia had been willing to believe it; after all, she was flighty. Even Grant had hoped it was true. He'd wanted to believe that she and his daughter were alive and well and living someplace without him. It was better than thinking she might be dead.

Selena stopped near the kitchen island. Her back was to them, her gaze on the stove and the pots still stacked there. "What did she tell you about that night?"

Finally Tony moved from the door. He'd repeated his conversation with Kathryn to both Selena and Grant days after it had taken place, adding a few details he'd picked up afterward. But telling it here, where it happened, wasn't the same.

"It was storming. Henry was in Montgomery. He'd come

down from Boston for a job interview with the police department there, and Grant was out of town. Before he left, he told Kathryn that he wanted a divorce. That didn't go over well. She was accustomed to getting her way. No one told her no. No one took something that she considered hers. That night she came here to bribe Amelia. She offered her ten thousand dollars in cash to leave before Grant got back from his trip, but Amelia refused. She laughed at her."

How livid had that made Kathryn? Facing public embarrassment. Disrupting her life. Losing her husband to another woman—a woman she considered most unsuitable. Common. Trashy. A woman she couldn't intimidate or buy off. An inferior nobody who had the nerve to laugh at her.

"There was a cast-iron skillet on the stove," Tony went on quietly. This was where details got sketchy. "Kathryn picked it up and hit Amelia in the head. There's no way to know whether the blow killed her or she died later from the injuries, but Kathryn thought she was dead, and she called Henry."

Selena moved a few silent steps closer to the island. "He took the skillet, too."

He'd taken everything—including her.

Stopping near her, Tony crouched to study the floor. Wood planks gave way to tile in this part of the room. There was a large rug underneath the dining table, smaller ones in front of the stove, the sink, the kitchen side of the island. This space was the only big area left bare. The tile was terracotta, the grout reddish brown, and showed nothing that shouldn't be there. Like bloodstains.

Selena crouched nearby, wrapping her arms around her knees. "Murder's usually a messy business," she murmured, a comment he'd made to her before. "Henry didn't paint." She gestured toward the cabinets that made up the island, with their everyday wear and tear. "He didn't have the tile replaced. He couldn't have removed every trace of blood."

"This one might not have been so messy. The blood splatter could have been minimal to nonexistent. It's possible the blow to the head caused bleeding in the brain without external bleeding."

Selena glanced at Grant, who'd gone to finger the dead flowers—a gift to Amelia from him?—then lowered her voice. "And it's possible the blow only left her unconscious and she died a slow, painful death wherever William left her." The softness of her voice didn't disguise her anger or her sorrow. For fourteen years, she'd adored and striven to please the man who, at the least, had covered up her mother's murder, and at most, had contributed to it. He'd saved her life, he'd boasted. She owed him.

If not for his sister, her life never would have been in danger.

Tony stood, then pulled Selena to her feet and into his embrace. "It's possible. Don't dwell on that, babe. It'll eat you up inside, and in the end, you can't change it. Focus on how Amelia lived, not how she died."

She held herself stiff for a moment, her gaze stony, then with a breath, she sagged against him, her face pressed to his throat, her muscles soft. "I'll remember how she lived," she whispered, then her voice grew stronger. "And I'll pray for William to die."

How Amelia had lived. That thought echoed through Selena's mind as she made her way through the rest of the house. She'd taken this little cottage and turned it into a warm, cozy, love-filled home. Every space bore the stamp of her personality, from the rugs on the floor to the fabrics on the bed to the stencils on the nursery walls.

"This was your room," Grant said as they walked through the door.

Her room. A bright, sunny space, with pale yellow on the walls and animals, toys, and the letters of the alphabet dancing over them. With furniture, a nubby rug, all the necessities and plenty of the luxuries.

She stood in the middle of the room and turned in a slow circle. "I was fourteen before I slept in a bed on a regular basis. I was eighteen and in college before I had a room that was all mine." A lump filled her throat. She wasn't prone to tears—nothing had pushed Rodrigo to violence quicker than that—but her chest was tight and her vision blurred. She blinked to clear it. "Did she do any of this herself?"

"The painting and decorating? She did all of it. That must be where you got your talent, because I can't draw a straight line."

Curly hair, bone structure, a strong resemblance, and artistic talent—things she shared with her mother. Satisfaction settled, small and quiet, inside her.

After more than an hour inside the house, they returned to the car. As they drove away, Selena twisted in the backseat to watch the house until it disappeared from sight.

They were only a few miles from The Gardens' service entrance when the rev of a powerful engine penetrated her thoughts. Glancing up, she saw that Tony's gaze was on the rearview mirror. She looked to see an old pickup, restored to better days, cut off the SUV carrying the security guards and bear down on them.

Switching his attention between mirror and road, Tony slowed to give the other driver an opportunity to pass. The driver didn't take it but stayed mere inches off the Cadillac's rear bumper. The pickup was so close that Selena could see the faces of the three occupants—boys in their late teens or early twenties. That, along with the fact that she'd never seen them before, sent a rush of relief through her, but it was short-lived.

As they rounded a curve onto a straightaway, the pickup crossed into the other lane and drew alongside them, then drifted back over the center line. Tony eased onto the shoulder, the wheels bumping over uneven pavement. "Hold on," he murmured an instant before stomping on the brakes.

Bracing herself, Selena eased her gun from the holster clipped to her waistband. As they fishtailed to a stop, the pickup sailed past, the young men laughing and yelling out the open windows, one of them bouncing a beer can off the Cadillac's hood. From behind them came the screech of the SUV'S tires. The driver pulled the wheel hard to the left, bringing his own vehicle to a skidding stop only feet from theirs.

"Damn stupid kids," Grant muttered. "They don't have the sense they were born with. They think it's fun to mess with people on the highway—" Abruptly he broke off to stare wide-eyed at first Selena, then Tony. "You don't think— They weren't trying to *hurt* us, were they?"

Her gaze met Tony's in the mirror, and he lifted one brow a fraction of an inch. She could tell Grant whatever she wanted, and Tony would support it. "I think you're right. They're just stupid kids who have had too much to drink." She would like to believe it herself. Knowing there were certain people who wanted to kill her was tough. Believing every single person out there was a threat to her was even tougher.

Sweat popped out on Grant's forehead and he sank back in the seat. "Oh, my God. People want you *dead*. I under-

stood that when you told me, but I didn't *really* understand...."

There was nothing like the adrenaline rush of a narrow
escape to bring the reality home, she thought with a thin
smile.

As he slowly put the car into motion again, Tony pulled
out his cell phone and called someone—911, the security
people back at the farm—and passed on the tag number and
a description of the vehicle and its occupants. When he
completed the call, he glanced at Grant. "Did you know any
of those guys?"

Grant shook his head. "I'm not very involved in things
around here."

He lived outside Greenhill. His family was there, he went
to work there, to church, did business, but Selena didn't
doubt what he said was true. By all accounts, he hadn't been
very "involved" in anything since Amelia disappeared. Other
than an effort to locate her and Amelia, he had withdrawn
into his own world. Continued the career he'd been about to
walk away from. Stayed with the wife he'd been about to divorce. For twenty-eight years, he'd lived without purpose.
Now he'd found some purpose in *her*.

She hoped she didn't let him down.

Back at the farm, Tony parked near the house, hustled
her and Grant inside, then left again. Still shaken, Grant
poured himself a drink from a decanter in the parlor, offered her one, then said, "If you don't mind, there are a few
things I need to take care of in the office."

"I don't mind at all." She was accustomed to spending
much of her time alone. Like him, she'd never been very "involved" in life, either.

He walked through the arch, suddenly came back and
embraced her, then walked away again.

The afternoon passed slowly, yet long before she was mentally prepared, it was almost time for dinner.

She sat on the bed in the room she shared with Tony, wearing the dress he'd surprised her with when he'd returned from town. The dress was crimson silk, sleeveless, with an asymmetrical ruffled hem that fluttered when she walked.

Finishing with his tie, he came to stand in front of her. She rose to meet his gaze levelly. "Are you troubled about this afternoon?" he asked quietly. "Because it looks like your father was right. They were just stupid kids. The sheriff says they have a history of drinking and driving and running people off the road. We'll question them once they sober up and go home, but it looks like it was just a random thing."

She shook her head. "I'm not worried about that."

"Then what—"

The doorbell pealed, echoing through the foyer and up the stairs. She didn't realize she'd stiffened until she saw it in Tony's grin. She wanted to push him away, to cling tightly to him, but in the end, she did neither.

"They're just people, Selena."

"They're my family."

"Okay, they're people who share ancestors in common with you. If they accept you, great. If they don't, then you'll be like most families out there—connected by blood but not much else."

She knew she had an idealized view of family because she'd never had one, and the Ceolas hadn't done much to change that view. They were close-knit and loving, and actually liked each other. They enjoyed their time together. The Hamilton family, on the other hand, most likely wanted nothing to do with her, shared ancestors or not.

Tony tucked a curl behind her ear. "I know you want

them to like you. That's natural. But the important thing is that Grant loves you. The rest of them are inconsequential. After tonight, if you don't like them, you don't ever have to see them again. It's no big deal."

"Easy for you to say. Your aunts, uncles, and cousins adore you."

"So do you."

"Yes, I do." She drew a breath, then placed her hand in his. "Shall we go?"

The guests were in the parlor with Grant: Rosalind, sitting like a queen on her throne, offering her hand for a regal shake; her younger son, Bryan, standing by the fireplace with a drink in hand; his wife, Eloise, at the opposite end of the settee; and their son, Marcus, looking bored in the rocker.

Bryan was a younger, softer version of Grant, who was soft enough in his own right. His hand was more tender than Selena's own when she shook it, his gaze less sincere than that of many of the criminals she'd met in recent months. Eloise, blond and lovely in a way that reminded Selena of Kathryn, didn't bother setting aside the drink she held but merely nodded in response to the introductions. Marcus didn't respond at all. It was questionable whether he'd even heard them over the tinny music coming from the buds plugged into his ears.

"So you're Grant's long-lost daughter," Bryan commented as she sat down. "We thought you were dead."

"Not yet," she replied with a taut smile.

He stared at her a moment, then turned to Grant. "How do you know she's your daughter?"

Grant scowled. "You knew Amelia. Look at her."

Knew, Selena thought. Hadn't liked.

"Oh, she looks like her mother, all right. But how do you

know she's *your* daughter? Amelia wasn't known for her responsible ways."

"Now, Bryan," Rosalind said chidingly. "Some things you just take on faith."

"And others require DNA," Bryan countered before turning his attention back to Grant. "You haven't done that, have you? Afraid of the results?"

"I don't need DNA," Grant said stiffly. "I *know*."

Tony spoke up, his voice mild, from his position nearby. "Kathryn didn't have any doubts. She was so sure she killed Amelia."

"Who are you?" Eloise asked. "Oh, yes, the boyfriend." She looked from him to Selena, then back again, shaking her head. "What *are* you thinking?"

"What *are* you thinking?"

Relieved the evening was over, Tony removed his holster from his belt and laid it on the nightstand, then hung his shirt and coat in the armoire. Selena had already changed into one of his T-shirts and was lying on her side on the bed, her expression impossible to read as she waited for his answer. He kicked off his shoes, peeled off his socks, then stretched out beside her.

"I'm thinking I don't care," he said, brushing his palm over her hair. "There are always going to be people who do care. Race is always going to be an issue, and people who say it isn't may have the biggest issues of all. But I don't care about that. I just care about you."

"I've been singled out all my life because I'm black. It's not always bad attention, but it *is* attention. When you and I go out, people look at us. If they're black, they wonder what I'm doing with you. If they're white, they wonder what you're doing with me. When we have children, they'll be singled out, too. They'll be noticed for nothing more than the color of their skin and the colors of their parents' skin."

"I don't care what other people think, Selena. Bigotry is a part of life. It's something we all face in one way or another. My northern Italian relatives didn't appreciate my southern Italian blood. Some people don't like Catholics. A lot of people don't like cops. Too many people don't like anyone who's different. But we can't live our lives for those people. We'll teach our kids to deal with it." He brushed a kiss to her jaw. "And just to be on the safe side, you can teach the kids to kick ass."

Her smile was slow, unwilling, but it spread across her face, transforming solemnity into pure beauty. Raising one slender hand to his cheek, she returned the kiss, along his jaw, across his mouth. She pushed him down onto his back, rose over him, and left a line of kisses down his chest. Eyes closing, he missed the gentle tickle of her hair, then forgot that as she easily undid his trousers, pushed aside the fabric, reached inside, and wrapped her fingers around his—

The sharp trill of the cell phone on the night table made him jerk. Selena looked up from where she'd settled between his legs, her expression soft and heated. "Go ahead," she said. "I'll amuse myself while I wait."

He couldn't read the information on caller ID because her gentle caresses were making his eyes cross. Flipping the phone open, he answered with a curt "Yeah."

It was one of the men at the guard shack out front. "Sorry to bother you, Mr. Ceola, but we've had a perimeter breach about halfway between the main gate and the service gate."

Selena's amusement lost its appeal in the chill that passed

through him. "I'll be right there." He closed the phone, tugged her hand away, and fastened his trousers as he swung to his feet. "Some of the alarms went off," he said as he shoved his sockless feet into his shoes, clipped on his holster, then yanked his shirt out of the armoire again. "You stay here, doors locked. If you hear anything, take the gun and go to Grant's room. I'll be back as soon as I can."

She didn't cling to him, didn't even look frightened. He pressed a hard kiss to her mouth, then left the room, waiting until he heard the click of the lock from the other side.

The house was quiet, dimly lit by sconces spaced along the hallway and down the stairs. He took them two at a time, keyed the alarm, then stepped outside. The night was warm, heavy with damp. There was activity—engines running, distant voices—but nothing that seemed urgent. No pounding footsteps, no shouts or gunshots.

The guard on duty at the front door, armed with an M4 automatic rifle, gave him a grim nod. "Whoever it was got away. Looks like he made it about a hundred meters in from the road before realizing he'd tripped the sensors. He hightailed it back out and took off."

"Anyone see his vehicle?"

"A pickup truck."

Thinking of the men in the truck that afternoon, Tony waited for more. Maybe their prank hadn't been so innocent. Maybe Long or Morgan had chosen them precisely because it would appear that way.

"Late model, white. We may be able to see more from the cameras."

The truck that had almost run them off the road had been green and at least forty years old. Maybe the stupid kids really were just stupid kids.

One of the guards' pickups made a wide circle in the

parking area, then stopped at the edge of the walk. Tony climbed into the passenger seat for a quick ride to the guard shack.

The monitors were already cued up with the footage from the service gate. The pickup that sped past was simply that: a white truck, nothing distinctive about it, occupied by only the driver. He was on the side away from the camera, little more than a shadow, and the tag light was out, making it impossible to tell anything about the license plate.

Tony stared hard at the picture frozen on the monitor. Was that blond hair like Luke Morgan's or just the glint of light on glass? It was impossible to say.

Armed with a heavy flashlight, one of the guards showed him where the man had pulled off the road and climbed the fence. The grass on the road's shoulder showed tracks from the tires, but no tread that could be cast and matched. There were no fibers caught on the board fence, and though they could follow his trail of broken weeds and twigs, they found no other sign of the trespasser.

"The least he could have done was drop his wallet," Tony said sourly. When the guard gave him a skeptical look, he shrugged. "Easiest rape case I ever solved. The guy's wallet fell out of his pants pocket and was left behind. Easiest bank robbery: The robber wrote the holdup note on a deposit slip for his own account."

But no one Long hired was likely to make that kind of mistake.

He shined the light into the woods, but even its million-candlepower beam couldn't penetrate to the hedge that surrounded the house.

The guard noted that, as well. "He didn't come anywhere near close."

"No, but closer than I'd like." Breathing the same air was closer than he wanted those bastards to Selena.

"We'll see if we can enhance the footage," the guard said as he and Tony made their way back to the driveway. "If we get anything, we'll let you know in the morning."

Tony turned down the offer of a ride back to the house and set out along the driveway. The air was muggy, making his shirt feel heavy against his skin, and smelled of flowers. Something plopped in the pond and, nearer, some small critter rustled in the undergrowth. One hundred fifty years ago, Selena's however-many-greats-grandfathers would have felt the same humidity, smelled the same smells, heard the same wildlife—both the one who lived in the big, fancy house and the one who labored in his fields. How did she feel, knowing that one of her ancestors had *owned* the other?

He could guess, but he could never really know. He came from a long line of working- to middle-class Italians. None of them had ever been rich like the Hamiltons, but they'd always had their freedom.

As he passed through the break in the hedge, the moon came out from behind the clouds, making the house damn near glow. It was impressive, and one day it would belong to his children. How did he feel about that?

More than a little uncomfortable, he admitted. He hadn't set out to fall in love with a rich woman...or a black woman...or a woman with enemies who wanted her dead. And he hadn't done any of that. He'd fallen in love with Selena. A woman. The rest of it was just complications.

The guard at the front door went on alert until he recognized Tony. Cradling the rifle in his arms, he waited until Tony reached the door to speak. "Everything okay?"

"It seems to be." He let himself in, reset the alarm, and

headed up the stairs. Knocking softly at the bedroom door, he murmured, "It's me, babe."

When Selena unlocked and opened the door, he told her what little he'd learned as he undressed. As usual, her expression was difficult to read. If she was afraid, uneasy, or even concerned, it was impossible to say. There was no doubt, though, that there was something else on her mind. When he'd shucked the last of his clothes, she pushed him down on the bed, following him, maneuvering until he was on his back and she was kneeling between his legs.

"I believe this is where we left off..."

"Can I get you anything else, hon?"

Charlize glanced at the meal spread before her—eggs over easy, hash browns, and grits, flaky golden biscuits and peppered bacon done just so. A dish of honey butter sat between a bowl of jelly packets and a tub of the cook's home-canned apple butter, and coffee steamed nearby in a white porcelain mug. "I think this is more than enough. Thank you."

"Once you see how good it is, you'll be surprised by how much you can eat." With a grin and a wink, the waitress headed off to see to her other customers.

The girl wasn't exaggerating, Charlize realized with her first bite. Her chefs, for all their training, experience, and ego, couldn't have improved on the simple dishes. And frankly, she was hungry. She'd spent the day before putting miles on the rental car and talking to every unsavory type she'd come across. She'd shown Damon's and Luke's photos to bartenders, waitresses, liquor store clerks, and punks on the street throughout much of the county, but she hadn't gotten so much as a flicker of recognition.

That wouldn't deter her from searching again today.

As she finished her breakfast and asked the waitress for the check, a farmer left the cash register, limping awkwardly to the door. She left a generous tip for the waitress, paid her bill, and left the diner. Her car was parked out back in a small gravel lot that opened off the alley. The farmer was fiddling with something in the bed of a pickup a few spaces away, his face shaded by the straw cowboy hat he wore. He moved like an old man, the limp suggesting an arthritic hip, but there was nothing old about the body encased in tight jeans and a white cotton shirt.

A chunk of gravel in the shoe gave a person a realistic limp—one of the tidbits of information Charlize had picked up from her father at an age when other girls were learning how to drive.

She stopped beside her car, fumbling with the lock, fumbling inside her purse. The footsteps approaching her were barely audible, but there was nothing subtle about the muscular arm that wrapped around her shoulders from behind. Everything in her tensed at the contact, but she maintained an icy calm as she turned and pressed her pistol into his belly.

"Hello, Luke."

He wasn't surprised by the weapon. "Nice to see you, too," he said mildly. "Careful there, Charlize. You don't want me to go off half-cocked, do you?"

She nudged, and he backed up a few steps, then leaned against the car next to hers, ankles crossed, arms folded over his chest. For a man who had a gun pointed at him, he looked remarkably unconcerned.

"I didn't say it was nice to see you," she pointed out. "It never has been."

"Never? I seem to remember a time or two when I first started coming around."

She could deny it, but what was the point? There *had* been a time in the beginning when she'd looked forward to his frequent visits. He'd been handsome, smart, and funny, and somewhere deep inside, in the part of her that had struggled for some semblance of normalcy in her life, she'd had a bit of a crush. She'd admired him. Gotten flustered around him. Had nurtured dreams of being rescued by him.

More important, when Luke was at their house, John Turner had left her in peace. He hadn't wanted his protégé—or anyone else—to know what he did to his daughter when they were alone.

She changed the subject. "Where is Long?"

"Don't know. I suspect he's around here somewhere."

So did she. It was part of the game to Long, to remain in the area even as people searched for him. He had great confidence in his ability to outwit them, deservedly so considering he'd been in the crime business for more than twenty years and hadn't even registered on the radar until the past few months.

"Do you have a way to get in touch with him?"

Luke gazed at her a moment before slowly smiling. "What's wrong, darlin'? Did he cut you out of the loop?"

There wasn't much she loved about men. Her father had seen to that. But Luke Morgan's smile was an exception. It was broad, and white, and reached even into his eyes. It was a wholehearted, satisfied-with-life smile that she'd never known. Nothing was wrong in his world.

All those years ago, she'd thought he could fix what was wrong in her world, but he hadn't. He'd called her a liar and scorned her for showing such ingratitude to John Turner. He'd destroyed her only hope for help.

No, that wasn't true. He'd only destroyed her faith in the goodness of others. She'd helped herself.

"You're not here to kill Selena McCaffrey, are you?" he asked.

She debated lying or not answering at all. Instead, she shrugged. "No, I'm not. I'm here to protect her."

"And how are you gonna do that?"

"By killing Long, if given the chance." Her smile was cool, practiced. "By killing you, if necessary."

She could see he wasn't surprised. Sentimentality hadn't been enough to stop her from killing her father. It wouldn't spare Luke's life, either.

"So why aren't you screaming? You could have everyone out of that diner in no time."

"Because it's not necessary." After letting that sink in, she added, "At this time." She didn't feel threatened. She had the gun, and she never hesitated to do whatever was necessary.

He grinned because that was what he did. He might kill people for a living, but that aside, life was one big joke to him. "What makes Selena so special?"

She shrugged.

"You think she's the sister you never had? What you could have become if things had been different?"

Though the questions struck too close for comfort, she answered carelessly. "I think she deserves to live. Long doesn't." Then, though she didn't mean to, she repeated, "If 'things' had been different? You mean if my father hadn't been a hit man? If my mother hadn't abandoned me to him when I was twelve? If he hadn't molested me for the next three years? If I hadn't been forced to kill him when I was fifteen?" She paused, her voice growing softer. "If you had helped when I begged you to?"

Finally there was a flicker of something in his eyes. Guilt.

Regret. Maybe just annoyance. Whatever, it disappeared just as quickly. "She isn't going to live. If I don't get her, someone else will. And if I have to kill you, too . . ."

Another flicker of emotion. Would he actually kill her? She didn't know or care, because she knew one thing for sure.

She *would* kill him. Without the slightest regret.

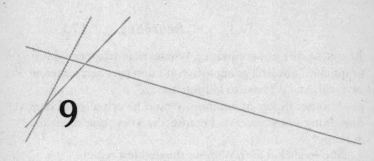

9

June was late getting out of the house Wednesday morning. She'd tossed and turned most of the night, and when she'd finally fallen asleep, even the alarm clock hadn't been enough to rouse her. Tardiness was irresponsible—so like Amelia—and it sent an already bad mood on a downhill slide. It wasn't helped when she walked out of the house, briefcase in hand, and found Luther waiting for her on the porch.

"I figured you'd gone fishing," she said, wondering why he hadn't awakened her when it became clear she'd slept through the alarm.

"Do I look like I'm dressed for fishing?" he retorted, rising stiffly from the rocker.

He didn't. He wore his Sunday best, including a tie.

"'Sides, I can go fishing anytime, girl. My old truck's acting up again. Can you give me a ride?"

She stifled an exasperated sigh. His truck wasn't acting up at all; he was just nervous about driving with his eyesight growing worse every month. Ordinarily she wouldn't mind making a detour on her way to work, but ordinarily she wasn't late. "Of course, Daddy. Where do you want to go? Miz Luella's? Little Jim's place?"

"Just the big house." He bent with some effort and picked up a box from the floor, tucking it under one arm. She recognized it as the one that usually sat on the shelf in his closet. It was filled with family photos, some dating back a hundred years or more, many of them pictures of Amelia.

A chill spread through June, locking her jaw in place, thinning her lips. He was going to The Gardens to show pictures of his precious Amelia to his precious Selena—to fawn over her as if she was something more than the bastard daughter of a married man and his mistress. "Maybe it would be better, considering the danger, if you stayed away from The Gardens—"

Luther laughed as he made his way carefully down the steps. "Danger don't mean nothin', girl. Spending time with my only grandbaby—that's everything. Come on now. We're already late. Baby girl's expectin' me for breakfast."

Grimly June turned back to lock the door. All he'd talked about the day before was Selena—how pretty she was, how smart, how sweet, how like her mother. He'd even shown June pictures, printed off the Internet in Grant's office, of paintings she'd done and bragged about her success as an artist.

She gets that from her mama, he'd said so many times that June had wanted to scream. *That Amelia always had an eye for colors and things. She was somethin', and that little girl of hers, ain't she somethin', too.*

June clomped down the steps and across to the car. When she tried to help him in, he shook her off. "I can handle it. I'm not so old as you think I am."

"Sorry, Daddy." She'd always helped him, and until Selena had come along, he'd always accepted. Maybe she just wasn't good enough for that anymore.

Dear God in heaven, she wished they'd never heard of Selena McCaffrey. She wished the girl would just go back where she came from. She wished that man would get past all the security and kill—

She paused halfway around the car. It was wrong to wish harm to someone. She'd been taught that practically from the cradle. But sometimes one person's harm was to another person's benefit. There was no denying her own life had improved vastly after Amelia's death. She'd had her daddy's attention, and his love. For the first time ever, she'd felt as if she'd mattered. She'd been important.

Once again she didn't matter. But if Selena was gone, dead like her mama...

June slid behind the wheel and took the back way to Grant's house. All the way there, Luther chattered. Selena this, Selena that, Selena Selena Selena. She was never so grateful to be shed of her father as when she stopped next to the veranda steps.

"I'll pick you up at lunch—"

Luther swung his feet to the ground, then grinned. "Baby girl's expecting me for lunch, too."

Of course she was. "I can pick you up on my way home, unless you get tired and want—"

"Baby girl will see to it that I get home. Don't you worry none. She'll take good care of me." He winked as he eased out of the car, closed the door, then started the laborious trip up the steps, box cradled close.

June watched as the security guard helped him the last few steps, then escorted him to the door, matching his pace to Luther's. Banging her hand on the steering wheel, she mimicked his words. "'Don't you worry none. She'll take good care of me.' *I* take good care of you, damn it! Where was she when you were sick, when you had to retire, when you needed someone to cook and clean and look after you? *I* did those things. *I* was there for you, *not* Amelia and for damn sure not 'baby girl.'"

A knock on the driver's window startled her. She jerked

around to see Tony Ceola bent to look in the window. With trembling fingers, she rolled down the window, then forced her quavering lips into a smile of sorts.

"Are you all right?"

"I'm fine. Just talking to myself. You know how us old folks are." Her hand fluttered, the gesture looking more nervous than careless, so she quickly lowered it to her lap. "I'm running late. I've got to get going. You keep an eye on Luther today."

"We will."

She rolled up the window again as Tony walked away, but instead of shifting into gear, she reached inside her purse, her fingers closing around the business card for *Modern South Magazine*. She knew now that the name on the card was fake, and the address, legitimate or not, certainly wouldn't lead her to David Jones, also known as Damon Long. But the phone number . . .

The phone number just might be the solution to her biggest problem.

Releasing the card, she drove toward the main gate. She had a lot to do today. Starting with doing something about Selena.

"She was beautiful."

The words were uttered by Grant, but everyone around the table, Selena included, nodded in agreement. They were looking at photos of Amelia, most of them accompanied by some small memory. *This was when she won that talent show. She could do anything but sing, but them judges didn't notice. They give her first place anyway.*

That was high school graduation. Her mama and me were

so proud. She was the first person in our families to finish high school.

There were other pictures, too—of Amelia's mother, of Luther's and Oda Mae's parents, their brothers and sisters, of grandparents and great-grandparents. Luther knew every face, every name, and Selena committed as many of them as possible to memory.

After twenty-eight years, she had a family history. She'd never had that, had never owned any photographs beyond a handful of herself. She could sort through these for hours without being bored, could listen to Grant and Luther reminisce endlessly.

She picked up an envelope, yellowed with age, and removed the snapshots inside. They'd been taken by Grant at some sort of celebration in town, and front and center in every one was Amelia. She wore a white dress, the bodice fitted, the skirt flaring to her knees. Her curls were pulled back and tied with a white ribbon, and the expression on her face was pure bliss.

"That was the Founder's Day celebration," Grant said. "You can't tell it, but she was pregnant with you. Three, maybe four months. We couldn't go together. We couldn't do more than say a friendly hello, as if I was just a lawyer and she was just a former client."

That was how they met. When Oda Mae died, there had been legal matters to take care of, and Amelia had hired Grant to handle them. Despite the fact that he was married, wealthy, and white, they'd fallen in love...and sealed her fate.

In the photos, she shopped, talked, and ate. June was in one, Luther in another. The people in the background covered the spectrum of Greenhill's social ladder. Women dressed for tea parties shopped alongside others in shorts,

T-shirts, and flip-flops. Little girls in sundresses and bonnets played with barefooted kids in hand-me-downs. Men in khakis and polo shirts mixed with farmworkers in worn jeans or overalls. Rich, middle-class, or poor; white, black, or Latino....

Selena's gaze caught on a figure in one picture. The man stood off to Amelia's side and watched her as she watched Grant behind the camera. He was Latino, dressed in faded jeans and a plaid work shirt. The cuffs were rolled back to reveal muscular forearms, and the look on his face was fierce, his brows drawn together, his eyes dark with emotion. He looked ... Dear God, he looked like ...

The picture fell from her fingers, drifting to the table top. "Rodrigo," she whispered, and a shudder passed through her.

"What's that?" Grant asked absently, but she ignored him, snatched up the picture again, and showed it to Tony.

"That's Rodrigo Acosta." Her finger shook when she pointed to the man. She clenched her free hand into a fist, willing the trembling, the fear, to pass.

He pried the photo from her hand for a better look. "Are you sure?"

Sure? She'd been nine years old the last time she'd seen the man married to the woman she'd believed was her mother. Nineteen years ago—a little girl. Could she possibly be sure?

He'd made her life hell. He'd hated the sight of her, had beaten her when he was angry or drunk or just bored. He'd bruised her body, broken her bones, and locked her for hours at a time in a cupboard barely big enough to hold her. To this day she still panicked in small spaces. How could she forget?

She scooped up the other five shots, shuffling through

them. He was in every picture, always near Amelia, always watching her. Selena laid the photos on the table in front of Tony and pointed him out in each one.

"That's him. I'm sure."

"Who is Rodrigo?" Luther asked.

Forcing air into her tight lungs, Selena shoved away from the table and paced the length of the room. Behind her, Tony quietly—carefully—answered.

"He and his wife raised Selena until she was nine."

Raised her in Puerto Rico. Lived in Puerto Rico. What the hell had he been doing in Greenhill, Alabama, when Amelia was pregnant with her? Why had he been watching Amelia? How had William come to place Selena with him? *Why?*

"Why would Rodrigo be in Alabama?" Tony asked.

Selena shrugged. She would have guessed the bastard had never traveled more than fifty miles from the village where he'd been born. He was ignorant, lazy, a drunk who needed help to make it home from the bars he frequented. What were the odds of his having been in Alabama twenty-eight years ago? Slim.

But she had been born in Alabama twenty-eight years ago. Had been taken from her dead mother and given to Rodrigo and his wife, Luisa, by William, who'd paid them to raise her. The fate he'd rescued her from was the fate *he'd* set in motion for her.

"Looks to me like he was one of the farmhands," Luther said. "We've always had a lot of Mexicans here. They're hard workers."

Rodrigo a hard worker. Selena couldn't imagine it. But before William and his money had come into his life, he must have held a job. He'd had to support Luisa and the children they'd already had before taking in Selena.

How had blue-blood William met immigrant farm-worker Rodrigo? Easy enough: William had had a knack for finding lowlifes to do the dirty work while he kept his hands clean. Maybe he'd paid Rodrigo to dispose of Amelia's body, just as he'd paid him to get Selena out of Grant's life.

How could he have put a helpless infant in the care of a stranger? He'd had other options. He could have left her at a hospital, could have turned her over to the police in Montgomery, where he'd been visiting, or in Boston, where he'd lived at that time.

But that would have attracted media attention and the risk that Grant would hear about it and identify his daughter. No doubt, William had thought it better to pay someone to take her away, to keep her away. Until *he* decided he had reason to bring her back.

Tony came to stand beside her, close enough for his arm to bump hers. She was tempted to lean against him, but kept her spine rigid, her arms folded across her middle. "Rodrigo might know something about Amelia's death," she said quietly.

"Like where her body is."

So the thought had occurred to him, too. William liked being in charge, giving orders, not carrying them out.

"He might know why William—" She broke off and clenched her jaw. Why had William given her to so unsuitable a father? Why had he condemned her to a life of misery? Why hadn't he taken five minutes to come up with a better solution?

Unexpectedly, a lump rose in her throat. "I know it's stupid after all that happened, but I feel betrayed."

Tony slid his arm around her and tugged her close. "It's not stupid. You loved William."

Loved him. Hated him. Wished him dead. For fourteen

years, she'd credited him with all the good things in her life. Now she knew that instead, he, along with Kathryn, was responsible for all the bad. All the pain. All the fear. All the sorrow. All those years of believing not even her parents could love or want her.

With a sudden surge of energy, she started toward the door. "I want to go to Puerto Rico. I want to talk to Rodrigo. To find out—"

She'd made it into the hallway before Tony caught up and swung her around. "You can't leave here."

"He knows something about Amelia. He watched her, stalked her. He knew my mother, knew William, and he very well might know what William did with her body. I need to talk to him." All those years he'd known, and he'd said nothing. Had let her believe she was the result of Luisa's one-night stand with some stranger. Had called her Luisa's nigger bastard. And he'd known.

"You don't even know if he's still in Puerto Rico," Tony said calmly.

"I'll find out when I get there, won't I?" She pulled free of him and started away, but he followed.

"Your father has spent a fortune making this place safe for you. If you leave now—especially when we know Long and Morgan are likely in the area—all that will be wasted."

She spun around to face him. Everything inside her was edgy, roiling, as if she might pop out of her skin. Everything about him was calm. Stubborn. "Rodrigo knows something, Tony. Maybe it's important. Maybe it's not. Either way, I need to find out."

"So we'll put that on our list of things to do when this is over. In the meantime, I'll contact the FBI office in San Juan and find out where he's living. I'll check with DMV and the Department of Labor here in Alabama and see if we can verify that he was here twenty-eight years ago. We'll ask around, see what we can find out about his time here."

Her breath came in short, heavy bursts as she stared at him. He sounded so damn reasonable, and of course, he was right. If she left the security of the farm, she was liable to pick up Long's hitter. If she made it to Puerto Rico alive, what would she do when she got there? She had been only nine when she'd moved to Jamaica. She didn't remember much about her years in Puerto Rico, not even the name of the nearest village. She had clear images of the beach where she'd played, the cupboard where Rodrigo had imprisoned her, and the whitewashed church they'd attended, but the island was surrounded by beaches and filled with churches.

"I hate it when you're so . . ."

Tony grinned. "Right?" He slid his arm around her, snuggled her to his side, and started back to the family room. "Tell me everything you know about him. The more we know, the better the chances of finding the right Rodrigo Acosta."

"He was a drunk who took money to raise me, and beat me damn near every day of my life." Then she forced a breath. "He didn't own a car. Didn't have a telephone. Didn't work regularly. He's probably in his late fifties, early sixties." Not too old for her to break him in two when she confronted him.

"Do you have any idea where the house was? What the closest town was?"

She shook her head, then stopped. "He used to point across the water and say, 'Jamaica's over that way. That's where the father who never wanted you lives.'"

"So it was the west coast? South?" He grinned again. "I should have paid more attention in Sister Mary Katherine's geography class. Or he could have been jerking you around. You were a little girl. You probably didn't know where Jamaica was."

She shook her head again. But Luisa had pointed in the same direction when Selena had asked where her father was. For all Selena knew, they could have been on the north coast and she might have been pointing in the direction of the United States.

"When we went to mass, we all sat together," she murmured. "Rodrigo, Luisa, eight little Latino children, and me. Sometimes people snickered and taunted him. The priest had to intervene more than once. I thought that was why he hated me—because I was biracial, and proof of his wife's infidelity. But after seeing those pictures...Maybe it was because Amelia had rejected him."

"She wouldn't have him, but he'd gotten her baby. He'd gotten to torment the child she loved so much." Tony shrugged. "It's sick, but it's possible." He stopped at the doorway and raised one brow. *Are you ready?*

With a tight smile, she walked past him and back to the table where Grant and Luther were waiting. The other pictures had been cleared away, except for the half dozen with Rodrigo, set aside for Tony, and new stacks were lined up for her perusal.

She had a family now, she reminded herself. A family history with family photographs she could sort through for hours. All she had to do was put Rodrigo out of her mind.

Until she was free to face him again.

"Hey, I've got a suggestion, Chee. Next time something like this happens, I'll run off with Island Girl and you stay here and do all your work, all mine, and everything I send you while I'm gone. Sound fair?"

Tony grinned. Bellyaching was Simmons's favorite activity in the world. He could be living a life of ease with more money, more food, more everything than a man could possibly need, and he'd still find something to bitch about. "Did you get anything on that list of farm employees I sent you?"

"Yeah, bored. It's your typical bunch of working-class chumps. A couple have protective orders against them, and one's in deep shit with the IRS for failure to report income. That's it. And I did some calling around. Charlize Pawley checked into the Azalea Inn in beautiful downtown Greenhill yesterday."

Tony grunted in response. They'd known Charlize would follow Long to town. Whether having her nearby was good or bad, only time would tell.

"Everything else around here is the usual shits and giggles. Workin' all day, not gettin' any at night. Suz is pissed. I told her you and Island Girl had headed south, and now she's whining that I never take her anywhere. She says we haven't been on vacation since the kids were born. Christ, I'd have to rob one of the casinos to pay for it."

"If it's any comfort, when this is over, I'm gonna need a vacation, too."

"Yeah, sure. I know, you're workin', too, but I bet you're still getting laid." Simmons's whine was replaced with moroseness. "Suz is threatening to make me start sleeping with Tucker."

"Remind me—is that your kid or your dog?"

"Funny. I'd rather sleep with the dog. At least he doesn't snore." His voice muffled, Simmons said something to someone else, then asked, "What else do you want me to do?"

Tony glanced at the top photo in the stack he held, his gaze fixed on Rodrigo. From the first time Selena had mentioned her childhood abuse, he'd wanted to jump on the first plane to Puerto Rico and beat the hell out of the bastard responsible.

Maybe he would get the chance.

"Hey, I've got one more thing for you. I need to know the whereabouts of one Rodrigo Acosta."

"Full name? Date of birth? Social Security number?"

"Don't know."

"Last known location?"

"Puerto Rico." Tony hesitated, then added, "Eighteen years ago."

"Christ, Chee. Puerto Rico's a big place with a lot of Rodrigos and a lot of Acostas."

"Isn't it lucky we only need one?" Tony asked drily. "We think he worked around Greenhill prior to returning to Puerto Rico. The state might still have labor or DMV records, which would give you his DOB and Social."

"Jeez, you know, I'm pulling double duty back here, working both your cases and my own. The least you could do is quit sending me new stuff to do."

"Yeah, I'll keep that in mind. Thanks, Frankie." Tony hung up, then spread out the pictures. Judging by the shadows, they'd been taken throughout the day, a fact Grant had confirmed. For Rodrigo to be caught in the background once would be no big deal. Even three times could be coincidence. But all six? Looking at her the same way?

Tony suspected Selena was right. Like everyone else, Rodrigo had fallen under Amelia's spell, but she'd had no interest in him, so he'd taken her rejection out on her daughter. What kind of sick bastard tortured a child because her mother didn't want him? And what kind of sick bastard put that child in his custody in the first place?

His gaze settled on Rodrigo again. He looked like a farmhand, Luther had said. Hamilton Farms was the largest farm in the county. What if Rodrigo had worked there? Would they still have his employment records?

When he ran into June downstairs and asked her, she gave him a long, level look. "The Gardens is a part of Alabama history. They have records dating back to the construction of the place. Every stick of furniture, every crop that was planted and harvested, every slave that was bought or sold—it's all documented. Recent records pertaining to the farm would be in the foreman's office, but he's gone for the day."

Tony glanced at his watch. It was a few minutes after five. "Do you know where I can get a key to the office?"

She gave him another of those looks, then her mouth settled in a thin line. "Come on. I'll let you in." After setting her purse on a chair in the foyer, she strode down the hall and through the kitchen. Luther's voice drifted from the family room as they passed.

Once they'd left the house through the back door, Tony moved to walk beside her. "You have keys to the foreman's office?"

Her no-nonsense strides didn't falter as she looked at him. "I *am* Grant's assistant."

"I didn't mean it as a criticism. After all, you're practically family."

That made her stiffen. "No, I'm not."

"He's your niece's father. If he and Amelia had married, you would have been his sister-in-law."

Scowling, she stopped at the office a few yards from the main barn and jabbed a key into the lock. The door swung open, but she didn't leave him there. She went inside, flipping on lights as she went, wrinkling her nose at the stale cigarette odor that hung in the air.

Tony followed her into a room that held tall gray file cabinets around its perimeter. She scanned the dates scrawled on the drawers before pulling one out. "Newer records are kept on the computer, of course. We've never taken the time to enter the older data. What exactly is it you want to know?"

"If a man named Rodrigo Acosta worked here any time before Amelia's death."

She thumbed through the folders before pulling out three and handing them to him. "That's every single employee for that year and the two preceding years, whether he worked one day or three hundred."

The lists were pages long, mostly typed with a few penciled-in additions. There were plenty of Hispanic names, but Acosta wasn't among them.

"Are there other farms in the area?"

June took the folders and returned them to their place, then closed the drawer. "Thirty years ago there were mostly family farms. A lot of them have gone out of business or been bought out by the bigger farms. I doubt any of them have records as complete as ours."

She waited pointedly at the door for him to leave, and he did, chasing away the smoke odor with fresh air. After she locked up, he pulled one of the pictures from his pocket. "Do you remember this man?"

She barely glanced at the picture, a muscle in her jaw twitching. "No."

When she would have walked off, he blocked her way. "Don't look at Amelia. Concentrate on him. Did you ever see him?"

When she didn't reach out, he took her hand and placed

the photo in it. Tension humming through her, she slowly lifted it and studied it for a moment, then shook her head. "I don't know...There was a Mexican farmhand who had a thing for Amelia." Her smile was thin. "Every man had a thing for Amelia."

"He's Puerto Rican. His name is Rodrigo Acosta."

She shrugged off his correction on ethnicity and thrust the picture back into his hands. Some people never looked beyond the color of a person's skin to see his face. June, it seemed, was one of them. "I don't remember. There were too many men vying for Amelia's attention."

And not enough wanting hers, Tony thought. Luther, in particular.

"Can I go now? I need to pick up my father and get home. I've got things to do."

"Sure."

Without waiting for him, she set off for the house. He followed at a slower pace. As he walked into the hallway from the kitchen, he heard Luther saying good-bye at the front door.

"Grant, thank you for the good food. That Nell can cook almost as good as my Oda Mae did. And you, baby girl..." There was a rustle, a shuffle, as Luther most likely gave Selena a hug. "I'll see you soon."

Tony walked into the family room and to the side windows. A moment later, he saw June holding Luther's arm as they made their way slowly down the porch steps. As soon as they reached the path, he shook her off and walked carefully but unaided to the car.

Tony had no doubt that June loved her father dearly, just as there was no doubt that Luther had preferred—still preferred—Amelia. Having Selena back reminded him of those better days when Amelia was alive.

It reminded June, too. But her memories weren't as sweet as Luther's.

Families were complicated things. If he hadn't already known that, he would have learned it in his first few years on the job. He was luckier than most. He not only loved his family, but he liked them, as well. It had been only a week since he'd seen the whole gang for dinner, but he missed them. He wondered how his father was getting along and how his mother was coping. He wished he could call her—hell, wished he was back in Tulsa where he could keep an eye on them, but he couldn't risk contact with them until this was over.

Until Long was dead.

Until Selena was safe.

Selena couldn't sleep. After checking the bedside clock for the tenth time in an hour, she slid out of bed and slipped out the French doors onto the balcony.

Sweet jasmine drifted on the humid air, and in a distant tree an owl hooted softly. Beyond the crape myrtles, the fields were quiet. The workers would arrive with sunrise and go about their jobs tending the earth, but she wouldn't know. The buffer between house and fields was adequate. All she might hear was the faint hum of a tractor, and then only if she concentrated. All she heard now were the sounds of the night, along with her own steady breathing.

A few steps along the balcony was a set of wicker chairs with bright cushions. She curled up in one, finding a comfortable position. They'd spent a quiet night tonight—just her, Tony, and Grant. It had been interrupted briefly by June, who had returned after dinner to retrieve the purse she'd left there when picking up Luther. She hadn't wanted to come in and talk.

Once she was gone again, Grant had asked questions about Selena's years in Puerto Rico and Jamaica. She had asked questions about everything else. Those years were like a bad dream. She knew they were real—the pain, the despair, the fear—but distance and circumstance had stripped them of some power. If she returned to Puerto Rico, if she found herself face to face with Rodrigo, would that power return?

It didn't matter. Curiosity had grown into need. The more she learned about her mother, about herself, the more she needed to know. Had Rodrigo known her mother? Had they been friends, acquaintances, or more? Had he known about her and Grant? Had he wanted her? Had he tormented Selena because Amelia didn't want him?

Had he been a part of Amelia's life? A part of her death?

Selena had questions. Rodrigo had answers.

Her breathing was slowing, her heart rate settling, when a sound disturbed the quiet night. Muscles clenching, she opened her eyes, looking to the left, then turning her head a millimeter to look to the right. Everything was still. She couldn't pinpoint where the noise had come from. Maybe Tony had awakened in the room behind her. Maybe it was simply the settling of the old house.

As soon as that thought faded, the sound came again. Rubber soles on wood at the front of the house. Someone was on the balcony. Grant, also unable to sleep? One of the guards assigned to stand watch?

Unmoving, she sat in the shadows, grateful for her dark T-shirt, and watched as a form turned the corner at the front end of the house. Dressed in black, too tall for Grant, too slim for Tony, too stealthy for a guard, he slid toward Selena's room carefully, staying close to the house, moving away only to skirt tables and chairs. The thin moonlight glinted off the pistol in his right hand, held close to his leg.

Heart thudding, Selena forced her breathing into a slow, steady pace and watched him pass the first set of French doors, the second, and stop in front of the next set, the doors she'd just come through. He shined a penlight on the knob, then reached out a black-gloved hand.

She eased to her feet, the small squeak of the wicker magnified by the rushing in her ears. Balancing her weight lightly, she asked, "Are you looking for me?"

The man spun around and the penlight went off, leaving his face in shadow. Once that momentary start was past, though, he didn't seem overly nervous. He didn't understand who he was dealing with, and that was to her advantage. "Thank you," he said, his tone flat, his accent New England.

"For what?"

She had the vague impression of a smile before movement drew her attention lower. He raised his weapon, aiming center mass. "For making this easy."

Angling slightly, she shifted her weight to her back leg, then executed a step-up side kick, the sole of her foot connecting with his right wrist with enough force to make him stumble back a few steps. Before he could regain his balance, she struck again, this time knocking him to the floor. The pistol hit the wood with a thud, but he didn't lose his grip on it.

He avoided her next kick, then rolled to the side and sprang to his feet. Switching the gun to his left hand, he gave his right hand a shake. "Damn bitch." There was no rancor in his voice. Risking injury or death himself was part of the job description. "Lucky for me, I'm as good a shot with my off hand as I am with the other."

Wishing for a weapon of her own, she dropped forward into a tumble, landing on her back in front of him, bringing both feet into his gut. He staggered back with a grunt, scraping a wicker table across the floor, sending the potted flowers it held to land in a crash of broken porcelain. Without a pause, she rolled up, knelt on his left arm, pinning it to the floor, and tried to wrest the gun from his hand.

Swearing, he punched her in the ribs, and her breath caught in a rush of pain. She pried one finger loose from the grips, then another, before he landed a second punch, slamming her against the wall. Her head connected with the wood, bringing tears to her eyes, making her vision grow blurry. Her leg stung, and she could smell the metallic scent of blood as it seeped along her skin.

The bulk of the fallen pot lay near her, its jagged edge responsible for the cut on her calf. She gripped the pot with both hands and flung it, showering loose dirt in the man's face. As he scrubbed at his eyes with his free hand, she forced herself to her feet, grabbed a second pot of flowers, and swung it at his head.

He raised his left hand to block the blow. The impact vibrated into her arms and knocked the gun from his hand. It discharged as it landed, the sound deafening, the bullet ricocheting off a pillar and shattering through a window.

"Goddamn," the man muttered. "You broke my fucking arm."

Cradling his arm, he looked for the gun, spotted it near the railing, and darted for it. Selena waited until he straightened again, then spun in a tight circle and kicked him hard on the chin. His head jerked back with a snap, and his body followed, toppling over the rail, arms flailing. She lunged to grab for him, but she was too late. His body hit the walkway below with a thud. He didn't move.

"Selena!" Tony covered the distance from their room in a few strides, glanced over the railing at the dead man, then gathered her into his arms. "Are you all right?"

She'd seen violent death before, but she'd never been the cause. Her stomach roiled while she silently willed the man to get up, to shake it off. He didn't. Couldn't. The unnatural angle of his neck told her that.

"Selena...babe." Tony gave her a gentle shake, forcing her to look from the scene below to him. He touched her cheek, scraped from its contact with the rough wood, felt the knot rising on the side of her head, then asked again, "Are you all right?"

A pickup skidded to a stop on the driveway, and two armed guards jumped out. Another truck was a few hundred yards behind them and, nearer, Grant was hurrying along the balcony. She gave him a weak smile before looking back at Tony. "Y-yeah. I'm okay."

He stared at her a moment as if confirming her words, then anger overrode concern. "What the hell were you doing out here? You're not supposed to come outside, and for damn sure not without me!"

"I couldn't sleep. I just needed—" She broke off as Grant reached them.

He wore a sloppily tied robe, his hair was disheveled, and his glasses sat crooked on his nose. He looked below, where more guards had arrived, paled, then reached out one hand to her, one to Tony. "I heard a gunshot. Are you all right? Did he hurt you? Is he...? My God...oh, my God..."

Keeping his arm around her, Tony gestured toward the open French doors. "Let's get inside and out of the crime scene."

It took a moment to make her feet move, but the pressure of his arm against her back finally propelled her forward. As soon as they were inside the bedroom, he switched on a lamp, seated her on the bed, and knelt to look at her leg. "How did this happen?"

"Broken flowerpot."

"I'll get some bandages," Grant said, striding across the room to the door.

Gazing up at her, Tony touched the mark on her cheek again. "Do you need to see a doctor?"

She shook her head. The knot was throbbing, but a few aspirin tablets would take care of that. Her ribs ached, too, but that was to be expected. After all, Sonny Yates had broken two of them little more than two months ago.

She expected his next question, but still felt a sinking in her stomach when he asked it, his voice low, his tone wounded. "Why didn't you wake me?"

Her attempt at a smile failed. "What? I can't sleep, so you shouldn't, either?"

He gestured impatiently. "When you saw this guy, when you realized something was wrong, why didn't you yell for me?"

The answer was simple, and he wouldn't like it one bit: She hadn't thought about it. She'd been taking care of herself for so long that not once during the fight had she realized that all she had to do was scream and Tony would come running. Even if she had realized it, though, she wouldn't have put him in danger, not as long as she had a chance to handle it on her own.

When she didn't respond, his expression turned grim. He didn't need her answer. He knew, and it hurt.

Her hand trembled when she lifted it to his cheek. Pain, she preferred to think, or delayed reaction over causing a man's death. Not fear. "I'm sorry, Tony. I just acted on instinct. All those months when I trained back at home, my instructor stressed that in a life-or-death situation, you can't count on anyone coming to your aid. You have to be able to protect yourself. That's what I was thinking about out there. Protecting myself. Not calling for someone else."

"I'm not just 'someone else,' and I was fifteen feet away. Hell, do you think if the situation was reversed, I wouldn't be yelling for you?"

This time her smile was genuine. "No, you wouldn't. You'd be thinking about protecting me. But..." She hesitated, then softly admitted, "I wasn't trying to protect you. I was just focused on staying alive."

He stared at her a moment. Once he finally opened his mouth to speak, though, he was stopped by Grant's return. He handed a first-aid kit to Tony, then wrapped the robe he carried around Selena's shoulders. The terrycloth was warm and smelled of him when she slid her arms into the sleeves.

Tony cleaned and bandaged the six-inch cut on her leg, then, as sirens sounded outside, checked the bump on her head. He gazed into her eyes—looking for answers or checking her pupils? she wondered—before pressing a kiss to her forehead. "That'll be the sheriff's deputies. I'm going down to talk to them. They'll want to take pictures and gather evidence from the balcony, so why don't you two wait in the parlor?"

Though the family room was more comfortable, the parlor was on the opposite side of the house from the man's body. Was he trying to protect Grant or her?

When she nodded, he kissed her again, then walked out.

She eased to her feet with a grunt of pain, tied the robe's belt around her middle, and gathered the excess fabric in one hand before offering her other arm to Grant. "Would you like to escort me downstairs?"

"I would be happy to. And when we get there, I would be happy to fix us both a drink." He took her arm the way a gentleman should, and they left the room.

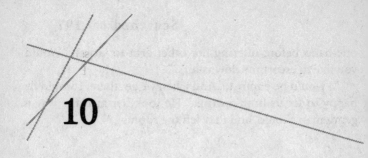

10

With the security guards back at the gates and two teams of men patrolling the grounds, Tony joined the sheriff, a potbellied man named McEntire, outside next to the intruder's body. Two of the sheriff's deputies were gathering evidence on the balcony above while a third did the same downstairs.

"He doesn't have an ID on him," McEntire said. "You recognize him?"

Tony looked at the man—blond, unseeing eyes, unshaven—and shook his head. The guy bore no resemblance to Damon Long and was ten years too old for Luke Morgan. Had Morgan subbed out the hit? Or had Long offered the job to others besides Charlize and Morgan?

"There's a woman in town at the Azalea Inn named Charlize Pawley. She might be able to identify him."

McEntire's gaze turned speculative. "And would she know him?"

Tony shrugged.

"Should we bring her out here or have her take a look in town?"

"In town." One killer had already gained access to the grounds. Tony wasn't giving the okay for another to come in.

Turning away, the sheriff murmured something to the deputy who, in response, summoned the two men leaning against the coroner's van. The body bag was nothing more than a shadow on the gurney they wheeled across the grass. As they began the job of collecting the body, McEntire said, "We'll need a statement from Ms. McCaffrey."

"Later, okay? She can't tell you anything more than I already have."

McEntire nodded. "How is she?"

"She's okay." On the surface, she was always okay. She could take care of herself. She didn't need anything from anyone.

That wasn't true, honesty forced him to admit. She needed *him*. She just found it difficult to remember and to communicate that. He couldn't blame her. She'd had twenty-eight years of being on her own, compared to only a few months with him. Eventually, though, her thinking would change. Being part of a couple would become natural to her. Her instincts would regear themselves to that new reality. He could be patient until then.

Standing back, he watched the activity outside the house, both on the ground and on the balcony. He'd been to more crime scenes than he could count, but this one hit closest to home. If Selena hadn't been awake, the bastard could have forced his way into their room, killed them both, and made his escape from the grounds while the guards were busy securing the house.

As the coroner's people left with the body, the sheriff lit a cigar and drew deeply on it before speaking. "They found the place on the other side of the house where he climbed up to the balcony with the help of a grappling hook and rope. Both guards at the front and rear doors were knocked out."

"Which explains how he got to our bedroom but not how he got onto the property." Security confirmed there had been nothing out of the ordinary since the night before.

"Either he came in through one of the gates or he dropped out of the sky."

McEntire glanced at the night sky as if contemplating it. "A determined man will find a way. But we'd have a parachute lying around somewhere, and we don't."

"So how did he get through the gate? Every employee was issued an ID. No one's supposed to get in without one." June Ravenel had complained about hers. Luther had been tickled by his.

"Maybe one of the guards slacked off. One of them took a bribe to let the guy in. One of the employees smuggled him in. When there's a half million dollars at stake, anything's possible."

Great. Tony had asked Simmons to look at arrest records. Now he'd have to check out financial records, as well. He was really going to bitch about that.

Leaving the sheriff and his deputies to their job, Tony went inside. Grant sat on the sofa while Selena was several feet away in the chair she preferred. In spite of the huge robe, she looked dignified. In spite of the fact that she'd fought off an assassin, that the man had died in the process, she looked serene. Unruffled.

A decanter sat on the table in front of the sofa, and Grant held a glass. Grant offered him the second glass. "Scotch? The best available. Wonderful for settling your nerves."

Tony shook his head.

"Of course not. You're a homicide detective. Your nerves don't get unsettled, do they?" Grant exhaled loudly. "I don't know how you two stay so calm. If this sort of thing happened very often, they'd have to lock me up in the psych ward with Kathryn."

"You're entitled to be shaken," Tony said. "Your home was invaded and your daughter could have been killed. But it won't happen again." He watched Selena hide a delicate yawn behind her hand, then closed the distance between them. "You need to get to bed."

"I don't..."

"Do what he says," Grant urged. "Rest will be good for us all."

Tony extended his hand to Selena. She hesitated, then capped the water bottle she held, took his hand, and stood with a grimace. "How's your headache?" he asked.

"Better. Did you find out anything?"

"Not much more than we knew to start. We'll figure it out in the morning."

With Grant a few steps behind, they slowly climbed the stairs to the second floor, saying goodnight there. When Selena would have turned into their room, Tony pulled her into the bedroom across the hall. She followed without comment, let him lead her to the bed, remove the robe, and tuck her in. When he lay down beside her, she turned on her side to face him, even though it was too dark to see.

"I'm sorry."

"Don't be," he said with less sincerity than he'd hoped for. "You're new to this relationship stuff."

"I love you."

She didn't say the words easily—had never said them to anyone before him, had never heard them from anyone before him. They went a long way toward easing the hurt still simmering inside him. "I love you, too."

Even if she still broke his heart from time to time.

"Hey, kiddo, it's time for bed."

Charlize stared so hard at the textbook open in front of

her that the words grew blurry. "I'm not done with my homework."

"You've been doing homework all night. If you're not done now, you'll just have to take the bad grade. Come on."

Underneath the dining table, her fingers clenched her pencil as she forced the fear and loathing down. The slender wood snapped, a sharp edge poking her palm, as she mumbled, "But I have a test tomorrow."

"Now, Charlize." The softness was gone from John Turner's voice, replaced by steel. He could go from loving to stern to regretful in the space of a heartbeat, from coaxing to forcing so quickly that she never stood a chance.

She laid the pencil pieces on the book, then pushed her chair back. As she stood, she kept her gaze lowered. She didn't want to see the look in her father's eyes—the hunger, the anticipation. She might be only thirteen, but she knew it was wrong for a father to look at his daughter that way. No matter what he said, it was horribly wrong.

Her feet dragged across the floor. She knew how many steps it was from the kitchen door to the bed he'd once shared with her mother, and they counted down in her head with an ominous beat. Twenty, nineteen, eighteen...

"Come on," he ordered from the hallway.

She wanted to refuse, to run away, to beg him to leave her alone just this one night. But if she refused, he would force her. If she ran away, he'd drag her back. If she begged him to stop, he did it anyway.

Five, four, three, two...

He touched her, and her skin crawled. Slid his arm around her, and her stomach heaved. He smelled of beer and cigarettes and death, and she prayed to God to save her from the things he intended to—

Charlize jerked awake, half rising from the bed, her

breathing loud and ragged in the quiet room. Where the hell—

Greenhill. The motel. Alone. She was safe.

She sank down again, shoved her hair from her face, and checked the bedside clock. It was nearly ten A.M. Sunlight seeped around the rubber-backed drapes, and the sounds of traffic filtered in from the street.

A sheriff's deputy had dragged her from a sound sleep at an ungodly hour that morning, sternly informing her that his boss wanted her to identify a body. *Can't it wait until daylight?* she'd asked. *He'll still be dead.* But she'd gone along with the deputy and, less than ten minutes later, had come face to no-longer-living face with Johnny Peretti at the local hospital.

Johnny had been a friend of John Turner's, a small-time enforcer who had, on occasion, helped out on bigger jobs. Charlize had never hired him herself, but William had. Luke had. Had he brought in Johnny this time? Or was a third person out there, trying to cash in on Damon's contract?

However Johnny had come to be there, now he was dead. Maybe that was what had prompted her dream, or maybe it was the sleeping pill she'd taken when she'd returned to the motel.

With a deep breath, she pushed back the covers and sat up. The chilly air raised goose bumps on the skin left exposed by her ice blue chemise. She rubbed her arms vigorously as she crossed to shut off the air conditioner, then went into the bathroom. She wasn't prone to bad dreams—thank God. This one had left a bad taste in her mouth that she scrubbed out with her toothbrush.

She'd showered, dressed, and was considering lunch

when the phone beside the bed rang. She sat primly on the edge of the bed, drew a breath, then answered.

There was no stab at a polite greeting, just a question. "You know where Harker is?"

Her stomach clenched, and new goose bumps rose on her nape and arms. She was the coolest, least emotional person around, but just the sound of Luke's voice . . . Her mouth thinned as her fingers tightened around the phone. "Small town. About fifteen miles southwest of Greenhill."

"There's a restaurant on the north edge of town, kind of a shanty, built on the riverbank. Meet me there in thirty minutes."

Before she could tell him no, he hung up.

Slowly, she did the same. She didn't have to go. She'd never taken orders from Luke Morgan, and there was no reason to start. But if he was in touch with Damon—and she would bet he was—he might be of some help to her.

Twenty-nine minutes later, she parked in the gravel lot of Cap'n Jim's Seafood Shack. "Shanty" was a kind description. The building looked as old as the dirt underneath it, but there were a dozen cars in the lot—none of them a white pickup.

She paused inside the door to let her eyes adjust to the dimmer light. A waitress hurrying past with plates of fried food greeted her with a nod. "Sit wherever you want, honey. The deck's awfully nice today. I'll be right with you."

Charlize didn't bother looking around the dining room. If outside seating was available, that was where Luke would be. He didn't like the confinement of walls and shuttered windows. Heels clicking on unvarnished wood, she wove between tables to the glass door, stepped onto the deck, and walked to the only occupied table. Luke's back was to the building, one foot propped on a chair, one arm resting on the railing. In jeans and T-shirt, with an orange Auburn ball cap pulled low over dark shades, he looked unremarkable.

Setting her purse, with its .22, on the table, she slid into the chair opposite him, crossed her legs, folded her arms, and waited for him to speak. It took only a moment.

"Is it true? Johnny's dead?"

"Yes. I saw his body myself."

"Goddamn. That sorry fucker..." He grimly shook his head.

His regret seemed sincere. Why shouldn't it? He'd met Johnny soon after going to work for John Turner. They'd been regular pals—Luke, her father, Johnny, and a few others.

Was that why Luke had refused to believe her? Because John Turner Thomas was his mentor, his partner, his buddy? Had he ever even considered the possibility that John Turner was capable of raping his own daughter, or had he simply written her off as a lying bitch?

"What happened?"

"He tried to kill Selena and failed."

"You don't seem too upset by it."

"Why should I be?" Her shrug was careless to match her tone. "You do seem upset. Did you send him there to do your job for you?"

The door swung open and the waitress came out, menu in one hand, glass of water in the other. She delivered both to Charlize and gave Luke an admiring look before leaving again. He didn't seem to even notice she was there.

When they were alone again, he showed no intention of answering the question. In the end, she reflected, it didn't really matter.

She scanned the menu, settling on broiled shrimp, then

fixed her gaze on him. "Have you ever wanted to do the right thing, Luke?"

He bristled. "I always do what's right for me."

"It's not a question of right for you or me or anyone else. It's right. Period. Morally, ethically." How could she discuss morals and ethics with someone who had neither? There was no honor among thieves, and certainly no honor among contract killers. Money and looking out for himself—those were the only things that mattered to Luke.

"I have an offer for you."

"I'm listening." Though he didn't straighten in his chair, remove his sunglasses, or show any interest at all.

"You help me locate Damon Long, and I'll pay you a hundred grand."

He snorted. "He's offering me five hundred grand to kill your friend."

"You and who else? He told me the contract was exclusively mine, but he lied. He'd hired you, too. And if you didn't hire Johnny, that means Damon did. If you get Selena, you get the money. If someone else does, you get nothing for your time. And if you keep trying, you stand a very good chance of dying yourself. However, if you accept my offer, you get a hundred thousand dollars for nothing more than information. That's better than nothing anytime."

He stared at her a long time. She could feel the intensity of his gaze in spite of the shades that covered his eyes. Abruptly, he shifted in the chair, letting his foot hit the deck with a thud, picked up his iced tea, and drained half the glass. "For two hundred grand, I'll kill him for you."

"I could put out a contract on him for half that, even less."

"Not to anyone who knows him. Certainly not to anyone who's currently in contact with him."

That was true. Those who knew Long knew he wouldn't be an easy kill, and those working for him at the present time wouldn't give up their shot at a half million for a fraction of it.

She shook her head. "I want to kill him myself."

"Why? You don't take things personally."

"I take some things *very* personally." Like betrayal. Disillusionment.

He shifted in his seat, though it was hard to say whether it was discomfort or natural movement.

"Are you going to risk your life for a chance at Long's contract, or would you rather have a sure hundred thousand dollars?"

"You keep talking about killing me, but I'm still kicking. Makes me think maybe it's just talk."

She smiled coolly. "I told my father on my fifteenth birthday that if he ever laid a hand on me again, I'd kill him. He thought it was just talk, too. One week later, he was dead." Softening her voice as the waitress reappeared, she finished, "I don't make idle threats, Luke. You should know that. So . . . do you want the job?"

For having survived a fight to the death with a stranger, Selena was little the worse for wear Thursday afternoon. Her physical aches had receded to mild nuisances. Emotionally . . .

She smiled grimly. The man had left her no choice. She wasn't responsible for his death. She had merely protected herself.

And if she repeated that often enough, maybe the regret would go away.

"Can I get you anything, Miss Selena?"

She glanced at Nell, standing in the doorway. While the housekeeper had warmed up to Tony immediately—who hadn't?—she had maintained a formal distance with Selena. This morning the formality remained, but it was softened by concern. She practically hovered.

"No, thank you, Nell. I'm fine."

With a nod, Nell left, humming to herself an old gospel tune. The sound was reassuringly normal.

Idly Selena fingered the knot on her head. Tony was upstairs in Grant's office, and Grant was elsewhere, returning business calls that couldn't wait. Only she was left with nothing to do but think about death. Life. Taking it. Preserving it. Drawing into the open Damon Long, Luke Morgan, and anyone else interested in killing her. Stopping them.

Killing them?

Before Selena could feel more than her normal revulsion for such an act, Nell came in again, carrying the cordless phone. "Call for you, miss. Actually, she asked to speak to Tony, but when I told her he was busy, she asked for you."

It was Charlize, of course. Who else knew to call them there?

"This is Selena," she said in greeting.

"I hear you had an eventful night."

"So did you." Tony had told Selena that morning about Charlize's identification of the man she had bested. Had Charlize known him well? Had it saddened her to see him dead? Or had she simply not cared?

"Losing an hour or two of sleep doesn't bother me." Charlize paused. "How are you?"

"I'm all right." *Liar.*

"He left you no choice. He would have killed you and

Tony, and believe me, he wouldn't have felt a moment's regret."

"Do you?"

"Do I feel regret for Johnny?"

"For any of them." The man Selena had killed, all the people Charlize had killed. After twenty years in the business, the number must have been substantial. For Selena, even one was too many.

"I can't say that I do."

No apologies, no excuses, just a simple truthful answer. Selena didn't understand it, but she appreciated the honesty.

"I called to tell you that Luke Morgan is in town. He was probably the one who sent Johnny after you."

"Do you know where to find him?"

"Not yet. Nothing on Long, either. He's gone to ground somewhere."

"If you find him, will you let us know?"

Charlize paused before replying, "You'll find out. Stay safe." The line went dead with a click.

They would find out when Damon Long's body was discovered. That wasn't the answer Selena had wanted.

She was still holding the phone when Tony came in, a paper in hand. He studied her face, then the phone. "Who was that?"

She told him, and his jaw tightened. Ignoring it, she repeated the conversation, leaving out only the part about regrets. His jaw was clamped harder by the time she finished. Wishing for a change in subject, she gestured to the paper. "What is that?"

His fingers flexed as he sat down beside her. "Frankie located a Rodrigo Alfredo Acosta living in Playa Vicente with his wife Luisa and the youngest of their thirteen children."

He offered a copy of a driver's license, but she didn't take it. Her fingers wouldn't unclench, and she could see well enough without actually touching the paper. He was older, of course. Fleshier. More dissipated. But there was no question it was Rodrigo.

No question that he was the man in Grant's photos.

Not sure she could find her voice, she simply nodded.

"He *was* in Alabama twenty-eight years ago, working on a farm on the other side of town, owned by a family by the name of Leland. He returned to Puerto Rico shortly after you and your mother disappeared, and he hasn't held a regular job since then." Tony's tone shifted, becoming taut, barely controlled, anger underlaying the words. "According to the local authorities, he mostly drinks while his wife works. He had an arrest record while he was here—petty stuff like public drunk, assault—and a couple more assault charges since he went back to Puerto Rico. They say he's a mean drunk."

Selena cringed inwardly. That was an understatement. It was pure luck that she'd survived his binges.

Tony pried her fingers apart, then gripped her hand. "He'll regret it."

She doubted it. People like Rodrigo—like Charlize?—didn't regret their actions. They only regretted getting caught. When this mess was over, the only ones who would feel remorse were the ones drawn in against their will—herself, for contributing to Johnny Peretti's death, and Tony, if stopping Damon Long involved killing him. No matter that Tony thought he was prepared for the consequences.

Footsteps sounded in the hall a moment before June came into the room, unaware of them until she'd covered half the distance to where they sat. She wore a navy blue suit with a white blouse buttoned to the collar. Neither the tailoring nor the color was flattering to her, no more than the chunky navy blue heels or the stockings that were a shade off for her. In all the pictures Selena had seen of Amelia, style had come naturally. She could have pulled off the outfit. June just looked dowdy, and knew it.

Her gaze skimmed over Selena, then Tony, before lingering on the photo Tony still held. Her eyes widened as fear flashed. Did she think it was a new threat for her to worry about? She stared at the photo before raising her gaze. "Grant asked me to wait for him here," she announced to the room in general. "I didn't know you were . . ."

Tony squeezed Selena's fingers before releasing them and standing. "I need to make another call. I'll be back later."

Selena wanted to ask him to stay—she was sure there was no call to make. He just wanted to give her private time with June. Considering the way their last conversation had gone, Selena wasn't sure she wanted another just yet. But he was already walking away, and she made no move to stop him.

June stood in the middle of the room as if she couldn't decide whether to stay or go. When the sofa creaked as Selena shifted, June started, then gave her a wary look.

"Have a seat, please. I'm sure Grant won't be long."

June sat on one of the chairs, rigidly perched on the edge, heels side by side on the floor.

"I missed Luther's company today."

Bad topic. The tension vibrating through June amplified. "He's not coming over here again. It's not safe. *You're* not safe."

"What happened last night was a one-time thing," Selena assured her, though she wasn't completely assured herself. If Peretti could sneak onto the property, who else might succeed? But the security team and their measures were both under scrutiny, and additional measures had been taken. The odds of a second incident had definitely been minimized.

"It only takes one time," June said sharply. "My father is frail. I won't let anyone place him in danger, especially you."

Not *your grandfather*, but *my father*. June had been so much more a part of Luther's life, and she wasn't about to let Selena forget it—or take her place. But Selena didn't *want* her place. She just wanted to know her family and, through them, her mother. "I'm not competing with you for Luther's affection."

June snorted. "As if you could."

But that was exactly what she was afraid of. Selena had seen the way June flinched when Luther looked at his new granddaughter, when he spoke to her—had seen the disregard he showed June when Selena was around. It wasn't intentional. Luther was a kind old man who loved his daughter. He was simply so caught up in having Amelia's daughter back again that he didn't realize his actions were hurtful to June.

"I'm new," she said with a bit of a smile. "Before long, Luther will get used to me, and things will go back to normal."

If it was possible, June's posture grew even more rigid. "Do you think I'm worried about you? Jealous of you? Let me tell you something, girl. I've always been here for Daddy. I was here when Mama died, when Amelia disappeared, when he needed nursing and someone to keep house for him and look after him. I've always been here for him, and I always will be, and he knows that. You think he's gonna count on *you* to launder his clothes and cook his meals and take him to church every week?" Her laugh was short, sharp.

"He may be old, but he's no fool. He knows he can't depend on you any more than he could your mama. Do you know she was late to our own mama's funeral? She didn't even have enough respect for the dead to show up on time. Told Daddy and me she was grieving in her own way. Ha! She was just too damn selfish to set aside her partying long enough to help out."

Grieving had nothing to do with being in a certain place at a certain time, Selena wanted to point out. Amelia had never had a funeral, had never been found to bury, but people had grieved for her. Grant and Luther still grieved for her.

But Selena kept that to herself and, instead, agreed. "She should have been more respectful." Yes, Amelia had lost her mother, but so had June, and Luther had lost his wife of thirty years.

June surged to her feet and paced to the fireplace. "The only thing Amelia ever respected was her own wishes. She excelled at this sort of thing." Her gesture took in the entire area, including Selena. "Going out, stirring up trouble, then running back home so that everyone else had to deal with it. Setting her sights on a rich white man, taking him away from his wife, having a baby with him...If anyone's to blame for Amelia's death, it's Amelia herself. You just can't do the things she did and not suffer the consequences. Everyone understood that but her."

"You didn't like her, did you?" Selena asked quietly.

June fingered a filigree frame on the mantel. It had been on display only a day or so, a snapshot of a heavily pregnant Amelia standing in the nursery of her house, curls pulled back and tied with a scarf, beaming a smile that could melt a glacier. "I loved her," June murmured, then her voice strengthened. "And I wished she'd never been born."

Wished, by extension, that Selena had never been born.

Picking up the frame, June cradled it in her hands. "She could light up the entire universe. It's no surprise Grant forgot his wife and his marriage when he met her. People adored her. All the girls wanted to be her best friend. All the boys wanted to date her."

And June had wanted to be like her. Had wanted some small part of that adoration for herself.

"Every man who ever knew her was in love with her. But she didn't care about none of them. She was wild and free, out for a good time, getting what she wanted, and to hell with everybody else. Until she met Grant. She said he was different, but no one believed her. She was too flighty, too dedicated to enjoying life. But she settled down. Got pregnant. Would have stayed . . . for a while."

"She would have stayed forever, if Kathryn hadn't intervened."

The frame slipped from June's fingers at the sound of Grant's voice, landing harmlessly on the rug. Nervously she ducked to scoop it up again and set it on the mantel, then smoothed her jacket before twining her unsteady fingers together. Startled though she was by his eavesdropping, she didn't retract her words. She said nothing at all as he came into the room.

Selena looked from aunt to father. June wanted to believe Amelia hadn't changed from the self-centered egoist she resented. Grant wanted to believe he'd mattered that much to her. Either could be right—or neither.

June took a purposeful step forward. "You wanted to see me, Grant?"

"I have a few things to go over with you. Selena, honey, do you mind?"

More touched by the endearment than she'd expected,

Selena excused herself from the room and went to the kitchen, where Nell was frosting a cake for the evening's dessert. If life was better—normal—she would be thinking about dinner now. Grilled chicken with mango, perhaps, or chilled shrimp marinated in salsa. She and Tony would clean up afterward together, then talk, watch television, or go for a walk. At bedtime, they would settle in—Mutt in the bedroom with them, the cats in their respective hiding places, and they would make love or sleep or both, without a thought to danger.

With a nod to Nell, she took a glass from the cabinet, filled it with ice, then poured mint-flavored iced tea to the top. Back in the hall, she could still hear voices from the family room, so she turned into the shorter side hall. At the end, a tall window looked out over the lawn; on the left was a door. It had been closed ever since she'd arrived at the house, and the space hadn't been included on Grant's tour. Opening it, she found a sunroom.

Windows lined both outside walls, hung with frilly valances that matched the fabrics on the wicker sofa and chairs. Ferns and ivies were scattered around the room, dead and brown in their pots; framed photographs covered the walls and marble-topped tables; and an oil painting hung over the fireplace. The artist was competent, the subject young, smiling, looking as if the world was his to command.

Jefferson Hamilton, better known to Selena as Sonny Yates. The drug dealer who'd tried to kill her. Her adopted brother. He'd lived in this house, been given every privilege denied her, and he'd chosen to throw it all away.

Distantly she was aware of Grant and June saying good-bye in the hall, of Grant's heavy steps, of his calling her name, then stopping at the juncture of the hallways. Slowly he joined her, laying his hand on her arm.

"Kathryn began talking about adoption maybe six months after you and your mother disappeared. I think she thought she could replace you and everything would be all right again. I knew it was hopeless, but everything was hopeless then. I eventually gave in because I just didn't care."

He continued to gaze at the portrait. "She got Jefferson through an agency in Atlanta. They were such a match—he needed someone, and she needed to be needed. He was five when she got him—too old, supposedly, to remind me of you. He was a quiet boy when he came here, all wide-eyed and afraid. He got over that after a while, though."

Sonny Yates afraid. It was hard to imagine the man who'd beaten her as a frightened young child. He'd been so brash, confident, conscienceless, and hadn't given a damn about anyone in the world besides himself, his mother, and Charlize.

"I wasn't a good father. It's one of my biggest regrets that I can't even say I tried. Jefferson wasn't my son. He wasn't a real part of my life. He was just *there,* he and Kathryn. Wallpaper. Background noise. I didn't do the things with him that a father should—didn't teach him or play with him or give him an example to follow. I ignored him, and gave Kathryn far too much influence over him."

Selena didn't tell him it wasn't his fault. It was. He'd had a choice. He had agreed to bring a child into his family, and he'd had an obligation to him, no matter that he was grieving for his own child.

After a moment, Grant released her and moved farther into the room. "This solarium was Kathryn's space. She entertained in the parlor or on the veranda, but this was where she came when she was alone. Her sanctuary, she called it.

She read here, arranged her busy schedule. Every day when Jefferson came home from school, he'd come here and tell her about his day. She planned here, dreamed here, schemed here."

As his voice faded, Selena moved, too, circling the room, skimming over the pictures that documented Kathryn's life. Childhood birthdays, high school, the prom. Family portraits with William, handsome and debonair, at her side. Jefferson, from childhood to adulthood. Her wedding day with Grant, scenes from their honeymoon, formal events, and holidays over the next few years, then no more of him. For all practical purposes, their marriage had ended not long after it started, but she'd never been willing to let go.

What if she had? If she'd let Amelia and Grant be together? If she'd tried to find happiness outside of Grant, started life anew both for herself and her son? Amelia might still be alive. So might Sonny.

But *what if*s were pointless. Nothing in the past could be changed.

Grant gazed around the room. "I haven't been in here in years. When I came back from Tulsa, I told Nell to just leave it as it was. I guess I should have her pack everything and dispose of it." He sighed. "I really don't want . . ."

Didn't want the reminders? Or didn't want to get rid of them?

"Don't do it on my account," she said quietly. "Kathryn was a part of your life for a long time. So was Sonny. They lived here. It was their home."

"It seems unfair to you. To Amelia."

"It's not. If these things bothered me, it would be a simple matter of staying out of the room. But they don't." Looping her arm through his, she started toward the door. Deliberately lightening her tone, she asked, "If I give you a list of art supplies I'd like to have, could you arrange for someone to pick them up?"

Relief at the change of topic was evident in his voice. "Anything you want, honey. I'll take care of it first thing in the morning."

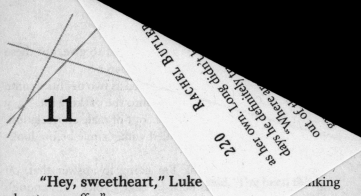

11

"Hey, sweetheart," Luke ⌁⌁⌁ ⌁⌁king about your offer."

Switching the cell phone to her o⌁⌁ ⌁and, Charlize flipped on her turn signal. Rush hour in Greenhill lasted about fifteen minutes, and she was right in the middle of it, which meant waiting for four cars to pass before she could pull into the nearest parking lot, which happened to be shared by the sheriff's and police departments. Not an ideal place to have a conversation with a man like Luke. "Of course you have. You're a smart man." About as trustworthy as a snake, but smart.

"You've got a deal. Half now, half when the job's done."

She eased into a parking space, rolled down the windows, then shut off the engine. "Deal. Where's Long?"

"Haven't got a clue. But he called a while ago and left a message. Something about having some inside information. I was, uh, otherwise occupied and didn't talk to him." His intimate tone hinted at exactly what had occupied him—no doubt female, large-breasted, and empty-headed. "When I call him back, I'll find out what I can."

"He's not going to just volunteer where he's staying."

"I'm not going to just ask."

Of course not. Luke had ways of getting information from people, ranging from charm to coercion to torture, and a working relationship with Long that went back as far

have much trust to give, but these
trusted Luke more than her.

"...e *you* staying?" she asked as two deputies came
...e redbrick building and into the parking lot. They
gave her a first and a second look, out of male appreciation,
not suspicion, and she responded with a smile before looking away.

"You don't really think I'm going to answer that, do
you?" The intimacy was back in Luke's voice. "It's enough
for you to know that I'm someplace where no one will find
me. You got a pen? Write this down."

Switching the phone to her left hand, she withdrew a
notebook from her purse, opened it to a blank page, then
made a note of the account number he gave her. She'd been
the recipient of numerous such transfers over the years. This
would be the first—and last—time she made one herself.

"I'll be in touch once I've confirmed the money's in the
bank." He clicked off, and after a moment, she closed her
phone and returned it and the notebook to her bag.

Though they'd just reached an agreement, she wouldn't
make the mistake of trusting Luke. Normally, his loyalties
were to the best deal, and hers was the better of the two, but
there was nothing normal between them. Any information
he gave might lead straight to Long or into a trap set *with*
Long. He could take these last conversations to Long and
persuade him to put out a contract on her. He could be bull-
shitting her, with no intention of turning on his current
boss. He could be planning to collect the payoff for killing
Selena, then turn Long over to her for a bonus.

But trust had nothing to do with using him. As long as
she stayed on her guard, she would be safe.

She never let down her guard for anyone.

"What's on your mind?"

Lying on his side on the four-poster bed, papers spread in front of him, Tony watched as Selena let the curtain fall back over the French door. She wore his T-shirt, along with the robe Grant had given her the night before, and looked beautiful and sexy and unsettled. She'd been distracted all evening—restless, he'd thought, and in Selena, that wasn't a good thing.

She moved from the door to the nearby bookcase, paying great attention to but hardly noticing the stuff it held. At his suggestion, they'd moved to a different bedroom for the night—their third in twenty-four hours. With lights on in every bedroom, no one but Grant knew which one they occupied.

Finally she turned to face him. "June said Luther can't come over here anymore. She says I'm too dangerous."

He grinned. "Luther's seventy-nine years old. I imagine he does pretty much what he wants."

Her smile came and went quickly. "I'd like to think she's being difficult because of Amelia, but being around me *can* be dangerous. If anything happened to him because of me..."

"Nothing's going to happen."

"You can't promise that. Neither can I. Maybe it *would* be best if he stayed away. Maybe it would be best if we left."

Tony shook his head. "You're safer here than you'd be on the run."

"But is anyone else safer? Luther? Grant? June?"

"I think any hitter who ran up against June would live to regret it."

That brought more of a smile. "She *is* a little..."

"Tough? Strict? Bitchy?"

"She's protecting her father. Maybe, by being here, I'm not." She came to sit on the bed, drawing her knees to her chest, resting her chin on them. "I feel sorry for her. She could never compete with Amelia. Everyone loved Amelia more than they did June—even June herself. It must have been tough, living your entire life knowing you could never measure up to someone else."

Tony reached for her hand, sliding his fingers between hers. "I guess. Being the best of the Ceola gang, I can't speak from experience."

Shifting sinuously, she lay on the bed beside him. "I don't know. Dominic is terribly handsome with those wicked dark eyes."

"Hey, his eyes are just like mine. Besides, he's too young for you."

"He's my age, isn't he?"

"Twenty-eight going on eight." One-handed, Tony worked open the belt on Selena's robe, then pushed the heavy fabric back. There was a faint chill in the air, but not enough to justify the robe. It was more of a security blanket, he figured, like sleeping in his shirt. "Don't worry about June. She'll come around—"

"Or not."

"And Luther will be back over here tomorrow, I bet. He can't stay away from 'baby girl' too long."

Heat flushed through her. "It's a silly nickname for a grown woman."

"It'd be silly if I called you that. Coming from your elderly grandfather, it's sweet."

"I think so, too," she murmured. For a moment, she looked supremely satisfied. Most of the people in her life had called her by other names, but none of them had been sweet. There'd been no endearments from the woman she'd believed to be her mother, no pet name more flattering than "nigger" from Rodrigo. How wrong was it that she'd had to wait twenty-eight years to get that kind of affection from someone?

With a sigh, she shed the robe, rolled onto her stomach, and picked up the papers he'd shoved aside. "What is this?"

"The sheriff subpoenaed the bank records for every employee of Hamilton Farms, and this guy popped up. He had a ten-thousand-dollar deposit to his account just today from a bank in the Caymans."

Damon Long preferred the Caymans for his banking. Maybe Luke Morgan did, as well, Selena thought as she studied the Alabama driver's license photocopy on the top page. It identified the man as Elpidio Vargas, age twenty-four, and gave an address in Greenhill.

The bank records showed little activity: a paycheck on the first and fifteenth, rent, car insurance, and two international wire transfers every month to Caridad Vargas. "Is Caridad his wife?"

"Mother. She's a widow; he helps her take care of his younger brothers and sisters."

"Ten thousand dollars could do a lot of taking care of."

"Yeah. But look at the deposit. The money was transferred around noon today. Peretti was already dead."

"Maybe he initiated the transfer before he died, and for whatever reason it took that long to complete. Or maybe he instructed someone else to make the deposit after he was sure Vargas had lived up to his end of the bargain." She fell silent a moment. "Or someone could be setting him up—Long or the person who was really responsible for getting Peretti onto the property."

"Or Charlize," Tony suggested. When Selena gave him a

chastising look, he shrugged. "I can't help it. I'm grateful as hell that she saved your life when Yates was trying to kill you, but it doesn't change the fact that she's a stone-cold killer. She murders people she's never even laid eyes on, and she does it for money. She needs to be locked away somewhere."

"Sometimes people really believe they have no choice. When William ordered me to kill you—"

"Huh-uh. Not the same. You never would have done it. You never *could* have done it. Charlize has done it. Repeatedly. For half her life. And it doesn't even bother her."

"You don't know what bothers her," Selena said gently as she continued to study the financial records. "You don't think Vargas is guilty."

He let her change the subject with some relief. "He knew almost to the penny how much money he had in the bank before the deposit. He didn't believe us about the ten grand until we showed him the bank printout, and he was either shocked or one hell of a good actor."

"Gut instinct," she prodded.

Tony didn't need to consider it. "I don't believe he's guilty. His crew supervisor says he's a good worker. He doesn't drink, doesn't get into trouble, hasn't missed a day of work since he started. He goes to church every Sunday morning. His neighbors hardly know he exists. He doesn't have family here, or any friends who would help or even care if he got into trouble. He doesn't speak much English."

"He's a perfect sucker."

He nodded.

"And if whoever's really guilty was savvy enough to set up a fall guy, then he's savvy enough to keep Peretti's payoff off the books."

Grinning, Tony wrapped one short curl around his finger. "I like it when you talk wise guy."

With a faint smile, she stacked the pages neatly and laid them on the night table, then lay back beside him. "I'm going to paint Luther's portrait," she announced, then ruefully added, "If June lets me see him again."

"You'll see him. He'll make sure of it."

She was silent for a time before softly asking, "What do you think William did with my mother's body?"

He'd been waiting for this question ever since they'd visited Amelia's house—had thought of all the places bodies could be buried, tossed, chopped up, burned, or sunk. Sometimes they were found right away. Sometimes, if the grave or the water was deep enough, they were never found. Sometimes there was nothing left to find.

He didn't want to discuss specifics with her. Didn't want to point out that her mother could have been buried in any isolated spot across the state or been devoured by wild animals or fish. Didn't want to tell her that the odds of ever finding enough of Amelia to give a proper burial were somewhere between slim and none. "I have no idea, babe."

"Her car was missing, too."

"He could have given it to someone. Pushed it into a lake. Sold it to a chop shop for parts or a salvage yard for scrap." He could have put Amelia's body in the trunk and watched as the car—and the proof of his sister's crime—was crushed into a two-by-four-foot chunk of metal.

"He had no regard for her," Selena murmured. "She was a human being—someone's daughter, someone's mother— and he disposed of her as if she were garbage."

"But he felt something for you," Tony reminded her as his arm tightened around her shoulders. "He didn't kill you. He gave you to someone to raise. He paid Rodrigo all those years for taking you."

"For beating me." Her tone became determined. "When

this is over, I'm going to Puerto Rico. I want to talk to him. I want to know what he knows."

If Tony were in her situation, talking to Rodrigo was the last thing he'd want. But he could only imagine her situation. As she'd pointed out with regard to Charlize, he couldn't know what was going through Seleña's head. He could empathize with her, stand by her, support her, and kick Rodrigo's ass for her—as if she couldn't do it herself—but he couldn't truly *know*.

"You know you can't trust anything he says unless you beat it out of him."

Her smile was thin, unamused. "I know."

"He won't have any apologies or regrets."

"I know that, too, but I still need to try."

Needed to know his connection to her mother, needed to hear whatever details he could fill in, even if it meant sifting through lies for truth. Though Tony had a large, close family of his own, or maybe because of that, he understood. "When this is over, we'll go."

She gave him a sidelong look. "You don't have to go with me."

"I know."

"After a week or two of Simmons filling in for you, they'll never let you have any time off again."

He chuckled. "Frankie's not such a putz."

"Sure, he is. But he's your putz." Gently she touched his cheek. "Thank you."

"For what?"

"Everything," she said simply.

Catching her hand, he pressed a kiss to the palm. "You're welcome." For everything. For always.

———

A pickup rumbled past on the highway, raucous music blasting out its windows, disturbing the night. June frowned until it was gone and continued to frown long after the quiet had settled again.

Normally she loved evenings like this, when the moon banished the darkness and the air was neither too warm nor too damp to make sitting on the porch uncomfortable. Lately, though, it seemed there had been nothing normal about life. Ever since Selena came to town.

June was dressed for bed, and had been for hours, in a plain ivory nightgown, terry-cloth slippers, and a housecoat. The robe was made of cotton in a horrid print—purple and red flowers on a pale green background—and it zipped up the front, had two patch pockets, and came to her knees. It was ugly, styled for somebody twenty years older to wear forty-some years ago, and Luther had thought it an appropriate gift for her on her last birthday.

He never would have dreamed of giving such a thing to Amelia.

When he'd fallen asleep in his recliner during *CSI*, she'd been relieved. He'd started harping about seeing Selena the moment she'd walked in the door, and he hadn't stopped until then. *I'm a grown man. You can't tell me what to do. You can't keep me away from my grandbaby. You're my daughter, not my boss. I've earned the right to do as I please.*

It wasn't safe, she'd explained to him over and over, but he'd been too stubborn to hear. *If the good Lord is ready to take me, then He'll take me, whether I'm with baby girl, down at the creek fishing, or here in my own bed.*

There's not people shooting guns at the creek, she'd argued.

There's not hateful old maids trying to run my life, either, he'd retorted.

Oda Mae was the love of his life, Amelia was the light of his life, and June was a hateful old maid.

Her hands gripped the rocker arms as bitterness threatened to choke her. For the past thirty hours or so, she'd felt as if she just might explode. Ever since she'd called that man. Ever since she'd offered to help him kill Selena.

It was wrong. Dear God in heaven, it was so horribly wrong, but she couldn't help it. A lifetime of never being good enough required that she do *something*, and that seemed the best, the safest solution. Luther would grieve, but he would deal with it, just as he'd dealt with losing Oda Mae and Amelia. Grant would grieve, too, but life would go on, just as it had since he'd lost her the first time. Tony would get over it and, before long, would find someone new—his own kind, this time.

And life would go back to normal for June. Luther would appreciate her again. So would Grant. All the talk about Amelia would stop. The questions would stop. Everyone would blame Damon Long, and June's secrets would be safe. Her life would be saved.

The floor behind her creaked a moment before the screen door did. Luther came out, two glasses in hand. He gave her one, then shuffled to the other rocker. He wore boxers and an old white undershirt—wife-beaters, people called them, though there wasn't a man alive less likely to raise his hand in anger.

The glass held warm milk, Oda Mae's remedy for sleepless nights. Luther's thoughtfulness sent a rush of love-inspired heat through June. He was her life. Always had been. Always would be. There was *nothing* she wouldn't do to protect him.

"That'll take care of what ails you, girl."

No, it won't. "Thank you, Daddy."

He sipped his own milk, then gazed around the yard. "Nice night. Hear that whippoorwill?" He gave a whistle, and off to the left, a bird replied. "Right after your sister moved into that house of hers, she called, wanting to know what whippoorwills looked like. I thought she was goin' to take up birdwatchin'. Your mama liked that, you know. She could get starlings to come up and eat out of her hand. Anyway, pretty girl laughed and said, 'Lord, no, Daddy, I'm gonna *kill* the darn things. They're disturbin' my sleep.'"

June had heard the story a dozen times before and had never been amused by it. It was classic self-centered Amelia.

After rocking a few moments in silence, Luther looked her way. "I know you worry about me, girl. I don't know where I'd be without you, probably in Pine Haven Nursin' Home. I didn't mean to call you a hateful old maid."

She forced a smile. "I am an old maid, Daddy. Fifty-three years old, and never married." Never asked by anyone she'd have. Maybe she wouldn't have been so picky if she'd known how it would feel to be fifty-three and alone. Maybe if she had a family all her own, she wouldn't care so damn much about the family she shared with Amelia.

Leaning across the space that separated them, Luther patted her hand. "You could have had a man. You just didn't want the right one."

"And Amelia did?"

He didn't take offense at her snide tone. As usual, he heard his precious daughter's name and everything else went out the window. "That girl was something," he said, his voice low and filled with wonder. "I remember when she was born. One thirty-eight on a Sunday morning. I held that baby for the first time and I knew my whole life had changed. She was the most important thing that ever happened to me—even more than your mama in some ways.

After your mama died, and then Amelia and baby girl disappeared, I had nothin' left in my life."

"You had me." June forced the words out through a tight throat, through anger and hurt and resentment.

His old eyes blinked, then focused on her. "Well, of course I did." He didn't have to go on. The rest was obvious: *She* didn't count. *She* hadn't changed his life. *She* hadn't given him a reason for living. *She* wasn't something.

"Every night before bed, I prayed for Amelia and her baby," he went on. "I prayed to Oda Mae to watch over 'em, and I prayed to God to bring 'em home again. I know we ain't ever going to see Amelia again. I think I've known that in my heart ever since she went missin'. But to have baby girl again . . . I feel like she's my reward for living all these years. She's the reason I'm still kicking." He drained the last of his milk, then pushed to his feet with a grunt. "G' night, girl. See you in the mornin'."

As he once again shuffled across the porch, then into the house, his soft voice drifted back on the still air. "Oh, yeah, my Selena. She's something. She's my reward, all right."

June stood up and walked to the edge of the porch, where she poured the milk over the pansies planted there, then drew back her arm and threw the glass as hard as she could into the night. An instant later, it shattered on the paved road, and for one moment, she felt as broken and worthless as it now was.

Then something inside her hardened. No more regrets, no more guilt. She'd lived half her life feeling sorry or guilty, and she was sick to death of it. She was going to continue doing what was right for her, and to hell with everyone else. To hell, especially, with Selena.

———

Damon was antsy. It was Friday morning, which meant he'd been at this fucking trailer ninety-six hours. That wasn't so long—in the past, he'd gone to ground in the same shitty place for weeks at a time—but he was tired of it. He wanted to move on. He had a business to rebuild, favors to repay, a few debts to collect on.

But he couldn't go anywhere, do anything, until Selena was dead.

He paced the length of the trailer, one long, filthy room with an even filthier bathroom stuck in one corner. Coming up against the wall in what served as a kitchen, he pivoted around. The only food was prepackaged, the only beer and bottled water as goddamn hot as the day. The ice he'd filled the cooler with had long since melted, and the generator was running low on gas. If Morgan didn't get off his ass and finish this job soon, he was going to need supplies, which meant leaving the trailer or trusting someone to get them for him.

He hadn't trusted anyone but Ruby Dee in a hell of a long time.

He was pacing back to the other end, aware of how he stank with every step, when sound outside stopped him in his tracks. He stared through the open door and saw nothing, but clearly heard the sound of an engine. It was a welcome distraction from the goddamn nature that had begun to grate on his nerves.

Smiling thinly, he touched the pistol holstered on his waistband, but didn't draw it. There was only the one vehicle, probably the bastard who owned this sorry place. The day he couldn't take out an unsuspecting hunter, or even three or four, without a gun was the day he'd waltz into town and turn himself in.

He closed the door, then moved to the nearest window,

separating two slats to peer out. The blinds were crusted with dirt, and a spider skittered along one of the slats until he squished it with his thumb.

The engine grew steadily louder, and finally the vehicle appeared from the surrounding woods. It was a beat-up pickup with dried mud splattered high on the sides. Two rifles hung on a rack across the back window, sharing space with a fishing pole, and there was only one occupant, a white-haired man.

He pulled into the clearing, saw the cot that Damon had dragged out under a tree, and got out muttering. "Goddamn, what's the goddamn bed doing out here? Those fucking kids. I told them to stay away from here..."

He lifted a cooler from the back of the truck and climbed the steps. Damon edged toward the door, his back flat against the wall. The man's keys rattled, and he swore again when he realized the door wasn't locked. He pushed it open, and it swung back, blocking Damon from sight.

He followed the man's movements by the sound of his footsteps—over to the kitchen, cooler dropping onto the counter, back to the door, boots clomping down the steps. Damon waited a moment, then left his cover to stand in the doorway. "Thanks for the food," he called.

The old man stopped in the act of lifting a box from the truck bed. Surprise quickly gave way to annoyance. "There's a goddamn sign out there says no goddamn trespassing. Are you too fucking stupid to read?"

He could kill with his hands, could kill quietly, neatly, when it was to his benefit. Instead, he drew his pistol and put a hole in the old man's head, nice and small in the front, big and ragged in back. The box fell into the bed with a thud, and the old man staggered back to the ground.

"I read just fine, old man." Damon walked down the

steps and looked inside the truck bed. The box held mostly snacks. He grabbed a can of Pringles, tore off the top seal and shook out a handful of chips, then ate them.

Blood had stopped seeping from the wound between the old man's eyes. Dead people didn't bleed. Damon searched his pockets, finding a cheap knife and a wallet with thirty-three dollars; he slid the money into his own pocket, then glanced at the driver's license. Eugene Watkins, with an address in Heavener, Alabama.

"You got family over there in Heavener?" he asked as he wiped the wallet clean, then eased it back where he'd found it. "Anyone who's going to miss you when you don't come back from your fishing trip on time? When would that be? Sunday afternoon? Monday morning?"

Goddamn. The way Damon's luck had been running, there was probably a Mrs. Watkins and she was probably the bitchy type who'd be raising hell if ol' Gene here was so much as an hour late. If she didn't send the sheriff out to check up on him, it would be someone else. Damon had to either move on or make it appear that Gene had never reached the trailer.

After double-bagging the old man's head with a couple of plastic grocery sacks, he heaved the body into the truck bed, then covered it with a sheet from his bunk. Next he returned the cooler to its place next to the snacks, rifled through the glove compartment, found a highway map, and located Heavener some forty miles to the north. He figured the most likely route for Gene to take, climbed behind the wheel, and made a wide turn in the clearing.

A mile away, he passed the place where he'd hidden his own car, marked by nothing more than the broken end of a branch extending a foot onto the road.

Even though he was on constant alert, it felt good to be

away from the damn trailer. Even the air smelled better. Once he was done with Selena, he was never setting foot in a trailer or Alabama again as long as he lived.

The road to Heavener was two lanes, winding through heavy woods, and wasn't much used. Damon chose a spot about fifteen miles from the trailer where there was plenty of room among the tall pines to get the truck off the road. After checking for traffic, he laid out ol' Gene on the ground, in pretty much the same position he'd died, then wadded the bloody plastic bags and rolled them inside the sheet. He used the pocketknife to puncture the right rear tire, watched it go flat, then cleaned the knife and carefully returned it to the old man's pants pocket.

He was interrupted twice by oncoming vehicles. He ducked out of sight each time, his fingers resting lightly on his pistol, but neither car slowed.

Using a corner of the sheet, he wiped down the interior of the truck, then rolled the sheet and the bags into a tight ball, tucked it under his left arm, and headed across the road and into the woods. According to the map, there was another county road only a few miles to the east. It wasn't the easiest of hikes, but he made it in under ninety minutes, including a stop to bury the sheet.

As cars whizzed past on the more heavily traveled road, he flipped open his cell phone and scrolled through the phone book to Luke Morgan's number. "This is Long," he said when Morgan answered. "I need a ride."

The supplies Selena had requested were delivered midmorning Friday. As she unpacked them in the family room, Grant asked, "When did you know you wanted to be an artist?"

"I guess I always knew." She couldn't remember a time when drawing hadn't helped her cope with the hurt, the fear, the feelings of worthlessness. "Rodrigo and Luisa lived a few hundred yards from the ocean, so I spent a lot of time on the beach." She'd learned at a very young age that the less he noticed her, the less he'd hurt her, so she'd avoided the house when he was home as much as possible. "Most of my early masterpieces were done in sand and washed away with the next wave."

Inconsequential—that was what her art had been. What she had been.

"Henry had a great appreciation for art. He must have encouraged you."

Her smile was thin. "Actually, no. He thought it was a distraction from my real talent for breaking the law. He had plans for me, and being an artist wasn't part of them."

The first time she'd entered William's big house in Tulsa was the first she'd learned of his appreciation for the arts. She'd seen his Monets, his Remingtons, his Roybals, and she'd felt such betrayal. He'd controlled her life, threatened her, blackmailed her. He'd let her believe that she'd killed a man—Damon Long in another guise—and had used her guilt and sorrow to demand that she kill a police officer. And yet she'd felt more betrayed by his private collection of great masters. He'd belittled her own artistic aspirations. He'd made her feel unworthy while he'd lived surrounded by such treasures.

"I'd like to have a Selena McCaffrey original in every room."

Arranging an assortment of brushes, she smiled in Grant's direction. "I'll have Asha send me a catalog. You can pick out what you like."

"Tell me about Asha."

She thought of the Haitian woman who'd walked into her life two years ago. Generous in stature and in spirit, Asha had encouraged and supported her from the beginning. She had been the first person to care about Selena and not what Selena could do for her.

"She's very capable, very good at what she does. I don't know what I'd do without her."

"Sounds like your aunt June. If she ever quit, my practice would go down the tubes and probably take the house and the farm with it. She's the best."

"Have you ever told her that?" Selena suspected it was something June hadn't often heard in her life. After all these years, she might be too jaded to believe it, but the sentiment should still be voiced.

"Every month. It's called a paycheck." He grinned at her chastising look. "She knows how important she is."

"It can't hurt to make sure." She took a step back and glanced around. The table and a nearby cabinet top had become a display for her paints and brushes. A canvas was mounted on the easel, and while talking, she'd automatically filled her palette. She was ready to paint for the first time in too long. All she lacked was a subject.

But not for long. Outside the south-facing windows, one of the farm's trucks stopped near the walk and Tony jumped out. He'd been out since breakfast interviewing employees, looking for information to support Vargas's innocence, looking for a finger to point at the real culprit. That person may have been smart enough to set up a fall guy, but he wasn't smart enough to dupe Tony.

He turned back to the truck to help Luther climb to the ground, holding the older man's arm as naturally as June did ... except that Luther didn't shake him off immediately the way he did June.

Selena wasn't sure whether the fuzzy, warm feeling seeping through her was brought on by the sight of Tony, his gentle care with Luther, Luther himself, or all of the above. All she knew was she couldn't stop smiling as she faced Grant. "Tony and Luther are here."

Grant's smile couldn't match hers, but it was filled with pleasure, too. He had a great deal of respect and affection for the man who would have been his father-in-law. "June should have learned by now that you can't stop Luther from doing what he wants. Why don't you decide where you want him to sit, and I'll get him something cold to drink."

Where she would really like to paint Luther was sitting on the bank of the creek at his favorite fishing hole, but she wouldn't waste her breath asking. A more formal portrait would be all right, but she would make time to visit that fishing hole with him at least once when it was safe.

She'd moved a comfortable chair near the windows by the time he and Tony had made the slow walk down the hall. When they came in the door, Tony greeted her with a wink. "Look who I found trying to wheedle his way past the guards at the east gate."

"And they wasn't havin' none of it," Luther declared. "All's they wanted was to see my ID badge, and that's the one thing I didn't have on me."

"Did you forget it?" Selena asked. The east gate was one-third mile from the Ravenel house—a long way for an old man to walk on a warm day.

"Heck, no, I didn't forget it. That girl took it to work with her today. Can you believe she did that?" Luther snorted. "All bossy like her mama. Thinks she can tell me what to do. Ha! I told the boys out there, 'You call Detective Ceola. He'll tell you to let me pass.' And they did and he did and he give me a ride the rest of the way, so here I am." He reached out one arthritic hand to tenderly touch her cheek. "You okay, baby girl?"

Though she still had some tenderness in her ribs and from the cut on her leg, she'd done her best to forget the run-in with Johnny Peretti. "I'm fine." Looping her arm through his, she started toward the chair she'd chosen for him. "I'm glad you decided to visit, but you should have called. Someone could have picked you up."

"Don't you start sounding like Junie. I've been walking for seventy-eight years now. I'm perfectly capable of gettin' from my house to here under my own power." But there was a hint of relief when he sank into the chair. He waved toward her supplies as if to distract her. "What's all this?"

"I'd like to paint your portrait, if you don't mind."

His grin stretched from ear to ear as he sat upright in the chair, straightened his tie, then slipped the fingers of one hand inside his suit coat. "How's this? Is it dignified enough?" Then he crossed his eyes and stuck out his tongue.

It felt remarkably good to laugh, easing the tension Selena had become accustomed to. "Just sit naturally."

"Now you know, at my age, if I sit still too long, I just might fall asleep, and then I just might snore."

"And then she'll poke you in the ribs with her elbow to wake you up," Tony teased. "At least, that's what she does with me."

Luther laughed, then looked from her to him. "Are you gonna marry my granddaughter?"

Tony didn't hesitate or look even slightly put out at the forward question. "Yes, sir, I am."

"Well, don't wait too long. I'm an old man. I'd like to see at least one of my girls get married before I die, and June, she give up lookin' twenty years ago."

Grant returned with a tray holding a pitcher of iced tea

nd four tall glasses. He greeted Tony and Luther as he tarted to pour, but Tony stopped him. "None for me. I've ot to get back." He caught Selena's gaze. "Walk with me to ne door."

As they went into the hallway, she reached for his hand. efore meeting him, she'd never indulged in casual touch-ng. She hadn't had the sort of friends who impulsively ugged or family who kissed or boyfriends who'd lasted nore than a few dates. She'd since developed a fine appreci-tion for a simple touch.

"How's it going?" she asked when they reached the door.

"Nobody who's worked with Vargas believes he's guilty. he financials on the rest of the employees didn't turn up nything unusual. Of course, if you take your payoff in cash, t's easy enough to hide. Too bad for Vargas, too."

"Why? You're convinced he's innocent."

"Yeah, but he's here illegally, and now he's come to the at-ention of law enforcement. He'll likely be turned over to mmigration and deported."

"Can you persuade them not to do that?"

His mouth quirked. "You expect a lot of me, don't you?"

"I do," she said with a slow, full smile.

"I'll talk to Sheriff McEntire." He agreed so readily that he knew he'd already intended to do just that. Tony was big believer in right and wrong, law and order, but he vas also compassionate. It made him a good person and a etter cop.

He bent to kiss her. "Have fun with your grandfather."

Reluctant to let him go, she clung to his hand when he vould have pulled away. "Are you sure it's all right for him to be here? Are you sure he'll be safe?"

He pulled free, then shook a finger in her direction. 'Don't you start soundin' like Junie," he mimicked Luther.

"He's safe. Trust me." He kissed her again, then opened the door and stepped out. She caught a glimpse of the security guard before the door closed again.

She did trust him, with everything in her. But she couldn't help worrying about her grandfather, her father, her aunt. June would be angry when she found out Luther had defied her, that Tony had helped him, that neither Selena nor Grant had informed her. She already had so much anger that they wouldn't be able to deal with it in their lifetimes.

So what was the harm of a little more?

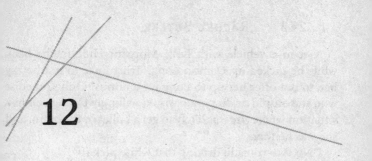

12

It was a normal Friday morning at the Azalea Inn. The housekeepers were going about their day, pushing over-sized carts of linens and toilet paper from room to room. A young Latino was mowing the strip of grass that separated the office from the street, and water was running in the bathroom next door to Charlize's.

She dropped the curtain, letting it fall into place over the window, as the cell phone rang. She crossed unhurriedly to the night table and flipped the phone open. "Hello."

Luke didn't waste time on a greeting. "I just got a call from your friend and mine. Seems he needs a ride, and he picked me to give it. I'm on my way to meet him now."

"Where?" she asked, pulling a county road map from the nightstand and spreading it open on the table.

"At some country store north of here on Highway 418. About fifteen, maybe twenty miles out of Greenhill. He wasn't sure."

She located the highway and traced it with one finger, estimating the distance. Straightaways in that fifteen-mile section were few and far between. One of them was a couple-mile stretch between two bridges spanning Tobacco Creek and Big Tobacco Creek. If there was cover alongside the road... "Where are you taking him?"

"He didn't say. Want me to pick you up? I'm coming up from the south. I'll be in Greenhill in about ten minutes."

Get in a vehicle with Luke Morgan? Hide in the back while he picked up Damon Long? Trust Luke to not betray her, to not offer her up to Long for a bonus? Only someone who was stupid or desperate would willingly put herself in a situation where she was likely to get a bullet in the brain, and she was neither.

"No. Are you still driving that white pickup?"

"Nope. Got a red Chevy Caprice. Looks like shit. Runs like a fucking dream."

"About twelve miles out of town, you'll cross two creeks—first Tobacco, then Big Tobacco. On your way back, call me when you reach Big Tobacco."

"You want me to just pick up the cell phone with Long sitting beside me and call you?"

"Put the number on auto dial. Keep it on your left side, out of his sight. Just dial, let it ring, then disconnect."

"What if we don't come back the same way?"

Good point. Long could choose to travel away from Greenhill, but instinct told her he wanted to stay close. According to the map, on that stretch of road between the estimated pickup point and the creeks, there was no place else to go.

"You will," she said confidently. "He doesn't want to leave the area, not yet."

"So I assume you'll have a little gift for Long soon after we reach the creek."

"Don't forget to call me."

"Don't shoot me by accident."

She smiled. "If I shoot you, Luke, it won't be an accident."

Tossing the phone aside, she went to the narrow alcove that served as a closet and pulled a pair of jeans from a hanger. She shimmied out of her pale blue dress, stepped into the jeans, and pulled on a long-sleeved T-shirt in muted green. She added socks and dark running shoes, tucked her hair up under a navy blue ball cap, grabbed the map and the phone, and left the room.

She picked up 418 a mile east of town, then turned north, driving five miles over the limit. Traffic was moderate, and the scenery varied from farmland to pine forests to close-growing scrub. The road curved this way and that, climbing an occasional hill before descending onto flat terrain again.

Just north of Big Tobacco Creek, she pulled onto the shoulder, swung the wheel in a wide U-turn, and drove back to the south side of Tobacco. There was a turnoff on the east side of the bridge, so overgrown that she'd missed it the first time by. She took it, easing the car over the ruts, following the faint trail into the woods and down a slope, where it ended at the creek bank. Beer cans and trash littered the ground.

Climbing out, she pushed the door shut, then, for a moment, just listened. An occasional vehicle on the highway. Birds in the trees. A plop or two in the creek. Nothing out of the ordinary ... except her.

She opened the trunk, undid the locks on an aluminum case, and lifted out the sniper rifle. Slinging the strap over one shoulder, she tucked a .22 into her waistband, then walked back to the highway. The hillside was maybe eight feet higher than the road—not the best vantage, but it would do. Leaves crackled beneath her as she climbed to the top, stretched out on her stomach, and settled in.

After adjusting the bipod that supported the barrel, she sighted on the driver of an oncoming pickup. Perfect. Then she waited.

She'd been in place about ten minutes, wondering if Luke would use this time with Long to sell her out, wondering how much—or how little—her life was worth to him, when a red Chevy Caprice passed below with a rumble of power that vibrated the very ground she lay on. Luke was wearing the Auburn cap again and appeared to be alone in the car. The windows were down, and his left arm with its tribal band tattoo rested on the door. No doubt, music was blasting from the stereo. The Doors or Jimi Hendrix.

She watched through the scope until he was out of sight, then checked her watch. She switched her phone to vibrate, slid it into her hip pocket, and scanned the route once again.

Minutes ticked past. Seven, eight, nine. A convertible passed northbound. A logging truck southbound. Then the cell phone began to vibrate and, seconds later, the Caprice appeared in the distance.

Charlize focused on the two men. Luke was talking. Damon Long wasn't. What was he doing out without a vehicle? Where had he been? What trouble had he caused?

As the car came nearer, the rumble started again. *Looks like shit. Runs like a fucking dream.* She preferred cars that didn't all but growl *Look at me,* but she could see where that macho power would appeal to Luke.

Her hands were steady, her heart rate calm, as she drew a bead on Long. The cross-hairs bisected his face, meeting right between his cold-snake eyes. Breathing evenly, she slowly, slowly squeezed the trigger, ending Selena's problems, ending Long's prob—

"What are you doing?"

She stiffened, and her finger jerked that last millimeter, sending the shot wild. Tires squealed as the Caprice swerved, then Luke accelerated out of sight.

"Goddamn." Wrapping her fingers around the pistol grips, she drew it from her waist as she turned, only to quickly shove it behind her again.

Two boys stood in front of her, probably no more than eight or nine, both looking like Opie Taylor straight from Mayberry freaking R.F.D. One wore shorts and a T-shirt, the other overalls and no shirt, and they each balanced a fishing pole on one shoulder as they stared wide-eyed at her.

Kids. Christ. Long wouldn't hesitate to shoot them where they stood. John Turner would have done the same. *You never leave a witness.*

She couldn't even consider it.

"Is that a real gun?" Overalls asked.

She picked up the 550, slapped down the bipod, and looped the sling over her shoulder. "What are you boys doing out here?"

"Fishing," Overalls said at the same time Shorts said, "Skippin' school." The first boy elbowed the second. "Shut up, stupid! You're gonna' get us in trouble!"

Shorts turned red and mumbled, "Sorry." Then he repeated the question. "Is that a real gun?"

Again she ignored it and started down the hill toward the car. "Skipping school, huh? What do you think your parents would say about that?"

The boys slid along behind her. "They'd take away our dirt bikes for good this time," Shorts said. "I bet you're a cop. My dad says there's lots of goddamn cops around here these days. Are you a cop?"

Why not? "Yeah. But"—she raised one finger to her lips—"don't tell anyone. I'm undercover."

At the bottom of the hill, Overalls ran to get ahead of her, then walked backward. His grin showed two missing teeth as he extended his hand. "We won't tell if you don't."

She shook it. "You've got a deal." When Shorts offered his hand, she shook it, as well. She had no clue whether the boys would uphold their end of the bargain—stumbling across a woman shooting a gun might be too good a story to keep to themselves—though the fact that telling meant losing their dirt bikes weighed in on her side.

But what did it matter if they told? Neither Luke nor Long was going to file a report with the sheriff. She wouldn't be charged with anything.

She locked the weapons in the trunk of the car, then faced the boys. "You two might think about going back to school soon."

"No way."

"Well, be careful out here." *You never know who might come along.* She got behind the wheel, fastened her seat belt, backed up, and bumped her way back to the road. The last she saw of the boys, they were heading for the creek.

It was too much to hope that Luke would go ahead and kill Long himself. It wasn't that he lacked initiative; he had plenty of it ... as long as it was preceded by large payments into his bank account. She'd screwed up, so he would put his work for her on hold and would instead do Long's bidding for the moment.

Damn it, she *never* screwed up. Fifteen years old, she'd killed her father and disposed of his body, and no one had even remotely suspected her.

Now Long's guard would be up. She would have to work doubly hard to get another chance. Another mistake would send him so deep into hiding that she would never find him.

So there wouldn't be another. No matter what.

"Pull over here," Damon ordered. "Into the trees."

Morgan braked hard, then steered the car into a stand of pines, bringing it to a stop about fifty feet off the road. He cut the engine, got out, and circled the rear of the car, bending to examine the damage. The goddamn bullet had entered the windshield high in the middle and exited the rear quarter panel, tearing a jagged hole in the metal.

It would have done worse damage to Damon's head.

As Morgan straightened, swearing, Damon slammed his fist into his face. Blood spurted from Morgan's nose onto his hand and made his grip slip when he drew his .45.

"What the hell—" Sprawled on his back, Morgan glared at him. "What the fuck is wrong with you? You call me to give you a fucking ride, and next thing I know, someone almost kills me! And you fucking blame *me*?"

Damon's aim was steady on Morgan's chest. "Who was it?"

"How the hell would I know? You're the one with all the fucking enemies."

"Who did you talk to?"

"Nobody. The cops are looking for *you*. They don't even know I exist."

"Charlize knows."

Morgan snorted, then spat out a mouthful of blood as he sat up. "That bitch would rather kill me than look at me. Besides, if it was her, she wouldn't have missed."

"Then who was it?"

Morgan shrugged. "Maybe that cop boyfriend of Selena's, or the fed you tried to kill up in Oklahoma, or some redneck who's wanting to collect on the reward out for you. There's more people looking for you than I even know."

Ceola would never take the law into his own hands. If he had had a clue where to find Damon, he would have called out the troops and tried to take him alive. Some citizen looking to cash in on the reward being lucky enough to get a shot wasn't fucking likely. Which left Charlize...and the question of how she'd found him. How she'd persuaded Morgan to sell him out.

Morgan got to his feet, spat again, then rooted in the backseat of the Caprice until he found a T-shirt. He crumpled it, held it to his nose, and turned to lean against the car, his head tilted back, his eyes closed.

It would be easy enough to put a bullet in his head and walk away. No great loss to anyone. But Damon had known him a long time. They'd partied together, gotten shit-faced drunk together, killed together. Morgan always did the job he was hired to do, he never screwed up, and he never left any loose ends.

And he knew what would happen if he even thought about betraying Damon. He might not give a damn about anyone else's life, but he valued his own.

Maybe Charlize had managed this on her own. She was like a goddamn bloodhound; she could find anyone anytime anyplace.

Or maybe she'd figured that Morgan was the one Damon was most likely to call on for favors; maybe she had been following him all this week. Which, in a roundabout way, still made Morgan guilty of betrayal through stupidity.

There were different levels of betrayal, but only one level of punishment.

"This bullshit's getting old. Enough dicking around. I want Selena dead. Tonight." He wanted to get the fuck out of Alabama, head south, and relax under the Mexican sun. He wanted his business back—wanted his life back. He wanted satisfaction.

Morgan lowered the shirt, found a clean spot, and wiped his nose again. Only a smear of blood came off on the cotton. "She's living in a goddamn armed camp," he said as he tossed the shirt back into the car. "One man can't do it alone."

"Charlize could," Damon replied, and Morgan's jaw tensed. "You can handle a few guards and Ceola. Do it tonight."

"I work on my own schedule."

"You've had a fucking week to do it on your own. This should have been an easy job, but after every failed attempt, she just digs in a little deeper. Pretty soon she's gonna be so deep no one will be able to touch her. I want it done now. If you can't, go home."

"Yeah, okay," Morgan said grudgingly. "Tonight."

Damon looked around to get his bearings. The trailer was three, maybe four miles south and west through the woods. He would hike back, pick up his car, and move on. If Charlize had pinpointed his general area, let her search it while he kicked back someplace else.

He turned back. "Go on. Get out of here."

"But don't you want a ride—" Morgan broke off and walked around the car.

The engine started with a roar that vibrated the ground. He drove slowly back to the highway, then accelerated onto the pavement with a squeal of rubber.

Damon listened until the engine's rumble faded, then set out through the woods. He kept to cover wherever possible, avoiding the occasional house, crossing the dirt roads quickly. Near the trailer, he retrieved his car from its hiding spot, then took a circuitous route southeast. On the outskirts of Montgomery, he checked into a hotel, not the kind of shabby place the cops would expect him to use, and he shaved his beard, gave his hair a drastic cut, and traded the glasses for contacts that turned his blue eyes drab brown.

Next he drove to a pay phone halfway across the city and dialed a south Alabama number.

Tommy LeFrancois had done small jobs for William over the years—had taken out Mitch Gautier and his crew. He didn't have the brains for anything complicated; he identified his target and took it out, usually with a lot of blood and gore. But this was one time where finesse didn't matter. Results did.

"I've got a job for you," Damon said after identifying himself. "In Greenhill, Alabama. Northwest of Montgomery. You interested?"

Different levels of betrayal. One level of punishment.

Tony climbed the veranda steps, then stopped next to George Baker, the on-site head of the security detail. They stood side by side, gazing across the lawn. Everything looked peaceful. A person might not even notice the guards patrolling the perimeter, or might mistake them for groundskeepers. A person might think everything at The Gardens was normal. Life as usual.

"We polyed everyone on my crew regarding how Peretti gained access to the property," Baker said at last. "They all passed."

Tony nodded. It would be nice if he could line up every person who worked for Grant and polygraph them all, but he couldn't. It was easy for the security firm, where regular polygraph exams were a condition of employment, but he couldn't compel the farmworkers to submit.

"We haven't found anything on the farm employees, either."

"So whoever it was got paid in cash and is smart enough to not spend the money yet."

"Or there was some other kind of payoff." Tony had considered the possibilities. Blackmail. The money could have gone to someone else or to a hidden account someplace else. It could have been a favor for a friend. Long or Peretti could have gotten to Kathryn Hamilton, who'd put him in touch with an employee who still acknowledged her as the boss's wife. Someone who held a grudge against Grant could have seen the opportunity to avenge it.

He had even considered the possibility that there had been no collusion—that Peretti had sneaked into the back of a vehicle and gotten onto the property without the driver's knowledge. He would be happier if that was the case—if no one on Grant's payroll had betrayed him, if Peretti had just gotten lucky. Without an inside source, the next hitter would have no such luck, especially with the vehicle searches they'd instituted.

A soft hum came from Baker's earpiece and directed his attention to the road. "Ms. Ravenel just came through the gate," he said.

She was driving fast, leaving clouds of dust in her wake. Tony went to meet her, reaching the top of the steps as she skidded to a stop. If it were someone else, he might think there was a problem, but it wasn't worry that tightened her features as she got out of the car and slammed the door. It was anger. She'd found out that Luther had come visiting despite her attempts to keep him away.

"Afternoon, June," he greeted her as she stalked up the steps.

She spared him the briefest of glances. "Why didn't you call me?"

"I didn't figure it was my place."

Stopping abruptly, she rounded on him. "Not your

place? You're in charge of security! You're supposed to be keeping everyone safe!"

"Luther is safe."

"Not if he's here, he's not! I told him—"

"June, you're his daughter, not his keeper." And she should be thankful for that. Tony and the rest of his family had become their father's keeper. The Alzheimer's made watching over Joe more stressful than babysitting Tony's twin nieces when they were toddlers. There were physical limitations to the trouble two-year-olds could get into. Not so with a grown man.

June stiffened to her full height. "I know exactly who I am and what my role is in his life. I don't need to hear it from you. Now, I'm taking my father home and I'm telling you, I don't want him over here again. You tell those guards at the gate not to let him pass unless he's with me."

"I can't do that." Her gaze narrowed, and Tony reworded it. "I won't do that. If Grant prohibits him from visiting, that's his business. But I won't."

She looked from him to George, standing nearby with the usual guard and doing a decent job of pretending to be deaf and blind. Her jaw tightened as her mouth creased into a thin line, then she strode off without another word.

Tony looked at George, too, rolled his eyes, then followed her inside. Her temper was obvious as she crossed the family room to stop near Luther. "Come on, Daddy, I'm taking you home."

Selena watched her warily; so did Grant. Not Luther. He smiled and patted the hand that reached for him. "Thank you, girl, but I'm not done visitin'. I imagine young Tony here will see that I have a ride home when I'm ready." Ignoring June's anger, he went on in his usual friendly tone. "Baby girl's paintin' my portrait. Can you imagine that? A famous artist wantin' to do a portrait of me, and me just a tired old farmer."

June's cutting gaze flicked toward Selena and the easel, then away as if both were unworthy of her attention. "That's real nice, Daddy, but she can do her painting from a photograph instead. You're going home."

Her fingers closed around his sleeve and pulled, but he resisted. His amusement was replaced by steel as he repeated, "I'm not done here yet. You're not done for the day, either. You need to quit botherin' me, get back to work, and earn that salary Grant's paying you. Go on now. Scat."

The tension in the air thickened. June dropped her hold on his arm and took a step back, looking harsher, more brittle; her lips thinned even more. Her breaths came in short, rapid puffs, and beneath the dull ebony of her skin, heat rose. "Scat?" she echoed, her tone edging toward shrill. "You tell me to *scat*?"

Before she could say anything else, Selena laid aside her brush and came around the easel. "Maybe we should take a break," she said quietly. "We've been at this half the day. You're probably tired."

"No, I'm not," Luther insisted. "All I've been doing is sittin' here and lookin' handsome for my granddaughter the famous artist, and I do it very well, don't I?"

"You do." Selena's smile was warm and gentle. "Truth is, I need a break. We can start again tomorrow."

Luther was considering it when June spoke. She just couldn't admit that Selena was trying to help her out. "No, you can't. He's not coming over here again. Grant, I don't want him here."

Grant rose from the couch and approached June. "I can't tell him what to do, June."

"Of course you can. You and your daddy and all the

Hamiltons before you have been ordering Ravenels around for two hundred years. Tell him he's not welcome here."

"I won't lie," Grant said stubbornly.

"Then tell *her* she's not welcome!" June gestured angrily at Selena.

With a grunt, Luther heaved himself out of the chair and faced his daughter head-on. "If anyone's not welcome here, it's gonna be you. What's wrong with you, girl? Your mama and I taught you better than to act like this. Carryin' on like you got no manners, embarrassin' me in front of family... You're right. It's time to go. Selena, Tony, I'll see you tomorrow. Grant, I apologize for my girl's behavior and her slackin' off from work. It won't happen again, neither one of 'em."

With a dignified nod, Luther walked from the room. Looking as if she might pop—the apology on her behalf might have been one push too far—June rigidly followed.

Long after they were gone, Grant heaved a sigh. "She doesn't mean to be difficult. She's just worried about him. She's all he's had since Amelia died."

But not anymore, Tony thought. Now he had Amelia's daughter, and that was the bigger reason for June's behavior. She was jealous.

Jealous enough to want Selena removed, not just from The Gardens but from Luther's life?

Tony moved to the windows to watch them leave. Luther walked on his own, head held as high as June's was ducked low. When they reached the car, she stood, hands hanging limply at her sides, as he moved slowly around the vehicle, then eased himself into the passenger seat. After his door closed, she remained there a moment, reached up to wipe something from her eye—a tear?—then got behind the wheel and slowly drove off to the east.

Could June want her only niece dead? Six years in Homicide had taught Tony that everyday, average people were capable of anything given the right motivation. Hatred, jealousy, resentment—all were powerful emotions, and June had definitely felt the latter two for her sister, had transferred them to her sister's daughter.

According to Grant, June was a loving, devoted daughter. Churchgoing, God-fearing, a kind, decent person. What would she gain from Selena's death?

Her father's attention. She would once again be all Luther had. He would once again rely on her.

Was that enough to persuade her to sneak a killer onto the property so he could murder her niece? They had checked her out, along with every other employee, and found nothing, not even a parking ticket, and certainly no unexplained cash. But, as he'd said to George just before she'd arrived, there were other kinds of payoffs.

"Tony?"

Selena's hand on his arm startled him. He turned from the windows to find her standing next to him, the cordless phone in hand. Clearly she'd asked him something, but he'd been too preoccupied to hear.

She smiled knowingly and repeated it. "It's Charlize. She has some news. She'd like to come here and talk to us."

He gazed into her dark eyes. What would it do to her if June was Peretti's accomplice, if her own aunt wanted her dead? She had so little family and had experienced so much disappointment. She didn't deserve more.

"Hello." She waved her fingers in his face. "Charlize? News?"

For a moment longer, he stared at her, then abruptly nodded. "Yeah. Sure. I'll notify the gate."

As she lifted the phone to her ear once more, he left the

room for the foyer and used his cell to call the guard shack. Then, as an afterthought, he called the sheriff. He would share whatever news Charlize had; it might as well be sooner rather than later.

He would share his suspicious about June, as well. If she was innocent—God, he hoped she was—Selena need never know.

If she wasn't, it would be one more heartache for Selena and Luther to bear.

Selena changed from the T-shirt and jeans she'd worn while working into a crimson silk tank top and a matching skirt of black swirls on a crimson background. Part of a wardrobe Grant had had delivered, the fabric floated lightly around her legs as she walked to the armoire to retrieve her jute sandals and reminded her of the days before Damon Long had decided she should die, when she'd worn little but silk in tropical patterns. Jeans, she'd discovered since, held a certain comfort and were well suited to the life she hoped to reclaim someday soon.

As she knotted a strip of fringed black silk at her waist, she glanced at Tony, looking out the window. "How long are we going to hide out here?"

He replied automatically, absently. "As long as it takes."

Sliding her arms around him from behind, she nipped his earlobe before murmuring, "Wrong answer. We need a plan."

"We have a plan."

"Holing up here in Grant's house, waiting for Long's people to make a move on me or for Charlize to flush him out and disrupting everyone's lives in the process isn't much of a plan."

"Beats the hell out of you waltzing down Main Street with a bull's-eye on your back."

She didn't respond. Her only idea was to basically do just that—move out into the open, go about her life as usual, and give Long a clear chance to take her out. But it would be risky, and she wasn't anxious to die, nor did she want to endanger anyone whose life happened to touch, however distantly, on hers.

Truthfully, though she hated the reason that had brought her to The Gardens, she was enjoying the time with Grant and Luther and even, in a perverse way, with June. She liked being in her father's boyhood home and loved hearing Luther's endless stories about Amelia. She even appreciated June's less glowing memories. For the first time ever, she had a family and was connecting with them.

But June was right about one thing: She'd brought danger into their lives. The sooner she was gone, the safer they might be ... unless Long threatened them to draw her back. It would be an effective ploy, and he was smart enough to know it.

Tony turned and wrapped his arms around her. "It's only been a week."

"But you can't put your life on hold to stay here forever."

He grinned. "Of course I can. You *are* my life. Besides, Long's not going to stay forever, either. His hitter will make a move soon or give it up."

"Long will never give up."

Tony's expression turned grim. "He'll have no choice."

Because the idea of Tony or Charlize killing Long in cold blood made her own blood run cold, Selena didn't mention it, but focused on something he'd said earlier. "Letting Charlize come here ... have you decided you trust her?"

"Not by a long shot. She'll be searched at the gate and

accompanied by guards." His cell phone buzzed, and he glanced at the screen. "She's here, and the sheriff's right behind her. Come on."

By the time they reached the first floor, Grant had escorted their visitors into the formal dining room. Selena thought the choice odd until she saw the oversized papers Charlize had brought with her. They covered the long table, overlapping at the edges, and appeared to be property maps of some kind.

Tony gave them a glance. "Why are we looking at plat maps for Chadwick County?"

"Not all of it. Just a few choice areas." Charlize smoothed out the last rolled page, then dusted her hands. "I heard from a reliable source that Damon Long was seen right about..." Scanning the maps, she pointed a perfectly manicured pink nail to a small *x*. "Here."

The spot Charlize indicated was alongside a highway north of town. It ran into the road that passed The Gardens about four miles from the house. The knowledge that Long had been that close while Selena had spent a lazy morning with Grant and Luther sent a chill down her spine.

"What was Long doing?" Selena asked. "Hitching a ride? Walking? Just standing there?"

"Actually, my source had given him a ride. That was where he dropped him off, where Long disappeared into the woods. That's why I got these copies of the plat maps. To see if we can figure out where he was going."

Tony swept his hand over the expanse of land west of the road. "So he took off this way?"

"I don't know. My source dropped him off, drove away, then sneaked back through the woods. Long was already gone. He could have gone any direction."

"Could another vehicle have picked him up?" Selena asked.

"He didn't see or hear any other traffic. He was under the impression that Long was going back to where he was staying. He wouldn't want anyone to know where that is."

Damon Long wasn't a fool. Like Charlize, like Selena herself, there were very few people he trusted.

"How did this guy happen to give Long a ride?" Tony asked.

"Damon called and asked him for one. He picked him up here."

Sheriff McEntire leaned closer to study the place where she pointed. "That's only a couple miles from where that man was found dead this morning."

Her stomach knotting, Selena shot a glance at Tony, but he looked surprised by the news. So did Charlize. "What man?"

"There was a body dump in the next county. I was going to tell you about it." McEntire leaned against the sideboard, beefy arms folded over his chest, and related the details. Eugene Watkins, retired plumber off for a weekend fishing trip, victim number who-knew of a conscienceless psychopath. If Long's need to see Selena dead hadn't brought him to Alabama, maybe Mr. Watkins would have lived to die of old age. If the FBI hadn't dragged her into this, if William hadn't dragged her into it . . .

"The sheriff up there is so wet behind the ears, he doesn't know what to think," McEntire went on. "He figured it was just a robbery gone bad—guy has a flat tire, pulls off the road to change it, someone kills him and takes the cash from his wallet—until a reporter for the local newspaper pointed out the absence of blood splatter and brain matter. Then he finally got a clue."

"Do you think it was Long?" Tony's voice was quiet, dark.

McEntire looked somber. "It seems awfully coincidental, doesn't it? A killer turning up in the area right after a man is killed. The wife says her husband was going fishing, but she doesn't know where. He had a bunch of favorite spots."

"Maybe he had a favorite spot in this county," Selena said, gazing at the maps. "Someplace quiet, out of the way, where he wouldn't be bothered by anyone. The kind of place that would appeal to someone hiding from the police. And when Watkins disturbed his privacy, Long killed him, dumped the body, and tried to make it look like a robbery. His hideout must be within reasonable walking distance of the drop-off point. Four, maybe five miles."

For the first time, Grant spoke up from his position at the far end of the table. "Four or five miles on foot is reasonable?"

Selena smiled at him. He'd always preferred intellectual pursuits over physical, though he admitted to, at one time, playing a hell of a game of tennis. Along with getting older, he'd gotten softer. Golf, complete with cart, was his sport these days. "Anyone can walk five miles with the right incentive."

Selena moved to Tony's side. "We need to find an isolated place with water, where the fishing may or may not be good."

"That covers an awful lot of places in Chadwick County," Grant pointed out.

"Lucky for us, we need only one." She watched as Tony and Charlize put the maps in order. "These maps don't show bodies of water, do they?"

"Only the big ones," Tony replied. "The river, a couple of lakes. I imagine there are creeks and ponds all over the place."

Grant left the room, then returned with a yellow high-lighter which he used to mark off sections. "This is The Gardens, this is Hamilton Farms, and Luther's property is here. We have a few ponds and creeks, including this pond behind Luther's house, but it would be impossible for any-one to set up camp around them. The crew goes everywhere. They would spot a trespasser."

With the sheriff's input, Grant marked more areas, iden-tifying the families or businesses who owned them. When he finished, much of the map was unmarked. They couldn't even rule out a lot of what he had marked because it be-longed to logging companies. Unlike on the farm, it would be all too easy for someone to go unnoticed in the forests; unless the crews were actively cutting, they were left more or less alone.

McEntire shuffled the pages together, then began rolling them into a tube. "I know an old boy who used to fly for the state police. I'll ask him to check out some of these places for us this afternoon. Odds are, he won't find any-thing. A plane could fly at treetop level over a pup tent in the trees and never see it. But it's worth a shot." He shifted his gaze to Charlize. "I don't suppose you want to tell who your source is."

Her smile was coolly polite. "It doesn't really have any bearing, Sheriff. Just take my word for it. It was Long."

McEntire didn't look as if he wanted to take her word for anything. With a muttered "Huh," he headed for the door. "I'll see about getting that plane up."

Grant walked out with him. When the door closed be-hind them, Tony said, "It was Morgan, wasn't it?"

Charlize's only response was a shrug.

"Long called Morgan and asked him for a ride. Morgan called you, and you . . ."

Hustled out of town to find a good place for an ambush, Selena thought. Charlize had tried to take action, but had somehow failed.

"Things didn't work out this morning," Charlize said, her features settling into a frown. She wasn't accustomed to failing. "But next time..."

"Next time call the police," Selena said. That would put Long's fate in the hands of the authorities. Neither Tony nor Charlize would have the chance to extract justice from the man. Neither would have to kill to protect *her*.

That was an outcome she could live with.

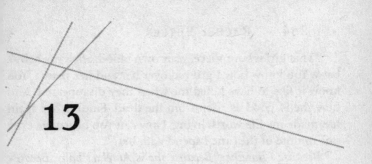

13

The slamming of a door echoed through the small house, making June jump. She turned from her place near the window, arms folded across her chest, and watched tight-lipped as Luther shuffled down the hall and into the living room. He'd changed from his Sunday best into a pair of faded work trousers in a nondescript blue and a white shirt that had seen better days, and he walked across the room to the door without so much as a glance in her direction.

"Where are you going?" she asked as he reached for the screen door.

He stopped short. "Tyrone is picking me up. We're goin' fishin'. Or do I need to ask your permission first?"

Closing her eyes briefly, she massaged the ache that had settled between them, then heaved a sigh and extended her hand to him. "Of course you don't. Daddy, I know you think I'm being unreasonable—"

He snorted.

"—but I'm just trying to look out for you. That's what we've done for most of our lives, isn't it? Look out for each other?"

"Lookin' out don't mean keeping me from my onliest grandbaby. It don't mean embarrassing me in front of Grant and treatin' me like a child."

Heat flushed through her. "I'm sorry. I didn't mean to . . . But if anything happened to you because of that girl . . ."

"That girl is your niece, your own blood. She's my baby's baby. You know how I grieved over her and her mama. You know it like to have killed me when they disappeared. And here she is, good as risen from the dead. Finding her again has made my life worth living. How can you begrudge even one minute of the time I spend with her?"

Because I hate her! Because she is *Amelia's baby. Because she's made me invisible to you.*

Through sheer will, June kept the words and the anger and the hurt inside. Instead she tried to sound reasonable and cool. "Daddy, people are trying to kill her. Every minute you spend with her puts your life in danger. *You* make *my* life worth living. Without you—" Choking up, she broke off and swiped at the tears that welled in her eyes.

Finally he removed his hand from the screen door and came to her, patting her awkwardly on the arm. "I'm an old man. Everything I do is dangerous—gettin' out of bed, walkin' down the steps, even settin' down to nap. When it's my time to go, I'll go, whether I'm asleep in that recliner or standing next to baby girl with hired killers around. You can't protect me from dying, girl, no more than I could protect your mama or pretty girl from going."

"No one could have protected Amelia," she muttered. "It was her own foolishness that got her killed."

Luther's fingers tightened painfully on her arm. "Don't you talk about her that way. Kathryn Hamilton bears all the blame for what happened to my girl. Amelia—she might have been young and a little reckless, but it was Kathryn's hatred and meanness that killed her and stole baby girl from us for all these years. It was Kathryn that broke my heart and left me with nothin'." His voice turned fierce. "And every night I pray to God that she burns in hell for what she did to my girls."

June stared at him, only vaguely aware that his fingers were biting into her arm. Emotion trembled through him and into her; her chest was growing tight, her blood boiling with guilt. If he knew what she knew, if he knew what she'd done...

Lungs burning, she raised her hand to his, prying his fingers loose. "Daddy, you're hurting me," she gasped.

The intensity in his eyes faded to dull brown, and contrition softened his expression. "I'm sorry, girl. I didn't mean..." He rubbed the spot for a moment, then lifted her arm and pressed a loud, smacking kiss to it. "All better?"

The action took her back to a time when she was little, when he'd still had the chance to love her and appreciate her and make her feel as if she mattered, when Daddy kisses had been enough to make any hurt all better.

That afternoon, it just made the hurt worse, because he'd turned his back on all those chances. Because he would never love her the way he'd loved Amelia and now loved Selena.

The sound of an engine broke the silence, and she glanced out the window to see Tyrone pulling into the driveway. He tapped the horn once, then jumped out. He was a good boy. He would help Luther down the steps and into the pickup, and Luther wouldn't resent him one bit for it.

All he felt for June, it seemed, was resentment.

Tyrone pressed his face to the screen door like a kid and grinned. "Hey, Junie. Hey, Uncle Luther. You ready?"

"You bet I am. We'll be home in time for supper, girl, and we'll be bringin' it with us. Just you be prepared." Luther gave her a wink before walking out the door.

She watched how effortlessly Tyrone tended to him, and how easily Luther let him. Accepting the boy's help was the most natural thing in the world to him, while accepting anything from her was apparently the most unnatural.

After he settled behind the wheel, Tyrone waved. Luther seemed to have forgotten she was there.

She watched until they were out of sight, then picked up her cell phone and dialed Damon Long's number. When he answered on the third ring, she didn't bother with a greeting. "Do something, Mr. Long."

Before it was too late. Before she lost Luther forever.

"Hey, son, how's it going there in beautiful sunny Alabama?"

With a glance at Selena and Grant, sitting on the sofa and paging through decades-old yearbooks, Tony left the parlor through the French doors and walked along the veranda. The night temperature was a few degrees cooler, the humidity less overwhelming. Something sweet drifted on the air, along with the faint scent of tobacco and the fainter scent of aftershave.

He nodded to the guard who'd disposed of the cigarette recently, then leaned against the nearest pillar. "All in all, I'd rather be in Tulsa. You have anything for me, Frankie?"

"Not really. Still nothing on Luke Morgan or Charlize Pawley. However, I talked to a guy who knows a guy, and there used to be a man down in Florida who turned up on a lot of known associates' lists. He was rumored to be a hit man, but they never could prove it. Then he went and got himself killed twenty years ago—shot in the head, one time, real neat and professional—and the cops forgot all about him."

"And this is pertinent because?"

"His name was John Turner Thomas."

J.T. The name Charlize used in her hired-killer business. "I'm guessing John Turner had a kid."

"He did." Simmons sounded more than pleased with himself. "A bouncing baby girl who would be about thirty-five now. Daughter stuck around long enough to bury her old man, then she left town and was never heard from again."

"Was she a suspect in his death?"

"Nope. She was just a kid, a pretty little blond thing, couldn't have had it in her," Frankie said, no doubt mimicking the detective he'd talked to. Then he snorted. "How could anyone work Homicide without learning that everyone has it in them? It's just the breaking point that varies."

Selena had killed Johnny Peretti to save herself. Tony would kill Damon Long to protect her.

What had been Charlize's breaking point? What had made her kill for the first time?

Tony had spent too many years in Sex Crimes to not make a good guess at the answer.

Too edgy to stand still, he headed down the steps toward the giant live oak halfway between the driveway and the fence. It was the only tree within five hundred feet of the house, a giant live oak, the trunk massive, its branches heavy with Spanish moss. It was more than a hundred years old, according to Grant, and could easily shade a dozen picnics under its dipping branches.

There in the dark, Tony felt more comfortable about broaching the next subject. "Did you check out June?"

"Yeah. Nothing to raise any red flags. No unexplained income, no excessive spending. I chatted up the dispatcher down there—says she's a dedicated employee, active in church, and that her daddy is blessed to have her. She works hard, gives money to charity, and never married, though she had her chance more than once. She doesn't even date anymore, and her last vacation was more than ten years ago."

Tony leaned against a solid branch that bowed to the ground before sweeping back up over his head. "You got all that from a chat."

Simmons chuckled. "People like to talk. All you have to do is listen. The only thing remotely interesting about Auntie June is a couple of calls in the past few days to a prepaid cell."

"Popular with criminals, teenagers, and anyone who doesn't want to sign a service contact." He was using a prepaid cell himself these days. It wasn't the red flag it had once been.

"You got it. Now let me get this straight, Chee. You suspect Island Girl's only blood aunt in the world might want her dead. Man, and I thought *my* family was tough."

"Everyone has it in them, remember?" June was certainly passionate about her father. Her sister. And her niece. But it was a long way from loving a parent, no matter how possessively, and being jealous of a sister to helping kill a niece. Maybe he was wrong. He hoped. "What about that homicide north of here?"

"The victim was shot with a .45. No prints on the driver's side of the pickup or on the wallet, not even his. The hole in the flat tire matched the blade of the knife found in his pocket, also cleaned of prints. ATM records show he withdrew seventy-five dollars at seven-eighteen this morning, and he spent forty-one dollars and change on the groceries that were in the back of the pickup. Grocery store receipt says he checked out at seven thirty-seven."

And the body was discovered about ten. "And nothing more than coincidence to tie it to Long."

"Not yet. If they catch him, Oklahoma gets 'im first."

Simmons said something to someone else in the room—probably Suz at this time of night—then added, "That is, if *you* don't get him first."

Tony gazed at the house. Dim lights now burned in each upstairs room. Was Selena getting ready for bed in one of them? Was she in the shower, washing the short curls that he was coming to like more each day? Or sitting on the edge of the bed, wearing something short and sexy—even if it was one of his shirts—and rubbing lotion over her legs?

She was lucky with her hair, she said, that it didn't require the time-consuming care that so many black women were committed to, but her skin did have a tendency to get ashy if she didn't pamper it. He was lucky for that, because he liked watching her, the way her hands glided along her legs, the way her long, strong fingers massaged the lotion into her skin, the way she stretched and rubbed and turned him on.

And he was standing outside in the dark talking with Frankie.

"How long are you planning to stay gone?"

"I don't know. As long as it takes."

"Sooner or later, the chief's gonna want you back. Hell, Chee, *I* want you back. This working bit is getting old."

"I'll be there when things are settled."

Simmons yawned loudly. "I'm heading off to bed. You need anything else, or do you think I've done enough work on a case that ain't even in our state?"

"If I think of anything, I'll call you."

"I'm sure you will, son."

Tony disconnected, then crossed the driveway to the house. After locking up, he took the stairs two at a time and walked into two empty rooms before finding Selena in the third. She was sitting on the bed, a half dozen pillows stuffed behind her, and the scent of cocoa butter filled the air. His shirt swallowed her and should have made her look impossibly young and innocent, but the legs that stretched forever beneath the hem were too shapely, the curves even excess fabric couldn't conceal too womanly.

Her expression was pensive until she saw him, when she smiled. "Did Frankie have good news or bad?"

"Just an update." Information that suggested June wasn't involved with Peretti...but his gut wasn't convinced. He didn't want her to be guilty, didn't want Selena's own aunt plotting against her, but what he wanted to believe didn't count for much. He needed proof.

He unholstered his pistol and left it on the night table, kicked off his running shoes, pulled his T-shirt over his head, then unbuckled his belt. As he finished undressing, he repeated the information about John Turner Thomas.

For a moment, there was silence, then she said, "I'm impressed. One would think, observing Frankie, that he wasn't exactly competent."

"He's better than people give him credit for. He uses that to his advantage."

"When we were in Savannah, I got Charlize's fingerprints for the FBI. They found out her identity went back only twelve years, but that was all. They didn't think about working the J.T. angle." Selena closed the magazine she'd been reading. "Of course, they'd never considered that the hit man could be a woman until they overheard the phone call Damon Long made to her."

"You have to admit, a woman isn't the first person to come to mind when you think 'cold-blooded contract killer.'" Though that kind of chauvinistic thinking could get a person killed.

"The night she—" Selena broke off, hesitated, then

started again. "The night Sonny Yates died, Charlize told me that her father had died of an illness. Later she said that he was killed. Do you think she killed him?"

Tony shrugged. If Charlize's father had abused or molested her, he'd deserved to die. And that sort of childhood trauma would certainly help explain some of the choices she'd made in life.

"Killing your own father . . . that's pretty cold."

"The job doesn't call for warm and fuzzy. Which makes me wonder why she's gotten so attached to you."

"Maybe it's not me at all," Selena said. "Maybe it's just her loyalty to William. Maybe she wants Long dead for a reason that has nothing to do with us."

Lying back, she drew Tony with her. For a time they just lay there, barely touching. The room was cool, the night was quiet, and the light was soft enough that it didn't bother tired eyes. If he didn't move for just a moment, he could fall asleep . . .

"You know Charlize tried to kill Long today."

"I know." She hadn't admitted it in so many words— *Things didn't work out this morning*—but the meaning had been clear.

"How do you feel about that?"

"Sorry she missed." Feeling Selena stiffen, he gave her a wry look. "I don't believe in vigilante justice. Law and order, right and wrong, black and white—I believe in that. I honestly do. But . . . There's an old joke that down in Texas, 'He needed killing' is a valid defense. In this case, it's true. If we arrest Long and he goes to trial, he'll be convicted. He'll go to prison, and he'll use up every appeal he can, and one day five or ten or twenty years from now, he'll be executed. In the meantime, the citizens of Oklahoma will spend a fortune on his prosecution, his incarceration, and his appeals. Or . . .

one of us can stop him now for the price of a bullet. It's wrong, I know, but it's also justice."

Selena's fingers tightened around his. "Can you live with that? Killing him or letting Charlize kill him?"

"I can." That wasn't to say he wouldn't feel some measure of guilt over it. Tony had felt guilty before; he would again. For all he'd done, for all he intended to do, Damon Long deserved to die. There was no question of his innocence, no doubt of his guilt. If he lived, others would die.

And if he died, Selena would live.

Tony squeezed her hand back. "Can *you* live with that?"

She was silent a long time, her expression troubled, but finally she nodded. It was a simplified answer—she would feel guilty, too—but for now, for Tony, it was good enough.

"Hey, Charlize."

Hairbrush in hand, Charlize switched her gaze from her reflection in the mirror to the cell phone, set on speaker, that lay on the counter next to the sink. It was late, and she was in for the night—or so she hoped. "Ruby Dee," she said in greeting. "What's up?"

"You know a guy named Frenchy?"

"Tommy LeFrancois? Sure. What about him?"

"He came by the bar this evening. Said he's got a job tomorrow up there around Greenhill. I thought you might be interested."

Charlize set down the brush and picked up the phone before moving to sit on the bed. "You're on speaking terms with LeFrancois? Don't you know—" She caught herself, biting off the question unfinished.

"That he's the one who killed Mitch? Yeah, I know." Bitterness sharpened Ruby Dee's voice. "He was given a job and he did it. He didn't find out until it was too late what was really going on. He felt real bad about it."

But William hadn't. He was the one Ruby Dee held responsible, along with Damon.

"Anyway, Frenchy's been coming around ever since I opened the place, looking out for me, trying to make it up to me in his own way. He's not a bad guy. He just took orders from the wrong man."

Charlize didn't think she would have been so generous. But she'd seen stranger things in her line of work. "So who's he taking orders from this time?"

"Damon."

"And I'm the target?" She was neither surprised nor frightened by the idea that someone would put out a contract on her. It was one of the risks of the job. She'd killed a lot of people. She'd expected that one day it would be her turn to become the prey. But, as she'd reminded Damon a few days earlier, sometimes the hunted became the hunter. Neither he nor LeFrancois would find her an easy kill.

"No. Luke Morgan is. I just thought you might like to know."

Charlize blinked. Damon and Luke had always been buddy-buddy, two of the guys, partners in crime. Damon must have blamed Luke for the botched shot that morning. Not that Luke didn't deserve to die a dozen times over, but damned if it was going to be because she'd screwed up.

"You say the job is for tomorrow?"

"Yeah, Damon was specific about that. Frenchy's not supposed to make a move before tomorrow morning."

Because Luke was going after Selena tonight. Damon wanted him to carry out the hit before he had him killed. His biggest problem would be taken care of, and for one hell of a lot less than a half million dollars.

"What information did he give LeFrancois?"

"A description, a car, and an address." The rustling of paper hummed like static on the line, then ceased. "Eleven-twenty-eight Oak Street in Leesville."

No doubt home to a pretty young woman with a higher sex drive than IQ.

Unfolding the map, Charlize traced south of Greenhill and found Leesville seven miles away. "Thanks, Ruby Dee. I owe you."

"I'll keep that in mind."

It was eleven o'clock when she hung up. The ideal time for a middle-of-the-night assault was around two or three A. M. Late enough for most people to be sound asleep, too early for even early risers to be up and about. But that was for the actual attack. Anyone good enough to do this job would want to be in place at least two or three hours earlier to get a feel for things.

A cell phone number would have come in handy, but she was lucky to have the address. If Luke wasn't home, she'd bet his temporary landlady would have his number.

The night was a tad cool for driving with the windows down, but she did it anyway, letting the wind whip her hair around her face. She passed only two cars on her way out of town and didn't meet the third until she was two miles south. Its bright lights sliced into the darkness, its engine rumbling. Muttering a curse, she squinted against the blinding light, then turned her head to watch the red Caprice streak past.

It was her lucky day.

Her car bounced and jerked as she steered onto the grassy shoulder, then swung the wheel in a tight turn. She bounced onto the other shoulder, hitting one rut deep enough to jar her teeth before straightening into the lane again. The Caprice's taillights were disappearing around a curve up ahead. She floored the accelerator until the vehicle came into sight again.

Luke slowed to the speed limit as he approached the city limits, then turned onto the road that led to The Gardens. He drove past the main gate and the service gate, as well, then made a right turn onto the highway that circled around behind the farm. Before making the same turn, Charlize switched off the headlights, counting on the darkness to keep him from noticing her.

When he turned off the road onto a narrow lane, she slowed to little more than a crawl and followed. His taillights were visible through the heavy growth of pines that closed in on both sides of the dirt trail, and the growl of the engine drifted clearly in the night. When he shut off the engine, the absence made the sound of her own well-tuned engine deafening.

Since Luke's motto was shoot first, ask questions later, she stopped fifty yards behind the Caprice, sheltered by brambles and bushes, and slipped out, careful to push the door shut with the softest of sounds. As she made her way around the brambles, she drew the .45 from its holster, thumbed off the safety, and held it loosely, finger on the trigger.

A thud sounded ahead—a car door closing—followed by a creak as the trunk lid was raised. Taking shelter behind a skinny pine, Charlize watched as Luke, illuminated by the trunk light, lifted a gun case from the car. He wasn't likely to get a long shot at Selena, but he would be prepared for anything. That was another of his mottos.

She left the safety of the tree, stepping lightly over the thick carpet of pine needles. Fifteen feet away, she raised the pistol until her arm was fully extended. Ten feet away, she eased back the hammer to make the first shot easier. If she had to take it.

She was almost in place when the case fell into the trunk with a clatter and Luke spun around, his own weapon pointed at her head. "John Turner's first rule," he said softly. "No aftershave, scented soap, deodorant, or anything else that might give you away. I smelled your perfume from thirty feet back."

"I could have dropped you from thirty feet without trying."

"You talk, Charlize, but you never seem inclined to carry through. Why is that?" Luke's grin emphasized the swelling of his nose, but didn't diminish his charm. "Maybe because you've got a soft spot for me?"

"Don't flatter yourself. I don't have any soft spots."

His gaze moved over her—the slow, heat-inducing look that made him so popular with women. "I can see a few."

Ignoring the tingling in her belly, she kept her aim steady. "I'll make a deal with you. Don't make me shoot you tonight, and I'll keep you from getting shot tomorrow."

"Why would anyone want to shoot me?"

With her free hand, she gestured toward his face. "Why would anyone want to break your nose?"

He touched it gingerly with his free hand. "The fucker sucker-punched me, then pulled a gun on me because *you* missed your shot. He thought I had something to do with it."

"You did have something to do with it. And that's why someone would want to shoot you. Specifically, Tommy LeFrancois, who's coming up from Mobile to splatter you into next week."

Luke stared at her a moment before his mouth flattened in a grim line. "Son of a bitch. He put out a hit on me? And he gave it to Frenchy? Are you fucking kidding?"

The disbelief, Charlize knew, was more for Damon's choice of hitters. LeFrancois was small-time. Luke would hope that a contract on him would go to one of his peers, not a fourth-rate wannabe.

"No, I'm not kidding. And he gave LeFrancois orders to wait until tomorrow." She gestured around them. "I'm assuming he gave you orders to take out Selena tonight."

"Yeah. He called this evening—said there's a rear gate that's hardly ever used. People tend to get bored when there's nothing much going on—even security guards. They relax, don't stay alert." He paced away a dozen steps, then turned to face her, the gun still pointing at her. "Jeez, he wants me dead *and* he's gonna stiff me for my damn money? Son of a bitch."

"No honor among thieves—or murderers," she said softly. "Imagine that."

Luke's gaze narrowed as he stared at her. "Why the hell are you telling me? You've threatened to kill me yourself a time or two. If Damon really has fucked me over, why not keep your mouth shut and let Frenchy do the deed?"

Tiny tremors rocketed through Charlize's arm. Slowly she lowered the pistol to her side, but she didn't take her finger from the trigger. She wasn't about to tell him that she felt responsible. If she hadn't missed her shot, all this would be over. Long would be dead, Selena would be safe, the hit never would have been put out, and Luke would be on his way someplace else. "I want Selena alive."

He didn't look convinced.

"Eleven-twenty-eight Oak Street, Leesville. I didn't know that until tonight, but you told Damon, didn't you? That's where you've been staying."

Disgust crossed Luke's face at his own stupidity. "Yeah. With a mutual friend."

He and Damon probably had such "friends" all across the South. John Turner had. Charlize never accepted help from anyone, not even a bed to sleep in. When she left an area after doing a job, no one could prove she'd ever been there.

"You might want to tell your friend to leave town for a while. Damon gave the address to LeFrancois."

"Fuck me." Returning to the car, Luke lowered his pistol, then sat on the open lip of the trunk.

It would be so easy to shoot him, Charlize thought, and let gravity carry him into the trunk, close the lid, and walk away with the keys. By the time his body was discovered, she would be long gone.

But she was here to save his life. Not take it.

Not this time.

"Do you know where Damon's staying?" she asked.

Luke shook his head. "I have a phone number. That's all."

He rattled off the number, and Charlize committed it to memory.

"What do you want me to do?" he asked grudgingly.

"Leave town. Go to ground until the contract is invalidated."

"Walk away and leave the fucker to you?" He shook his head. "He put out a hit on me—with Frenchy, for God's sake."

"Would you be as offended if he'd offered it to me instead?"

Abruptly Luke grinned. "You're one hell of a step up from Frenchy. He's got no talent. His kills are messy and clumsy." Then the grin faded, and he eyed her speculatively. "I'll give you forty-eight hours. If Long's not dead, I'm going after him. I'll kill him and Frenchy and anyone else who gets in the way. Understand?"

"I understand."

He holstered his weapon, secured the gun case that had fallen into the trunk, then closed the lid. When he turned, he closed the distance between them with two steps, slid his hand into her hair, and kissed her. Her mind went blank for the instant it took to realize what he was doing, then, muscles tensing, she raised her free hand to push him away. He stepped back first, though, and flashed that shit-eating grin again. "Thanks, J.T.," he said. As he strode to the car door, he called back over his shoulder, "I owe you." And he winked.

She stood numbly as the engine roared to life, then he executed a turn in the tight space. As she started back to her own car, she shook off the kiss, the grin, the wink, but it was harder than it should have been. Luke Morgan didn't mean a thing to her, she reminded herself. Since the day twenty years ago when he'd refused to help, the day he'd let her down when she so desperately needed him, he'd been less than nothing.

All that mattered now was Selena. Keeping her safe. Keeping her alive.

Tony braced himself with one hand on the dashboard, the other gripping the handle above the SUV's door. He'd been halfway through breakfast when one of Sheriff McEntire's deputies had come to take him to a site in the woods where Damon Long had apparently been holed up. They'd spent the past twenty minutes bumping over some of the worst road Tony had ever seen. Considering that he lived in Oklahoma, that was saying a lot.

"Jesus," he muttered when the top of his head narrowly missed connecting with the vehicle's roof.

"Rattles your fillings, doesn't it?" the deputy asked, looking as if he was enjoying the ride too much.

Finally the road ended. What looked like an old construction site trailer sat under the trees, listing toward the back. Cinder blocks stair-stepped to the door, and a generator sat under a structure that was one breath short of blowing away.

"How the hell'd they get that in here without it shaking apart?" Tony asked, still feeling the jolts in his bones though they weren't moving.

The deputy's only response was a shrug. He didn't know, and, more important to him, he didn't care.

McEntire met Tony at the front of the vehicle. Several other deputies were already working the scene. "We're about three and a half miles as the crow flies from the drop-off point marked on the map," the sheriff said. "Tire tracks over there appear to match Eugene Watkins's pickup. There's a significant amount of blood a few feet away, brain matter on the ground, fingerprints all over the trailer—oh, and a can of Pringles by the door. The grocery receipt shows that Watkins bought a can of Pringles that morning. It wasn't in the box of food found in the pickup bed."

Over the sound of the birds, Tony heard running water. "And a creek out back for fishing. How did Long find this place?"

McEntire shrugged. "Maybe he got lost. Maybe someone told him about it."

That wasn't as far-fetched as it sounded. People tended to be chatty. Ask the right questions, display the right affect, and a good interrogator could learn all kinds of things that his subject didn't realize he was telling.

"Did your pilot friend spot it?"

McEntire nodded.

"Any other tire tracks?"

"Nah. Presumably Long was smart enough to hide his car nearby. If someone came around, he could take off through the woods and get away."

"Or put a bullet in the poor guy's brain." Maybe Watkins had surprised him. He hadn't had the opportunity to escape unnoticed, so he'd taken the easy way out.

McEntire shook his head in disgust. "He could have let Watkins live. Could have said, 'Hey, I'm sorry, I just needed a place to stay, I'll leave now.' He could have just walked away."

Not Damon Long. If killing was in his best interests, he did it. Right or wrong wasn't an issue for him. Expediency was.

But McEntire was right. Long could have walked away from Eugene Watkins. The odds that the old man would have taken time from his weekend sans wife to report a trespasser were probably nonexistent. Long could have let Watkins live and moved on to a new hiding place—which he'd done anyway. But he'd killed the man because he could. It was second nature.

McEntire circled the deputies gathering blood evidence and climbed the steps into the trailer, careful not to touch anything. Tony followed a few paces behind. The place was shabby—worn linoleum on the floor, holes punched in the brown paneling that lined the walls, a musty smell that permeated the very structure—but Long wouldn't have noticed any of that. Four walls and a roof, far from the nearest nosy neighbor. That counted.

Fingerprint powder dusted the door, the counter, and fresh smudges on the window blinds. Tony gazed at the patterns for a moment before heading outside again in need of fresh air.

Not too long ago, another deputy had taken him out to

another isolated murder scene. That scene had stunk, too. The barn on the property had housed a meth lab, and the killer had set the place on fire, leaving nothing but charred remains of the two men inside. One of them had been an informant of Tony's, the other his cousin.

And the killer had been Damon Long. Death followed wherever he went.

"DNA will show whether all that blood belonged to Watkins," the sheriff said.

"And the fingerprints from the trailer will match Long's. After Oklahoma gets through with him, you can have what's left." If Long made it to trial.

"How many homicides does this make?"

Tony shrugged. "I doubt even he knows."

"Too damn many." McEntire drew a cigar from his breast pocket, then used it to gesture toward the nearest deputy. "Take Detective Ceola back to The Gardens when he's ready."

"I'm ready now." Long hadn't left behind anything but evidence of murder, and Tony couldn't help collect that. He could only watch and feel frustrated.

He followed the deputy back to the SUV and settled in for another bone-jarring ride. They were over the worst of the ruts and back on the paved road when his cell phone rang. He fished it from his pocket and flipped it open, answering with a curt, "Hello."

"Good morning, Detective."

Charlize. "I'll have to talk to Selena about giving out this number to just anyone," he said drily.

She didn't respond but got straight to the point. "Luke Morgan has left the state. If he comes back, it won't be for Selena."

Suspicion raised the fine hairs on the back of Tony's

neck. "He leave voluntarily? Or did you have something to do with it?"

"I didn't kill him, Detective, if that's what you're asking. He had a falling-out with the boss. Damon decided he couldn't be trusted and should be removed from the picture—permanently. Luke decided it was in his best interests to lie low for a while." Charlize sounded so cool and businesslike. No one would ever guess from her tone that she was talking about murder-for-hire.

"And you know this how?"

"I imagine my sources are even more wide-ranging than your own, Detective. Something else I thought might interest you: Yesterday afternoon Damon told Luke about a rear entrance to The Gardens, one that's rarely used. If there is such an entrance, I'd wonder how Damon found out about it. I'd also shore up security there."

"Thanks. I'll do that." Tony hung up, then glanced at the deputy. "Are you familiar with The Gardens?"

"Sure. We took field trips out there in school, and Miss Kathryn used to hold an annual barbecue and invite everyone in town. I even worked there one summer." He shook his head ruefully. "I decided real quick that farmwork wasn't for me."

"How many entrances are there?"

"Two. The main one and the one for deliveries and employees."

The deputy didn't know about the rear entrance, and why should he? It was a dirt trail barely wide enough for a car. There were trees on both sides of the road, blocking it from view from the nearby fields, and, as Charlize had said, it was rarely used, only by June for quick trips to the house and, since Selena's arrival, by Luther. More often than not, according to Grant, June used the main entrance—because she could, Tony thought.

If the deputy who'd once worked at the farm didn't know of the rear entrance's existence, odds were good not many others did. Among those who did were Grant, of course, his foreman, the security detail, Luther . . . and June.

Tony flipped open the phone again and punched the only number on speed dial. When Simmons answered, he didn't bother with a hello. "Real quick, Frankie. Those pre-paid cell calls from June's phone records—when were they made?"

"Christ, Chee, it's Saturday, and I'm babysitting."

"I've seen what passes for babysitting with you—cereal and the television. It doesn't matter whether you're there or not. When was the first call?"

The cartoon blare faded and was replaced with the shuffling of papers. "Wednesday."

The night Peretti gained access to the property. June had come back to the house that night to pick up something she'd left earlier. Security hadn't been doing vehicle searches then. Had she brought a hired killer with her? "The next one?"

"Thursday. Twice."

The day ten grand appeared in Elpidio Vargas's checking account—and June had access to the employment records for the farm. Pulling a name and direct-deposit info off the computer would have been easy. "And yesterday afternoon?"

"Yeah. For three minutes, seven seconds."

A person could pass on a lot of information in three minutes.

"Has Auntie June been up to no good?" Simmons asked.

"Yeah, I'm afraid so." Tony sighed. "Thanks, Frankie. I'll call you later." He slid the phone into his pocket as the main entrance to The Gardens came into sight ahead. "Just drop me at the gate," he instructed the deputy. He could borrow a pickup from Security and drive to the Ravenel home without having to face either Selena or Grant. No need to trouble them. Yet.

But if June was guilty...Christ, with family like that, Selena didn't need enemies.

14

The knock at the door startled June. She hadn't heard a vehicle approach, not since Brother Hawkins had stopped by to pick up Luther for the weekly men's fellowship breakfast at the church. Of course, she'd been running the vacuum and the dishwasher, with the radio on the kitchen windowsill turned loud for company.

Now she switched off Aretha Franklin mid-tune, dried her hands, and went into the living room. The front door was open, the screen door latched—pitiful protection if someone dangerous showed up on her doorstep. Lucky for her, the most dangerous person in her life wasn't allowed to leave The Gardens.

She stopped at the door but made no move to unlatch it, instead folding her arms over her chest. "Can I help—"

The man standing there grinned when she broke off. She'd seen him only once before, and he'd changed his appearance since, but changing the color of his eyes did nothing to disguise that greedy, sly look in them. "Ms. Ravenel. Can I come in?"

She looked past him. She hadn't heard a car pull up because there wasn't one out there. Either someone had dropped him off or he'd come in on foot. "What the hell are you doing coming to my house in the middle of the day? You're taking a big chance being out like this."

"Then you'd best unlock the door and let me come in before someone sees me standing out here."

Grudgingly she did so, backing away as he stepped inside. Knotting her fingers in the dish towel she held, she watched as he slowly circled the room, taking in the furnishings, the souvenirs of Luther's years with Oda Mae, the crocheted doilies and the angels and the framed picture of Jesus. He stopped in front of a display of family photographs, his gaze going automatically to Amelia. He looked from the photo to her, back to the photo, back to her.

June knew that at her best, she couldn't compete with Amelia, and she looked far from her best this morning. She wore a cotton skirt so old that its floral pattern had faded to nothing but a swirl here and there, with a blouse that had lost its shape long ago. Her comfiest old terry house shoes were ripped, and she'd tied a ratty scarf around her hair. No competition at all for beautiful Amelia looking her finest.

"I see why you hated your sister. Why you hate your niece."

Bitterness flared so strong that it left a sour taste in her mouth. It was nothing so simple as looks. She wasn't that shallow. She had a whole world of reasons for feeling the way she did, but she didn't contradict him. Her reasons were her own business.

Getting rid of Selena—that was his business.

He got down to business right away. "I thought it would be best to minimize my chances of getting captured and let someone else take care of your niece for me, but so far all I've gotten is screwed. So fuck this bullshit. I'm gonna handle it myself." His grin was sudden, unexpected. "With a little help from you, Miss June."

———

Glass of iced tea in hand, Selena went into the family room, crossed to the easel where the portrait of Luther sat, and studied it. She rarely did portraits; her talent lay in landscapes. She did have a self-portrait in progress—vivid colors, long black curls, café-au-lait skin, but no features. It had been "in progress" for months, though she rarely even looked at it. Before Tony had asked her to stay in Tulsa, she'd shipped it to Key West, where it remained.

She'd always thought she'd found it impossible to finish because she hadn't really known who she was. Now she did know. Her parents had names, faces, histories, families. *She* had a history. A father who loved her, a grandfather who adored her . . . an aunt who resented her. Life couldn't be too perfect.

Sighing, she turned away from the canvas. Tony was out with the sheriff, Grant was on the phone with a client, and Luther had other plans for the morning. She wished she was free to make plans. First, she would finish her tea outside, with the morning sun warm on her face. Next, she would explore the farm, and then the town. She would visit Luther's church, his house, and Oda Mae's grave, and meet some of the extended family she shared with the Ravenels and the Hamiltons.

And she would be looking over her shoulder the entire time, watching for Long, for Morgan, for strangers whose faces meant nothing to her. Suspecting anyone who looked twice at her.

The house was cool and relatively quiet. The clock ticking in the foyer. Nell singing in the kitchen. Beyond the hedges outside, the fields were quiet. Only the security staff worked twenty-four hours a day. The other workers were enjoying their weekend off.

When movement outside caught her attention, Selena

lifted the curtains for a better look. It was June's car driving along the lane, and she was alone inside. Disappointed that she wasn't bringing Luther for a visit, Selena left the family room for the foyer anyway. At the moment, even hostile company was better than none.

The doorbell interrupted Nell's singing. "I'll get it," Selena called, and after a beat, the tune started again. She undid the locks, turned off the alarm, and opened the door.

It was the first time she'd seen her aunt looking less than polished. June's purple pants and white shirt were unflattering, her hair had been hastily and badly fixed, and she wore no makeup, revealing a sprinkling of freckles across her nose.

She gave Selena a measuring look that managed to convey disapproval as well. "They're letting you answer the door?"

"I was closest."

"There was a time when our people always answered the door for Grant's people. Back when they owned us." June stepped into the foyer and her gaze swept around. "Where is Grant?"

"In his office."

"And Tony?"

"Out."

"So . . . you were probably expecting Daddy."

"I was hoping," Selena replied, and watched June's jaw clench. She'd had Luther to herself for nearly thirty years. Was it really so hard to share him now? Or was it sharing him with Amelia's daughter that bothered her so much?

"He's at the church. He had a life before you came along, you know. You can't expect him to give up everything to be at your beck and call. So . . ." June's smile was forced, uneven.

"I thought I'd come by instead. I thought we could have that talk you wanted."

"About what?"

Another unsteady smile. "Amelia, of course. The only thing anybody wants to talk about since you showed up."

Selena closed the door, then gestured toward the hallway. "I'd like that. I'd like to talk about you, too."

June's laugh was brittle. "There's nothing to talk about. I'm nothing special. Ask Luther. He'll tell you."

Selena didn't know whether to lead June to the family room, as if she were the hostess and June merely a guest. She wound up walking awkwardly a step or two behind her aunt.

Once inside, June headed for the easel instead of a seat. Selena was accustomed to Tony seeing her work, and she hadn't minded Grant's occasional glances over her shoulder the day before, but her nerves tightened as June stood back to study the portrait. She made a good living with her art. Her paintings hung in homes, offices, galleries, and a few museums around the world. Did it really matter what her aunt thought?

Yes, she admitted with a thin smile. Though June would rather eat dirt than compliment her on the one talent she shared with her mother.

After a moment, June turned away from the easel without comment and looked around the room. "The first time I came to this house, I called ahead, and I was told to go to the back door, where Nell left me waiting on the stoop in the rain while she made sure it was all right to let me in." She feigned a Deep-South accent. "Miz Kathryn was mighty particular about who she let into her home. Who knew what someone like me might do?"

Her sigh seemed to well up from deep inside her. "She

was right to be suspicious. I wreaked a lot of havoc in her life. In everyone's life."

"How?" The comment intrigued Selena. By all accounts, Amelia had been the hell-raiser. June had been too quiet, too lost in the shadows, to even make much of an impression.

As if she hadn't heard her, June picked up a photo of Amelia from the mantel and gazed at it. "When I was a little girl, I idolized Amelia. She was the best big sister anyone could have. Oh, she had her flaws. She had to be the center of attention, had to have everyone's eyes on her, but I loved her anyway. We all did. But the older we got, the more people ignored me, the harder it got to love her. She was just so *much*. She charmed everybody into forgetting that I even existed. I was an afterthought, hardly worth noticing."

Hands trembling, she set the photo down, then turned to face Selena. "You want to hear some stories about your mama? I've got some to tell you. When I was little, I called her Melie because I couldn't say her name. When I got older, she called me P.J. Short for Plain June. She used to tell me, 'There are more important things in life than being pretty.' Easy for her to say, when she was the prettiest girl in Chadwick County. 'You've got brains,' she used to say. 'You've got a good heart.' But having brains and a good heart didn't get me anywhere...and look what being pretty got her."

Selena wanted to believe that Amelia's words had been meant to comfort, not wound. But she knew from experience that people could be thoughtless and outright cruel. Amelia, like so many beautiful, spoiled women, could have had a mean streak that anyone not on the receiving end couldn't see.

"I was seventeen when I got my first boyfriend. I had a crush on Robert that, oh, was not to be believed. When he asked me to go steady with him, I just about fainted. He went to church and sat with me on Sundays, and he hung out at our house every chance he got. Even Mama, who was so thrilled that a boy had finally noticed me, was getting tired of seeing his face every evening. 'I didn't take him to raise,' she used to say, but she didn't mean it. She was happy for me. She'd thought no boy would ever look twice at me.

"Amelia had thought so, too. She flirted with Robert every time she saw him. She just couldn't believe that the male existed who preferred me over her, and she had to prove it by taking him away from me. He was three years younger than her, still in school. She only wanted him because I had him, and she got him. He fell hard for her and damn near forgot my name. It broke my heart... and she broke his heart. Once he dumped me, she lost interest in him. She was always like that, wanting what someone else had."

Women always accused pretty girl of flirting, Luther had said with a chuckle. *But she wasn't flirting. That was just the way she was. When she looked at you, it was like you was the most important person in her world. She made you feel good about yourself. Made you feel special.*

But she hadn't made June feel special. Had she known how much her little sister disliked her? Had she accepted any of the blame for June's resentment or tried to make amends? Or had she been too caught up in her life to bother? She'd been young, in love, with a baby and a bright future. Maybe she'd thought there would be plenty of time in the future to make things right with June.

June fixed her gaze on Selena, the look in her eyes one of malicious satisfaction. "Not the sort of stories Daddy and Grant tell, are they? Not the sort of thing you want to hear."

"I told you before, I want to hear everything. I know they

idealized her. They couldn't see her flaws." And June couldn't see her virtues. Selena was surprised that June could admit to ever having loved Amelia. She was so angry.

Selena wanted to shake her, to tell her to get over it. Amelia had been dead for more than half of June's life. Enough was enough.

But they didn't call the early years "formative" without reason. Everything June was today had been shaped in those years. The bitterness had hardened; the anger had turned poisonous. Getting over it would require work and desire, and June lacked the desire. If she didn't blame Amelia for everything, who would she blame? Luther? Herself?

In the foyer, the clock chimed the hour, the first bong making June flinch. She hugged her arms to her chest, rubbing her hands briskly over her arms as she gazed around the room as if seeing it for the first time. "I hate this house. I hate coming here to work, to eat. I hate that Grant tries to make Luther and me feel as if we belong here. We don't. If he would have just stayed in his world, and Amelia had stayed in hers, I never would have had to..."

Selena moved a few slow steps nearer. "To what?"

June's gaze jerked back to her. "Come for a walk with me. I don't want to...I can't..."

When she started toward the door, Selena extended one hand to stop her. "I'm not supposed to go out. You know that."

After staring at the hand in front of her for a moment, June smiled slowly. "If anyone ever told your mama she wasn't supposed to do something, she'd turn right around and do it just out of spite. Mama would say, 'You be in by midnight,' and Amelia would smile that bright smile of hers and say, 'I will.' Then she'd come dragging in at four or five in the morning. And Mama would just shake her head. If I'd disobeyed her like that, I'd have gotten a whipping for sure, but when Amelia did it, it was just cute." June's smile remained in place as she shook her head and murmured, "Everything about her was just so goddamned *cute.*"

The venom cloaking the soft words was enough to chill the air. Keeping her voice steady, her tone level, Selena asked, "What was it you never would have had to do, June?"

For a moment June remained utterly motionless, hardly even breathing. The stillness was abruptly shattered by a shudder, one that she calmed with a deep breath. "Come for a walk with me," she said, taking Selena's hand, tucking it tightly between her own. "I'll tell you everything you want to know about your mama. How she lived. How she loved. How she died."

Damon crouched behind a tangle of underbrush. The muscles in his legs were cramping, but he ignored them and focused on the guards.

The guard shack was small, knocked together in a few hours. There were windows on two sides, one facing the gate, the other looking toward the Ravenel house, and a door on the third side. Both windows and the door were open, with a box fan in one window to move the warm air. Both men sat inside, one reading the paper, the other watching a movie on a portable DVD player. They probably thought they'd pulled the easy duty, with no cars but June's coming in or out, no one to question, no threat.

They were fucking wrong.

He'd been watching them since June passed through the gate twenty minutes earlier, and little had happened. The guy with the newspaper had poured himself a cup of coffee;

the one watching the movie had practically pissed himself laughing. They were complacency at its finest.

Easing to his feet, Damon moved into the shadow of the nearest tree. His .45 was holstered in his waistband in back, but it wasn't much use here. He couldn't risk a gunshot alerting any of the fuckers who patrolled the grounds regularly. Couldn't risk alerting his prey. Instead, he'd chosen his weapon for availability and lack of noise: a hunting knife that belonged to June's old man. Pissed off as he was, he could use his bare hands, but there was something sweet about all that blood. . . .

He made his way back a few yards, then to the edge of the road. At the other gates, all the growth had been cleared away. Not here. There was plenty of cover until he was only ten feet from the shack.

Damon paused in the last of the cover for a moment, until the one guard burst into a belly laugh, then, fingers loosely gripping the knife handle, he strolled right up to the door. Stepping inside, he stabbed through the paper with one swift slash and plunged the knife into the guard's chest.

"Jesus Christ! What the hell—" The second guard tried to jump to his feet, but stumbled.

Leaving the knife where it was, Damon wrapped his arm around the man's neck, squeezing tightly, using his own weight as leverage. The man clawed at his forearm, drawing blood, his ragged gasps laced with fading curses, before he went limp.

Damon let go, leaving the man to fall to the floor. He took both men's weapons, then dragged the second guard's shirt over his head, stripped off his own shirt, and pulled it on. The polo shirt bore the logo for the security firm on the left chest, and the navy blue made the flecks of blood splatter hardly noticeable.

Around the curve on the other side of the gate appeared two figures on foot. The short hair on the taller one threw him for only an instant. He would recognize Selena anywhere. She was the only person who'd ever drawn blood from him and lived to tell the tale, and she'd managed more than once. Today, finally, she would pay.

The first guard made a gurgling sound, drawing Damon's attention to him. His eyes were rounded, and blood trickled from his mouth. He was dying, and knew there wasn't a damned thing he could do about it.

After taking the ball cap from the man's head, Damon gave him a shove, toppling him onto the floor on top of the other guard's body. He put the cap on, added the dark glasses he found sitting next to the DVD player, and pulled the door shut.

June was holding onto Selena's arm as if she feared she might make a run for it. She wouldn't. He'd told June what to say to get her out there. Selena had obsessed about one parent or another all her life. She wouldn't turn down the chance to learn more, especially from her aunt June.

As they drew nearer, he pushed the button that swung the gate open. Selena held back, saying something to her aunt. Probably that she shouldn't leave the grounds. She was good at doing what she was told. William had always been pleased by her malleability, right up to the time she'd refused to go to work for him.

Whatever misgivings Selena had, June didn't let go. She said something that got the bitch moving again, though reluctantly. They came through the gate, and he nodded respectfully through the window as he pressed the button again. The gate slowly closed, stopping with a clang, and he turned to watch them through the rear window. Selena looked back over her shoulder, her gaze connecting briefly with his before June tugged her arm, making her stumble. She turned her attention back to the ground ahead of them.

At his feet, the gurgling stopped and the guard grew still. Soon Selena would be dead, as well. Damon would put the past behind him and start taking care of the future.

Selena dug in her heels, sliding a bit in the loose dirt before bringing June to a stop. "June, we really shouldn't be here. We need to go back to the house."

Impatiently, June frowned at her. "I told you, I can't talk about this in Grant's house."

Selena pulled. "Why not?"

June resisted. "Because I need to tell you...I need to show you...It's not far. Don't worry. Tony will never know you disobeyed him unless you tell. I certainly won't."

When she tugged again, Selena reluctantly began moving. They weren't going far—just another hundred yards to the pond. For much of her life, it had been June's favorite place in the world. She'd spent hours on its banks, reading, thinking, daydreaming, planning. It was where she'd cried out her heartbreak over Robert, where she'd schemed about a future where people would say, "Ain't she something?" about *her*, not Amelia. She was going to go to college, have a successful career, make a lot of money, take care of her mama and daddy, and people were going to be impressed.

Thanks to Amelia, June hadn't set foot near the pond in twenty-eight years.

Her heart was thudding in her chest. Excitement or fear? Dread or anticipation? It wasn't too late to stop this. She could tell Selena she'd changed her mind. She'd said all she had to say. She could walk away.

But it *was* too late. Selena would never let it drop. She

would tell Tony and Grant and Luther, and they would question her, pester her. They would never give her a moment's peace until they uncovered her secret, and then everything would be ruined.

This was the only way to hold onto Luther. To save herself. To stop Amelia from destroying her even from the grave.

Years ago she'd tromped through the trees to the pond so many hundreds of times that she'd worn a path into the weeds. It was long since gone, but she knew where to turn, which direction to maneuver between tall pines and scrubby undergrowth.

"Where are we going?" Selena asked.

"To the pond. There I can tell you..." Deliberately June trailed off. She would tell her secrets, and then Damon Long would kill Selena. Luther would grieve, but he would get over it. He would never suspect his own daughter.

"Were you sorry when she disappeared?" Selena asked.

"Of course." Though not for the same reason everyone else was.

"Were you sorry that I disappeared?"

The smells of water and damp growth, accompanied by the plop of a slow trickle, signaled the clearing as they topped the last rise. The pond was spring-fed, with an overflow pipe that fed a slip too tiny to be called a creek. Cattails grew at the edge on one side, and a metal lawn chair rusted in the nearby shade. June had pulled the chair home from the neighbor's when she was only ten, proud of her find despite its sorry condition. Amelia had been sitting on the porch with some friends and had called to Oda Mae, "Junie's dragging home trash now, like some stray dog."

Amelia had laughed, and her friends had followed suit.

For weeks after, they'd called June "trash girl" when they'd seen her.

"June?"

June glanced at Selena and saw Amelia, heard Amelia's voice. Shaking her head to clear it, she shrugged. "Of course I was sorry you were gone." A lie. She'd never felt kindly toward Amelia's daughter. With her light-colored skin, the baby was a living symbol of Amelia's sins and good fortunes. June had done everything right, with nothing to show for it, while Amelia had lived a selfish and shameful life and was about to be richly rewarded for it. Her baby would have been rewarded, too.

The pond covered two acres and was deep enough to hide all manner of mysteries. On the west side where they stood, the trees grew almost to the banks, providing shade and a carpet of pine needles to keep the weeds down. Releasing Selena's arm, June picked up a pine cone and tossed it into the water, then watched the ripples of its passing until they dissipated.

"You're lucky that she died," she said at last. "She wouldn't have been a good mother. She didn't share attention gladly. She would have come to resent the affection your father showed you. She would have seen you as competition, and she couldn't bear competition."

"She loved me," Selena said evenly.

"She wasn't capable of loving anyone but herself. She got pregnant to bind Grant to her. She used you to convince him to leave his wife and run off with her. She never cared if she hurt someone else, if she broke someone's heart, just as long as she got what she wanted."

"You never forgave her for breaking your heart, did you?"

"I never forgave her for any of the wrongs she did me.

She was breathtakingly beautiful on the outside, but her inside was ugly and mean and rotted, and no one ever saw it but me. Mama and Daddy, they thought she was perfect. They looked at her and looked at me, and found *me* lacking. Because I wasn't pretty like her, because I wasn't flighty and flirty like her, I didn't measure up. They loved and spoiled and doted on her, and hardly noticed I existed. They never held her accountable."

June closed her eyes briefly, listening to the overflow trickle, feeling the heat and humidity on her skin, remembering that night so many years ago. It had troubled her, haunted her, but standing there just feet from the water, she knew she'd had no choice. Just as she had no choice today.

Opening her eyes again, she looked at Selena, whose resemblance to Amelia was always startling, whose voice was even starting to sound like Amelia's. No choice at all.

"So I did," she said with a faint smile. "I held her accountable."

The Ravenel house sat off the road, shaded from the morning sun. The yard was too dark to grow grass, and no flowers softened the lines of the foundation. But June wasn't a soft person.

Tony parked next to a pickup that looked as if it could have been a teenage Luther's first car. There was no sign of June's car. She could be running errands—Saturday mornings were prime time for that.

Or she could be working against Selena. Making more phone calls, maybe meeting with Long in person.

He climbed the steps and knocked on the door, then walked around back, making note of the dirt tracks that led into the woods and, eventually, to The Gardens. The grass in the backyard was neatly trimmed, and at the far edge, chickens scratched and clucked in their pen. An unpainted picket fence circled Luther's garden, mostly at rest now.

Maybe Luther knew where to find her. He'd had something going on at church, he'd told Selena the day before, and couldn't see her until the afternoon. Tony had passed the small white building a mile back, cars parked in small clusters under the live oaks.

He climbed into the truck and backed around Luther's pickup before pulling onto the road. His fingers were tight around the steering wheel, his knuckles turning white. He was probably overreacting. The mere fact that June was away from the house meant nothing. She was a busy woman with a job, family, and volunteer activities. Like him, like most people, she probably spent more time away than home.

He wasn't sure what made him look to the left—instinct, hyperawareness. He stomped on the brake, bringing the truck to a squealing stop, then shifted into reverse. He stopped again, even with a wide spot leading off the road. It might have once been a driveway, but now there was nothing at its end. Just thirty feet of weeds . . . and a car.

It was an early nineties model and bore a strong resemblance to Simmons's car, with fast-food trash covering both front and rear floorboards. Sections of a newspaper were scattered across the back seat. The Dallas *Morning News,* dated a month ago.

Damon Long had been in Dallas a month ago.

Damon Long had left the car, the trash. He was somewhere in this area, less than a half mile from Selena's grandfather's house, little more than that from The Gardens.

Tony looked around the area, wishing he knew something about tracking. Was that faint disturbance in the weeds a trail or courtesy of the wind? Had Long set off through the woods? Had he gone toward June's house or directly toward The Gardens? Or had someone picked him up in another vehicle? How did he plan to get onto the farm? Would he take out the guards, or was June going to help him?

Maybe he didn't intend to deal with the guards. Maybe he planned to lure Selena away from The Gardens. Tony would like to be one hundred percent sure that he couldn't do it, but if he threatened her family, if he told her he was holding her aunt June hostage and had June there to play the frightened victim...

He raced back to the truck, climbed in, and peeled out of the drive. Fumbling his cell phone from his pocket, he called Security first, instructing them to lock down the property, then left a message for the dispatcher to pass on to Sheriff McEntire. His next call was to the house. He counted rings impatiently before Nell picked up. "It's Tony. Let me talk to Selena, please."

"Hang on a minute," Nell said, "and I'll get her."

One minute crawled past. Two. Three. His grip on the cell phone tightened until his fingertips went numb, and the tightness spread to his chest, making it difficult to draw a full breath. He was muttering silent prayers when the phone at the other end clattered an instant before Grant came on the line. His words were laced with fear.

"Tony, we can't find her. Selena's not in the house."

15

An edgy feeling prickled along Selena's spine. The pond wasn't as isolated as it appeared, she assured herself. The road was only fifty yards behind them. The roof of Luther's house was visible through the trees to the east, and the guards were within shouting distance to the west. There was no reason for her to feel so anxious.

Except the bands tightening around her chest. The knot in her gut. The unexpected little tremors that rocketed through her. The malice in June's voice, gleaming in her eyes. The sick feeling that Selena, like everyone else, had underestimated her.

June wasn't *just* an angry, bitter woman. She was filled with hatred, jealousy, possessiveness, and fear. She hated Amelia as intensely as she loved Luther, and she hated Selena, too. Not resented. Not disliked. Hated.

Disappointment welled in Selena. She knew "family" didn't automatically mean friendship, love, and caring. But she had so little family and had gone through so much to find them. She had hoped...

"How did you—" Her voice was unsteady; she swallowed hard, then tried again. "How did you hold Amelia accountable, June?"

Her aunt paced to the edge of the water, gazing into its depths at memories only she could see. After a time, she gave

Selena a curious look. "If Tony was being unfaithful to you, would you want to know?"

Selena didn't point out that Tony would never be unfaithful; it simply wasn't in his character. Her faith in him would only make June more hostile. "I suppose so."

"I would, too. Knowing is always better than not knowing. At least, then you can prepare yourself. But not everyone agrees. Take Kathryn Hamilton. Everyone in town knew Grant was stepping out on her with Amelia, but she didn't want to know. She was deaf, blind, and dumb when it came to that. Until I made her face it. I *made* her hear it. How they'd been together for years. How they'd had a baby together. How he was planning to leave Kathryn and they were going to run off together.

"She cried. Can you imagine that? Miss High-and-mighty Kathryn, boo-hooing like a baby—for about two minutes." June smiled. "That saying, 'Don't get mad; get even,' was made up with Kathryn in mind. She decided right there in the solarium that she was going to put a stop to their affair, and I was happy to help her do it."

The sick feeling intensified. Selena eased a step back. June wasn't going to confess something that could affect the way Luther felt about her and leave Selena free to pass it on. Confession might be good for the soul, but, in this case, only if it died with the telling.

She could run. She'd seen no sign of a weapon, unless the decaying branches here and there on the ground counted. She was younger and in better shape. Even in flimsy sandals, she could outdistance June easily. She could also beat her in a one-on-one fight. June might have weight and passion on her side, but Selena had years of training.

And she had the .9-millimeter pistol holstered on her

waistband beneath her shirt. But could she use it against June? Against her own family?

Before she could make any decision, though, she needed to hear whatever June was willing to tell. "What did you do?"

June shrugged breezily. "I told Kathryn where to find Amelia. That house was pretty much a family secret. Grant, Daddy, a few other people, and me—we were the only ones who knew about it. So I drew Kathryn a goddamned map."

"Did you know she intended to kill her?" There was no denying that Amelia had shown poor judgment in having an affair with a married man, bearing his illegitimate child, and agreeing to run off with him. But she hadn't deserved to die for it. She hadn't deserved to have her death set in motion by her own sister.

Something flashed across June's face. Guilt? Regret? Whatever, it disappeared just as quickly. "It didn't matter to me what she did as long as she did something. As long as Amelia got what was coming to her. Everything always went her way. She skated through life, breaking rules, breaking promises, breaking hearts, and she never had to pay for it. She never suffered for her bad choices, and she always got what she wanted. But for once, thanks to me, she was going to get what she deserved."

"Having an affair and a baby doesn't justify murder," Selena said quietly.

June gazed into the pond. "She was so smug. 'Grant's leaving his wife. He's looking for a house for us right now. As soon as he gets back from his trip, we're moving. He's divorcing her, and we're getting married, and we're going to live together like a real family.' As if she had the right! She didn't care that it would kill Kathryn to lose him, that it would hurt Miss Rosalind, that it would bring shame on the whole Hamilton family. She didn't even care what it would do to Daddy, for her to move away and take his grandbaby with her. She was getting what she wanted, and as far as she was concerned, that was all that mattered."

"So you told Kathryn where to find Amelia, and Kathryn killed her."

"Yes . . . no." The malice was in her eyes again when she brought her gaze back to Selena. "Kathryn hit her in the head with the skillet, but that wasn't what killed her."

Selena stiffened. Her first attempt to speak failed; the second sounded strangled. "Then what did?"

June looked around, arms wide as if to embrace the place. "Growing up, I spent more time here than at the house. This was my sanctuary, though it didn't belong to us then. It was part of The Gardens until after Amelia died. But nobody ever came here, so whenever I needed solitude, whenever life just got too much to bear, I'd come here. Sometimes I even slept right here. Amelia wouldn't set foot out here for fear of getting chiggers or mussing her clothes or something. It was all mine. I brought that chair. I built that fire ring. I brought that little table."

The ancient chair sat askew, as if its bolts had rusted away, and the table was a pile of rotting wood. The rocks that had made up the fire ring were blackened and scattered haphazardly across the ground.

"There was a terrible storm that night. When it passed, I slipped out of the house. I liked it here when the grass was wet, when everything smelled so fresh and clean. I brought a plastic sheet to keep me dry, and I laid down right here and stared up at the sky. The stars were so bright, the night so clear. And then they came."

Selena imagined the scene from that long-ago night. It had been July, so even at night, the air would have been heavy with heat. She saw how starlight could change the pond from mundane to magical, blurring the hard edges, reflecting off the water. The drip of the overflow pipe must have become a steady stream as it cast off rainwater, and the moisture must have intensified the scents.

"Who came?" she asked, keeping her voice soft, her prompt unobtrusive.

"Two cars pulled through the weeds to that side of the pond." June gestured toward the northwest. "There used to be a road over there years ago. I didn't recognize the second car, but I knew Amelia's car. She was so proud of that flashy little red car. She was always offering to take me places in it just so she could remind me that Grant had given it to her."

Stopping for a moment, June seemed lost in the past. Had it ever occurred to her that Amelia had offered her a ride because she needed to go somewhere? Had she ever given Amelia the benefit of the doubt?

"The man driving Amelia's car stopped right at the edge of the water, and he got out. I thought he was Mexican, but Tony says he's Puerto Rican. As if it matters. Anyway, Kathryn's brother got out of the second car, and together they pushed Amelia's little Camaro over the bank and into the pond. They stood back and watched until it sank, and then they got in the second car and left. They never knew I was over here. They never knew I saw . . ."

June swiped at her face, then stared at her hand as if the tears there were an alien substance. She had likely cried over the years because of Amelia, but had she ever cried *for* her? Had she ever regretted that her sister had died so young? Or had she always believed that Amelia brought about her own death?

"Kathryn told the police that she killed Amelia, and I guess she always believed it. But she didn't. I laid here in the shadows and watched those men. I watched the car slide out into the water and start to sink, and I saw her. I saw Amelia banging on the window and trying to open the door. She was screaming—I could tell just by looking, but I couldn't hear her because there was tape or something across her mouth. I watched her until the car went under the surface, and I kept watching until all the bubbles stopped, until the water was calm again. I watched until the sun came up the next morning, and I shook out my sheet and went home and never came back here again until today."

Selena's stomach heaved. "You left her there to drown? You let her die because it fit your warped idea of justice?"

"There's nothing warped about believing you should pay for your sins."

"All these years Luther and Grant have mourned for her, wondering what happened, whether she was alive, and the whole time you knew. You knew her body was right here, between their houses, and you never told them."

"They would have blamed me. It wasn't my fault. Amelia brought it on herself. But if I'd told them what I'd seen, they would have blamed me anyway. She would have ruined my life even in death. Do you know how things changed with her death? People began noticing me. They began seeing that I was smarter than her, more dependable, more capable, more responsible. They began valuing *me*. I never would have had that acceptance if I'd told."

Selena tried again. "Don't you think Luther deserved the chance to give her a proper burial?"

June's shrug was edged with impatience. "What does a burial matter? She's dead either way. He's going to mourn either way. Except this way he had his devoted daughter June there to help him through it."

Selena glanced at the water, then away. She didn't want to imagine the car resting on the bottom, didn't want to think about Amelia trying desperately to free herself. The blow Kathryn had given her must have left her unconscious; she'd awakened in pain, terrified, her mouth taped to mute her screams . . .

Dear God, William had known she was alive. He hadn't merely disposed of her body, as Kathryn claimed, but he'd killed her. He'd murdered Amelia just to keep her from accusing his sister of assaulting her.

And the Mexican—*Tony says he's Puerto Rican*—could only be Rodrigo. He'd helped kill her mother, then had taken Selena to Puerto Rico and tormented her for the next nine years.

Tears welled in her eyes, but she blinked them back and focused on June again. "You couldn't risk letting Luther know what a horrible daughter you were twenty-eight years ago. You're not going to let him find out now, are you? Do you plan to kill me, the way you killed Amelia?"

"I didn't kill her! And I was never a horrible daughter! I was always the best daughter he and Mama could have asked for. They just never noticed because of *her*." June's gaze shifted somewhere behind and to the left of Selena. "But, no, I don't intend to kill you. I just brought you here so he could."

Prickles of awareness rose along Selena's spine too late. Slowly she turned and saw a stranger leaning against a tree, one ankle crossed over the other, a pistol grasped in one hand.

No, not a stranger. Damon Long.

Tony's last call was to the Azalea Inn. He didn't give himself a chance to consider the wisdom of it. He didn't trust Charlize, but he did believe she was no threat to Selena. The thing that made him so suspicious also made her his best ally: She was a killer. She wouldn't hesitate to shoot Damon Long where he stood. Tony couldn't say the same about the sheriff or the security guards. He wanted Damon dead.

Long's at The Gardens, he'd said.

I'll be there in five, she'd replied.

He stopped at the gate long enough to clear Charlize for entrance, then sped along the drive to the house. He was out of the pickup before the dust settled, jumping out at the end of the sidewalk, where Grant and Nell waited.

His face pale, his eyes rounded, Grant burst into speech. "She's not in the house, Tony. We checked every room twice, but there's no sign of her. Just a glass of tea she left in the family room. I don't know where she could have gone, I don't know why she would have left without saying something—"

"What about June?"

Grant looked at him blankly, and Tony gestured toward her car, parked off to the side. Grant stared at it as if he'd never seen it before.

"I told you June came for a visit," Nell said. "I was in the kitchen when the doorbell rang, and Miss Selena called that she would get it, and then I heard June's voice. I told you."

Grant nodded. "Of course. I just didn't think . . ."

A lot of people just didn't think when it came to June.

"How did Long get onto the property?" Grant asked. "Where would he have taken them? How could he have gotten them past the guards?"

"I don't think he did get onto the property," Tony replied grimly as Charlize parked behind the truck. "I think June lured Selena off."

Nell's eyes widened and she clapped one hand over her mouth to muffle her gasp. Grant stared at him, shaking his head side to side. "No . . . they're family. She's Amelia's sister, she's Selena's aunt, for God's sake. She wouldn't . . . she couldn't . . ."

Charlize took two weapons from the trunk of her car, then came to stand beside Tony, offering him a choice between a sniper rifle and a shotgun. He took the shotgun, and she slung the rifle strap over her shoulder. "Someone's coming," she murmured with a nod to the east.

A pickup was approaching at a fast clip. It skidded to a stop ten feet away and the driver jumped out, the color in his face on the sick side of green. "Brown and Dobson . . . oh, God . . . they're—" Whirling away, he bent at the waist and heaved up his breakfast.

"Who are Brown and Dobson?" Charlize asked.

"The guards at the rear gate." Tony felt pretty damn sick himself.

"Then that's where we need to start." Charlize circled the truck and climbed into the passenger seat. As Tony pulled away from the house, she pulled her pistol from the holster, moved the safety to Off, and gave the barrel a damn near sensual caress. Then her gaze shifted to him. "Just to be clear . . . Damon dies. Even if he tries to surrender. Right?"

Tony swallowed hard. "Right."

Everything appeared quiet and normal when they reached the gate. One of the firm's pickups was parked off to the side, in the shade of a live oak, and chatter came from the guard shack, but no one was visible through the windows. Tony climbed the gate and approached the guard shack slowly, knowing what he would find, hating it like hell.

The chatter came from a portable DVD player, obscenities and canned laughter that couldn't dispel the unnatural stillness. The guards were slumped on the floor. One was covered with blood; the other bore no obvious signs of trauma but was just as dead.

Charlize glanced at the two men, then turned in a slow circle to study the area. "What's down this road?"

"Luther's house."

"He wouldn't take Selena far."

Tony knew she was right. Long would want them to find her—her body. He could hardly think the word. Couldn't imagine Selena dead. Couldn't consider the possibility and still breathe.

"His car was through the woods about a half mile north," he said, his tone harshly controlled. "Probably two or three hundred yards east of the fence line."

"I'll go there and start back this way. See what you can find from this end."

Nodding, Tony turned away from the dead men and focused his attention on the road. It was soft, sandy, and showed two sets of indistinct footprints in the middle. They were on top of the last set of tire tracks, which meant they'd been made after June went to Grant's house earlier.

Hardly noticing the rev of the engine as Charlize drove away, Tony headed east, following the tracks. There was nothing but woods and a pond between The Gardens and the Ravenel house. Plenty of places for Long to settle old scores, then make his getaway.

But this time he wasn't getting away.

Nothing in the warm morning indicated that anything was wrong. Birds sang in the trees and flew overhead, gnats buzzed, and a squirrel darted across the road ten feet ahead. It looked like a normal Saturday, no disturbances, no troubles. It looked like one hell of a day to die . . . but a damn fine morning for ridding the world of scum like Damon Long.

Long's beard was gone, his eye color had changed, and his hair was little more than stubble beneath the ball cap he wore. Like the shirt, the cap was embroidered with the security firm's logo. He'd been at the gate when Selena and June had come through. She'd looked over her shoulder at him after they passed, but hadn't recognized him.

"Interesting tale, Miz June," he said, his tone conversational. "When I told you to get her out here by offering her some story about her mother, I didn't know you had such a good one just waiting to be told. Treachery runs in your family on both sides, doesn't it, Selena? Your stepmother tries to kill your mother; your aunt lets her die. Kind of makes you wonder why you cared so damn much about finding them in the first place, doesn't it?"

About twenty-five feet separated Selena from Damon, with maybe a third of that between her and June. There was no cover but the pond, and everything in her rebelled at the idea of going into the water that had been both her mother's death and her grave. But maybe she wouldn't have to. There was still the pistol, hard against the small of her back. If she could pull it out before he realized what she was doing...

Slowly she shifted so she was facing him. Her hands were limp at her sides; she raised one to brush back a curl, then resettled it at her waist. "You're taking a big chance coming here."

"You think? Who's gonna know? You'll be dead. And Miz June's not gonna say a word to anyone, are you, June?"

"They'll know, June," Selena said quietly. "Your car is at the house. Nell knows you came to visit. They'll figure out that I left with you."

"I'll tell them you didn't."

"But they won't believe you. Luther won't believe you. He'll believe you helped Long kill me, and he'll never forgive you for it."

Uncertainty flashed across June's face before she determinedly shook it away. "Daddy would never believe me capable of hurting anyone."

"What other explanation is there? Tony will know I would never leave the house alone. They'll know that the only person who came onto the property was you." Selena eased her fingers a bit closer to the holster. "Luther will believe it, June, and he'll hate you for it. He'll wish you'd died all those years ago instead of Amelia. He'll wish you'd never been born."

June shook her head in agitation. "He won't believe it! He loves me!"

"He does," Selena agreed. "And it'll break his heart to know you helped Long kill me."

Long snorted. "Yeah, like it ain't gonna break his heart even more to find out that she helped William kill her sister."

Selena glared at him before returning her attention to June. "He doesn't have to ever know about that, June. I won't tell him. It's enough for him to know that she's dead. He doesn't need to know how it happened."

"She'll tell," Long said. "You think she's gonna leave her mother's bones at the bottom of a farm pond? She'll tell, and they'll want to know how she found out, and she'll—"

"Say that he told me." She jerked her head in his direction. "They'll believe me, June. He worked for Kathryn's brother for twenty years. William confided in him. Trust me, June, once I mention his name, they won't look any farther."

He pushed away from the tree and ambled toward them. He'd probably killed the two guards and had come here to kill her and, quite likely, June, too, but a person could never guess it from watching him. He was all easy grace, as if he was there for nothing more than enjoying the fall morning. He had no conscience, no heart, no soul.

"She's right about that," he agreed. "They won't have any problem believing William told me about dumping your sister's body here. But you know what, June? Your daddy finding out what you did isn't your only problem here. *She* is. Luther might tolerate you. He might even like you. But in his eyes, you're nothing compared to her. She's the only child of the daughter he loved more than life itself. As long as she's alive, she's going to be everything to him and you're going to be nothing. You don't want to go back to living like that, do you? Ignored. Forgotten. Second-best."

June's gaze shifted slowly between them, her look calculating. Selena held out little hope that she would change her mind. June couldn't change what had happened twenty-eight years ago, but she *could* protect her secret. She could remove Selena from her future and ensure her place in Luther's affections.

Her decision showed on her face, in her thin smile, her nod. She moved a few steps closer to Long. "Go ahead." Her voice was cold, empty, sounding like a stranger's. "Kill her."

"He'll kill you, too," Selena said sharply.

"Nah," Long said. "June's been good. She's the only person I've dealt with in a long time who's done what she said she would do. Besides, there's no reason to kill her when I know she won't talk. After all, I know her secrets."

Fear shivered through Selena. This wasn't the first time she'd faced death, but it was the worst. She had too much to lose—Tony, her father, her grandfather, their future. Tony wasn't going to save her this time; neither was Charlize. She had only herself to count on.

Long gestured with the pistol. "Go over there and search her, June. Find that weapon I know she's hiding."

Selena swallowed, shifting nervously. There was no way she could give up her gun. If she did, she might as well close her eyes and wait for Long to pull the trigger.

June came to stand in front of her, laying her hands against Selena's middle. Selena slapped them away. "Don't touch me, P.J.," she ordered. "Plain June. Trash girl. You weren't forgotten, June. You were everyone's favorite joke."

"Bitch," June spat out, her flat palm connecting with Selena's cheek in a stinging blow.

The slap knocked Selena off balance. She stumbled backward toward the pond, managing to turn and dive just when she would have splashed in. Behind her, she heard an angry shout and curses, but she swam deeper, angling to one side. Her lungs were bursting, eyes burning, as she fumbled the pistol from its holster, then stroked toward the surface. Filling her lungs with a hasty gasp, she submerged again as a shot rang out, slicing into the water a few feet away. Knowing Long would expect her to resurface elsewhere, she waited a moment, then came up again in the same place and squeezed off three shots before diving deep.

The shouts from the shore were distant, barely distinguishable from the rush of water in her ears. She was swimming toward the north side of the pond, hampered by the gun in her right hand but moved along by powerful kicks, when her foot connected with something hard. Toes throbbing, she drew up short, squinting in the murky water, barely able to make out...

Dear God, it was the back end of a car. Amelia's car.

She kicked toward the dim light of the surface, stopping just before she reached it. Slowly she eased her face from the water. Long was standing ankle deep in the reeds, his gun braced in both hands, and June was behind him, wringing her hands and shouting. "You told me you would kill her! You can't let her get away! She'll ruin everything! You find her and you kill—"

Long turned the pistol on June, pulled the trigger, and watched disinterestedly as her body jerked backwards in a graceless fall. He turned his attention and his pistol back toward the water, and Selena pulled the trigger. One head shot. One kill.

Treading water, she slid the pistol back into the holster, then swam toward shore.

Spurred by gunshots, Tony raced through the woods. He charged to the top of a rise and burst into the clearing unexpectedly, skidding to a stop.

Damon Long lay dead in the water, his feet tangled in weeds at the shore, keeping him from drifting out. A few yards away lay June's body, her white shirt turned red with blood.

And slicing through the water, one tired stroke after another, was Selena. Tony waded into the pond and she fell into his arms. Scooping her up, he lifted her, sodden and made heavy by the water, and carried her to shore. When he lowered her to her feet, she leaned against him, eyes closed, fingers knotted in his shirt.

"I'm sorry, babe," he murmured, holding her tightly. "I'm so sorry. I should have told you...I should have warned you..."

Finally she lifted her head. "You knew she was working with Long?"

"I suspected it. Just since yesterday. I wanted proof

before I told you. I didn't want you to think she hated you if I was wrong."

She smiled thinly. "I would have come out here with her even if I'd known. She promised to tell me how my mother died. She showed me where...."

Tony looked at the pond, then back at her. "Henry dumped her body in the pond?"

"Not her body. Her." Her voice quavered, and emotion darkened her eyes. "She was alive, Tony, when William and Rodrigo pushed her car into the pond. *They* killed her, not Kathryn. They left her there to drown. And June watched." A shiver rippled through her, making her huddle more tightly against him. "I saw the car. I touched it. My mother's car. And she's inside."

With that, she laid her head against his shoulder and wept. Not great sobs but tiny cries that were heartrending in their softness. There was nothing he could say to ease her pain, and so he simply held her, containing her shudders within his embrace.

The tears that she'd held inside for so many years lasted only a few moments, then she became still. She raised one hand to swipe at her eyes before looking at him. "At least now she can be buried. Grant and Luther can have a grave to visit."

And so could she. She could have some sort of closure.

Movement sounded to the north, then Charlize burst into the clearing. Slowing to a walk, she holstered her pistol, then came to stand near them. "At least you look better this time than before. I see only one mark."

Selena touched her hand gingerly to her face, then lowered it again and drew back her shoulders. "June and I went for a walk to talk. We ran into Long near the gate, and he forced us to come here. She gave me a chance to escape, and he killed her for it, then tried to kill me, but I was able to shoot him instead. That's the story we have to tell."

Charlize glanced at June, then nodded. "She died to save your life, like a good aunt."

Selena nodded, then both women looked at Tony. He nodded, too. That was the only story Luther ever needed to hear.

"We'll need some divers out here," he said. "And a wrecker. Amelia's car is in the pond." And Amelia herself. After all these years, there would be nothing left but bones. Not much to bury, but better than nothing. As Selena had said, at least those who loved her could have a grave to visit.

Taking a few steps away—but holding tightly to Tony's hand—Selena gazed at Long's body. With a bullet dead center between his eyes and a chunk of the back of his head missing, he wasn't a pretty sight anymore. Was she wishing they could have turned him over to the authorities, could have sent him back to jail where he belonged? Regretting that she'd had no choice but to kill him?

Tony didn't have any such regrets. "Dead" was where Long belonged. Where he couldn't hurt anyone else. Where he couldn't hurt Selena. Tony's only regret was that she'd been forced to kill him herself. Either he or Charlize would have taken that shot and never wasted a moment's sorrow for it. Selena would always regret it.

"How many deaths do you think he's responsible for?" Selena asked of no one in particular.

"More than anyone would want on his conscience," Charlize replied.

How many deaths were on her conscience? Tony wondered. She wasn't a psychopath, like Long, but she killed people for a living. But she'd done the right thing by Selena. That counted for a lot with him.

Selena looked at the body a moment longer, then turned away. Her features impossibly solemn, she said flatly, "He's better off dead. We're all better off with him dead."

Then she extended her hand to Tony, and when he took it, she held on tightly.

"Let's go home."

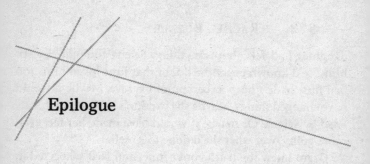

Epilogue

"Halloween's my most favorite time of the year."

"Dom's ugly mug is scary enough without a mask."

"Just what I need—four kids on a sugar high for the next week."

The night was chilly, but the bonfire burning in the clearing took the edge off. Wearing jeans and one of Tony's Tulsa Police Department sweatshirts, Selena stood near the flames, absorbing the heat along with the conversations, the laughter, and the sheer pleasure in the night. It was the last Saturday in October, and they were at Tony's Uncle John's place at Keystone Lake for the annual Ceola Halloween cookout. They'd roasted wieners and grilled burgers to go with baked beans, salads, and incredible desserts prepared by Tony's mother, sisters, and aunts—and by Selena, too. She was a part of the family. She'd contributed, too.

On the far side of the fire, Luther sat in a lawn chair, with Tony's father on one side, an elderly aunt on the other. Heartbroken by June's death, he'd decided after the funeral to accompany Selena and Tony to Tulsa. With his girl gone, there had been nothing keeping him in Greenhill, he'd declared. That old house would be too lonely for an old man, at least for a time.

He'd believed the story Selena and Tony had told him—had accepted as fact that June would sacrifice her own life to save her niece's. He'd never really known how his younger daughter had felt about anything, Selena thought. Except him. He'd known beyond a doubt that June loved him. Too bad June hadn't been as certain of his love. Maybe it would have changed things. Maybe she wouldn't have felt so threatened by Selena. Or maybe it would have made her feel even more guilty over what she'd done to Amelia.

Grant knew the truth about June, and Nell suspected it, but loyalty to Grant and affection for Luther made the housekeeper keep her suspicions to herself. No one else knew. Selena, Tony, and Charlize had told the same story, never wavering, and everyone had accepted it as fact.

A log popped, sending tiny wisps into the air that flamed before dying away. Little more than a week ago, Selena had been standing in another clearing, outside a small white church, with twin graves awaiting twin caskets. Two sisters, two burials, one service. How June would have hated that not even her funeral was hers alone. Amelia had intruded on everything in her life, even that.

Amelia, Selena believed, could have been one of the best parts of June's life, if only June had let her.

Tony's twin nieces ran past, garbed as cartoon characters, making him swerve to balance the two cups of hot chocolate he carried. Good-naturedly admonishing them not to run near the fire, he handed one cup to Selena, then gazed across the fire at Luther and Joe. "They're good together."

Selena nodded. Luther was patient with Joe's forgetfulness, Joe with Luther's arthritis-slowed movements. Neither required much conversation, and neither cared whether that conversation made sense.

Warming her hands on the foam cup, she looked at Tony. "*We're* good together."

He grinned. "We're way better than good. Want to slip off into the shadows so I can prove it?"

She knew what was beyond the shadows in the direction he gestured—a narrow trail that wound through the trees to the lake. Joe's generation had created the beach on the rocky shore there, while Tony's maintained it. It was the subject of a painting she'd done a few months earlier. It was also the place where she and Tony had made love for the first time.

"Tony," she chided. "There are at least a hundred Ceolas running around here."

"Go with me and we'll work on making it a hundred and one."

Something warm and tempting shivered through her. At the beginning of the summer, she'd never considered having children. She'd never had a mother or a father worthy of the name, had never had the kind of relationship where children were a possibility, had never known the love. She'd thought she would always be alone, as she had always been.

Then she'd met Tony.

He pulled one hand free from the cup and twined his fingers with hers, giving her a tug. She figured he was kidding—he wouldn't really risk making love to her with his entire family nearby—but who could blame them for necking a little on a moonlit beach? Luther was keeping an eye on Joe, Joe was doing the same for him, and Anna was watching them both. No one would notice that she and Tony had slipped away for a while.

"All right," she said, and he rewarded her with the boyish grin that always made her heart beat faster. "But first you have to tell me something."

"I love you," he said promptly, making her grin.

She squeezed his fingers hard. In a creditable imitation of Luther's drawl, she asked, "Are you gonna marry me?"

His gaze turned darker. *Yes, sir, I am,* he'd replied without hesitation when Luther had asked the question in Grant's family room. He didn't hesitate this time, either, but his response was different. "That depends on you."

A group of kids ran by—a Britney Spears lookalike, an ogre, and a furry blue monster, chased by a caped vampire. Their shrill laughs and shouts faded into the distance, along with everything else. All Selena could hear was the thud of her heart, the hush of her breathing. All she could focus on was Tony, looking handsomer, sweeter, and more serious than she'd ever seen him.

His hand nudged hers, and she tore her gaze from his face to look down at a small velvet box. The firelight showed its age, the nap marked and worn away completely in places. He opened it to reveal a gold band set with a pearl, small but lustrous, simple and beautiful.

"This is the ring Luther gave Oda Mae when she agreed to marry him." Tony's voice was husky. "On the day she died, she took it off and told him to give it to whichever of their girls got married first. You want to be that girl? Will you marry me, Selena?"

Another woman might shriek her answer, throw her arms around him, and dance around with pure joy, but that wasn't Selena's style. Swallowing hard over the lump in her throat, blinking away the dampness in her eyes, she held out her left hand. He slid the ring onto her finger, closed the box with a snap, and returned it to his jacket pocket.

"I take it that's a yes," he said, pulling her near.

"Emphatically so." She wrapped her arms around his neck and kissed him, nothing too intimate, nothing to draw attention to them. Then, moving her mouth to his ear, she murmured, "Let's find those shadows, Tony. Show me just how good we are."

How good they would always be. She wasn't sure of much else in life, but she knew beyond a doubt that she loved Tony and that he loved her back.

As Luther would say, she was blessed.

About the Author

Rachel Butler lives in Oklahoma with her husband and son, where she is at work on her next novel.